MW00721311

Cry:

The Shattered Crystal: Book 1

By
James Funfer

Branch Hill Publications
Readsboro, Vermont

This is a work of fiction. All of the characters, organizations, countries, and events portrayed in this novel are the work of the author's imagination.

Cover art: David Baumgart
Cover typography: Megan Seely

Acknowledgments

Although there are many individuals who gave me encouragement and inspiration along the way as I wrote and edited *Crystal Promise*, there are a few who deserve special recognition for helping me turn a fantasy into reality.

Kelsey Anne Swanson, your first-round edits were wonderfully thorough and professional. Genie Rayner, you are an incredible editor and one of the most genuine, sweetest people I know. Your anecdotes and smiley faces made the grind of editing bearable! I must also tip my hat to my mother, Kathy Funfer, who helped me polish up the manuscript before I sent it to Branch Hill. Thanks Mum!

Jim Vires, I would be a lost child in the big, scary world of publishing without your guidance and support.

David Baumgart, thank you for your incredible artwork. I hope this isn't the only time we work together.

Tara Juneau, thank you for your camera, your photographer's eye, and your laughter.

Last but not least, thank you, Damian Gray. You welcomed me to an amazing community and believed in me when *Crystal Promise* was a hastily-written fifty thousand words.

for Becky
who taught me that being ambitious
is nothing to be ashamed of
and
for Travis
my irreplaceable best friend

Prologue

The night the Great Crystal awoke was as silent an evening as the city of Captus Nove had seen in years. It was The Reverie, a night of quiet observation and private reflection that preceded the first day of autumn. In the country of Novem it was a tradition stretching back over two thousand years.

The gentle breeze of the Southron Sea had stilled that eve. No ill wind came as portent of Novem's coming doom. The sea stretched onto the shores of Captus Nove in lazy waves, silent and cold as a wraith's fingers. Although the skies were clear and the moon was full, the sea seemed as black as the night sky above.

In Avati Hill Park, no nightingales sang that night. Its proud whiteoaks, planted centuries before during the Reunification, cast long shadows on the valley by the light of the full moon. The cobblestoned streets of the Avati slums were barren and silent under the shadows of the whiteoaks. It was a night of shuttered windows, not moonlit walks.

Past the slums of Avati was Crystus Hill, sister hill to Avati and home to the Old Temple and the Parliament of the Republic. Beyond the tight security patrols of the Crystus district, a lone figure crept along the shadows of the alleyways and among millennia-old marble pillars. A cloak was wrapped tight about the figure and seemed to pull the darkness in from the crannies and crevices, the corners of walls and even the ebon sky above. The shadow of shadows glided along with confidence, and more than once a guard on patrol passed his eyes right over the creeping form. Had the guard been able to espy the figure, he would have noticed a crystal ring hanging from a slender silver chain wrapped around the neck of the cloak.

Before long, the Old Temple loomed ominously over the cloaked figure, as stately and impressive as it had been since its construction during the Mosind occupation. Evidence of both Mosind and Novem influence could be seen in the temple's design, from the gilded marble pillars and Novem arches overlooking

5

Temple Square, to the stained-glass Mosind dome atop the temple itself.

Sidling up to the great whiteoak doors, a hand fished into the folds of the cloak and produced an ornate brass key. It was pushed into the lock and given a quarter-turn almost inaudibly, and the twelve-foot tall door opened just wide enough to allow the figure to slip on through.

Moonlight spilled through stained glass to form a rich colour tapestry on the marble floor of the Old Temple's great hall. On the left window, the prophet Markus knelt and shielded his eyes from the awe and majesty of the Great Crystal. On the right was a set of panes that had been replaced several times. The lone body in the cloak took a moment to gaze up at the scene of the controversial Abdication of Queen Celesta. Echoed in darker tones on the white marble floor, Celesta - dressed all in white with scarlet hair tumbling down across her shoulders - casts her crown into flames to be melted as she looks in the direction of the Crystal Hallway.

The light of a lantern peeked around the corner to the great hall. The figure, startled out of wistful pause, skulked over to the other end of the hall and around a pillar as the footsteps went by. The shadowed form let a few seconds go by and then passed under the arch to the Crystal Hallway.

Sombre faces of keepers past looked down at the shadow reprovingly as it passed by. The portraits ran down the entire right length of the hallway and halfway up the left. The temple interloper was moving at a swift jaunt and paid them no mind. The dead could not harm the intruder. Only the living could pierce or bruise the flesh. The dead broke no hearts.

The hallway split into two winding corridors that followed the spherical centre of the temple around on either side. The entrance to the Crystal Chamber was at the other end, but the lone intruder knew that it was guarded at all times. Instead, a doorway of the inner right corridor was chosen, this one with a crystal lock. The figure paused to listen for footsteps, then leaned down to the small blue crystal beside the knob and whispered a phrase into the silence. The crystal briefly glowed with an azure luminescence, allowing the intruder time enough to turn the knob and step inside.

The office was sparsely decorated. A painting of a rural Noven riverside was on the left. On the desk was a heavy obsidian placard engraved with the name 'Keeper Orvin' in white. The crystal-speaker showed no interest in the office or its contents, and strode quickly across the floor to the inner door that led to the Crystal Chamber.

Another whisper to another crystal lock, and the way to the legendary room was open.

The Crystal Chamber was an enormous interior space, easily the size of a two-storey house. A pillar of Noven religion and society, the Great Crystal took up most of the chamber like a great behemoth of reflective rock. To many Novens it was merely a symbol, to others a religious tool or a remnant of a fading way of life. The cloaked figure knew that it was much more. The Great Crystal had a purpose.

It ruined lives.

The temple intruder spent a few moments staring silently at the crystal. The moon peered in from high above the glass dome, and its beams refracted in the crystal to send dark rainbow streaks across the bare polished walls. The faithful often claimed that the crystal wove the threads of fate. If society believed it to be true, the cloaked one supposed, it became true like any self-fulfilling prophecy. A shaky hand inched toward the crystal's surface. If the tapestry of life was woven by the Great Crystal, a crystal-speaker could in turn weave the destiny of every citizen of Novem.

A glance into the reflections of the crystal revealed that there was somebody else inside the Crystal Chamber.

"You ..."

Across the Crystus district, the muffled sound of wandshot echoed in the night. Blood had been spilled on the Great Crystal, for the first time in centuries.

Angry waves crashed against the shoals and boats on the docks of Captus Nove. The wind howled through the leaves of the whiteoaks of Avati Hill. Clouds gathered and thunder rumbled in the skies above the city, and the nightingales cried shrilly on their branches. A brilliant white flash shone from the dome of the Old Temple. For a moment, night became day.

The fate of the nation was sealed.

Chapter 1
One Year Earlier

Jacoby took a fist to the chin.

"Dully!" Grig called out. He'd had it in for Jacoby since their first year of school. Little had changed between them since then, except that at some point Grig realized he could do more damage if he brought friends around with him. Jacoby was facing off against three broad-shouldered boys, and the only exit from the alleyway was blocked. There was a wall of hot bricks at his back. Escape was not an option. Jacoby was used to fights, but he was not used to winning them.

Another swing came at Jacoby as Grig's pals caught up to him. Jacoby tried to duck in the hopes that his attacker's fist would hit the bricks behind him, but the boy had swung carefully and pulled his meaty hand back in time. Jacoby tried in vain to disengage along the wall before he was completely surrounded, but Grig's friend, a lanky boy Jacoby did not recognize, caught him in a grapple and gave him a firm knee in the stomach. Jacoby fell to the street coughing and clutching his guts, tears streaming from his face. If Jacoby was lucky and the fight went as he expected, he would get kicked as he lay on the ground for a while, then the bullies would get bored and disperse after spitting on him and calling him a few more names. Jacoby buried his face in his arms and prepared for the worst.

"Fuckin' dully," Grig said. He followed the insult with a stomp to Jacoby's head. The boy's boot landed on his arms. Each of the other kids proceeded with kicks to Jacoby's sides.

"You think you're one of us now? Fuck you and your dirty miner family."

Jacoby groaned and tried to curl up as tightly as possible. He didn't like being such a coward, but any time he'd fought back on his own it hadn't gone very well.

Jacoby heard quick footsteps coming down the alleyway as his former classmates continued to kick him and call him names. He prayed that it was an adult come to tell the boys to 'go on and git'. Peering through his arms, Jacoby witnessed a pair of legs no longer than Grig's come to a halt. The next thing he knew, Grig's feet were leaving the pavement and his compatriots had stopped kicking. Bouts of shouting echoed through the narrow alleyway as Jacoby got to his feet and took stock of what was happening.

"Don't just stand there, Jake, ya idiot," Timori called out as he planted his knuckles across a boy's face. Although no heavier or taller than his foes, Grig and his buddies seemed to fear Timori regardless. Jacoby shook off the pain and leapt on Grig, who had been in the process of getting to his feet until Jacoby's knee found his diaphragm. Jacoby may have been a coward, but he knew how to fight dirty when he thought he could win.

Although he had the advantage of being on top, Grig was much heavier and easily pushed Jacoby over after receiving a few punches to the head. Instead of continuing the fight, Grig glanced at Jacoby's ally, who was holding his own against both of Grig's friends, and stuck an angry finger in Jacoby's face.

"This isn't over, ya fuckin' picker." Then the boy turned and ran.

Jacoby tried to think of a witty response to Grig's threat but couldn't find the words. He sniffled and tasted copper in his throat as he watched his saviour chase down the alley after the other two boys. Jacoby waited for the three of them to round the corner, then he slunk down against the wall and checked his ribs for bruises. He closed his eyes and let out a heavy sigh. He had been hoping never to run into Grig again since they were likely to go to different finishing schools. As his father had always told him, however, 'wishing for something doesn't make it come true'.

"Fancy running into you here," said a nasal voice from above him. Jacoby opened his eyes. Timori was stockier than Jacoby, and taller by a good three inches. His clear blue eyes were gentle as he regarded Jacoby, who was still slumped against the brick wall.

"Tim," Jacoby replied with a smile. Without a word, Tim offered Jacoby a hand to help lift him to his feet. The pair fetched

Jacoby's bike that had been abandoned where Jacoby had crashed it against the garbage cans of the alley. They left the alley for the blistering sunshine of Corti Street and Tim's house down the way.

The summer of 1894 was a sweltering one. Several temperature records were broken that year, and historians would later say that the only summer hotter on record was in the year of the revolution, A.C. 1736. It was a lazy kind of heat that seemed to come from underneath as the stones of the city baked. The walls pulsed with it.

That sort of slow boil was not kind to a city already on hard times. Dockhands gave more sweat each day, so they drank more in the evenings and got into more fights. The politicians in Parliament bickered and swore at each other across their party divisions and few laws were passed. The economy, which had ground itself to a near-halt in 1885, was supposed to be pulling itself back out thanks to President Gergovi's 'Class Action' plan. It was not going as planned. The rich blamed the poor, the educated blamed the Great War, the miners and the alchemists blamed each other, and everyone blamed Gergovi. Only those who had miraculously climbed the class ladder were happy about any of it, and most of them feared for their lives from the disdain of those who wanted to stay on top and the jealousy of those who had been left at the bottom.

A riot broke out in the month of Maya over the price of bread, followed by a miners' union strike. In the oppressive heat of the month of Yuna, the miners brought the city to its knees as they picketed against the heavy workloads of crystal ore that were being undervalued in the global markets, and their families starved.

Nothing of the heat wave or political turmoil mattered much to Jacoby Padrona that year. It was that glorious, bittersweet summer between grade school and finishing school. It was the summer of last freedoms. He was between adolescence and adulthood, carefree times and responsibility. He was waiting to discover if he would be accepted to Central School, the best finishing school in the nation, or if he would have to be satisfied with something less prestigious. He was between all possible worlds, and it was where he wanted to stay.

On the day Jacoby discovered his educational fate, school was the farthest thing from his mind. He had awakened casually late and refried some bacon that his mother had left in the icebox. His younger brother, Marco, was listening to the radio in the common room. Jacoby avoided him and snuck around to the back door. He didn't want his little brother trying to tag along. Jacoby grabbed his bike and was off and down the hill as quickly as he could pedal.

Timori, Jacoby's best friend, lived in Avati Valley. Neither of them liked to call it 'the slums' because they had grown up there, and as a matter of pride most residents referred to it as 'Avati Valley'. Jacoby and Timori used to live right next door to each other, until a stroke of luck under Gergovi's 'Class Action' plan saw Jacoby's father brought into the alchemists' guild. Befitting a man of the alchemist class, Jacoby's father had moved his family to Cateli Hill, a 'decent' neighbourhood for 'decent' citizens. Jacoby remembered being told by his father that it was a good compromise – Cateli Hill was a safe place, but not so affluent as to alienate old friends. Jacoby had cursed at his father and said that they were abandoning their friends in Avati. His father had struck him across the face and called him ungrateful, then sent him to his room without any supper.

Later Jacoby would admit to himself that he was only angry about having to move so far away from Timori. Cateli was a long way from Avati – half an hour by bike – but Timori and Jacoby had both agreed to spend time together whenever they possibly could. It was on the way to Timori's house in the slums that Jacoby had run into broad-faced, meaty-armed Grig while taking a shortcut through an alley.

As he'd crashed his bike against the tin trash cans in panic, Jacoby had thought to himself that it was fate mocking him. You could take the kid out of the slums, but you couldn't take the slums out of the kid ... and Grig would never let him forget it. Jacoby could only console himself with the fact that Grig was not the type of student who got accepted into Central School. His parents may have been high-born, but he was an idiot.

Thoughts of Grigori Marsa quickly faded in the company of Timori, after the pair had regaled each other with all of the 'clever moves' they had used during the fight. Jacoby let his friend do most of the talking. It was a silent understanding between them that they didn't have to point out who was a better scrapper.

Timori and Jacoby walked leisurely down Corti Street, side-by-side in the intense heat. Neither one found the sun too hot that summer. They basked in its glow as though it was the last summer that they would ever see. They both knew that in some ways it truly was their last. Miners' sons like Timori rarely afforded finishing school.

Jacoby found the familiarity of Corti Street soothing after the fight. Smells of cured ham and baking bread filled his nostrils, and he took in the welcoming sight of the bright, freshly painted wooden signs outside every storefront, mainstays of his childhood. Men and women strolled leisurely down the street taking in the sights, some of them with children in tow. All were sweating. The women used lace fans and many of the lower-class men went shirtless. To either side of the crowds, row upon row of shops boasted baskets of fruits and baked goods, racks of summer dresses and barrels filled with parasols. Displays of toys for small children teased from store windows, but crying about them did the youngsters little good. Everything in Novem was overpriced in the depression, even down to the potatoes. Shopkeepers were often seen out on the street, both to peddle their wares and discourage thievery, which had spiked in the years since the depression. Some eyed Jacoby and Timori warily as the pair strolled down the lane. Boys from the valley were notoriously nimble-fingered.

As they walked in comfortable silence, Jacoby decided on a lark that he would treat Timori to a soda once the sun climbed to its sweltering zenith. Timori seemed to be the only person who understood that Jacoby's change in social status wasn't his fault, and would not scoff at the generosity. There was nothing like a flavoured soda from Belaggio's Deli to beat the heat.

Timori's house was just off of Corti Street, a little shack that he shared with his two younger sisters and his mother. Jacoby had vague memories of Timori's father, but it was a subject best left untouched. As the pair walked down the street talking of all the pretty girls they were going to charm at Central School together, Jacoby glanced over at the house beside Timori's, where he used to live.

Jacoby stopped to stare at the faded green bungalow, dwarfed on either side by two-storey apartment houses that most families had to share in order to afford rent. He could tell by the broom at the front sidewalk and the ugly, drawn yellow curtains behind the dirty windows that somebody had moved into the old shack recently. Dirty houses fallen into disrepair were a familiar sight in Avati Valley, but through the fog of nostalgia Jacoby seemed to remember the house being cleaner, brighter when he had lived there. Jacoby's mother and father had kept the house ruthlessly clean, and had forced their children to do the same.

As he stood there wistfully, gazing at his old home, he could hear his father's voice in his mind: 'You should always be proud of where you live'. Jacoby wondered idly if his father was more or less proud than he used to be. 'Class Action' had been a blessing and a curse. Old family friends were venomously jealous of his new station, and the upper classes had not been very welcoming.

"Yeah, someone moved in," Timori said, breaking Jacoby's reverie. "It's not the same without you, pally. However ..." he raised his eyebrows suggestively, "their daughter is clear pretty."

Jacoby looked over at Timori and a smile broke on his face. He could always trust in his best friend to bring him back to reality.

"True? I'll have to visit you more often, then." He barked a laugh. "I'd start wooing soon if I was you, or Jake is gonna swoop in and ..."

"Hey, you get enough doves following you around already," Timori protested. "At least leave the girl next door for me."

"Depends on how clear she is," Jacoby said as he leaned his bicycle against Timori's house. The two friends entered the small

14

dwelling through the front door. The foyer led to a series of four apartments, each a two-storey home with separate interior entrances. The communal foyer was always dusty. Nobody seemed interested in volunteering to sweep out the dirt that was tracked in from the street. Timori's door was the closer one on the left.

As Jacoby stepped through the doorway, he noticed that a few stacks of books had appeared in the entryway, in and amongst the shoes that had been placed haphazardly about the welcome mat. Timori's mother was likely 'organizing' again, Jacoby figured. A casual glance in the direction of the kitchen revealed that the pots and pans from his last visit had probably not been cleaned, but Jacoby had no way to be certain. The pile was high enough in the sink that it was impossible to discern what lay underneath the stacks of chipped cups and soiled plates. Jacoby wondered if he would be able to smell the mould accumulating. It would not have been the first time.

The common room was the same as it had been the last time Jacoby had come to visit. The broken rocking chair was still leaning against the window next to the radio that Timori had to fix about once a week. The coil spring in the ratty old yellow couch was still pushing stubbornly past the patch that Timori had sewn in it. Jacoby suspected that the couch had been white, originally. Timori's youngest sister, Carlotta, was playing with dolls on the frayed brown rug of the common room. Her dolls were arranged about her like an army, ready to do her bidding.

"Hi Jake!" Carlotta said. She gave a friendly wave and her dark curls of hair bounced jovially. Jacoby waved back and followed Timori to his room.

As usual, Timori's room was much cleaner than the rest of the house. A pile of dirty clothes littered the floor and stacks of old papers covered the surface of Timori's tiny desk, but other than that the box-like room was free and clear of extra detritus. Timori didn't spare his room a glance but quickly changed his bloody shirt and lent a clean one to Jacoby as well. Jacoby went to wash his face in the washroom basin and fix his hair, which had a habit of getting messy after even the slightest physical activity.

Jacoby and Timori left the house and returned to Corti Street to buy sunflower seeds and sodas. Timori protested when Jacoby offered to pay for his, but he relented after Jacoby insisted several times. When they had finished the sodas, the pair shared Jacoby's bike down to Memorial Bridge.

The boys wove in and out of motorcoach and stagecoach traffic until they were at the foot of the bridge. Although it was the newest motorcoach bridge in Captus Nove, the Great War Memorial Bridge had been made of marble and stone in the old Noven style. At the centre of the bridge, more easily seen from below, the crest of the Noven Republic was carved in the marble: an eagle held aloft the crest in its claws, wings spread wide. Ironically, the eagle had been the symbol of the old Noven Empire which the republic had overthrown at the end of the Great War. The traditional Noven symbols of the key and the crystal, representing knowledge and spirituality, were engraved on the crest. These were tempered by the republican symbols of the whiteoak and the wheel, which implied peace and prosperity. Beneath the crest the republican motto proclaimed in old Noven, *Par Tradiziona, Ordina*, which Jacoby had been taught meant 'Through Tradition, Progress'. Jacoby had always found the motto to be a bit self-contradictory. He gazed at the bridge, which was supposed to be a reminder of those who had lost their lives in the Great War. Jacoby never saw anybody looking at the crest, the motto, or the relief of the Noven soldiers marching off to war. To most Noven citizens, it seemed to be just another part of the road.

To Jacoby and Timori, the bridge meant something else entirely. From the time they were little, the boys would go to the Great War Memorial Bridge after football games and chew and spit sunflower seeds until their tongues hurt from the salt. Jacoby's mother had joked that one day they would bury the tunnel under the bridge with all of those seeds. This had prompted Jacoby and Timori to save up for as many bags as they could buy and spit them all in

16

one afternoon onto the street below the bridge in the hopes that something interesting would happen. They knew they would never have enough seeds to bury a motorcoach, let alone the tunnel, and to their dismay, all they managed to do was make a mess, which had only lasted for two days until the street cleaners came.

Jacoby sometimes wondered what the people in their motorcoaches and on their bicycles thought as the pair of boys with the identical comb-over haircuts spat sunflower seeds at them. He liked to imagine that passers-by assumed that they were brothers, even though they were too close in age and not similar enough in facial features for it to be so: Timori's jaw was much stronger, his nose longer and straighter, hair lighter and more wiry than Jacoby's.

"Did you get your letter yet?" Timori asked. Jacoby thought he detected a note of anxiety in his friend's voice.

Jacoby shrugged and spat out a seed. "Not yet. You?"

Timori shook his head and popped another seed into his mouth. He would always chew them one at a time, no matter what.

"No, not yet, although I doubt that I'll get into Central. My mom can't afford it, even with the 'Class Action' subsidy."

Jacoby felt his heart sink. Even if neither one was accepted into Central, Jacoby would wind up going to a decent finishing school and Timori would be stuck with whatever his mother could afford. Even worse would be if Jacoby had to go to a boarding school somewhere else in the country. He would only be able to see his best friend during the summer. He decided to think positively, instead.

"Timori, you're the smartest person I know. Didn't you even say you feel like you did well on the exam? You're bound to get scholarships."

Jacoby's words brought to mind his own exam, which he wasn't nearly as optimistic about. Every student at the end of grade school had to take one, and it was considered to be the most important test of every child's life, which hadn't helped Jacoby feel any less nervous about the whole thing. The science and history questions hadn't been much of a problem, but the portion of the test

17

that combined empathy and crystal-speaking had been one of the most bizarre experiences of Jacoby's life. They didn't teach either discipline to children, so Jacoby had gone in blind, which he felt had been more than a little unfair. The teacher just told him to go with his gut. 'What are *you* feeling?' she would ask, followed by 'what am *I* feeling' and 'what colour are *you*, on the inside?' 'Look at this crystal. If it had a mouth, what would it be saying to *you* right now?' It had all been very confusing for Jacoby.

"Yeah, maybe I'll get a scholarship," Timori replied. "It probably won't be enough money to get me into Central, though."

With an air of dejection, Timori spat a seed and promptly put another one into his mouth. Jacoby couldn't find any words, so the two of them continued in silence for a moment. Jacoby grabbed a handful and shoved them into his mouth, chewing without trying to get the seeds out first, making a pulpy mush instead. Sometimes when he was upset he would try to spit the whole mess onto cars and it made him feel better.

"That's disgusting," Timori muttered without looking up from the road below. His casual remark made Jacoby chuckle, which sounded funny when his cheeks were puffed up full of seeds. The sound made Timori laugh, and soon both of them were in hysterics until Jacoby couldn't control his lips and bits of seed and mush were coming out of his mouth, which made them laugh even harder. Eventually, Jacoby spat the whole wad out onto the street underneath the bridge with a *puah* and they both laughed again.

Suddenly it occurred to Jacoby that soon he and Timori might not be able to spend every day together. He grew silent. Timori also stopped laughing and the boys looked at each other.

Timori spoke first. "Listen, Jake. I don't want this to sound really dull, but ...." He paused, struggling for words. Even a poetic youth like Timori could find it difficult expressing himself to another male. "Let's be friends forever."

Jacoby nodded his head and smiled. "Tim, you know we will be."

"Just indulge me, make it official. Let's promise. Friends forever, no matter what happens. If we go to different schools, if one of us moves away, anything. Friends for life. Promise?"

Jacoby nodded. It was purely for ritual's sake. There was no doubt in Jacoby's mind that Timori would be his best friend for as long as they both lived. They looked in each other's eyes, and shook hands the way Jacoby imagined that great men would shake hands, men of character and importance.

With an air of solemnity, Jacoby and Timori returned to Timori's house. Jacoby was required under house rules to return home in time for supper, so he bade Timori farewell and grabbed his bicycle. As he turned to face home, he noticed that he was being watched.

She was sitting on the steps of the house where Jacoby used to live. Her nose was deep into a book, and her skirt was draped across the dusty steps as though she didn't care if it stayed clean or not. Jacoby strained to read the title of the book, but it was obscured by blonde, wispy locks that tumbled down to her knees as she crouched down on the steps.

She looked as though she didn't want to be disturbed. Since he couldn't get a good look at her face, Jacoby decided to head for home. As he started to pedal off, he glanced her way and saw her watching him over the tops of the pages. Although unnerved by the intensity of her gaze, Jacoby stared back and saw that her eyes were an ocean shade of blue.

"Hi," he blurted as he gave an awkward wave with his hand. He had wanted to sound confident, but the greeting came out timid and uncertain.

"Hi," the girl said, her eyes downcast once more. Jacoby looked away from her and stared at the olive green wall of the house where he used to live.

"What are you reading?" Jacoby asked as he dared a second glance.

The young lady pulled the book away from her face and read the title as though it was the first time she had laid her eyes on the front cover. To Jacoby's disappointment, her hair still obscured her features.

"Um, it's called *Tales of the Crystal Speakers*."

"My name's Jake." He took a step toward her. She withdrew slightly and tensed her shoulders. Jacoby stopped and gave his best disarming smile.

"What's your name?"

"I'm …"

"Crystara!" a man bellowed from inside the green house. Crystara stiffened and froze like a startled animal. She shot Jacoby an apologetic look, which to his delight offered a full look at her face. She had delicate, pointed and well-proportioned features, high cheekbones, and a clear complexion. Timori hadn't been wrong about his neighbour's looks.

"Nice to meet you, Jake," Crystara whispered with a pretty smile. She turned and dashed inside the house. Jake heard the door slam and the man yelling from inside. Jacoby mounted his bicycle and began to pedal for home. He thought of Crystara's smile as he rode.

Riding over the Memorial Bridge, Jacoby stopped pedaling and took a moment to admire the view of the valley. Jacoby was at an age where he was prone to feelings of wistful romanticism. Often he would stop wherever he was to watch a sunrise or sunset, or pause while riding down Corti Street to hear the rest of a song he liked that was playing on a store radio.

Jacoby got off his bike and leaned over the railing. Memorial Bridge was the boundary between affluence and poverty. Up the hill, the road led to the houses of the wealthy classes. Down in the valley were the slums. It seemed fitting to Jacoby that he could look down on Avati Valley from the bridge – the place in the middle – caught as he was between the life he had left and the one he wasn't accustomed to. Although his father's new job offered more money, security and opportunities for Jacoby and his family, he felt as though he had somehow betrayed his friends, especially Timori. People like Grigori had certainly made it clear that Jacoby wasn't welcome amongst them. He knew that he would always be an outsider, even if the law stated that he was not.

Jacoby breathed a heavy sigh and turned his gaze away from the valley below. He had to get home in time for supper.

It always took longer for Jacoby to return home after visiting the valley than it did to get there since his house was up the hill. Even so, Jacoby found taking a bike the whole way there and back preferable to not seeing his best friend at all. Jacoby's father didn't own a motorcoach yet. Anytime Jacoby urged his father to purchase one, his father listed all the reasons he couldn't afford one. Since his household owned no motorcoach, Jacoby was stuck using his bicycle if he wanted to see his best friend at all.

As he neared home, the familiar aroma of savoury tomato sauce filled his nostrils. His stomach gurgled in response. It occurred to Jacoby that the only things he had eaten all day were some bacon and sunflower seeds.

Jacoby parked the bicycle in the back yard and entered the house through the back door. Instantly, his senses were suffused with the smells and sights he'd become accustomed to from as far back as he could remember: freshly baked bread in the oven, his mother testing a sauce and adding more parsley, his father yelling at her to 'stop puttering around and set the godsdamned table already'.

Unlike most traditional Noven families, Jacoby's mother and father cooked dinner every evening together. With any of his friends' parents, Jacoby had always seen the mother have dinner ready on the table by the time the father came home from work. At Jacoby's house, they ate at a much later hour, but every meal was a work of art. Even when they had been poor, Jacoby's father made sure they ate well, even if it meant sacrifices elsewhere. Jacoby wouldn't have traded his parents' meals for anything.

Jacoby's grandmother liked to tell the story of how his parents met every time she came to visit. Jacoby's father, Gilliermo Ligari, had been born to a poor family in a small crystal mining town called Muli. Gilliermo had outshone his heritage by saving enough money while working in the mines to pay the acceptance fee for an engineering academy. Graduating at the top of his class, Gilliermo was nevertheless restricted by his social caste, and the highest position that he could ever hope for was that of supervisor in the mines. He had once told Jacoby that he had gone to an academy 'just to prove a point'.

Gilliermo met Jacoby's mother while on a job in the city. Katarina Di Catalari came from a moderately wealthy Captus Nove family whose importance came primarily from overseas trading. She was attending the Noven Academy of Art, studying to be a painter. Her father had told her that she could be anything that she wanted to be, so Katarina grew up free-spirited and headstrong. She and Gilliermo met entirely by accident. The surveyor for Gilliermo's team had consumed too much wine the night before and sent Gilliermo in his place. At the intended site of the dig, Gilliermo discovered a lone young woman in the countryside painting a landscape. Apart from a friendly 'hello' to each other, they both went about their business and Gilliermo left as soon as he had finished his survey. It had taken him longer than usual. The artist had been distracting.

Jacoby's mother always referred to it as 'that fateful day', when she ran into Gilliermo Ligari a couple of months later at a café during lunch. Both of them were eating alone, but Katarina recognized the miner immediately and on a whim invited herself over to his table. They talked the whole lunch through, and were inseparable afterward. Two months later, they were engaged.

The rest of the Di Catalari family was less than enthusiastic. Jacoby's grandfather, Marcosi Di Catalari, had never set foot inside Jacoby's father's house, even after Gilliermo Ligari had been renamed to Gilliermo Padrona to reflect his status as a member of the alchemist class. Gilliermo and Katarina chose to elope rather than risk persecution from Marcosi. Once the papers were signed and crystal rings exchanged in a temple, the Di Catalari family had no choice but to recognize the union. Eventually they all forgave him, except for Marcosi.

Jacoby could tell from the aroma that greeted him at the back door that supper was going to be homemade spaghetti with Aranyan meat sauce. The table was already set. His mother stirred the pot of sauce, singing to herself. His father fetched the loaf of bread from where it was cooling by the windowsill. Gilliermo turned and looked at Jacoby with a smile.

"There you are. Do me a favour and get the bread knife, would you Jake?" he asked. There was an odd look on Gilliermo's face. His moustache twitched as it did when he was deliberately trying to hide something. Jacoby wanted to point out that he knew his father had a secret, but although his father was not a large man, he was still intimidating enough to have his requests followed when given.

As Jacoby grabbed the serrated knife from the drawer and handed it to his father, a pit formed in the base of his stomach. He knew immediately why his father seemed strange: the letter had arrived from Central School. Gilliermo Padrona was either waiting to congratulate his son formally over dinner, or waiting until he could tell Jacoby privately that he was disappointed in him. Jacoby approached his mother with all the subtlety that he could muster.

Jacoby had always thought that his mother was beautiful, even though she was larger and greyer of hair than in the photographs of when she was young. Her smile still carried the same radiant, unconditional benevolence that Jacoby remembered from when he was a small child. Although more cunning than she appeared, Jacoby knew that his mother was easily manipulated if he applied the proper amount of boyish sweetness.

"Mother," Jacoby began, eyes wide, "did my letter come today from Central?"

"Your father would like to discuss it over dinner, Jake."

"Fine," Jacoby sighed.

"Go wash up before dinner, please," his mother said. Jacoby nodded and resigned himself to the wait despite the anxiety growing in his chest. He hurried up the stairs to the bathroom to prepare for dinner and the news he'd been waiting all summer for. Grabbing his comb from by the sink, Jacoby fixed his hair and splashed some water on his face. He looked at himself in the mirror and shot a hopeful grin at his reflection. Jacoby found himself wondering what girls thought of that grinning face.

"Jake!" his mother called. "Marco! Dinnertime!" Jacoby heard his brother's pounding footsteps racing down the stairs. Jacoby gave himself one last hopeful look in the mirror and tried to remain calm as he followed his brother down the stairs.

All was neatly prepared as usual: main course and salad bowl in the middle of the table, a slice of bread already on each plate. Jacoby noticed that his parents had brought out the crystal wine glasses, a wedding gift from Katarina's mother. His mind was set at ease. They would not bring out the fine crystal if Jacoby's hopes and dreams were about to be shattered.

Marco and Gilliermo were already seated. Katarina came out of the kitchen carrying a freshly uncorked bottle of wine just as Jacoby was seating himself. To Jacoby's surprise, she approached him with the bottle first, rather than his father.

"Jacoby, would you like some wine?" his mother asked with a sparkle in her eye.

"Yes, please," he replied. His mother poured him a generous portion of wine and then went around the table, finishing with her own glass. She sat down and looked at Gilliermo expectantly.

Gilliermo Padrona cleared his throat. "Well everyone, before we start dinner, I have an announcement to make." He produced an envelope from beneath the table and held it up. "Jacoby has been accepted to Central School this fall. Congratulations, son." He began to applaud, and Jacoby's mother and brother followed suit.

Jacoby felt a sense of pride welling up within him. Gilliermo lifted a glass in toast. "Here's to you, Jacoby. I'm proud of you."

Jacoby was so excited that he could barely put the glass to his lips to sip from it. Toscetti wine had never tasted so good.

"However, that doesn't mean you can slack off, Jake. You're a damn smart kid and you wrote a good test, but Central is really tough about schoolwork and grades, and you won't be able to get by

24

just on your brains anymore. This school is very expensive and I expect you to succeed. I know it's not going to be easy on you if any of these kids know you used to be a Ligari, but this school is the gateway to your future, Jake. You need to take it very seriously. You can't be a kid anymore. Do you understand?"

Jacoby stared at his father, then at the tablecloth. He knew what his father wanted to hear – telling him that part would be easy. Committing to it was a different matter. Jacoby had no idea who or what he wanted to be. He was not ready to decide.

"I understand, Father." Jacoby said. He drank some more wine and then reached for the salad.

Chapter 2

Racquela dreamily followed a popcorn-shaped cloud through the sky as her tutor droned through the weekly history lesson. She didn't understand why it was so necessary for her to receive tutelage during the summer. She was going to Central come the month of Sexta. Although it was convenient to hold her lessons in the secluded gardens of the De'Trini manor, she felt stifled by her tutor's presence.

"And so, in a controversial move that shocked scholars and, truly, everyone in the day, the Queen stepped down as monarch of Novem and handed its rule over to the republic. The Queen, having been declared a prophetess by the church, prepared to enter a life of seclusion behind the doors of the Old Temple. She was, as you recall, considered to be the greatest speaker of her day and desired to study the Great Crystal to the best of her abilities."

Racquela yawned and tried half-heartedly to make it sound like a muted note of interest. Her tutor, a fairly alert man despite his rheumy eyes and ears overstuffed with white fringes of hair, caught on and gave her a disapproving glare over his spectacles.

"Racquela, please, this is a very important part of our history. If you put as much effort into listening as you did pretending to listen ..." He did not finish the sentence. It was one he had repeated to her several times before.

Racquela wondered why he bothered. He was being paid by her father regardless of how well she listened or how well she did at her studies. What did he care for her education? Racquela rolled her eyes and sat up straight, as if to appear willing to receive boring information. Old Tevici would get carried away talking about something useless like the effect of the fish tax revolt on continental economic policies, and she could go back to daydreaming about something far more interesting.

Racquela looked up and to the left as her tutor cleared his throat and re-entered the realm of her own imagination. At fifteen years old, there was only one thing that she wanted to think about.

"Men," the old scholar rumbled, "are fickle in love, unlike women. While a woman is unwavering in her devotion to one man, a man's tastes can change as quickly as the wind."

Racquela sat up straight. Suddenly the old man seemed to be speaking her language. "Pardon me, teacher, but I thought we were talking about Queen Celesta."

Her tutor's face morphed rapidly from irritation to surprise at her interruption. He adjusted his spectacles.

"So you actually were listening, then? Well, I am glad to have finally caught your attention. It is like catching a gnat with a butterfly net. If you would but allow me to continue, young lady, you will see that I am, indeed, speaking of the prophetess Celesta."

Racquela sat attentive on her parents' garden lawn. She was always careful to use a blanket to keep her skirts from accumulating grass stains. She would always listen to the parts of her history lessons that dealt with love: the tragic romance of Adrian of ancient Novem and Ma-hep of Novem's Southern Empire, the ballads and old plays of the bard Raffino, the many love affairs of the kings and queens of the Rebirth. It was all the boring parts of history that she didn't care to retain.

"Now then," the educator continued, "although Celesta was beloved by her people, many saw her abdication as abandonment, even though she was still alive and a part of Novem's well-being, if privately. Can you think of why that is?"

Racquela furled her brow and absently played with a dark lock of hair. Her tutor had skilfully tricked her. The discussion was not about real love, but about public adoration. Although she felt cheated, she humoured the man.

"Um, because the republic didn't do a good job after she left?"

Tevici pursed his lips as though he found her response surprisingly thoughtful.

"Well now, that is a matter of some debate, my lady Racquela. To this day scholars and nobles, and indeed, even the lower classes discuss this, sometimes with much fervour. However, one must always remember the situation not of the present, but of the world in which our subject lived. In Celesta's time, the church was much more powerful than it is today and many, especially the burgeoning middle classes of Novem, saw them as coinmongers and profiteers of misfortune. With the advent of Vespici's Laws of Science, which we discussed two weeks ago – I hope you recall at least some of that – as well as the splintering of Novem during the Holy Wars, faith in the church was dwindling and they held onto their dying power tightly. With a mistrust of the church spreading amongst the people, many viewed Celesta's choice as her turning her back on the people. Thus, the mutable love that men feel can change swiftly. That particular chain of events, which I will relate in detail in just a moment, culminated in the anti-crystal rebellion of 1691 ..."

Racquela swiftly lost interest again. As her gaze wandered over to her mother's blooming rose bushes, she wondered what it would have been like to be Queen Celesta, torn between her duty to her kingdom and her love of the Keeper of the Old Temple. Although her tutor had glossed it over because he didn't believe that it had really happened, the love between Celesta and Keeper Lucianus was legendary. Even after all of the songs and stories that had been written about it, a consensus had never been reached as to whether or not the love affair had been real, or whether Celesta had truly become a prophetess merely to study the Great Crystal.

Racquela preferred to believe in the love story. Not only was it more interesting, but it was far more likely. Who wouldn't sacrifice everything that they held dear for the one they loved? It would have been forbidden for a woman to marry any priest under any circumstances. Abdication and declaring herself a prophetess would have been the only way for Celesta to remain close to her true love. Racquela pondered if Keeper Lucianus had truly been as handsome as the stories claimed.

"... and mercenaries from Kilgrun. Are you paying attention, my lady?"

Racquela nodded sagely, her favourite tactic. Old Tevici would frequently ask her if she was paying attention, but Racquela was often more stubborn and could silently convince him that, since he was the one being paid for the service, Racquela could listen or not as she chose. Tevici chose not to press it that day, and continued on in a flat voice.

Racquela absently plucked at blades of grass and found herself thinking about Central School and how thrilling it would be to attend the most prestigious finishing school in the nation. Many of her old friends would be there, and she was hoping to make many new ones as well. More importantly, according to the old customs, every year six first-year students would be chosen for the crystal betrothals. It was an exciting time for Racquela. The prospect of having the gods themselves deign to choose for her a true love was exciting enough to make her giggle aloud if she thought about it too deeply. Racquela had always believed in true love, and a decision handed down by the Great Crystal would only confirm it further.

Racquela's mother's advice from earlier that year, after she had received her acceptance letter, didn't stop her thinking about the crystal betrothals.

'Spend time in the company of many men,' her mother had told her. 'You are a beautiful girl, Racquela, and unlike many of our station are actually more interesting than you appear. Many will shower you with their affections and desire that you show them exclusivity. How are you ever to find the man who is right for you if you do that? You must experiment. Discover your likes and dislikes when it comes to men. The last thing that you want, my darling child, is an unhappy marriage. Men will try to stop you from this because they are jealous of each other, but it is your right as a woman and as a De' Trini to be picky and to take your time.'

In a subsequent breath, Racquela's mother had noted that she would be proud of Racquela regardless of who she chose, or even if she chose to disregard the dying tradition of marrying at the end of finishing school. Racquela knew, however, she was truly her mother's daughter. She planned on falling in love, as fully as though it were a thing that could be mapped out and sequenced to ensure success. Though she had not yet experienced it with a man, love to Racquela was not a thing of spontaneity. It was a necessary part of her life to come, and she would find it by any means necessary. The engineers of old had once proclaimed crystal sounding a 'haphazard process at best', but eventually a formula was discovered to ensure success. Racquela, surprised that she actually remembered something obscure that Tevici had once said, knew that there was a formula to finding love. She intended to do just that.

"Senior Tevici," she interrupted. Racquela had no idea what she had even interrupted, or if Tevici had just finished a sentence. At that moment she didn't particularly care. Her question was monumentally more important than whatever Tevici was talking about.

"What do you know about the crystal betrothals?"

The old man gave a long-suffering sigh and tugged at his white ponytail. It was a question Racquela had already posed several times. She was certain that Tevici knew more about it than he let on, and since she was going to Central in the fall it became even more crucial that she knew all that there was to know about the crystal betrothals. She hoped that that by pestering him enough he would reveal more information.

"Crystal betrothals..." he began. Racquela could see the shrewd look in his eye, the struggle between being an honest educator and a tactician who tried to protect Racquela from potentially harmful information. "You are asking because you are going to Central, I assume, my lady?"

Racquela hated rhetorical questions. "I must know all that I can about it, Senior Tevici. What is the purpose of education if some knowledge is deliberately hidden?"

Tevici rubbed his temples with his thumbs and leaned back on the wrought-iron bench. "Some knowledge is more danger than it is worth," he said in a tired voice. "However, you are indeed paraphrasing something that I have said to you before, and I must remain true to that. As I mentioned before, the crystal betrothals are a tradition that stretch back even to the early days of Novem, before the empire. Nowadays, the only remaining legal crystal betrothals are performed at Central School, three betrothals every year to be exact. The Great Crystal chooses three boys and three girls and in pairs they become legally betrothed."

The pause lengthened after Tevici's sentence. Racquela got the impression that it was all he wanted to divulge on the subject.

"Yes, you have told me all of this before," Racquela said. She tossed a handful of plucked grass aside. "What I really wish to know is this: who gets chosen and why?"

Tevici nodded gravely. He seemed to understand what his pupil was after. Racquela had a hopeful look in her dark eyes, and she knew that it was hard to resist.

"The church would know more of this than I, my lady, or perhaps a book on the specific subject might suit you better. However, seeing as how we will not be able to press forward with our actual lesson until your curiosity is satisfied, I will tell you all that I know about the types of people who are chosen for crystal betrothals. Most, throughout history, have been gifted in some way, both the men and the women. Often the women are beautiful and artistic. Many of the men were said to have been handsome and athletic, like the marble statues on Avati Hill. Even more common are speakers or empaths who get betrothed this way. It is said that the Great Crystal chooses pairings that are likely to produce gifted offspring, and this theory is supported both by physical evidence and by the Old Temple itself. Many of those children go on to become betrothed at the behest of the Great Crystal, themselves. Does that answer your question? Most regard it as a method to keep the bloodlines of Novem strong. It is a part of our national identity and our culture, my lady."

Racquela nodded. Her teacher had told her nothing that she hadn't already known, but it was likely that he had actually exhausted his knowledge of the subject. Tevici's areas of historical focus were less mystical in nature.

"But is there any way to know who the Great Crystal will choose each year?"

"None that I know of, my lady. Those secrets are known only to the priests of the Old Temple, or perhaps not even them. Perhaps only the Great Crystal knows. It is, after all, considered to be a very spiritual ritual."

Racquela accepted that as Tevici's final say on the matter. She would have to look elsewhere for her answers. As Tevici picked up his lesson book and cleared his throat, Racquela's eyes returned to the clouds.

***

Racquela tied a blue ribbon into her ebon locks of hair and looked at her reflection in the vanity mirror with a critical eye. Appearances were crucial, even during a small jaunt to the Avati library. Racquela's social circle was a cutthroat one in many ways, and she tried hard to stay on top of things at all times, in fashion and beauty especially. Her social graces must be above reproach if she were to come out on top at Central School.

Despite the difficulties she faced in strictly maintaining appearances, Racquela was by all accounts lucky in more than just her birthrights. Blessed with not only a healthy, clear complexion for a girl of fifteen, Racquela possessed the wavy, raven locks and burnt umber eyes so fondly looked upon as the traits of the true ancestors of Novem.

Carefully brushing her hair in front of the vanity, Racquela sang *Costimara*, her favourite song to hear on the radio. It was an old folk tune, recently made popular again by the famous Faxon singer Mary Marion. Racquela hoped to one day record a song as popular as *Costimara*. She knew that it was possible if she tried hard enough. She was certainly prettier than Mary Marion.

Racquela changed into a lacy, cotton black-and-white summer dress that complemented her curvy figure nicely. She had filled out more than a little in the past year, and was still not entirely comfortable with her body, despite the attention it garnered. She felt fat and awkward, even though her parents and every boy she spoke to tried to convince her otherwise.

After applying her makeup and checking it in the mirror several times, Racquela telegrammed for a coach. Motorcoaches were expensive to take anywhere since they were a relatively new invention and the depression had hit the crystal industry quite hard, but Racquela wouldn't be caught dead hiring a smelly, horse-driven stagecoach when her family could afford better. Racquela's family owned a motorcoach, but her father would be out working and her mother was shopping so she was left to find her own way to the other side of Avati Hill. Racquela was not allowed to drive her father's motorcoach. It had cost him over a hundred thousand dinari.

As she sat on the green divan beside her bedroom window reading a book of love poetry, Racquela saw the sleek, black coach coming up the driveway. It had arrived much sooner than she had expected, but most of the Pirelli Motorcoach Company's drivers knew that the De'Trini family always left a tip. As the coach pulled up to the front doors of the De'Trini estate, Racquela heard a knock at her bedroom door.

"Come in," she said as she put her book down on the divan. The door opened and Maria, the family stewardess, entered.

It was rare for nobles to keep a female steward, but Maria's family had served the De'Trinis for over a century. Maria's father had served Racquela's grandfather. When the old steward produced no sons, it seemed certain that a new steward would have to be found, but Mercurio De'Trini asked his steward's daughter to apprentice for the role. Racquela often saw more of Maria's family than her own parents. Maria's husband, Mario, was the De'Trinis' chef, her son Lucius tended the gardens, and Lucius's wife Sarai had once been Racquela's nanny. Racquela used to play with Maria's grandchildren until Racquela's father had agreed to send them to boarding school.

The wrinkled old face of Maria smiled at Racquela until it looked as though her eyes would disappear under folds of eyelids and crow's feet. Although stooped from age, Maria's presence still commanded attention. As a little girl, Racquela had often felt nervous around the old woman.

"Mistress Racquela," Maria said, "your motorcoach is here. May I ask where you are going?"

Racquela stood and walked over to the old stewardess. "Please tell Mother and Father that I'm off to the library if they return before I do. I am ... doing some research for my studies with Senior Tevici. I shouldn't be more than an hour or two."

"Of course, mistress. Don't forget your purse."

Racquela turned around and grabbed her small leather purse from the vanity. She gave Maria a kiss on the cheek to thank her for the reminder and took the stairs down to the foyer. She slipped into a pair of black pumps (which her father was finally letting her wear after a year of begging) and left the manor. She had been hoping for the young driver with the kind eyes, but it was the old man with the liver spots on his skull. Racquela pretended to be occupied with the contents of her purse to avoid conversation.

Motorcoaches had come a long way since their invention by the commonwealth entrepreneur Jonn Larsin. Originally shaped like a horse-drawn buggy and powered by a steam engine, the creation of the electron crystal had changed everything and Jonn Larsin capitalized upon it immediately. Within a matter of years, every sufficiently wealthy person owned a motorcoach. Infrastructure and industry changed rapidly to keep up. Racquela remembered her father telling her once that it 'seemed like it had happened overnight'.

That had been when Racquela's parents were in their youth, during the Great War. After the economic boom of the 1880s, horses were a thing of the past, 'out to pasture' as Racquela's father laughingly put it. Every decent street corner had a lamp powered by an electron crystal, and what had once been the mount of kings and nobles became, instead, the transportation of the poor. Urbanization gripped the continent.

Racquela smiled as she stared out the window. Despite her indifference to history, she would often surprise her tutor with how much she actually remembered of his lessons. What kind of highborn child didn't overachieve, after all, unless rebellion was the goal? She was not only expected to be clear-minded, she wanted to be. Racquela had never willingly made friends with girls who feigned simplicity because 'the boys preferred them that way'. Her father had taught her better than that.

Avati was a big hill, and the library was on the other side from the De'Trini estate. Even by motorcoach it took fifteen minutes to get there.

One of the ancient buildings in the city and considered a national monument, the library was old Novem style with none of the Mosind influence on the structure. The outer edifice was built entirely of white marble, similar to Parliament, and was kept brightly painted in sky blues and cardinal reds, the same way that it had been coloured for centuries. The library was flanked by the National Museum of History and the campus of Captus Nove Academy, one of the three finest academies in the country. Across the street from the library entrance was the eastern edge of Avati Hill Park. Racquela loved strolling through the park in the summertime. It was the best time to see the Avati artists painting landscapes, or to watch boys play football.

Racquela paid the coach driver and hurried off toward the library entrance. She wasn't entirely certain which section to look through, but she imagined that 'history' would be a good place to start. She rifled through the card catalogues until she came to books about the Great Crystal. It was a large section. Not intimidated, Racquela pulled her notebook out of her purse and found an inkwell for her pen. She wrote down the numbers for several books that seemed like a good start: *Rituals of the Great Crystal 354 – Present*, *The Great Crystal of Captus Nove*, *The Great Crystal and its Role in*

Noven Society, and a few others. Carefully wiping her pen dry with a cloth, she returned it to her purse and strode purposefully over to the massive stacks of books.

Before long, Racquela was seated at a quiet table near the back of the library with a generous stack of books in front of her. She searched through the volumes for the answer to her question. After an hour and a half of reading and note-taking, her eyes were sore, her hand was cramped and stained with blue ink. She was much the richer for knowledge of the Great Crystal, but she had yet to find the information she was searching for. Racquela chuckled to herself. If Tevici ever found out that she had spent a summer afternoon in a library doing research, his heart would likely give out from pure shock. She vowed to herself that she would never tell him about it. Although he would be proud of her, she had an appearance of nonchalance to maintain.

After another half an hour Racquela grew frustrated. She returned several of the books to their shelves and picked out a few more. Her luck turned out to be no better with the new volumes, and she nearly cried when she discovered an ink stain on the front of her dress. Racquela cursed herself for a dully. Her note-taking had been too frenetic.

Frustrated, she got to her feet and looked around for someone who could help. She approached a middle-aged female librarian who was typing up reference cards. Racquela smiled politely and waited until the librarian stopped typing.

"Hello, pardon me. I was wondering if you could point me in the right direction of something specific."

The librarian looked up over her spectacles at Racquela, her face expressionless. "That depends on what you're looking for," she replied simply. She had an odd way of shaping her words that Racquela found annoying.

"I'm looking for books about the traditional Great Crystal betrothals. Unfortunately all of the books that I've looked through don't seem to have enough information. Is there some other section I should be checking?"

"Well, what section did you check?" she asked in that same, haughty tone.

Racquela suppressed her impatience. "History."

The woman nodded and arched both eyebrows. "That's the right section. And you didn't find anything?"

Racquela shook her head. "Nothing specific enough."

The librarian furled her brow and got up out of her chair. "Come with me," she said. Racquela followed her over to the card catalogues and watched as the librarian dextrously flipped through them. She stopped at a particular card and pulled it out of the drawer to show Racquela. "Did you read through this one? *Crystals and the Church*?"

"No," Racquela said, taking a moment to recall the books she had looked through. "No, that one wasn't on the shelf, I looked for it. If it's checked out I can come back next week."

"It might not be. Most people are lazy when they return the books to the shelves and don't follow the system," she said, her voice dripping with disdain. Racquela found herself wishing to be away from the woman almost as much as she wished to find her answers. "I'll take a quick look and see if I can find it for you." The shrew plodded off at an awkward gait down the aisle to the history section.

Racquela's eyes wandered as she awaited the librarian's return. As impatient as she was to find the proper information, she was also anxious not to miss out on the rest of a summer's day outdoors. Her eyes glazed over as she watched the dust motes floating in the sun's rays that came in from the second floor atrium windows. When they returned to focus, Racquela realized with some embarrassment that she was staring at another person unintentionally. Luckily, the girl that she was looking at didn't seem to notice since her nose was buried in a large and very old-looking book. Racquela looked away before the girl took notice that she was being watched, but her gaze returned to the girl every so often. Blondes weren't very common in Novem. Out of curiosity, Racquela squinted to read the title on the spine of the book the young girl was so interested in: *Crystals and the Church*.

"Well, I don't see the book anywhere on the nearby shelves," the librarian said.

Startled by the sudden reappearance, Racquela nearly lost her composure. She stepped back slightly and smiled as best as she could manage at the woman.

"You know what? Don't worry about it. Thanks for all of your help, you've been really shiny."

With a curt nod, the librarian left. Racquela turned her attention to the blonde girl, who looked as though she couldn't have been any older than fifteen. Like any discerning teenager, especially one of important status, Racquela made sure to carefully evaluate the girl she was about to speak to before approaching. Although Racquela thought that the girl was very pretty, her skirt and blouse were horribly out of fashion. Racquela also thought she spied some grass stains and dirt on the long, white skirt under the table. The young woman's posture was slouched, which, combined with her clothing, made it painfully obvious that her class was very low.

Racquela wasn't sure whether to feel pity or apprehension. She had no idea how to interact with someone who was obviously so lowborn, especially when she wanted something they had. Regardless of how she felt, she knew that the only way to acquire the book was to go up and talk to the girl.

The chair whined against the marble floor as Racquela took up the seat opposite her target at the large table. The noise made the girl look up immediately with a startled expression on her face. She noticed Racquela across from her and stared back. "Yes?" she asked.

"Hi," Racquela began. She hadn't thought far enough ahead to decide what exactly she was going to say to the mysterious girl, or how she was going to ask to borrow the book. "Um, this might sound like a dull request, but can I take a look at that book you're reading?"

The girl shrugged and examined the spine of the book, as though she weren't entirely certain what it was that she had been reading. Then she handed it over to Racquela.

"Sure."

Racquela sat stunned for a moment with the book in her hand. "Shiny. Wow, um, thanks." She stood up to leave.

"You won't find it in there."

Puzzled, Racquela turned back to the strange blonde. "Excuse me?"

The other girl's face was still as stone.

"You won't find it in there. I already looked."

Racquela tried to suppress a scoff but it came out anyway. She put her hand on the table and looked into the girl's eyes, which had an intensity that Racquela found discomforting.

"And what exactly am I looking for?"

The girl's face remained passive. "You're Racquela De'Trini, aren't you?"

Racquela was taken aback. How on Earth would a lowborn girl know exactly who she was? Something seemed very odd about the girl hiding behind wheat-coloured curls.

"I don't ... know you, do I?" Racquela inquired.

Racquela was startled when the girl grabbed her hand across the table and began to examine it. The waiflike teenager pointed to a large signet ring on Racquela's right middle finger. "That's the De'Trini crest, isn't it?"

"Well ... yes," Racquela replied as she pulled her hand back in an indignant gesture. "How did you know that?"

She felt like a dully, giving insipid, echoing responses to everything the stranger across from her did or said.

In response, the girl shrugged nonchalantly and made a face that would have been comical had Racquela not been so flabbergasted by the entire situation.

"I read a book on Noven nobility and heraldry once," the girl said. "I recognized the De'Trini crest when you walked up, and since Joven and Jessica De'Trini are known to have only one daughter ... well, I made an educated guess. Your family is kind of famous, after all."

Racquela couldn't argue with that. Even so, something seemed to her to be missing from the equation. "Wait, wait," she said, "I still haven't told you what I'm looking for in that book."

The other girl gave a sly smile. "Well, I don't actually know," she admitted. "But I have a good guess. You're going to Central in autumn, aren't you?"

Racquela nodded, too intrigued by that point to be annoyed.

"So am I, possibly. I was just reading about the crystal betrothals. What else would you be looking for if you're going to Central School?"

Racquela was dumbfounded. She realized that her mouth was hanging open, which was very unladylike, and closed it.

"I've read a lot about the Great Crystal," the odd girl continued. She seemed aware that she had put Racquela off with her strange manner, as her tone had become more apologetic. "There isn't a whole lot of useful information in that book," she said as she pointed at the heavy tome, "but I still might be able to help you."

"What's your name?" Racquela asked as she took a seat.

"My name's Crystara," the girl said without smiling.

"So ..." Racquela was lost for words. Her opinion of Crystara wavered between intriguing and disturbing. "You really think that you can help me?"

Crystara nodded. Racquela glanced around her. For reasons she couldn't explain it felt as though somebody was watching them.

"Hey, why don't we go to the park? It's a clear day out, might be a better place to talk."

Racquela could have sworn she saw a smile creeping onto the corners of Crystara's lips. She wasn't sure whether it looked endearing or bizarre.

"Sure," Crystara agreed.

Avati Hill Park was bustling with life as Racquela and Crystara picked their way across its winding cobblestone paths to find a quiet spot. A marching band tromped through the central square of the garden to the delight of onlookers, blaring a rousing rendition of Novem's national anthem, *The Crystal Skies of Novem*.

The whiteoak blossoms were soft underfoot, and the pair found their niche among a sequestered patch of black birch.

"I love this park," Racquela exclaimed. Crystara merely shrugged. Racquela wished that she'd brought a blanket to sit upon, or that her companion would appear less apathetic to everything around her.

"I never come up here," Crystara said after an awkward moment of silence. "I always wind up in the library." She followed the statement with a small, brief laugh.

"You read a lot, then?"

"All the time."

Another silence followed. Racquela wondered if being nice to Crystara was just a vain attempt to feel better about needing information from her. She decided to drop the pretense.

"Well. So you said you could help me. What do you know about the Great Crystal betrothals?"

"Lots. What do you want to know, specifically?"

"Well ..." Racquela felt nervous about revealing too much, but she knew that she didn't have a choice if she wanted accurate information. She only hoped that the girl was as knowledgeable as she claimed to be.

"Do you ..." she dropped her voice to a whisper, "... know how the Great Crystal chooses the betrothed?"

Crystara didn't seem surprised by the question. "Well from what I know the crystal chooses'the best' of each year. It doesn't pick based on class. I read once that in older times it was the only way for cross-class marriages to be considered socially acceptable. Some people say that the crystal chooses compatibility based on who would have the best children, but a lot of the books that I've read claim that it has more to do with true love, and who is meant to be together according to the gods."

Racquela raised an eyebrow in surprise. She had heard that before, but recalled that most people passed it off as romantic fancy. She felt a knot in her stomach and hoped that there was some truth to the claim.

"So it's more of a spiritual thing, then?"

"According to a lot of people. The church says that it's both. Why, do you think that you'll be picked?"

Racquela couldn't easily meet Crystara's gaze or the question. Would she be picked? If she were certain of it, she never would have gone to the library in search of answers in the first place. She knew that she was beautiful and of high station, but according to Crystara, station wasn't what was important. She was talented at music, but had absolutely no aptitude for crystals. Her parents had sent her in to be tested for empathy twice. Both times the test came back negative. When she was honest with herself, Racquela knew that she was a prize in terms of marriage, but when only three girls were chosen every year for betrothal, would her assets be enough? She wasn't certain.

"I have no idea," she answered.

"You could always bribe the church. You're rich, right?"

Racquela's head turned up sharply. "What?"

"Bribe the church," Crystara said again, nonchalantly. "People have been doing it forever, not just for crystal betrothals."

"But ... people actually do that?" Racquela asked. "I thought that the Great Crystal chose the betrothed."

Crystara nodded sagely. She had an absolute confidence in what she was saying that Racquela found attractive. Racquela wondered idly if there would be any social consequences to befriending somebody like Crystara. A person this knowledgeable would certainly come in handy. Besides which, Racquela mused, Crystara seemed very unique, and that was refreshing and fun. One could never have too many friends, and somebody had to assist Crystara with some fashion sense. Even if Crystara couldn't afford it, Racquela could spare a few of her old dresses to help the other girl out.

"The Great Crystal is the church, and the church is the Great Crystal. What I mean is, the big question that theologians, philosophers and rebels ... and, well, everybody have been arguing about for the last century has been whether or not the Great Crystal is actually a sentient thing, a speaker for the gods. The point is that it doesn't matter. If the church simply controls the actions of the Great Crystal and it's just a figurehead, then you just have to bribe them as you would bribe any public official. If the Great Crystal runs the church, giving a sufficient amount of money supports the church's goals, which are subsequently the crystal's goals. Therefore it should amount to the same thing."

Wheels turned in Racquela's head. Bribe the church? Her father would never agree to such a thing. He would be too worried about his reputation if such a thing was exposed to the public – but she didn't have to be completely honest with him in order to get the money. Then the Great Crystal would find her true love for her. She knew in her heart that everyone had a true love, but the crystal betrothals were the most effective way to ensure that she met hers. She had seen enough miserable relationships amongst her relatives to know that not everybody found their true love, and Racquela would never accept that fate.

She looked back at Crystara, who was attempting to coax a robin to approach her by using whistling sounds. Crystara appeared so peaceful – almost happy as she spoke in soft words to the small bird – that Racquela no longer found her intimidating.

"Are you hungry, Crystara? I'm starving."

The robin suddenly flew up to the branch of a black birch nearby. "I don't have any money."

"Oh, that's all right. It's my treat. I know a great place on Corti Street to get a gyro."

Chapter 3

Until Racquela came into her life, Crystara spent nearly every day reading. Since as far back as she could remember, which was about right after her mother died, Crystara read anything that she could lay her eyes on, sometimes from dawn to after dusk. She had no idea why she loved reading so much, but suspected that her penchant for it had grown out of the desire to avoid other children her own age, who never seemed to like her much. Crystara couldn't even remember how she had learned to read or who had taught her, but it was likely her mother, since she found it impossible to conjure up an image of her father lifting anything other than a whiskey label to his eyes.

After meeting Racquela that day in the library, Crystara found that she was reading less and less. Although Racquela professed to have other friends (who were very infrequently spoken about and never seen – at least not by Crystara), she seemed to prefer Crystara's company almost exclusively, which suited Crystara just fine. She hadn't had a friend in years, ever since she had punched Bruno in the nose for trying to kiss her. At some point she had decided that books were far less effort and heartache, and a much better diversion from how simultaneously frustrating and dull life was.

That was before Racquela. Nearly every day that summer after their first meeting, Racquela sent Crystara telegrams detailing where they should meet up for the day, or she would simply show up on the doorstep and away they would go. Crystara was more than happy to get out of the house as much as possible. Ever since the miner's strike her father could find nothing to do other than drink himself into a stupor by noon. He wasn't even picketing with the other workers, but in a moment of soberness he had told Crystara that he'd 'rather be working for table scraps than not working at all.' She couldn't decide if it made her respect him more or less, but Crystara couldn't deny that it was Racquela's generosity that kept her belly full that summer, since there was usually nothing in the icebox at home except hard liquor.

Excursions to the five-and-ten store were frequent when the two of them got together, as were picnics in Avati Hill Park. Racquela seemed to have no issue with spending money on Crystara. Initially Crystara felt guilty about that, but she soon discovered that there was no sense in arguing about it. Money was nothing to Racquela. Sometimes Crystara would grow angry at how frivolously her new friend spent dinari, but she kept those feelings hidden.

After that first day, it took Racquela almost a month to mention the crystal betrothals again. Crystara had nearly forgotten about it, but she could tell that Racquela, who had an obsessively romantic view of love, would only put it aside for so long.

On the first day of the month of Sexta, Crystara and Racquela were enjoying a picnic of freshly baked bread, fancy cheeses (some of which Crystara didn't even know the name of) and olives under the shade of their favourite whiteoak in Avati Hill Park. It was sweltering even in the shade, which made their cotton dresses feel like wool.

To pass the time, the pair had devised a game that they would often play wherein each of them would rate a male passerby for his attractiveness, on a scale of one to ten. Crystara couldn't remember which one of them had thought up the game, but it was a fun way to spend a day in the park. They would even rate the incredibly old or overweight, which was followed by giggles as soon as the man in question was out of earshot, although sometimes Racquela gave older men a more favourable score than Crystara.

"Seven," Racquela whispered as a well-dressed young man, probably an academy student, passed by. Crystara wheeled her head to look, but all she got was his backside. Not a bad view, in Crystara's opinion, but she had missed out on his face, which was the usual basis for the rating system.

"Shatters, I missed him," Crystara exclaimed when the young man was far enough away. She had to admit to herself that she had been very distracted that day. Ever since her letter from Central School had come in the mail, she could not keep her mind off of it.

If she had left it up to her father, Crystara wouldn't have thought about going to a finishing school, let alone Central. She'd had to go through the entire application process herself. All that her father had to do was sign the papers, which he did begrudgingly even after Crystara explained that unless her test scores were high enough to merit scholarships she wouldn't be going to a school that cost money anyway.

The letter had sat on Crystara's desk for a week now, unopened. Sometimes when she awoke in the morning she would stare at it, but she could never summon up the courage to tear open the envelope and face the inevitable rejection she was sure to find inside.

Other finishing schools had already accepted her, but none so prestigious as Central, which represented Crystara's best chance to make something of herself. Central School, however, was among the many finishing schools that Crystara could not afford. Her primary school grades and entrance exam scores were well above average, she knew, but she doubted if they were good enough to merit scholarships.

Crystara knew that so long as she didn't open the letter, she could hold on to the shard of hope that she would go to Central and make a future for herself, after all.

"You've been distracted lately," Racquela noted. "Are you thinking about the letter again?"

Crystara shrugged. "It doesn't matter, I can't afford to go. Summer will end and you'll go to Central and I'll wind up going somewhere that they stick poor students, like Gallari, and I'll probably never see you again." She hadn't intended to sound petulant, but it came out that way regardless.

Racquela beamed her usual benevolent smile. "Crys, we'll still be friends if you don't go to Central, I promise. Why don't you just open the letter and set your mind at ease already? Eight, solid eight."

46

Crystara turned her head in time to catch a glimpse of another student-type walking by, at least as handsome as Racquela had rated him to be. Wealthy academy boys were not in Crystara's future if she didn't go to Central, she knew.

"Uh, eight and a half." Crystara drew a slightly rumpled envelope out of her satchel, the one that usually carried books. "I can't do it," she said as she tossed the envelope in Racquela's direction. "You open it for me."

Racquela said nothing, but picked up the envelope from where it sat innocuously on the grass and turned it over in her hands.

"See, it's not very thick," Crystara reasoned, "so I think it's just a rejection letter."

Racquela raised her eyebrows. "Mine was the same. They don't send you much, Crys, just a letter. The rest of it, entrance exam scores and the like, you receive at Central, I think. Are you sure you want me to open this?"

Crystara shut her eyes tightly. "Do it, before I change my mind."

As she heard the paper tearing, Crystara imagined that it was her heart tearing in two as the letter confirmed her being torn away from her only friend and her only real chance to make something of herself.

"Uh, hmm ..." Racquela mumbled.

Crystara cringed. "What does it say?"

"Wow."

"It says wow?"

"No, I said wow."

"I can't take it anymore!" Crystara exclaimed. She tackled her friend onto the picnic cloth and wrested the letter from her hands, which elicited peals of laughter from Racquela. Crystara's heart pounded as she read the letter over, and then over a second time. "Due to your high crystal-speaking score, we are proud to offer you a full scholarship to ..."

Crystara's hands were shaking. "High crystal-speaking score ..." She looked over at Racquela, who had the widest grin Crystara had ever seen.

"You got in!"

"Aah!" Crystara screamed. She and Racquela sat on the picnic cloth and hugged as tears of joy streamed down Crystara's face. She had a future, after all.

After a minute or so, Racquela pulled away. "Well, we have to celebrate!"

"Celebrate? How?"

Racquela flashed a mischievous grin. "I have a great idea."

***

It was a great idea until Crystara began to feel ill.

It had all started out fine. Racquela swore that her parents would never notice the missing wine since their cellar was always well-stocked. They would be away all weekend anyway, Racquela added, and Maria the stewardess wouldn't bother them if Racquela demanded privacy. It had taken the girls a while to find a corkscrew, but once they figured out how to work it, it wasn't long before they were into the second bottle. The radio blared, and they danced and sang along as loudly as they could.

Racquela's parents' house was enormous. Crystara couldn't begin to imagine what somebody would need all that room for. She imagined that Racquela could spend a week in the same house as her parents and never see them, or the hired help. There were three floors, balconies in almost every bedroom, a huge manicured garden in the back, even a coachport. A coachport! Crystara's jealousy was diffused by how much fun she was having.

The wine didn't taste all that great to Crystara, but she felt amazing. She had no idea why her father was so angry all the time when he drank. She felt better than ever.

Around the middle of the second bottle of *Costimara Grigia*, however, Crystara had to sit down. Perhaps it was how tiny she was, or just how much she drank, or all the spinning around. Luckily, she managed to make it to the toilet before she got sick.

Racquela was there to hold Crystara's hair back after the initial dash to the bathroom. "All right, stop, you're gonna make *me* sick," Racquela said jokingly.

Crystara laughed despite herself. She felt miserable and joyful all at once. "I guess I learned my lesson. I don't know how Dad does it. I ..." she stopped mid-sentence to heave into the toilet bowl. She couldn't remember the last time she had felt so embarrassed.

"I'm sorry, Crys, this is all my fault," Racquela admitted. "It was my idea."

Crystara breathed heavily, trying to control the roiling feeling in her stomach and the spinning sensation in her skull. "Ugh ... that's all right. This is still ... the best day of my life." She managed a weak smile, which she imagined made her look hideous given her insobriety and the spittle coming off of her lower lip.

Racquela laughed. "Aww. Well I'm glad I'm here to share it with you, then, upset stomach and all."

Crystara threw up again in response.

Later on, once Crystara's stomach had settled down, she and Racquela sat on the balcony under the stars, drinking tea. Crystara was feeling rather subdued and no longer intoxicated, and more than anything else glad that she was not feeling ill. Racquela still appeared to be under the influence of the wine – she had finished the second bottle by herself – but was handling it much better that Crystara had. She was quite animated, waving her arms about as she spoke, and Crystara was content to just sit and listen, occasionally adding a word or two here and there or simply nodding in agreement. They spoke of everything, from boys to fashion to their future at Central School together and back again. It was a night of philosophy under the stars. It was a night of looking forward.

"Do you believe in true love, Crys?" Racquela asked. She craned her head backward over the wooden patio chair to ask the question. She was a caricature of laziness, yet her expression suddenly grew serious, which Crystara found amusing.

"I dunno," Crystara replied honestly. She had never given it much thought before that moment. "Never been in love. I've only had one boyfriend, even, and that didn't exactly end well."

Racquela sat up suddenly, rapt with interest. "What happened?"

"I bit him."

"What?" Racquela burst into peals of laughter.

"I was eight," Crystara explained. "And he was being a dully. So I bit him. I guess I've never had a real boyfriend, so I don't know about love."

"What about your parents?"

Crystara shot her friend a glare. Racquela should have known better than to ask. It was probably the wine's fault. "I don't remember my mother ... and I hate my dad. So, no. I've never experienced love."

"But do you believe in it?"

Crystara shrugged. "I dunno. It's hard to believe in something you've never seen or felt, like the gods or the Great Crystal."

Racquela didn't reply immediately. Crystara could see the wheels turning in her companion's mind by the expression on her face.

"I believe in true love," Racquela finally replied. "And the Great Crystal. Do you still think that you can help me? With the Great Crystal, I mean?"

Crystara's heart felt heavy. A part of her had hoped that Racquela would forget about her plan. She didn't understand how something like love could be forced like that, but her feelings about the Great Crystal were much more ambivalent than Racquela's. It wasn't that she didn't want to help her friend, but the thought of contacting the church with the intent to bribe them tied her stomach in knots. Whether or not it was rational, she felt as though her friendship with Racquela was somehow linked to her success with the bribery attempt.

"Of course I can, so long as you can still get the money from your parents."

"I'll just tell them I need money for new clothes."

Crystara suppressed the urge to call Racquela spoiled.

***

Crystara couldn't approach just any old priest. The priest had to be from the Old Temple on Crystus Hill. Preferably it would be the keeper himself, the crystal-speaker who looked after the Great Crystal. As the nominal head of the church he would be the prime candidate, and likely the one who was bribed the most, Crystara figured. The trouble was finding a way to meet him in person.

According to most of the books that Crystara had read on the subject, the Church of Novem, despite its diminishing power, was still an incredibly wealthy and influential force in affairs of state. Traditionally, the Great Crystal had been consulted on most important decisions undertaken by the nation of Novem, especially when it was a central symbol to the First and Second Empires, but after the holy war and the subsequent democratic revolutions it was no longer the end-all and be-all that it had once been.

Despite the Great Crystal's limitations, it and the church were the only influences that mattered when it came to the crystal betrothals. If Racquela was as abyss-bent on finding her 'true love' the old-fashioned way, Crystara was certain that between her own tenacity and Racquela's family money, the ambiguously mystical Great Crystal would find a way to choose Racquela as one of the six.

Crystara had spent a few days pondering how best to approach the Old Temple of the church and find out, through some means of subterfuge as yet unknown to her, how to bribe the Keeper of the Great Crystal. She was not the most outgoing girl she knew, and her extensive research into the subject of secret politics did not count as real-world experience. At times Crystara wondered why she had ever made the promise to Racquela in the first place, since she seemed to be no better equipped to make it all happen than Racquela herself. But then she remembered Racquela's wide-eyed naïveté and the fact that the promise had made them friends. Crystara had always appreciated the value of a promise.

While loitering about on Crystus Hill one afternoon alone, watching the crowds of wealthy tourists and street vendors who congested the area around the old fountain, Crystara pondered the best way to turn her timidity into courage and approach a priest. From her bench, Crystara noticed that a large flock of people were entering the Old Temple through the front door. She was close enough to blend in with them before they all passed through the great marble archway, so Crystara bolted across crowded the old square and nonchalantly insinuated herself into the cluster of people.

Most of them looked like students. They were young and carried notebooks and pencils. One of them even had a big clunky camera with a light crystal set into the top. Crystara realized belatedly that she had found a tour group. Her timing couldn't have been better if she had planned it.

Nobody objected to her presence, although several of the boys in the crowd took notice of her as they all passed through the big double whiteoak doors into the main foyer of the temple. Crystara was used to it, of course. Her father had always told her that a blonde in Novem was like coal in a crystal mine. The coal was just as important as the crystals, but everybody acted like they didn't want the coal there. Crystara never had the guts to tell her father that with new advances in crystal technology, coal was becoming less and less useful. Crystara was used to being treated differently for being blonde. She had surpassed the difficulty of it sometime in her childhood to emerge confident enough in her own appearance not to care. She knew that some people would treat her like less of a person for being blonde, while other people would treat her like a delicate flower. To Crystara, neither type was worth her time.

The tour guide began to tell the throng about the history of the Old Temple, which Crystara might have found interesting if she wasn't concerned with more urgent things.

"These ancient halls that we stand in are over two thousand years old," he began. The short, piebald man had an officious look about him. Crystara wouldn't have been surprised if the tour guide was actually a priest. "Built during the First Republic to honour Jova, our lord and creator, this temple was and always has been the central administration of the Noven church, to which all other Noven temples dedicated to all other gods owe their fealty."

Glancing around the great marble foyer, Crystara took note of the security guards in the Jovan temple colours of blue and white who were ahead and behind the tour group, as well as the two who stood under the archway that led to a much larger hall. Crystara reasoned that speaking to a guard wouldn't do any good. She would have to wait until she actually saw a priest, if she were even lucky enough to find one on the tour. The sightseeing of the Old Temple likely skipped many of the administrative or 'restricted' areas, including the Great Crystal and the keeper's offices. As far as Crystara could remember reading, the general public was not allowed to see the Great Crystal. To be permitted to do so was considered a high honour bestowed by the church.

The tour guide continued. "To your right is the great hall, which we'll visit later and is probably the most popular part of the tour. If you'll follow me, we'll head through this door and out of the building so we can get a better look at the amazing architecture of this ancient structure, as well as a view of the temple gardens, which are absolutely gorgeous this time of year."

Crystara suppressed a yawn as the crowd began to herd itself out of the foyer and into the heat of the afternoon. Architecture was about the last thing that Crystara cared about. The tour group followed the white marble wall of the Old Temple around on a pathway bordered by rose bushes.

"Are you a part of this class?" a male voice said right beside Crystara. "You don't look familiar."

53

Startled, Crystara turned slowly to see who was speaking to her. The voice in question belonged to a man who looked like an academy student. He was decent-looking and young, but Crystara was more concerned with not being discovered than with flirting, though she cursed herself for a dully for having to make that choice. She consoled herself with the notion that the young man would likely find her awkward or strange within a minute or two of conversation.

"Not speak much Noven," she said, not meeting the man's eyes directly. She had no idea where the made-up accent came from that she had tacked onto her broken speech, but she hoped that it would at least convince the man to leave her alone.

To Crystara's dismay, her reply seemed to make the man more interested. "Oh, so you're not from around here, then? Seeing the sights, are you?"

"Uh ..." she stared at the flowers.

The man made a pacifying gesture. "Oh don't ...don't worry, I'm actually learning a language or two at Captus Nove Academy. Maybe we'd have more luck if I tried your tongue? Where are you from? Faxon?"

Crystara was stunned. Were all men out of finishing school so bold? She switched tactics and pointed at the tour guide up ahead of them, who was gesturing at a flowerbed as though it were the most exciting thing on the tour.

"Tour man talking. Please quiet." She folded her arms and turned a cold shoulder to the man, hoping that he would take the hint.

Instead, the man followed her around as the tour continued, going so far as to introduce himself as 'Tomasi' and asking if he could show her the best places to go for dinner in Captus Nove. Flattered as she was, Crystara found Tomasi's forwardness a bit off-putting. As the group passed by a doorway that the tour guide said led to 'the temple library and other administrative areas', Crystara decided to try something a little more drastic.

The man with the camera was still in sight just ahead of Crystara in the tour group. He was tucking the camera and tripod under his arm after having just taken a picture of the bell tower to the

54

north of the temple. Crystara plunged her way forward through the milling crowd, leaving Tomasi behind her. All she had to do was touch that crystal on the top of the camera and ...

The crowd exploded in a frenzy of confusion. It sounded as though a wand had gone off. Great flashes of light and bangs of sound were coming from the camera, and half of the crowd stood staring at it, wondering what was wrong with the abyss-damned thing, while the other half turned and fled as though they were being shot at.

In the chaos Crystara made her way to the side entrance of the temple and slipped inside, unnoticed. Her heart was pounding and her hands were shaking. Never before had she done something so rash. Behind the door she could hear a muffled voice amidst the shouts: "Oh shatters, the crystal light broke!" Crystara began to chuckle and then clapped her hands over her mouth.

Crystara looked around to get her bearings. A long hallway stretched out before her, with a wide set of double doors at the other end, and two smaller doors closer to her, one on the left and one on the right. Crystara was almost certain that the area she was in was restricted to priests and temple staff only, but she had no idea how else to find a temple priest.

"What are you doing back here?" a voice said right beside her. Crystara was so startled that she screamed out loud. Her head jolted to her right to behold a stooped old man in very fancy-looking blue and white robes. His beard was full, white and fluffy and his eyes sparkled a kind blue, but at that moment he was the most terrifying thing on the planet.

"I ... I ..." Crystara was stunned. A part of her tried to think of an excuse, but her brain was as shocked as her body seemed to be. She thought about fleeing, but her legs couldn't seem to summon themselves out of their paralysis. Only at the mercy of her father had she ever been more terrified. A small voice in her mind mused that she would probably go to jail for trespassing. Her father finding out about *that* was the scariest part of all.

"I'm afraid you'll have to come with me," the old man said.

Although his tone was not immediately threatening, Crystara was on the verge of tears. She fought them back. To cry would have betrayed her fear to the priest, and she wanted to see if she could still swing the situation to her advantage. After all, she had been looking for a priest all along.

The old man gestured for Crystara to precede him down the hallway. Slowly and shakily, she made her way along the creaking wooden floor. When they arrived at the whiteoak double-doors, Crystara hesitated and looked back at the priest. He came up beside her and opened one of the doors to reveal another hallway that curved around and away from Crystara on both the left and right sides. There was also a guard in blue and white standing right beside Crystara in the hallway, which made her even more nervous.

The priest nodded to the guard solemnly. "Follow us, please," he commanded. "Make sure she doesn't try and leave."

The guard shot him a confused look, but followed his orders and walked behind Crystara. Her guts clenched with every boot clomp the guard took behind her.

Stooped as he was, the old priest was remarkably quick on his feet and Crystara had to hurry to keep up with him. He led Crystara and the guard around the winding hallway, past a set of doors only slightly smaller than the ones at the temple entrance, and then over to a small door with a crystal lock. The priest produced a small crystal key of a cobalt blue out of his pocket and turned it in the lock, which made the lock itself go from a neutral white to the same shade of blue. Then he entered the room. The guard ushered Crystara in behind the priest.

The office was small and tidy. The priest took a seat behind the desk, and gestured for Crystara to take the one on the opposite side. She did so quietly and waited for the priest to speak first.

"Thank you, Anton," he said, looking at the guard. "You may go."

Crystara couldn't see the guard's response, but she heard the door behind her close, leaving her alone with the priest. Although she was somewhat fearful, she was excited as well. The old man's voice made him seem hard as a crystal blade, but there was a softness to his eyes, and Crystara could have sworn she could see a corner of a smile underneath the shaggy curls of his beard. He was completely inscrutable, and it made him compelling.

A long, uncomfortable silence followed the guard's departure, and Crystara's eyes nervously darted about the room. They rested upon a black name-plate that was on the edge of the desk, and her eyes widened.

"You must be dabbling in crystal-speaking at finishing school," he said finally, "although I have no idea why you caused that scene outside, or what you were doing in the hallway, for that matter. What exactly are you looking for here, young lady? Not the Great Crystal, I hope?"

Crystara took a deep breath. "Not ... exactly." She chose her next words very carefully, for she was certain that she could still find trouble if she said the wrong thing. "I'm here for a friend of mine. She's interested in the crystal betrothals."

The man raised an eyebrow inquisitively. "Oh? Interested? So interested that she sent you in her place?"

"She was afraid," Crystara said. She folded her shaking hands in her lap to keep them steady. She found that she could not think fast enough to make something up. Her tension forced her to be honest. "I offered to find out more for her and so I came here."

"And you are not afraid?"

"No," Crystara answered, although she could not meet the priest's eyes when she said it.

"What is your name, child?"

Crystara knew that it would have been foolish to give out her own name when there was a possibility of incrimination for trespassing on church property, but in her nervousness she couldn't think of any other name than Racquela's off the top of her head, and she had no desire to betray her friend in such a way in case the bribery attempt failed.

"Crystara. Crystara Mita."

The old man smiled, sitting back in his chair. "Crystara. I am Keeper Orvin, Crystara. It is a pleasure to finally meet you."

It was Crystara's turn to raise an eyebrow. "You ... you know who I am?"

Keeper Orvin stood and beckoned Crystara to follow him to the door at the other end of the office. Being far too intrigued to consider doing anything else, Crystara followed as the keeper produced a second crystal key from somewhere within the folds of his robes, this key a brilliant emerald green. Keeper Orvin opened the unassuming door and guided Crystara through to a massive circular space, most of which was taken up by the largest crystal that Crystara had ever seen in her life. She could only assume that she stood before the Great Crystal itself.

It sat like an iceberg, half-buried under the stones of the temple. It was hard to deny how real the thing was as she stood before it. It was harder still simply to shrug off the religious belief that the Great Crystal was more than just an imbued rock. Crystara always thought of the Great Crystal as a larger, multi-purpose version of the crystals used in everyday life. The church simply claimed it had greater, more esoteric powers, to maintain their dominance over Noven society. Yet standing before the towering rock, Crystara couldn't decide if it was merely a symbol of old Noven prosperity and cultural dominance, or a fallen piece of the heavens. Cut with a complex and symmetrical brilliance that seemed to outdo even the greatest feats of engineering, it was statuesque. Shining down from the clear glass skylight, the unrelenting sun's rays struck the massive thing and burst into all the shades of the rainbow.

Mesmerized by the prisms of colours that shimmered in the air and across the bare circular wall of the chamber, Crystara had no words for how she felt. Although the Great Crystal's circumference was separated from the walkway by a brass railing, it was easily within a reachable distance. She found her hand slowly inching toward its smooth, pure surface. It seemed to call out to her silently, summoning her to press her palm against it and uncover its mighty secrets.

"Don't touch it," Keeper Orvin commanded. His words pulled Crystara out of her trance and she looked at him.

"You can feel its power, can't you Crystara? Yes, I read your transcripts that you sent to Central School."

He began walking around the Great Crystal at a leisurely pace, and Crystara found herself following along. "The church is privy to many things that might surprise you. We get copies of the transcripts from the entrance exams every year, so that we can start grooming certain individuals for a life of service with the church. Most skilled speakers go on to become engineers, but there are many other avenues available to a speaker of decent talents ... someone such as yourself."

He turned to look back at Crystara and his gaze was heavy with suggestion. "It's not often that somebody comes along who can speak to crystals without first receiving proper instruction, Crystara. Or is there something that I should know about?"

The truth of the matter was that Crystara had always possessed a knack for crystals, ever since she could remember. Nobody had taught her, unless it was her mother, whose memory had long since faded into the background shadows of her mind, places that she couldn't or wouldn't consciously go.

"Nobody taught me," she replied to the keeper. "I've just always seemed to know how to manipulate crystals. The simple ones, anyway."

To Crystara's surprise, the Keeper smiled, then continued to pace around the Great Crystal. Again she could feel its presence, more than just the visual sight of the thing beside her, but she didn't dare touch it or even look at it without the keeper's permission. There was something about his voice that compelled her to obey, or at least respect his wishes.

"That is very uncommon, but not unheard of. The prophetess Celesta was similar in her childhood, did you know that?"

Crystara had never read much about the Queen-turned-prophetess, but she remembered hearing something about her being gifted with crystals at an early age. She nodded silently to Keeper Orvin and her thoughts turned apprehensive. She was beginning to understand why the keeper was trying to draw a parallel between herself and the long-dead monarch.

"I'm not interested in working for the church, Keeper Orvin," she said flatly.

They had circled the entirety of the Great Crystal and were back at the door that led to the keeper's office. Keeper Orvin looked disappointed but not upset.

"I see. Well I suppose that might make it difficult for me to help you with whatever it is your friend wants," he replied as he opened the door to his office. He ushered Crystara through ahead of him. Keeper Orvin returned to his office chair and pressed a hand to his lips in a thoughtful expression. He gazed at Crystara patiently, as though he were waiting for her to reply.

"My friend is interested in being one of the betrothed this year at Central School," Crystara admitted as she took a seat across from Keeper Orvin, just as she had before. She didn't want to play any more games, and Keeper Orvin turned out to be quite different from what she had expected, not intimidating or nefarious-seeming at all. At the worst, he would turn down her request, but Crystara expected that to happen regardless. At least at that point she could go back to Racquela and admit that she had tried her best. Nobody could fault her for that, or so she hoped.

"Your friend. Not yourself?"

Crystara shook her head.

"Crystara, you must understand that I don't make decisions on behalf of the Great Crystal. It chooses the betrothed. However, I can ... influence that decision. But I require something in return."

"She can pay."

Keeper Orvin nodded. "Yes yes. A token gift of wealth is fine, but do you think the church really needs money that badly? I am interested in something additional and a little more substantial if you want to make this deal with me."

Crystara shook her head again. "I'm sorry, keeper. I am not interested in joining the church after finishing school. Isn't there some other kind of deal we could make?"

Keeper Orvin looked up at the ceiling. As he pondered, he stroked his beard and played with the crystal keys in his pocket. Finally he looked back at Crystara, and it seemed to her that a different kind of smile had found its way to his lips, hidden by the great white billows of beard.

"There is, actually."

Keeper Orvin told Crystara the deal. She wondered if it would be worth it.

Chapter 4

Timori had read once that Central School had originally been a prison. He found the fact both ironic and amusing.

When it was erected in the dark ages, Central was the largest prison that had ever been built on the continent of Titania. Originally it was simply referred to as *La Prigiona,* and it housed the the majority of Novem's murderers and political insurgents. Structured out of deepstone masonry, it took seven years to complete and could house two thousand prisoners, a considerable achievement for its day. It was larger even than Renaldi Castle on the northern tip of Novem, the first line of defence against the Nilonne Empire.

La Prigiona remained a prison until the first republican revolution of 1736, when it was sacked and temporarily converted into an administrative building for the republic in the ensuing confusion. The respite from its origin was short-lived, however, and when King Matia assumed the throne in 1756, *La Prigiona* resumed its original function. Most of the administrators of the Third Republic found themselves in *La Prigiona* before being summarily executed for treason against the crown.

La Prigiona suffered extensive damage during the revolution of 1822 that led to the Fourth Republic. Two years later, the city planners needed a finishing academy for their central district, since the Aestala Hill district lacked a facility large enough to house its students. They decided to capitalize on the vast space of *La Prigiona*, now abandoned and rife with squatters. After some renovations, *La Prigiona* became Central School, the finishing school for the Aestala Hill district in the centre of the city of Captus Nove.

Until Central School was finished, Avati School was considered the most prestigious in the city, and most of the noble classes sent their sons and daughters to Avati for their education. Declining test scores at Avati and a rise of the second merchant class – the 'entrepreneurs,' as they were dubbed – led to Central's rise as a more illustrious school. With each passing year, more and more nobles sent their children to Central.

Additions were made to the original prison building in 1863 as the need to create additional classrooms and house additional students grew, and, over the course of thirty years, especially after the population boom that followed the Great War, Central School's massive deepstone fortress was buried under brick and limestone. Although the school had lost its fearsome appearance, its reputation could not be ignored.

It had come as a surprise to Timori not so much that he had been accepted to Central School, but that somehow he had earned a scholarship from the republic in order to cover the cost of his education there. His mother nearly fainted when she read the news, and Timori couldn't figure out whether to laugh or cry, so he merely sat in a chair in his tiny kitchen and shook with excitement. He would be going to the best school in the country with his best friend, after all. He had no idea how he had managed to earn a scholarship. He had barely studied for the entrance exams, and he knew damn well that he had failed the empathy/crystal test. Timori wondered if it was a part of the 'Class Action', to select random lower-class students to attend Central. He would never question it, of course. It was the greatest blessing he had ever received.

Timori stood beside Jacoby and gazed up at the pell-mell collection of white-and-taupe blocks used for classrooms that clustered around the old brown stones of *La Prigiona* like bees around a hive. Like most fifteen-year-olds out to prove themselves, Timori wasn't afraid of much, but the barred windows and thick whiteoak doors of Central stood out ominously. He knew that he would soon be looking out of them from the inside, and that in many ways a school wasn't much different from a prison. As a member of the lower classes, Central would chew him up and spit him out if he didn't keep his wits about him.

Jacoby, beside him, grinned from ear to ear. Nothing could keep his best friend down, which Timori found enviable at the same time he found it naive. In some ways he knew that Jacoby would have an even harder time at Central than himself. A son of 'Class Action' was like a wolf without a pack. The dullies at the bottom and the spoiled socialites at the top were both going to treat Jacoby like dirt.

"You know," Jacoby said with a smirk, "it's actually kind of an ugly school."

Timori laughed. "That's putting it mildly. But it's what's inside the school that matters, Jake. The best teachers in the country are here." Timori watched as other new students passed the pair on both sides. "Come on. Let's go register before it gets too crowded in there."

The hallways were large and confusing, completely different from the primary school designs that Timori was used to, but there were signs posted to direct him and Jacoby to the right place. Before long they stood in the assembly room, a great stone chamber with vaulted ceilings that Timori knew from his research about Central was actually the centremost room of the original fortress of *La Prigiona*. In the days of the prison it had been the courtyard. The ceiling and floors had been added later as a decision by the administrator during the Third Republic. Timori remembered reading something about how the administrator had been agoraphobic and chuckled to himself.

"What's so funny?" Jacoby asked as he looked around with excitement.

"Nothing," Timori said. He watched the throngs of students milling around and travelling from table to table, writing down classes on their registration sheets. "This is gonna take a while."

Jacoby nodded and the two of them went over to the table with the banner labelled 'registration' to get their class selection sheets.

The teacher handling registration, a bored-looking woman with her hair done up in a bun, asked Jacoby and Timori for their names, then searched through a large stack of papers and handed them each a few sheets. Upon the front page was a great deal of personal information, and the subsequent pages listed in detail their test scores and achievements since the first grade. Timori rifled back to the final page to find his test scores from the Finishing School Achievement Test he had taken at the beginning of summer. He was pleased with what he found, and couldn't help but smile to himself.

"So where to first?" Jacoby asked. "Football?"

Timori's smile widened. He had forgotten all about football. "Yeah, we should get that out of the way first. They might have a limited number of spots available for tryouts."

Football had been the boys' passion since they were old enough to kick. Although they had dabbled in other sports while they were growing up together in primary school, the most popular sport in Novem for the past fifty years or more had been football, and every boy who didn't want to be considered a pansy played the game. Timori and Jacoby always played together, in school or in the junior leagues during summer, and were glad to consider themselves among the best players wherever they went. Jacoby had a keen eye as a goalie, and could always tell which way the ball was going to go. Timori could charge and weave through his opponents with a ball, and his footwork was almost unmatched. Dreams of grandeur in the National League had filled the boys' heads since they had won their first divisional championship together in the second grade.

Timori had become more realistic about the possibilities of being a football star as he grew older, but it was fun to indulge in the fantasy once in a while. The importance of the game, if only as a bond that he shared with Jacoby, was not lost on him. Timori was pleased to find that there were plenty of spaces left on the list when he and Jacoby wrote their names down. He recalled that few highborn indulged in the sport. Skill at the game of football was a poor kid's ticket to success.

As Timori and Jacoby crossed the assembly hall to register for engineering, a voice called out at them:

"Hey! Aren't you going to register for empathy?"

Timori turned to look. The teacher in question was an aging man with a ponytail, the mark of the generation that had lived through the Great War when they were young.

"I didn't score high enough to register for empathy," he said sadly. Timori had been disappointed when he discovered that he had no talent for empathy or crystal-speaking. His secret wish from the time he was a small child was to be discovered as a prolific speaker. It was a common dream for youth, however, and Timori knew it.

"Not you," the teacher said with a scoff. He pointed at Jacoby. "You. You're Jacoby Padrona, right? I saw you when you came here to do your achievement tests. Aren't you going to register for empathy?"

Timori looked at Jacoby with incredulity. Jacoby an empath? Timori tried to suppress his jealousy and let his surprise show through instead. Jacoby didn't seem to believe the teacher either.

"Me?" he asked. "Are you sure you have the right person?"

The teacher tilted his head down and raised an eyebrow. "You are Jacoby Padrona, aren't you?"

"Well ... yeah," Jacoby replied. "But how could you know that I'm an empath? Wouldn't I have heard about it first?"

Timori rolled his eyes. "Didn't you look through your test scores when you got those sheets, dully?" He tapped at the pieces of paper Jacoby was carrying for emphasis. "What do they say?"

Jacoby skipped to the back page and scanned through it. His eyes widened at what he saw. "Ninety-six on empathy?" he practically screamed the words. "Shatters, how did that happen? I had no idea what I was doing."

"That's the point, it's a blind test," the teacher said as he pushed his spectacles up his nose with his middle finger. "Nobody knows anything about it when they go in because they don't teach empathy to children. It's an intuitive thing. Either you have the ability or you don't."

"Seems like a load of horseshit to me," Timori muttered. It was loud enough in the room that nobody heard him. He noticed that Jacoby was particularly elated by the news that he had empath potential, which quelled Timori's jealousy somewhat. He clapped Jacoby on the back.

"Well congratulations, Jake," he exclaimed. "At least one of us has the potential. To tell you the truth, no offense meant, but I'm still surprised."

Jacoby nodded. "Me too." Smiling like a dully, he walked up to the table to register for the class. Timori wondered what Jacoby would drop in favour of empathy. He hoped that it wasn't football.

Timori heard a female voice nearby. "Hold on, I need to register for this class."

"Oh, you're an empath too?" another girl said. "There's just no end of surprises to you, is there?"

Timori turned to see two girls standing behind him. To his surprise, one of them was the girl who lived next door to him, whose name he hadn't yet managed to discover. It was his neighbour's friend, however, who caught his attention, and he found himself dumbstruck when he looked at her. She looked back at him with dark, seductive eyes and smiled warmly. He smiled back like a grinning fool.

"Hi," the girl said with a friendly curtsy. By then, Timori had completely forgotten about the girl next door.

"Timori," he blurted.

The raven-haired girl tilted her head to the side. "Pardon me?"

Timori silently cursed himself and extended his hand in the proper custom – if somewhat sporadically followed by the youth of Timori's generation – to kiss hers.

"That is, uh, my name. Timori. But you can call me Tim if you like, or not if that's too personal. Uh ..." He awkwardly planted his lips on her fingers and stepped back respectfully, almost too quickly. "And who may I have the pleasure of ..."

"Oh!" Jacoby exclaimed, interrupting Timori. "Crystara. Remember me?" Timori glared daggers at Jacoby.

"Jake. I remember," Crystara replied. She didn't seem interested in customs, because she offered her hand to neither Jacoby nor Timori. However, the girl whose hand Timori had just kissed offered the same one to Jacoby. Timori hoped that it was just out of politeness.

"I am Racquela De'Trini," she said as Jacoby kissed her hand. "It's nice to meet you, Jake. Timori."

She turned back to Timori as she said his name and he felt light-headed. Elated, Timori knew that another hopeless romance was beginning. His attention to his poetry would likely double.

Crystara, meanwhile, had gone up to the table to register and returned in the time it had taken for Racquela to introduce herself. "I have to register for speaking, Racquela," she said. She turned her gaze to Jacoby. "You should do the same, Jake."

Jacoby gave Crystara a quizzical expression. "I should?"

Crystara nodded and gave Jacoby a look as though he were a fool of a dully. "Of course you should. Every empath can speak to crystals."

With that, she turned and left. Racquela shot the boys another smile and followed her.

Timori waited until they were well out of earshot. "She's mine."

"Which one?" Jacoby asked.

"Racquela."

Jacoby barked a laugh. "What happened to the girl next door?"

"She's yours, if you want her. Seems like you've made headway already. Just don't touch Racquela, she's mine. I know how you like to steal all the girls, Jake." He punched Jacoby on the arm playfully.

Jacoby rubbed his arm. "Tim, you do know who she is, right? Racquela De'Trini?"

Timori shrugged. Jacoby had become much more aware of customs and important names since his last name had changed to 'Padrona'.

"Not really. Should I?"

"Her father is the head of the alchemists' guild. The guy who tells my dad's boss what to do. Their family name goes back to the First Empire. She's really highborn, Tim."

Timori's face darkened. "What, are you trying to dissuade me already? Who cares if she's highborn? This is Central. Anybody who gets here deserves to be here, and abyss with all the rest."

Jacoby nodded and made a pacifying gesture with his hands. "I know, I know. I'm not trying to dissuade you, Tim. I'm just ... well, just don't get your hopes up, is all. She's highborn and probably looking to court up, not down. She'd turn either of us down quick as a glint."

Timori watched Racquela from afar as she introduced some of her highborn friends to Crystara. Timori knew that if Racquela would associate with an obviously lower-class girl such as Crystara, there was hope for himself. He was not one to give up easily.

He glanced back at Jacoby. "Well, are you registering for speaking or what, pally? Crystara sure wants you to."

"Do you think so?"

Timori rolled his eyes. "You dully, can't you tell when girls are interested? Register for speaking. You'll regret it if you don't. Just don't drop football."

Jacoby shook his head. "I would never. Maybe I don't need engineering after all."

"Engineering? Won't your father be upset?"

Jacoby shrugged. "He expects me to follow in his footsteps, but I never imagined that I would have the potential to be a speaker. There's no way he can't be proud of that. You go ahead over to engineering. I'll catch up with you."

Timori watched Jacoby wander away. He spun about and tried to find Racquela's face in the crowd once more. She and her friend Crystara could not be found, so Timori made his way to the engineering table.

The line-up for engineering was much longer than it had been for empathy. Engineering was a trade that anybody could learn if they had the brains or the gumption, unlike the pass-or-fail, inborn talent way that empathy and crystal-speaking operated. When Timori reached the front of the line, he noticed that the teacher watching the engineering table was staring at him as he wrote down his name.

"Good," the teacher said gruffly. Timori dropped his pen and stared back at the man. The teacher's bespectacled face was covered in a thick salt-and-pepper beard, and he sported a tweed cap on his head. Absently, Timori was reminded of the fairy-tale elf who granted wishes, Papanina. The teacher, however, had a serious countenance, and his bloodshot eyes regarded Timori with all the gravity of a bird of prey about to strike.

"You better study damn hard in my class, boy," the man continued. "Won't pass you if you don't do your work, don't care if you're smart or not."

Timori looked up at the man. Never one to back down from a challenge, he nodded to his future engineering teacher. "I'll do the work. Central is the best shot I have at getting somewhere."

The teacher nodded. It was an unspoken understanding that Timori was lowborn. It didn't need to be addressed directly.

"Come to class, do your work, you'll go far, son. Engineers are always needed, and students from Central can go anywhere they want. Economic depression doesn't last forever, and when it's over you'll be the front line of new recruits to work with crystal."

Timori smiled to himself as he handed the registration sheet back to the teacher. In the educational setting, it didn't matter a damn if you were highborn or not. In the brave new world of crystal technology, brains were what mattered.

***

Timori's and Jacoby's impromptu football game that afternoon was more intense than Timori had expected. The empty field they had played on since childhood seemed smaller, a place meant only for idle fun and not for any kind of serious competition. Two sweaty hours later, Timori was declared the victor by fifteen points. He always won when he put his mind to it.

70

After the game, Jacoby bought sunflower seeds from a general store and they went to the bridge.

A seed left Timori's mouth and spun in a wild arc down to the street below. Despite the excitement of the day, Timori and Jacoby had said little to each other since their game.

"Still going for Racquela?" Jacoby asked.

Timori nodded and spat out another seed. "Yes. No doubt in my mind about it. She's beautiful, Jake. Don't you think? And I just ... I feel something when I look at her. I felt it when she talked to me. I know she's the one for me, Jake. It was meant to be. Don't you ever feel that way? About Crystara, maybe?"

Jacoby gave a casual shrug and spat out a wad of seed. He laughed when it struck the windshield of a motorcoach and ducked with Timori behind the railing. Jacoby looked at Timori as they were chuckling.

"She's clear, Tim, I'll give you that. Why, do you think I should court her? You seem really interested in the idea, which is funny, considering how a while ago you told me to stay away from your 'girl next door'."

Timori popped a seed into his mouth. "I changed my mind, Jake. Just promise me that you'll let me go after Racquela with no interference. I don't mean to be rude, but sometimes you ..."

Jacoby put up a hand. "You're right. If you really like this girl, Tim, I won't get in the way. I'm not sure about Crystara yet, but I will stay away from Racquela if you want me to. I promise. Besides, she doesn't really seem like my type."

Timori breathed a sigh of relief. He knew that he could trust Jacoby when it came down to it.

***

Timori knocked on the door of the green house next to his own and held his breath. The idea of speaking with Crystara made him nervous. Although he was no longer attracted to the mysterious girl next door, the idea of actually talking to a person with such an intense glare still made him uncomfortable. Even worse, Racquela could be visiting Crystara. Timori tried not to think about it.

The door opened and Timori stood before a large, hairy man who was wearing a white undershirt and undershorts. Timori assumed the man to be Crystara's father. He didn't look impressed to have been disturbed.

"What?"

Timori looked up at the tall, swarthy man and gave his most polite smile. "Hi there, good afternoon. I was wondering if I could speak to your daughter for a moment."

The older man's glare narrowed even more. Timori wondered idly if it would have been less trouble simply to find out where Racquela lived and gone to speak with her directly, but he had no idea where or how to begin the search.

"What's it about?" Crystara's father demanded.

Timori knew the best way to convince Crystara's father that he had no intentions upon her.

"Well it's just ... she has this friend that I need to speak to regarding this class that we'll be taking together, but I'm not sure where she lives. Really it's very important. Otherwise I wouldn't think to bother you with something so trivial. Is Crystara available, just for a moment?"

The man folded his arms. If his eyes had narrowed any farther, Timori would have thought him to be blind. He started to feel sorry for Crystara. A father like the one in front of him would not be easy for any teenaged girl to deal with.

"You can talk to her out here," the father decided with an air of authority to his voice, as though his word were greater than Noven law.

Timori was pleased with the result. It didn't matter to him where he spoke to Crystara so long as he got the information he needed. He watched as the bear-shaped man turned his head and bellowed into the house, "Crystara! Door!" He then plodded down the hallway and out of sight, leaving the door wide open. The experience made Timori wonder more about what his own father had truly been like before he left.

There was a long pause, and Timori had time to grow bored as he waited for Crystara to appear. The hallway that he could glimpse from the porch reminded him of his own house: messy. Instead of toys and books, however, the hallway was cluttered with empty liquor bottles and unpacked boxes.

As Timori waited he wondered if he was making a mistake. Girls had a tendency to tell each other everything, and the last thing he wanted to do was hurt his chances with Racquela. He dismissed the thought as paranoia. What girl wouldn't want to know that boys were interested in her?

Crystara's sudden appearance made Timori jump a little. She didn't say anything, but stood in the doorway and stared at him as though she were silently asking him to explain why he was bothering her. Timori couldn't quite put his finger on why, but whenever he saw Crystara she seemed perturbed somehow. She tossed some wispy hair out of her face and continued to stare.

"Crystara," Timori said. He had no idea how to broach the subject of Racquela without making it obvious. He supposed that beating around the bush was pointless, anyhow.

"Racquela likes to be romanced, but she's very picky," Crystara replied, as though Timori had already asked a question.

"What? I didn't even ..."

"Why else would you be here? You've never spoken to me before and I know you like her. Don't pretend to be nice to me just to get information. If you want Racquela you'll have to prove yourself to her, but don't come on too strong. That's all the help that I can give you. Bye."

As suddenly as Crystara appeared, she disappeared and firmly closed the front door. Timori scratched his head, then shrugged. Crystara may have been unorthodox, but she had given Timori the information that he needed. He walked next door to his own house in high spirits, and tried to think of words that rhymed with 'beauty'.

Chapter 5

*Letters of correspondence between Private Julio Vellize and
Ramona Scaletti during the Great War, 1874-1879*

16 Octobra, 1874
My Beloved Ramona,
*It feels as though a lifetime has passed between us, though it
has been scarcely a week since I left the warmth and security of your
arms for the fear of the unknown here at basic training down in
Sabeccus. Would that my draft notice had been bestowed upon some
other poor soul, but I would not wish that upon anyone, even though
the thought of pointing a wand at another human being fills me with
a great dread. If only that aversion to violence would convince them
to send me home, but alas, I would be incarcerated if I refused to
join the service.*

*I am not alone in my resentment against the empire's
expansion, and many of the other recruits speak quite openly of their
disdain for the war. It seems as though the commanding officers care
nothing for the opinions of recruits, so long as we all follow orders.
One fellow in particular, a man by the name of Largo Mita, has told
me that he follows the works of Nigel Hornsby, the socialist. Though
Largo and I have quite differing viewpoints on certain things, we
have become friends rather quickly. He too has a girl back in Captus
Nove, and he speaks of her often.*

*Basic training has been brutal so far, my love. They
humiliate us daily with drills that only the miners and finishing
school footballers can perform well, and beat us with the butts of
their longwands at little to no provocation. I am bruised and sore,
but it is thoughts of you that keep me going. I will not fail you, no
matter the punishment my body may take.*

*I miss you dearly, Ramona, more than ink on scraps of paper
could ever express. I would swim across the sea back to you this very
moment if I knew that I would not be caught and court-marshalled. I*

miss your smile, I miss your kiss, I miss your gentle wisdom that reminds me to be strong. Without your quiet strength I never would have made it through the academy, and it is that same strength I rely on now.

Please write back soon, my love. I will be in basic training until at least the end of the month, possibly longer. They say the boats might not brave the Southron Sea in wintertime, but I think that is just wishful thinking. We will be sent to the front lines regardless of what mood Neovus and the other gods of the sea are in this winter. If only the war would end by the spring, but that is likely more wishful thinking upon my part. A war of this magnitude is not likely to last less than a few years, if history has taught me anything about the world. It will go on until the empire falls or we reclaim all that we once had. Sometimes I wonder if Emperor Longoro will stop at just Titania.

I must retire for the evening, my dear Ramona. I pray to the gods this eve for dreams of you.

Julio

P.S. I am sending most of my pay home to you. I need very little here that they do not provide, and since your father's death I know that finances have been a concern. That pay, and my love go to you.

24 Octobra, 1874

My dearest Julio,

It's already cold here in Captus Nove, and I miss your warm embrace. The city feels barren since you left, devoid of hope and happiness. I miss your lips, both for the sweet kisses they provided, and the beautiful words that come forth from them for only me to hear. By all the gods, you should be here chronicling the war with that mind of yours, not out there fighting it with the uneducated!

You must receive better news of the front lines than I do, but the papers here scream their optimism from the front page while the wives read the killed-in-action list. Every week at least one of the women at the factory goes home in tears. I couldn't bear it if that *happened to you. It can't. You mustn't let it. I would die on the spot to be with you.*

What do they tell you of the war? Is it true that Nilonne is already half-defeated? I wonder sometimes if it's right for us to reclaim an empire that hasn't stood for fifteen hundred years. Are we truly better than they are?

It's nice to hear that you're making friends. You always do, wherever you go. I'm sure that with their help and the love that I send to you, you'll survive basic training. I'd kiss every bruise away, if I could.

Thank you dearly for the money, my love. The factory pay is awful, as you know. However, I can't simply live off of your generosity. I'm saving a quarter of everything you send me for our wedding. What do you think about a honeymoon in Los Maros?

Write back as soon as you can, my dearest, and be safe.

Love, Ramona

33 Octobra, 1874

Ramona, my love,

A honeymoon in Los Maros sounds like a dream, but please do not refrain from spending the money if it is needed. I would not want you to starve.

Basic training is almost over, and then they are sending us away to bolster beleaguered troops. I am not permitted to tell you where we are going – they check every letter I write and I have already been reprimanded for writing disparaging words regarding the empire. Oh, the things that I would write in these letters if they didn't read every single one! Things to make you blush at the very least. Things that I miss about being with you, beyond just the kisses.

Despite the horrors of basic training, though, I have survived thus far, and the drill sergeant has begun to treat us less like unruly children and more like men. He said that if he did not brutalize us, we would never be prepared for the front lines. I wonder if he is cruel or kind for his actions.

They tell us of the war, but the news that we receive is usually vague at best. I do not doubt that we are winning ground against Nilonne, but the Alliance will not sit idly by and watch it fall. We do not have an endless supply of men, and we cannot simply enslave our conquests as we did during the days of the First Empire. How I miss the peaceful republic of my youth!

On the subject of chronicling history, your words prompted me to start a journal detailing the events that led to the war, and the war itself. Perhaps someday I may publish it once I return to claim my Master title. You are, as always, an inspiration, my love.

I miss you. I miss your flawless, smiling face. How did I not think to get a picture taken before I left? There is naught but sweet memory. It may be selfish, but could you spend some of this pay I send on a photograph to send back to me? It would mean the world to me, and would keep me sane once I am in the trenches.

I fear for the future, Ramona. I fear for mine, and yours, and Novem's. This war will claim much before it is over, and I feel unprepared for what lies ahead. Only a fool would raise his wand in bravery and not fear.

I do not yet know what company I will be placed with, but I hope that I am placed with Largo. He is a quiet man, but he is honest and on more than one occasion has defended me to the sergeant to save me from a beating. He is a much better soldier than I am, since he is a strong young miner, and we have promised to protect each other if we find ourselves stationed together.

Please keep yourself warm as the winter season approaches, and do not refrain from buying extra coal with the money that I am sending if it is needed. I do not want you to catch a chill.

I am afraid to leave the training camp, but I will be brave for you. I love you, sweetheart. More than words could ever say.

Julio

***

**Excerpt from 'The Rise and Fall of the Second Empire'
by Master Julio Vellize**

The study of the Second Empire of Novem is, out of necessity, a study of Noven traditions and values, a look at the Noven psyche itself. We must examine the historical facts and causes of the Great War, naturally, but what is history if not a glimpse into the lives of our ancestors?

By ancestors, I of course refer not just to those of us who lived through the Second Empire, but our families and friends, and those historical world-changing individuals who were the driving force behind the war to pacify the globe. Emperor Longoro immediately springs to the mind of any of us who remember than stern but charismatic face, and we remember also the promises that bound him to us and us to him. History is written by us all, commoners and rulers alike.

When I began what would eventually become this book, it was a journal that I was writing during the Great War, on the front lines. I was a junior historian then, eager to make sense of the misery and death that surrounded me. I do not claim to be the sole authority on the Second Empire of Novem, or the Great War, but I lived through them both.

***

4 Novembra, 1874
My dearest Julio,
I hope this letter finds you well. I worry about you more and more every day, ever since I knew that you were leaving for the front lines.

I did as you asked, my dear, and the photograph is enclosed with this letter. What do you think? I think that I look sad, though I tried my best to smile for you.

They're pushing us harder at the factory every day. They always need more uniforms and textile supplies for the war effort, and there are almost no men remaining here on the factory floor, except for the supervisors and the boys who are still too young to go off and fight. I don't prick my fingers anymore, though. They're all calloused. I feel like an old woman! I hope that my photograph suggests otherwise.

Another set of draft notices was sent out the week that you wrote your last letter. They're taking boys as young as fifteen now! Little Antonio from down the street was called to war, and he's still just a child in my eyes. The city grows quieter by the week.

Have you been stationed with your friend Largo? I hope so. You're not a fighter, love, though you're brave when you need to be. The gods won't protect every soul during a war, and I worry that if Longoro goes too far, then they might abandon us.

Is it nice in Nilonne, where you are? I bet right now it's not as beautiful as it could be. Still, I've always heard that Nilonne is a wonderful place to visit. Maybe once the war is over, if the empire succeeds, we could visit Nilonne as easily as any neighbouring Noven city.

Look after yourself, my love.
Ramona

***

The city of Captus Nove felt as barren as Ramona's heart.

Julio had been away for scarcely two months, but it felt like a lifetime since Ramona's love had left for basic training. His letters were the only bit of warmth she seemed to be able to find in what looked to be a long and dreary winter.

Ramona was thankful for the extra money that Julio sent her, for it meant that she and her mother were able to eat properly. Ever since the death of her father, Ramona and her mother had barely been able to survive. She had been forced to take extra shifts at the factory, and Julio hadn't had a job since before his studies at the academy. The money that he sent was the one clear side to the fact that he had been drafted into the military.

Ramona walked through the market plaza with her basket, noting how much quieter the marketplace had become since the war had begun. Most of the shops were run by merchants' wives instead of the merchants themselves, many of whom had been sent off to the war or to the mines. Gossip revolved around the war and Emperor Longoro, and though many remained optimistic, all Ramona could feel was the dull grey of winter around her.

Ramona returned home with a full basket of fresh produce and bread and went to the tiny kitchen to make supper for herself and her mother before she had to go to the factory for her night shift.

"Emilio? Is that you?" Her mother called from her bedroom. Ramona sighed as she chopped tomatoes. Her mother hadn't dealt with the death of her husband very well, and Ramona was beginning to worry that it was more than just the trauma of losing her spouse. She reminded herself to pay a visit to the doctor and ask him if there was anything to be worried about.

Ramona's mother shuffled into the kitchen, dressed heavily in a shawl and sweater despite the heat from the fireplace. "Did you hear the door?" she asked Ramona. "I thought I heard your father coming in."

"Mother, why don't you sit down?" Ramona suggested as she lit the stove with a match. "Supper should be ready shortly, and then I have to go to work."

"Work?" Lissana Scaletti muttered as she slowly took a seat at the small round kitchen table. "At this hour? What are you up to, child?"

Ramona went back to chopping vegetables as she waited for the water on the stovetop to boil. "I had to start taking extra shifts at the factory, remember? The factory has been open in the evenings ever since the war began."

Ramona watched her mother nod slowly, a look of confusion still on her face. Ramona wondered if Lissana Scaletti even remembered that a war was going on.

Ramona finished making supper without any further comment from her mother, and sat down to eat as quickly as she could. She never considered herself to be a versatile cook, but the fresh bread and ham made up for how small and tasteless the vegetables were in wintertime.

"Have you heard from Julio lately?" Lissana inquired as she picked through the tomatoes and carrots on her plate. She seemed more lucid than earlier.

"When is that boy going to marry you and start providing for us, hm? What is he waiting for? If he takes too long, somebody else is going to swoop in and steal your heart away. You aren't getting any younger, after all, and most girls your age are already married."

Ramona rolled her eyes. It was the same tirade she had heard from her mother since she was sixteen years old.

"Julio is away at war, Mother, just like Emilio. We can't get married right now. As soon as he returns, we promised each other. I should be getting a letter from him any day now, and then I can let you know how he's doing."

"Hmph," Lissana Scaletti replied. "You two should already have cut the crystal, don't know why you waited this long."

Ramona was rapidly losing her appetite over thoughts of Julio and her own loneliness, but she forced herself to shovel down the food on her plate so that she wouldn't get hungry at the factory. "Because Julio was at the academy so that he could get his Master's, Mother." Ramona tried to put things in a way that her mother could understand. "So that he could provide well for us."

As soon as the last bit of food was off of her plate, Ramona quickly threw the dishes in the sink and gave her mother a kiss. Throwing on her shawl, she left the house. It was a cold evening, but clear, and she hurried to keep herself warm.

The factory was a dreary place. It was an old brick building with large windows that never seemed to let in enough sun, and at night half of the crystal lights on the factory floor didn't work properly so Ramona had to strain to see the buttons as she sewed. Even before the war had broken out, most of the clothing that was made at the factory was for the military. Most of the workers operated the sewing machines, but Ramona's eyesight was good and her hands deft, and so she was a sewer of buttons. She worked at her own table, which gave her supervisor plenty of time to bother her.

He was a short, round man, about Ramona's age although he looked to be at least ten years older than she. Ramona could barely tolerate the way he loomed over her as she worked, partly because his breath was always terrible, but also because she was more likely to make mistakes with another person watching.

"Ramona," he said that evening as he hovered just behind her, watching every pull of the needle, "your hands must get so cold here in the factory at night. Why don't you take a break and let me warm them up for you? I wouldn't want you to prick your finger, after all."

Ramona hoped that he couldn't see her wince. "No thank you," she said as politely as she could manage. She didn't want to jeopardize her job by being rude to Ralfi Andari, but she certainly wasn't about to lead him on.

"I'm a little behind anyway, Mister Andari. I don't think that I can afford to take a break this evening or else this shipment might not go out on time, and I wouldn't want that to reflect upon either of our positions."

Ramona could see Ralfi Andari shrug out of the corner of her eye. He came around and leaned on the work table so that Ramona could see him clearly.

"I'll make sure they get done," he insisted. "We have others who can sew, but none are quite as delicate as you are, Ramona. Have you thought about my offer?"

Ralfi Andari's 'offer' had stood for almost as long as Ramona had worked at the factory. Within a month after her first shift on the floor, he had asked for her hand in marriage, claiming that she was the most beautiful girl he had ever laid eyes upon. Ramona had struggled between disgust and flattery, but ultimately she told him that she was engaged to Julio Vellize, even though they hadn't been at the time. Ramona was thankful that she hadn't lost her job then and there, but Ralfi had kept his eyes on her every day since.

"I'm sorry, Mister Andari," Ramona replied, never taking her eyes off of her work, "but my answer hasn't changed. Julio and I are to be wed as soon as he returns from the war. I appreciate the offer, but my answer must remain 'no'."

Ramona was startled when Ralfi grasped her hand in his. She almost pricked herself with her sewing needle. She trembled but forced herself to look him in the eyes.

"What if he doesn't return?" Ralfi Andari said. "Wars claim many lives, Ramona. Besides, you might be waiting years for him to come back. He might not love you by then."

Ramona felt her cheeks burning and pulled her hand away. "He will return, Mister Andari, and I can wait as long as it takes because I love him, and he loves me, and nothing is going to change that."

Chapter 6

Timori arrived early for the first day of school, book bag in tow. He had spent the night at Jacoby's house, and the two of them had stayed up until well past midnight talking. Despite his lack of sleep, Timori was not tired. His excitement overruled it completely.

Timori glanced over as he and Jacoby marched up Aestala Hill to see Jacoby admiring the new book bag his parents had bought him as a gift for getting into Central School. Timori examined his own book bag and its contents with shame. All of the notebooks within were old and half-used from previous school years, and the bag itself had already been stitched back together by Timori twice, on each end of the shoulder strap. Jacoby's new book bag was made of finely-worked black leather with a silver clasp and was filled with fresh notebooks and a new pen.

Timori could remember the days when the two of them would share notebooks because they didn't have enough paper between the two of them for all of their classes. Jacoby seemed to have forgotten all about those old times.

"Guess we won't be sharing notebooks anymore like we used to," Timori remarked. He immediately felt like a dully. He had just wanted to ignore the fact that Jacoby was no longer poor and pretend like nothing was any different, but he'd let his mouth get ahead of his thoughts.

Jacoby shrugged. "Well we'll be taking a lot of different classes."

As usual, he didn't seem to notice Timori's jealousy. Timori wondered how Jacoby was supposed to be good at empathy if he never picked up on things like that.

"But I probably don't need all these notebooks my parents bought. You can have a couple of them if you like."

Timori swallowed his spite. "No," he said. "That's fine. I have enough."

As they reached the crest of the hill, the school loomed ahead in the serious shades of buildings associated with ponderous matters of adulthood: the dull red of brick, the sad grey of deepstone and the sun-faded pale orange of adobe. Its doors were open, beckoning like portals that promised to lead Timori from that place where nobody took him seriously and everyone looked down on him into the land of adulthood, the land of freedom of personal choice.

As Timori stared back at those blank windows that regarded him like so many uncaring eyes, he wondered if he was ready to grow up.

"What are you waiting for?" Jacoby exclaimed. He beckoned Timori to follow, and the two raced their way to the long concrete front steps.

Students streamed into the building on either side of Timori. Signs pasted on either of the opened whiteoak doors directed students to the gymnasium, where an assembly of all students and faculty was scheduled before classes officially began for the school year. Timori let Jacoby lead the way and kept one eye on him. The other was searching for Racquela.

The gymnasium was rapidly filling with students. Timori hadn't seen so many people gathered together in one place since the time he had snuck out of the house late at night to watch the fireworks on Crystus Hill for Republic Day. Chairs were arranged in neat rows from the front to the back of the gymnasium, and the faculty were sitting upon chairs on the gym stage, muttering to each other as they watched the beginnings of another school year.

Timori tapped on Jacoby's shoulder and pointed out a free set of chairs in the back row, where it would be easy to watch for Racquela's entrance. He had already scanned the gym for her, and found it unlikely that his eyes could accidentally pass over a girl with her beauty.

"Why the back row?" Jacoby asked. "We might not be able to hear what the teachers are saying."

Timori raised an eyebrow. "Do you really care about long-winded speeches from the schoolmaster?"

"Good point."

They grabbed the chairs and sat down before somebody else picked their spot. Timori noticed that there were a lot of older-looking students in the back rows, so he puffed up his chest a little and sat up straight. All the while he kept his eyes peeled for Racquela.

A knot of despair rose up in Timori's heart as the gymnasium continued to fill. What if she had decided to go to a different finishing school? What if her parents had sent her off to an all-female boarding school somewhere else in the country? He had been told once that such a thing was very common amongst the upper classes. He turned to Jacoby.

"Keep an eye out for her, will you?"

"Who?"

Timori pressed a palm to his forehead in an exasperated gesture. "Who do you think, dully? Racquela De'Trini."

"Wouldn't it be easier to look for Crystara?"

Timori silently applauded his best friend's good sense. He had been so focused on Racquela De'Trini that the thought had never occurred to him. His eyes began scanning the massive crowd for blondes. There were a couple of blonde girls, but neither of them had the straight hair and fairy-like frame of Crystara. He despaired once more.

"I don't see her," Timori said as he shifted restlessly in his seat. "What if she's not coming?"

"Just relax," Jacoby said. "I'm sure she's going to school here. We saw her at registration. Besides, even if she isn't, it's not like you even really know her, Tim. What's the big deal?"

Timori scowled. "Jake, don't be such a picker. I've ...." He stopped mid-sentence as he saw a face out of the corner of his eye and turned his head. Racquela had entered the gymnasium. She was wearing a fashionable green dress with wide skirts and had a matching bow tied in her hair.

"There she is!" Timori exclaimed. The gymnasium din drowned out his voice, so he slapped Jacoby repeatedly on the shoulder until Jacoby looked where he was pointing. Crystara followed along behind the heir to the De'Trini fortune. She wore a nice white cotton dress that seemed a size too big for her, like a hand-me-down.

Beaming, Timori watched as Racquela made a show out of selecting good seats for herself and Crystara. A part of him was certain that the wealthy young socialite was showing off with her dress and fashionable airs, but he didn't really care because it afforded him a good long look at her. Timori stared in amazement as Racquela's dark locks swayed from side to side as she scanned for a seat. It was awe-inspiring. Racquela seemed to *project* her beauty rather than merely possess it.

"Close your mouth," Jacoby whispered to Timori. "You don't want her to catch you staring at her like a dully, do you?"

Timori didn't even look back at Jacoby. He merely made a dismissive gesture with his hand and continued to stare. "Don't ruin this for me. After today everyone will be wearing school uniforms, remember?"

Suddenly Racquela locked eyes with Timori from across the gymnasium and a look of recognition crossed her face. She gave a friendly wave and Timori melted. Hastily, he scanned on either side of him for any free seats, but the back few rows of chairs had already been spoken for. By the time Timori looked back up, Racquela had found a seat somewhere and he couldn't pick her out of the crowd of seated students, despite his insistence to himself that she was unique from all angles. Crestfallen, he sank into his chair and folded his arms.

"Timori, don't worry about it," Jacoby said reassuringly. "You'll be seeing plenty of her, I bet."

"Yeah, maybe," Timori muttered. "I just ...". He fumbled with something in his book bag, making sure it was still nestled between two old notebooks so that it wouldn't get crumpled. "... Never mind."

Jacoby opened his mouth to reply just as the old schoolmaster cleared his throat to address the assembly. Jacoby promptly shut his mouth and turned his attention forward. Timori did the same. The last thing either of them wanted was to get a reputation as troublemakers on their first day of school.

The speech was the most boring Timori had ever heard. The schoolmaster, a small bald man with thick glasses, began a long, dry lecture about the history of the school and its legacy of producing students with the highest aptitudes in the country. Although Timori was somewhat interested in the crystal projectophone the schoolmaster used so he could be heard by the entire assembly, he quickly let his mind wander to Racquela.

His attention drifted in and out of focus the longer the schoolmaster droned on. He rambled through Central's history, from the School's role in the formation of the Fifth Republic, to the proud tradition of the crystal betrothals, to the importance of education in the face of an economic crisis and a famine. Timori rolled his eyes at the mention of the depression the country (and the rest of the world, for that matter) was facing. That kind of thing only mattered to the rich. The poor were always poor, depression or no.

Jacoby was falling asleep beside Timori, but Timori remained alert and watched the rest of the assembly on the off chance Racquela might turn around and look at him. He was disappointed that she did not, but Timori told himself not to fret about it. He was certain that if he kept his wits about him, he would manage to find her before the end of the first day of school.

After what seemed like hours, the schoolmaster concluded his speech.

"... looking forward to another successful year here at Central School. As for the first year students, on behalf of all the faculty and returning students, I want to welcome you once again to the best finishing school in the nation. Now, if you could all please rise and join me in the singing of our national anthem, this assembly shall conclude. Upon its completion, first year students please note the homeroom number printed on your registration papers and schedule, which you should all have with you. After the national anthem, please leave the gymnasium in an orderly fashion and proceed directly to your homeroom. All rise."

Timori had to nudge Jacoby awake, even amidst the cacophony of hundreds of shuffling feet and the wood-on-wood scrapes of chairs along the gymnasium floor. As the senior band's trumpets began to blare, Jacoby yawned and placed his right hand in a fist over his chest to join in the singing of *The Crystal Skies of Novem.*

Timori, not much of a singer or a patriot, half-heartedly mumbled along to the words, but Jacoby got right into it. His voice drowned out those of other nearby singers in a crystal-clear tenor timbre. Timori shook his head, amazed at how his friend could go from asleep to fervent in a matter of seconds.

Timori was glad when the song concluded. Jacoby's enthusiasm seemed to draw contemptuous looks from some older students. As the throng of students began to disperse, Jacoby clapped Timori on the shoulder.

"See you at lunch, Tim," he said with a friendly nod. As Jacoby turned to leave, Timori tried to see if he could get one last glimpse of Racquela before everyone cleared out of the gym.

Unfortunately for Timori, she was nowhere to be seen, and he found himself at the back of the exit line-up. Many of the older male students shoved their way around, either to get to the exit faster or just for fun, while teachers looked on and waved disapproving fingers.

After a painstakingly slow exodus, Timori found himself in a hallway and quickly followed the signs to his homeroom that had been put up for new students' benefit. Somewhere along the way the plaster walls gave way to stone, and Timori knew that he was somewhere in the original prison complex. Weaving amidst the bustle of other students, who were for the most part much taller than he was, Timori made his way up two flights of mason-worked stairs to a narrow hallway with a vaulted ceiling. The room that he was seeking was halfway down the corridor, guarded by a heavy darkoak door that bore a brass plaque which read '313'.

He pushed the heavy door open to reveal a very dark classroom already filled with students. The only natural light came in through three tiny barred windows that were much too high for the average person to reach, even at a jump. For additional illumination, crystal lights had been placed into the ceiling, bare and brazen.

Timori wondered where all the money that was thrown at the school went if they didn't even bother to invest in decorations. On the plus side, the deepstone made for excellent insulation and thus the room and old prison area were much cooler than the rest of the school in the sweltering heat of late summer.

Timori quickly scanned the room but found absolutely nobody that he knew. He quietly found a seat next to the wall and waited for the homeroom teacher to arrive. As he waited, his eyes wandered over the stacks of textbooks and school uniforms that lined the far wall of the dingy classroom. He winced at the thought that his uniforms were going to be faded old rentals. Even with the scholarship that he had earned, he couldn't afford to buy his own uniforms. Not for the first time, Timori cursed his low birth.

The teacher who entered the classroom turned out to be none other than the heavily-bearded man who had spoken to Timori when he had registered for engineering class. The man was wearing the same tweed cap, as well as a worn-looking brown suit. He regarded the students as though the lot of them were some sort of trial that he had been unmercifully subjected to.

"All right, let's not waste any time here," he said abruptly as he shut the door behind him. "I've got a lot of textbooks and uniforms to give out and not a lot of time to do it in. You are also each going to be assigned a locker. They should be just outside of your homeroom, so once you get your key you can keep your textbooks and what-have-you in there ... on your own time, that is, not mine. Everybody grab a chair behind a desk immediately. Any goofing off and I won't hesitate to send you straight to the schoolmaster's office for disrupting the proceedings. You can tell them Doctor Ruveldi sent you. As for your names, I'm not going to bother to try and learn them all. I teach hundreds of students like you every year. Show yourself to be exceptional and maybe I'll remember."

Doctor Ruveldi seated himself slowly in the chair behind his desk and pulled a sheet of paper out of his book bag. "When I call out your name, come up to the front of the class and grab your textbooks and uniforms. Then sit down and shut up."

Under Doctor Ruveldi's efficient method, along with the threat of discipline for disruption, the proceedings went quickly. When Timori's name was called and he went up to the front of the class, the teacher said nothing, but Timori could have sworn he saw the old man's head inch down slightly, as if to acknowledge Timori. Timori dismissed it as idle fancy, but he went back to his seat feeling satisfied. Timori shoved his textbooks into his old book bag, hoping that it wouldn't fall apart from the added strain.

"I will remind you only once, students," said Doctor Ruveldi after the last student had received her uniform and books, "that by tomorrow you are all expected to be in full uniform at all times while on campus. If it's cold, wear a school jacket. If it's hot, too bad."

He checked his pocket watch. "It looks like we have a few minutes left before the bell will toll for your next class. You may use this time however you wish, provided you do not speak to each other or get out of your seats." A smirk appeared on a corner of the teacher's lips. "You've been very cooperative thus far. See that it stays that way."

Many students, out of desperation, began reading their textbooks to stave off boredom. In the grim silence, Timori's mind wandered. He wondered what Racquela was doing at that very moment. He wondered if the bell was close enough and large enough to be heard through the tiny windows of the deepstone room. He thought about Doctor Ruveldi. Why would a man with a doctorate be teaching at a finishing school, instead of at an academy?

The bell pealed, deep and resonant. Timori had not seen the bell tower from his views of the exterior of Central School, but it had to have been close. It thrummed in his chest as it rang. Timori's fellow students looked up at the sound of the bell as though it were a thing of mercy. They exited the classroom in a less-than-orderly fashion. Once again Timori was the last to leave.

"Mister Stravida," the doctor intoned.

Timori turned around to see the man staring at him over the top of his small, round spectacles.

"Yes, Doctor Ruveldi?"

"Good to see you made it here. I'm only singling you out because I expect better from you than the usual narcissistic, over-privileged dullards who come through these doors. The fact that you're here proves that the republic isn't completely useless. Just mostly useless. So don't fuck around in my class."

"I ..."

"Go, get to your next class."

"Um ... yes, sir. Doctor," Timori stuttered as he backed out of the room. He checked his schedule and made his way through the hallways of Central with a smile on his face. He had been singled out because he was *special*.

His next class was physics, which Timori had hoped would become one of his favourites. It was also one of the science classes that were necessary in order to become an engineer. Timori had never been afraid of difficult mathematics and was expecting the first year class to be a breeze for him.

As he entered the classroom, he was surprised to find that the teacher for the class was a woman, and a relatively young one at that. In Timori's experience, it wasn't often that women were interested in physics. All the predominant physicists were men and always had been. Timori supposed that perhaps it had something to do with women's suffrage, which had only successfully lobbied for the female vote in Novem just after the Great War, right around when Timori was born. Most Novens still felt that a woman's place was at home.

As a boy of fifteen, Timori didn't give too much thought to women's rights, but he saw no issue with an attractive woman teaching him physics. Her style of dress was modest, and her dark hair was tightly done up in a bun. Timori didn't say a word to his teacher as he entered the room, but he did choose a seat at the front of the class.

"Good morning, class," she said in a soft but stern tone after the last of the stragglers had entered the room. "I am Miss Tricchio, your teacher for physics. While I do realize that your aptitude levels are likely concurrent with the tests you just took in order to get here, I would like to ensure that you are all still at a reasonable level of knowledge in the sciences so that I won't have to slow the class down for anybody. Please open your textbooks to page thirty-one and write out the answers to the small quiz on a piece of notebook paper."

A few groans were heard amidst the ruffling of papers and book bags, to which Miss Tricchio replied with the click of a button atop her pocketwatch. "You have half an hour," she said, "and this quiz, like everything you will do in my class, counts toward your grades."

Timori suppressed a chuckle as he gave the quiz questions a once-over in the textbook. The questions were about as basic as physics could get. The book, like most of the ones he had received that morning, seemed relatively new. At least, Timori figured, he knew where *some* of that money Central accumulated was going. He finished the quiz in five minutes, took the page up to the teacher before anybody else, then returned to his desk and skimmed through the textbook as he occasionally stole glances at Miss Tricchio.

Once the half-hour was up, Miss Tricchio demanded the rest of the quizzes and marked them rapidly with a pen dipped in bright red ink. When she was finished, she arranged the pieces of paper in a neat stack and folded her hands together to address the class.

"Well," she exclaimed. "My intuition was right. You *do* need a review. In fact, only one student answered every question correctly." She looked straight at Timori as she said it, and he turned bright red.

The rest of the class was spent reviewing the physics basics that the students had learned in primary school, which Timori found utterly boring. Miss Tricchio didn't seem concerned by the fact that he wasn't paying much attention, at least not to the lesson itself.

In no way had Timori forgotten about Racquela, however. Miss Tricchio may have been attractive, but she paled in comparison to Racquela, as far as Timori was concerned. Besides which, Timori reasoned, crushes on teachers were just idle fancy. He didn't want to get too distracted once his physics class started to get interesting, after all.

When the lunch hour bell pealed, Timori was off like a wandshot and out the classroom door before anybody else. Miss Tricchio was all but forgotten. He had to find Racquela before the hallways grew too crowded.

Unfortunately for Timori, the interior of Central School was dauntingly vast. It felt as though he were searching for diamonds in a crystal mine. Timori raced through the hallways as they filled with students, hoping for a glimpse of the beautiful young woman he intended to court.

His search was not in vain. Timori spotted Racquela across a crowded hallway near the west entrance to the school, which was part of an older brick addition that made up the array of early expansions to the original prison fortress.

Racquela was busying herself piling books into a locker. Timori wanted to shout out and get her attention, but his voice caught in his throat. A sudden nervousness gripped him, and a sheen of sweat formed on his brow.

"Timori, you dully," he muttered to himself, "summon your courage and go talk to her. You'll never get her attention otherwise."

He reached into his book bag and brought out the item that he had absentmindedly toyed with all day. It was a folded note. Much to Timori's shame, he didn't have the money to buy an envelope.

Timori looked up from his book bag to find that Racquela had disappeared into the crowd. "Shatters," he mumbled.

As Timori made his way through the congested hall to Racquela's locker, it occurred to him that his venture to find

Racquela hadn't been a complete loss. He had discovered the location of her locker, which Timori considered to be a major victory in being the first to win Racquela's affections. He had no doubt that he would not be the only boy at Central School to notice the young heiress. Timori deftly slid the note into the crack of the locker door and walked away casually, whistling. It was turning out to be an excellent first day of school for him.

Timori's next objective was to find Jacoby, which wasn't nearly as difficult as tracking down Racquela had been. Jacoby was likely to be enjoying his lunch either in the courtyard (which, as Timori recalled, was no longer truly a courtyard) or somewhere outside in the sunshine. Timori decided to try the courtyard first.

It was packed with students. Timori squinted to get a better look but still couldn't spot his best friend. Timori would never admit that he needed glasses. There was no way to afford them.

"There you are, pally," said a voice behind Timori. "Been lookin' for you."

"This place is full, Jake," Timori said as he turned around. "Let's go outside."

Timori and Jacoby found a spot on the vast expanse of grass that surrounded the school and sat under the shade of a black birch. Timori noticed that the grass seemed greener at Central. They likely spent a lot of money on water to keep it that way. The drought had turned most of Captus Nove's lawns and parks a slightly yellow tinge, and there were water restrictions in place. Timori wondered how much money the school had to pay in order to maintain their lawn.

As they sat down, Jacoby produced a brown paper sack from his book bag and began to remove its contents. Within it was a jar of apple juice, sealed, some of his mother's bread baked the previous day, some olives and a few generous slices of ham. Timori's stomach growled as he watched Jacoby unpack the lunch. Luckily, having stayed at Jacoby's the previous night, they had each packed identical lunches. Timori felt somewhat guilty for mooching off of Jacoby's parents, but Mrs. Padrona had insisted. Timori produced a brown bag from his own leather satchel and devoured his lunch long before Jacoby had finished his. Food didn't last long at Timori's house. After his father had left, everything had to be rationed, and there was never enough to fill him up. Timori loved the feeling of a full stomach from eating too fast.

"Did you run into Racquela?" Jacoby asked, his mouth full of a combination of bread and meat.

"Almost. I left a surprise in her locker, though."

Jacoby raised an eyebrow suggestively.

"It was a note, you jerk," Timori replied with a laugh.

"Writing poetry again, Tim?"

Timori pointed a finger at Jacoby. His gaze was grave, though his tone was not accusatory. "That girl will be mine, Jake. I'll do whatever it takes."

"Well, I hope she likes poetry then."

"I have it on good authority that she likes to be romanced."

Jacoby pursed his lips. "Romancing a noble is expensive, I'd imagine."

"That's not very encouraging," Timori said sourly.

"You're right, Tim. I'm sorry. I'll help you in whatever way that I can."

"It's not money I need, Jake. Love isn't about class. Reading the poetry of Raffino taught me that. I just need ..."

"A miracle?" Jake offered.

Timori gave Jacoby another dirty look. "Fuck you, Jake. You're not being very helpful."

Jacoby looked apologetic. "I'm being realistic, Tim. This is the heir to the De'Trini fortune we're talking about here. You're gonna need the charm and wit of the gods if you think money won't matter to her ... or her family, for that matter."

Timori cursed under his breath. He hated to admit when somebody else was right. "Don't forget the gods' own luck, pally."

Jacoby popped an olive into his mouth. "Also don't forget there's a chance that one of you will be selected for betrothal and ruin any possible chance at courtship. This is Central, after all."

"Yeah, but what are the odds of that happening?" Timori asked. Jacoby shrugged.

Timori and Jacoby spent the remainder of the lunch hour discussing classes, teachers and new students they had met. Jacoby told Timori about the boys he had met in his homeroom who were trying out for the football team, then he laughed riotously when Timori related the tale of how he instantly became the teacher's pet of the most attractive educator at Central.

"So, something's been bugging me," Timori said near the end of lunch. He and Jacoby were lying on their backs, watching the sparse clouds go by. "How is it that a finishing school employs doctors? Seems to me they would be teaching at academies."

Timori was surprised to find that Jacoby had an answer. "Oh, my dad told me about this. Apparently Central is really competitive with the other finishing schools. They offer these professors more money than the academies do, in order to entice them to teach at a lower level. That's why the school still looks like it's falling apart. All the money goes to the staff instead."

"Huh," Timori remarked, just as the bell rang.

The first class after lunch was history, which was Timori's and Jacoby's only shared class that semester. Timori and Jacoby found adjacent seats and awaited the arrival of the teacher.

Within a few minutes, the classroom felt like the inside of an oven, even though all of the windows were open. It was not nearly as cool in the outer buildings as it was in the prison area of the school, and the heat seemed to have reached its peak for the day. Timori could feel the sweat darkening the back of his shirt. The students grew restless and irritable as they waited for the teacher to show up. Many were arguing or shoving to get some fresh air from the open windows.

They heard their teacher coming long before he entered the classroom. The heavy, uneven shuffle-and-stomp of his footsteps inspired a foreboding sense of gravitas and sent the students scrambling to their desks.

The door creaked open ominously, and a shiver ran down Timori's back. The teacher's cane entered the classroom first, held by a metal hook in place of a hand. When his face appeared, Timori's mouth dropped open in shock. Half of the man's face was missing.

The left side was shredded and melted into a gruesome mix of deep red scars and angry splotches, the remnants of burnt tissue. His left eye was completely missing, and the empty socket was not even covered by a patch. His teeth were all visible on the one side, even with his mouth closed. His hair was a mess of tangled grey wisps that sprung out haphazardly from his misshapen head as though they were trying to escape from the man entirely. By comparison, the fair side of the man's face should have seemed placid, but to Timori, that good eye gazed at the students with a look that suggested it had seen the far side of the abyss.

Nobody so much as whispered as he laboriously made his way to the chair behind the desk. The misshapen teacher sat down with a heavy sigh and regarded his class with his one good eye.

To Timori's surprise, the haggard teacher smiled. It was a gruesome smile, but not an unkind one.

"Good afternoon," he greeted them with a whispery, reed-thin voice. "I am Master Vellize, your teacher for Noven history. Your first-level class is modern Noven history, followed by ancient history next year and world history for level three. Before I take attendance, are there any questions?"

It was so quiet that Timori could hear his breath coming in and out of his nose. Nobody dared to pose the question that was on every single student's mind. Suddenly, Jacoby raised his hand. Timori looked over at his friend, hoping to the gods that Jacoby would not say something insensitive.

Master Vellize nodded in Jacoby's direction. "Yes, you there. Please state your name and stand up as you ask your question, so that I might become familiar with you."

Jacoby stood eagerly. "Jacoby Padrona, Master. Will we be following the textbook for this class? I forgot mine in my locker."

Giggles and snickers filled the room. Timori shook his head. Jacoby's honesty came out seeming like insipidness sometimes. Jacoby turned as red as a whiteoak blossom, but the laughter relieved some of the tension in the room. Timori noticed that Master Vellize was laughing as well, in a barely audible rasp. He turned the unmarred side of his face to Jacoby and his smile disappeared.

"You forgot your textbook. Why is that, Mister Padrona?"

Jacoby's hands began to shake. Put on the spot, he was no doubt embarrassed. "I ..." Jacoby's voice was shaking, as well. "I don't know."

"Well, I do," Master Vellize offered. "You forgot it, Mister Padrona, because you do not need it. None of you need it."

He stood abruptly and limped around to the front of his desk, then leaned on his whiteoak cane with his only hand. "In this class we are going to *discuss* history. We are going to read first-hand accounts, not distant, dry facts that have little context or meaning. History is not about names and dates. It is about people and places. Now don't get too excited, because you will be taking a lot of notes in this class, and I am required to push the limits of your intellects because Central has been the best finishing school in Novem since 1859. However, I would like you all to follow Mister Padrona's example and leave your textbooks in your lockers. The schoolmaster and the Education Bureau ask that all faculty provide a standardized textbook to students, but that is just for appearances. Here, in this classroom, I am the boss, and I say that textbooks are dirt. With that out of the way, who would like to offer a guess as to when, historically, the Great War became inevitable?"

The remainder of the class was spent discussing recent Noven history. Timori wasn't accustomed to speaking to a teacher without first raising his hand, but somehow Master Vellize led the discussion without allowing too many interruptions or off-topic comments. By the end of class, Timori was enjoying the discussion as he defended Emperor Longoro's pre-war policies to the noble kids who had no idea that it was the farmers and miners who *really* kept a nation running. Timori used to think he hated history, but he wondered if it was because of the way it was usually taught.

After history class, Timori went to mathematics. His teacher's Eltan accent was almost impossible to understand, but the subject matter wasn't. Timori flipped through his textbook as the thin, hairy man reviewed basic algebra and told strange jokes about Nilonnese priests.

Math class passed by painfully slowly, but once it was over Timori had his free period where he was allowed to work on special projects or visit the library or study hall. He spent the first part of the hour sketching ideas for a wand that could hold multiple crystals, loading a fresh one if the first crystal shattered. Soon he got distracted doodling stick-people firing wands at each other. He was in the middle of writing a poem for Racquela when the bell rang. Timori packed up his papers in his ratty old bag and went to his locker to get his football shorts.

Football tryouts were held after classes on the school field. The boys had already changed into shorts. It would have been too hot to walk home in slacks during the afternoon even if there hadn't been tryouts.

The field was already dotted with students from all three levels of study who had come to try out. Some were running around the field, some chatted with their friends or pushed and shoved each other to show off for the small group of girls who had come to watch. Racquela wasn't among them, which was a blessing in disguise. Timori was already nervous enough about tryouts.

Jacoby turned to Timori as they approached the field. "So Master Vellize wasn't quite what I expected."

"You mean his face wasn't quite what you expected?"

"That too, but when he first came into the class I thought he was going to bite my head off for forgetting my textbook, but he actually seems very calm. I don't think I could be that benevolent if I'd been through what he undoubtedly has."

Timori shrugged. "He's a war veteran. He's had a lot of time to deal with it."

"So is my uncle," Jacoby replied, "and he's anything but calm. What I don't understand is why Master Vellize doesn't wear a prosthetic mask."

"Why don't you ask him?" Timori suggested with a chuckle.

"Because I want to stay on his good side."

Timori spotted two boys approaching at a jog. One of them waved and Jacoby waved back. As they came to a halt, each of them covered in a sheen of sweat, Timori knew right away that they were brothers. Their hair curled and framed their faces in the exact same way, their noses had the same blunt mushroom shape, and they even tilted their heads the same way as they regarded Timori for the first time.

"Hello, Jake," the shorter brother greeted. "This must be Tim." He offered his hand to Timori with an amicable smile. Timori shook it, then the other boy's.

"I'm Mariano, and this is my brother, Filippo. You might not remember us, but we used to play against each other in the junior leagues."

Timori could recall a vague memory of two lanky players of Filippo's and Mariano's likenesses.

"Right, I guess we haven't spoken much off of the field," Timori remarked. "You went to private school, right? Saliara up north?"

Mariano nodded emphatically. "That's why we only played in the summer leagues here in Captus Nove."

Timori nodded in response. The brothers seemed nice enough, but he was always waiting for the other shoe to drop when dealing with rich kids.

Jacoby looked at Filippo, the taller, older-looking one. "Any advice for tryouts, Fil?"

Filippo was more than eager to share his wisdom and experience. "Coach Lagheri is tough as darkoak." Timori noticed that Filippo directed his advice to Mariano, as well. "He'll try to run you into the dirt because he's looking for your ability to keep up with the older players as much as he's testing your skill. I hope you guys have been playing over the summer."

"We have," Timori and Jacoby said in unison.

Filippo barked a laugh. "Are you two brothers as well?"

"No," they answered at the same time.

Filippo's and Mariano's laughter was cut short as the coach blew on his whistle to bring the team hopefuls in line.

"All right, bring it in, no dawdling!" he yelled. His voice could have cut through a scattershot's boom. "Form a straight line so that I can see what I've got to work with this year. That goes for everybody, move it! Just because you were on the team last year don't mean nothing."

Coach Lagheri's face turned bright red when he shouted, but Timori was too busy scrambling into a line-up with the other students to find it amusing.

The coach looked them over as they lined up, strutting up and down the line with all of the authoritarian haughtiness and discerning eyes of a drill sergeant. He was a barrel of a man, as wide in the middle as he was at the shoulders and bald as a potato.

"Hmph," Coach Lagheri uttered after a lengthy inspection of the potential footballers for the 1894-95 finishing school circuit. "They get bigger every year," he quipped, more to himself than anybody else. "Some of you should be trying out for Commonwealth rugby. Football is a sport of finesse. It's not made for pudgy giants like some of you soft-bellied, spoiled brats. This is the sport of the poor, those barely able to afford the ball it's played with. Football is the sport of the lowly and the thin." Timori wondered if Coach Lagheri's speech was the same every year.

"Lowly and thin?" a student somewhere to Timori's right piped up. "Doesn't that exclude you from your own game, coach?"

No doubt the student was trying to be funny and hoped to impress everyone, but Timori could scarcely believe that somebody was be stupid enough to interrupt a man like Alonzo Lagheri. His temper had been legendary since his heyday as a professional footballer during Timori's early childhood.

"What did you say?" Lagheri demanded. He walked right up to the student in question until their noses were practically touching.

Timori watched as a bead of sweat travelled from Lagheri's forehead to the boy's nose. He had to bite his lip to suppress his laughter. Lagheri stared at the boy until the he looked ready to faint.

"Nothing," the boy squeaked.

"Nothing," Lagheri echoed. "I will remind you – all of you – that I was once that dirt-poor child dreaming of becoming a football star, thin as a rail and starving most nights as I practiced my footwork by the light of the moon and clung to the small glint of hope that one day I might make something of myself rather than be stuck as a poor miner's son until the end of my days." Lagheri's rant was overwrought with his own self-importance, but Timori found himself empathizing nevertheless.

"I'm retired from football now, which means that I can get as fat as I damn well please, eating fancy cheeses and caviar with the rest of you privileged little snots, but you might have forgotten that I was once the best footballer in Novem, which is why I now teach at the best finishing school in Novem. I use the term 'best' loosely, of course. Do you know why?"

Nobody dared to answer his challenge.

"Because it's filled with lazy rich dullards like most of you. Your grades are the best in the nation, but I'm always stuck running a dirt football team that gets beat every year by the poor schools who actually want to earn their victories instead of having them handed off on a crystal platter. So! I want to see how many of you can actually handle an honest two hours of training. As for the dullard who thought that it would be wise to make fun of my size, get off my field."

"What?" the boy whined in protestation, "But I ..."

"I said get off my field," Coach Lagheri said again, with much more weight behind his voice than the first time. Timori imagined how frightening the man would have been if he were fully incensed. "If you're lucky, I'll forget your face by next year and you can try again."

The unfortunate student hurried off. Timori could scarcely imagine the humiliation that the boy must have felt, but figured that it was his own fault for mouthing off.

"As for the rest of you, start running around the field. You've been standing still for too long. I will let you know when to stop."

What followed were the most physically gruelling two hours that Timori had ever known. By the time Timori's shoe actually touched a football, forty-five minutes into the first hour, he was so exhausted that he could barely kick. Thankfully for him, all of the other students seemed just as weary, even the second and third-level ones.

By the end of the two hours, most of the team hopefuls were lying on the ground, panting. Three students had abandoned all hope of making the team and had quit the field entirely, sneaking off with shame during the drills. Two had thrown up, one boy passed out, and another had twisted his ankle and was helped off the field by Lagheri's assistant coach. The assistant coach, a young man who looked as though he might have been Lagheri's son minus about thirty kilograms, seemed just as afraid of Coach Lagheri as the students were.

Coach Lagheri looked quite pleased with himself at the end of it all. "Get up, you lazy sacks." He separated everyone into two groups. Timori and Jacoby found themselves in the group on Lagheri's left, along with Filippo and Mariano.

"The group on my right ..." Coach Lagheri began, smirking mischievously as he spoke. Timori's heart leapt into his throat. He knew that he was either slated for football that year or failure in the eyes of the entire school. To be rejected from the football team would be an alienating experience, beyond the personal sense of failure that he would feel.

"... has failed me," Lagheri said after an absurdly long pause. "Better luck next year. Go home."

Timori felt the tension leak out of his muscles. He had made the team.

"As for the rest of you, the next practice will make today's look like a walk in the park. It will sort out the crystal from the rock. I am going to write your names down on the roster before you go, if you dare to face another practice with me. Before this season is through, I am going to push you so hard that you might wish you hadn't passed tryouts."

Timori clapped Jacoby on the back. "We made it, pally!"

"Was there ever any doubt?" Jacoby huffed in reply. "I'd say we did a damn sight better than most of 'em."

Mariano strode over to them. "Looks like we're on the same team now," he pointed out. He dropped his voice to a whisper. "Even if the coach is a lowborn ass who would just as soon see every worthy noble booted off the team."

Timori was about to make a smart reply, but thought better of it. It was too soon to make enemies.

***

It had cooled down by the time Jacoby and Timori marched toward home, and they stopped at the Memorial Bridge for a spell despite their lack of sunflower seeds.

"What a mouth, that Mariano kid," Timori remarked with spite. "I woulda beat him up if it wouldn't have got me kicked off the team."

"You have to admit he plays well," Jacoby said in Mariano's defence. He was leaning with his back to the railing, staring up at the sky.

"That doesn't matter, Jake. He's just one of those noble dullies who thinks they're better than we are. You heard what he said."

Jacoby threw up his hands. "I think that remark was directed more at the coach, Tim."

Timori's face grew hot. "It doesn't matter. He feels the same way about all lowborn. Or are you starting to forget what it was like growing up in the valley?"

"Calm down, Tim. Of course I haven't forgotten. It's just that ... well, we're at Central now. We can't go around antagonizing all the rich kids or they'll gang up on us, just like they used to. Better to make friends anyway. We're in their world now, like it or not."

Timori scoffed. "You are, maybe."

Jacoby turned around and stared up at the hill where he lived, which was casting its shadow over the valley as the sun approached the horizon. "You know I can't help that."

Timori felt a pang of guilt. He knew that it was no easier for Jacoby, dealing with the animosity that the established nobility seemed to hold against him. "You're right. I'm sorry."

"Me too. Mariano is a jerk. I was just excited to make new friends. Nobody will replace you, though, especially not some dully of a noble."

Jacoby looked back toward his house. It was almost his suppertime, that sacred ritual that Timori wished his own family shared. "Anyway I'd better get home before Dad kills me for being late to supper. I'll see you tomorrow, Tim."

Timori's stomach growled as he waved goodbye to Jacoby. He was glumly aware that there would be little to eat back home. Even so, there was nowhere else for him to go. He did not want to play on Jacoby's generosity. He kicked a pebble off of the bridge and made his way down Corti Street toward home.

Timori's street was quiet as he approached his doorstep. Crystara was not out on her front step reading and there were no sounds coming from her house. Timori's house was silent as well, which likely meant that his mother was out selling the late catch at the docks, or putting in extra hours at the typing pool. Timori wondered if his mother had saved enough money to buy groceries that morning, or if her daily wage had already been spent on cigarettes. He hoped it wasn't going to be old fish again for breakfast tomorrow, but it was better than nothing.

Timori pushed the front door open with a heavy sigh, exhausted from the football tryouts and all of the things weighing upon his mind. He wondered whether or not Racquela would get his

106

poem. He thought about how long it would take before he came to blows with Mariano, and whether or not he would get kicked off the team.

The entryway and tiny living room were a mess, as usual. Carlotta was playing with her ratty old doll on the worn couch that faced the window. His youngest sister had the enviable ability to amuse herself in the simple and imaginative way that only the very young could usually manage. Nicola, Timori's other sister, was doing schoolwork at the kitchen table. Both sisters jumped up to greet and hug their brother as he entered the house.

"Mother's working," Nicola said as she tried to squeeze the breath out of Timori.

"What's for supper, Tim?" Carlotta asked as she looked up at her older brother with her impossibly huge, green eyes. "I'm hungry."

"Me too," he admitted as he tousled his kid sister's hair. She stuck out her tongue at him. "Let's see what's in the icebox."

He shuffled wearily over to the small container by the back door and threw the lid open. Inside were a few pieces of bread and two eggs, nothing more. It was the same as the day before, minus the eggs that Timori's mother had likely cooked the girls for breakfast. It was barely enough for one person, and certainly not enough for three.

"Looks like it's eggs and toast again," he said, trying in vain to sound cheerful.

Carlotta made a pouting face. "I'm tired of eggs. We had eggs this morning."

"It's that or go hungry tonight, Lottie," Timori said. Tears welled up in Carlotta's eyes, and Timori could feel his patience wearing thin. "I'll make them into a sun for you."

Carlotta's pout warmed into a smile. "Okay."

Timori lit up the stove from their paltry supply of wood and fried the eggs as he toasted the bread directly on the stovetop. Nicola preferred her eggs right on top of the toast, but for Carlotta he placed the egg in the centre of the plate, then cut up the toast into thin slices

107

and arranged them around the egg to make a facsimile of a sun. Timori knew this was one of the easiest tricks to appease his finicky little sister.

Timori placed the two plates on the table in front of Carlotta and Nicola. Nicola looked up at him. "Where's your plate?"

"I ate with Jake after football practice," he lied.

Nicola frowned as she stared at her egg and two pieces of toast. "But you said you were hungry just a minute ago."

"I'm fine. Eat your dinner and I'll remind Mother to buy groceries tomorrow morning. Before it gets cold."

Nicola continued to stare at her plate as though she was no longer hungry. Carlotta happily plunged a piece of toast into the yellow yolk and drowned it in the viscous liquid, but Timori could no longer lie easily to Nicola the way he did when she was younger.

"You can have half of mine," she offered with a warm smile.

Timori slammed his fist on the table, his patience suddenly at an end. "I said eat your fucking supper!" he yelled in Nicola's face.

There was a moment of stunned silence, and time stood still in the messy and cramped kitchen. Then Nicola burst into tears and fled the table. Carlotta, frightened by her brother's outburst, began to cry as well. Timori forced himself to take a breath and calm down. He looked at Carlotta, who was salting her meal with her tears.

"I'm sorry, Lottie."

Carlotta's lip trembled but she nodded, accepting the apology. Timori gave her a hug. His sisters didn't deserve to be burdened by his issues, and he hated losing his temper. He hated how much he was beginning to hate himself. He hated his poverty and the world that had created it. He loved his sisters so much, but he was afraid that love would turn into hate and resentment if things continued as they were.

"Finish your supper, please, Lottie, and then I'll read you a bedtime story, okay?"

Lottie had stopped crying and had turned her attention back to the half-eaten sun in front of her. Timori was thankful, at least, for a child's ability to shift emotions so quickly.

Timori grabbed Nicola's untouched plate off of the table and went to lock the front door. Then he made his way up the stairs and knocked on the door to Carlotta's and Nicola's shared room.

"Go away," he heard through the door. "I hate you."

The words stung, and Timori feared that Nicola would actually mean them one day. He wasn't about to let his sister go hungry, however.

"But you don't hate eggs. Or toast. Or apologies."

"Yes I do," she insisted, but Timori could hear the resolve in her voice waver.

"Can I come in? I would push everything under the door but you might not want to eat it after that."

He heard a giggle from behind the door and knew that he had won. Nicola opened the door. Her eyes were red and puffy and she wiped her nose on the sleeve of her blouse.

"How come you're always the one to go hungry?" she asked as she took the plate from Timori with a guilty look on her face.

"Because I'm the oldest, that's why. Three more years, Nicky. Three more years and none of us will go hungry anymore. I promise."

Chapter 7

29 Novembra, 1874

My love,

It is snowing here. I have not seen snow since I was a child, and it does make the city beautiful, even though more than half of it has been obliterated. There is a peace that comes with the falling snow, as though there is still beauty to be found amidst the wreckage. It is a haunting kind of serenity. I wish that you could see it, though this is no place for a lady right now.

Your photograph is beautiful. I look at it every night before I go to sleep. How I long to look upon you, your true beauty that a slip of film can never catch, but still it brings me comfort. I can almost hear your voice in my mind, telling me to be strong, to be brave. You are, as always, my reason for being.

I have indeed been placed in the same company as Largo. We are a part of B company of the 103rd infantry battalion. The night watch is long in the wintertime, and I have made friends with many members of my company. We pass the time by telling stories or playing cards for cigarettes, though lately I have begun to debate politics with some of my friends.

Our commanding officer in the company is Captain Lazarus Di'Zotto, and he is not anything like what I would expect from a man in charge. He does not shirk any work that the men are doing themselves, and disciplines only when necessary. He comes from an old noble family, a military one. I have grown quite fond of him.

Our junior engineer is Corporal Roberto Ruveldi, a somewhat taciturn man and a staunch imperialist, but he is smart as a whip and we have many interesting discussions.

We have more than one speaker in the company, but Lieutenant Pietro Garus is certainly everyone's favourite. He is very young for an officer, and sometimes has difficulty getting the men to follow his orders, but he is friendly and will tell a joke at his own expense if it makes somebody smile.

Please do not work yourself too hard at the factory. I worry about your health. I know you insist that you are not a delicate flower, but all the same you must look after yourself.

I must finish this letter, my dear, for my night watch shift is beginning. I love you with all of my heart.

Julio

***

Emperor Longoro was not just the ruler of Novem during the Second Empire. He was a symbol of the return of Noven prosperity. Born to Paula and Titus Longoro on the fifteenth of Martia, 1832, Maximus Longoro's lineage could be traced back to the original emperors of the First Empire.

His was a family steeped in tradition: his ancestors were emperors, kings, engineers, artists, priests and bankers. Longoro knew the key to the hearts of the commoners, however. Many of his promises to the poor were fulfilled in the early days of his empire, such as lifting the fishing tax in 1864 and implementing plumbing to the Avati Valley district the subsequent year.

Nobody could have guessed that the unruly youth of Aestala Finishing School would go on to rule, or even to rise to greatness. Letters from his teachers to his parents speak of 'a poor attitude, and even worse manners' as well as his 'tendency to start fights'. By the age of twelve he had already been banned from three primary schools. According to the historian Piatto, 'he seemed determined, destined to squander the fortune of his family and tarnish their good name'.

Even after finishing school, Longoro remained resistant to responsibility. He refused to attend an academy, and showed no interest in the family businesses, which were eventually bequeathed to his younger brother Casto upon Titus Longoro's death. Maximus Longoro seemed perfectly content to frequent cabarets in Nilonne and be seen with women 'far below his station', according to Casto's famous incomplete memoir.

The element of change in Longoro's life was Leonardo Posco, the struggling merchant's son whom Longoro happened to meet in a Riti city bar on the twenty-sixth day of Quinta, 1853. Many of my contemporaries argue that Posco was the true architect of the Second Empire. My research suggests that it was both of them, and that neither one could have succeeded without the other. The understanding of that principle is an understanding of the Second Empire itself.

***

"Fuck," Lieutenant Pietro Garus muttered out of the corner of his mouth. There was a cigarette pressed between his lips in the other corner. "Twosies." He threw his cards down on the barracks table in exasperation.

"Language, lieutenant," Captain Di'Zotto scolded. He set down his cards face-up beside Pietro's. "Fives and Eights. Twenty-six points."

"Damn," Pietro exclaimed before he could stop himself. He pushed the four cigarettes that were lying on the table in his commanding officer's direction. Lazarus Di'Zotto gave Pietro a stern look but accepted the cigarettes.

Julio rubbed his hands together and drew his trench coat closer around himself to keep out the chill. It was a cold night in Cime, and the small heat crystals placed around the barracks did little to dissuade Farus, the God of Winter, from pressing the cold deep into Julio's bones that evening.

Julio gathered the cards and began to shuffle. In the silence, Pietro Garus put out the butt of his cigarette in the ashtray and promptly lit another one using the oil lamp in the centre of the table. He was always short on cigarettes because of the way he smoked and gambled, and Julio often traded the young officer his cigarettes in exchange for paper and ink.

"You really think Nilonne will fall before the year is up?" Pietro asked his fellows. Julio wondered if the lieutenant was actually curious or if he was simply filling the silence. The young speaker was rarely interested in the why and wherefore of the war, even though he had attended the military academy.

"Of course it will," the captain replied with confidence. "Fresh troops were just sent from Mikos."

"Ha!" Pietro laughed. "Better them than us!"

Julio began to deal the cards clockwise, first to Largo, then Pietro, Lazarus, Roberto, and finally himself. "They're people too," Julio reminded Pietro as he finished the four-card deal. "It's not their fault they got pulled into this war."

"Yes it is," Roberto interjected. "They accepted the empire with open arms, thus subjugating themselves to our sovereignty. Emperor Longoro can place them wherever he likes, where they're needed the most. And deal some better cards next time, Jules."

"Dirty deal, huh, Rob?" Pietro quipped, his smile devious. "I raise a cig."

"Fold," Julio said as he rolled his eyes. He only played when his cards were a sure bet. It didn't win him many cigarettes. "Mikos welcomed the empire because we strong-armed them into it. Besides which, the citizens had no choice, just like those of us who were drafted."

"It's better than the mines at least," Largo said in his rumbling bass. "And wait your turn to bet, kid. I'm in for this one." He added a cigarette to Pietro's.

"Kid?" Pietro whined. "I'm your superior."

"You're a pipsqueak," Roberto retorted after Lazarus added a cigarette to the pile. "And I fold. Jules, you forget that once upon a time all of these places belonged to Novem. They are unenlightened compared to us, especially when it comes to crystal technology, and they have abandoned the gods. You don't think we have a responsibility to show them a better way?"

After the betting, Largo, Lazarus and Pietro each had the option to discard one card and draw another. Largo was the only one who did not exchange a card, and the three soldiers continued with another round of betting.

"These aren't hut-dwelling barbarian tribes anymore, Rob," Julio argued as the others each tossed in another cigarette in turn. "They have a right to govern themselves, which we are trying to take away."

Another round of card exchange occurred, then a final bid. Largo surprised everyone by bidding an additional three cigarettes. Pietro and Lazarus met his bet.

Roberto blew warm breath into his hands. "Longoro made our nation great again, Jules. The republic was dirt."

"But he took away our right to vote!" Julio yelled, incensed. "What kind of a nation is it that doesn't offer freedom of choice to its citizens, freedom to decide whether or not they even want to go to war?"

"Calm yourself, private," Lazarus warned. "Well Mita, what's your score?" He looked pointedly at Largo.

Largo, expressionless as always, laid three tens and an errant six on the table. "Thirty. And you're both wrong. The empire took away freedom of choice for the wealthy only. Those of us who were fooled by Longoro's promises to abolish the class system didn't see much of a change after he was elected between the lies of the republic and the lies of the empire. We had to fend for ourselves, as always. Sure, Longoro did a bunch of stuff to improve quality of life for the empire's lower-class citizens, but he didn't balance out the disparity between wealth and poverty like he said he was going to. Now I'm not gonna gripe about the war because it's better pay than I'll ever get in the mines, but the only truly fair system is neither imperial nor republican. A system where all are equal and classless and every citizen has the right to vote, that is the way."

There was a profound silence. Largo rarely spoke so freely.

"Thirty," Pietro muttered. "You dirty shoveller. I got fifteen."

"Call me that again," Largo warned, "and I'll show you just what a shoveller can do."

Captain Lazarus Di'Zotto stood up. "Well gentlemen, it has been fun, but I cannot be in the presence of anti-imperial sentiments without handing out discipline, so I must take my leave."

He threw his cards on the table: twos and fives for fourteen points. "And for the gods' sake, lieutenant, show some backbone."

There was another silence as their commanding officer walked away stiffly. It was always the same: they would each hold firm to their political opinions and never waver. Eventually the captain would leave once they got too loud so he would not be implicated, but the debate would continue.

"Well," Julio sighed. He grabbed the stack of cards with cold fingers and handed it to Largo. "Another round? I wouldn't mind winning some of the lieutenant's cigarettes to sell back to him later."

"We'll see about that," Pietro replied. "Hey guys, I've got a joke for you. A republican, a socialist and Emperor Longoro walk into a bar ..."

Chapter 8

In the days of the First Empire, every citizen of Novem tithed to the gods in order to earn their favour. The church was trusted unequivocally as the source for guidance, not just in matters of spirituality but for financial woes, health, protection in times of war, and, of course, matters of the heart. All children born to noble families had their future partner selected by the Great Crystal. Family alliances were strengthened and the bloodlines of Novem were kept pure from the taint of those lesser barbarian peoples who encompassed most of the slave and lower-class populations the Noven Empire had brought into its fold. Although not always from the noble classes, skilled speakers and empaths were sometimes included in the betrothals because of their abilities.

The traditional age of marriage rose over the centuries, and so did the age at which betrothal was acceptable. In the Dark Ages, when threats from other kingdoms were at their greatest, the betrothals were used for political positioning. Family alliances continued into the Rebirth, and when schooling became commonplace for children of the day, the betrothals were set to occur at the beginning of finishing school, sometime between the ages of fifteen and sixteen.

Centuries passed. Faith in the church began to dwindle as science brought to light facets of crystal lore that the church, if it had ever possessed such secrets, had refused to share with the subjects of Novem. The merchant class rose up and began to buy their way into the nobility and thus into the sacred tradition of the crystal betrothals.

With the democratic revolution, many other radical ideas came to the fore, and old traditions were swept away in favour of bringing Novem into the modern era. Novem had lagged behind other nations ever since the Sundering, when the proud peninsula was divided into warring kingdoms. Historians later claimed that The Sundering was the pivotal event that brought about the Dark Ages in

Titania. Although the Rebirth saw culture and refinement return to Novem, it was a divided peninsula, and money was spent on wars instead of colonization and trade.

The Reunification and a lack of colonial interest turned the nation's focus inward, toward modernization. The church was forced to adapt as well. In order to fill its coffers, the church opened the crystal betrothals to any family who could pay the price.

It wasn't long before the republic repealed the laws surrounding the crystal betrothals, and the democratic ideal of freedom to choose a partner became the norm. Central School was the sole remaining institution that maintained the tradition after the Great War. The nobility arranged their betrothals privately, if at all, and the Great Crystal held sway over the fates of only six students a year. Only the church and the owners of Central School knew of the details that maintained the arrangement that never successfully abolished the law linking Central School to the Great Crystal, although it had been put to a vote several times. Some said that it was the will of the gods that kept the ties between the Great Crystal and the famous private school, others that it was the coin of the church.

That was what old Tevici had taught Racquela, at any rate. Racquela's father had always impressed upon her the importance of respecting the gods, and she had never failed him in that regard. Lying to him about money, however, was a betrayal of his trust. She saw no other choice. How else to ensure the favour of the gods so that they could find for her the one that she was meant to be with?

When Crystara told her the agreed-upon price that had been worked out with the keeper, Racquela knew that there was no way that her father would believe she needed that much money for clothing. She and Crystara had to work out an alternate plan. Joven De'Trini would never agree to a betrothal that wasn't of his choosing unless it was the will of the Great Crystal.

It had taken some time, but during the first week of classes Crystara concocted a devious scheme. At first Racquela was fearful that her father would instantly become aware that something

117

untoward was going on, but he read the forged letter 'from the Schoolmaster' rather briskly and signed the cheque for fifteen thousand dinari without thinking to question the sudden increase in school fees. Joven signed much larger cheques nearly every day of his life, and private schools were notoriously expensive. Joven was a discerning man, but he would never question or doubt his own daughter.

Everybody knew Racquela at her father's bank, and it was easy for her to convince the teller that her father had simply made a mistake when writing the name on the cheque. Racquela told the young man that her father wrote numerous cheques in a day – sometimes hundreds – and couldn't be faulted for writing the wrong name now and then. Racquela batted her eyelashes to cement her point, and the teller was more than happy to cash the cheque for her. With fifteen thousand dinari and a heart full of guilt weighing her down, she and Crystara made their way to Crystus Hill after dark.

The shadows were long and deep on Crystus Hill that evening, and Racquela felt cold for the first time that summer. She had always respected her gods, but the Old Temple was sacred in a way that frightened her. It was absolute. It was the home of Novem's link to the divine.

A guard followed the girls with his eyes as they crossed the plaza, but he did not leave the shrouded comfort of his post under an archway. Racquela and Crystara would be safe from thieves and lowlives within the district, but if the keeper was not there to meet them at the temple they would likely be questioned by the guards about their business.

Crystara turned to Racquela as they passed under the giant whiteoak that overshadowed the plaza fountain. "Are you sure you still want to do this?" she whispered. "What if your father finds out what we've done?"

Racquela shook her head. "It's too late now to second guess this, Crys. Besides, my father won't question the Great Crystal once this is all done, as long as we can trust the keeper's word."

"We can trust him," Crystara said quickly. She and Racquela skulked over to the north wall of the temple, where Keeper Orvin was supposed to meet them.

The wall was as dark as the abyss on the north side of the temple. There were no crystal lamps and the moon was nowhere to be seen. The deepstone jutted up from the ground beside Racquela like a sea of solid pitch, black as coal and darker even than the night sky above.

Keeper Orvin was leaning against the wall, unaccompanied. His white face was stark against the deepstone thanks to the illuminated crystal that he wore around his neck. His garb was simple and un-priestly: a pair of cream-coloured slacks and a blue button-up shirt, and Racquela immediately felt silly for wearing her cloak to the rendezvous. Belatedly, she realized that a secret encounter should not appear secretive.

As Racquela regarded the calm, smiling face of the keeper for the first time, she noted that he looked much as she would have expected from an old priest, if a little less sombre. Still smiling, the Keeper of the Great Crystal nodded at Crystara with a surprising amount of familiarity and then turned to Racquela.

"Crystara tells me you wish to curry the favour of the Great Crystal," he said, completely ignoring the protocol of proper introductions. "Is this so?"

Racquela swallowed her anxiety. "It is," she said after a moment's hesitation. The keeper had an intimidating amount of presence, despite his small stature and placid demeanour. "Um, that is, yes. I would like the Great Crystal to find my true love for me."

"Your true love," the keeper repeated. There was a small pause. "The Great Crystal can do this for you, provided you have the proper tithe."

With shaking hands Racquela withdrew the paper bank notes from her purse and offered them to the old priest. He nodded and took the stack of notes, examined one by the light of his crystal necklace, and did not bother to count the rest. They were hidden within his pants pocket a moment later.

"The gods will hear your plea, Racquela De'Trini," Keeper Orvin said in an officious tone. "They will be pleased with your offering. I will inform Central School of the Great Crystal's decision at the appropriate time. Have a safe journey home."

Racquela took the words as a dismissal and turned to leave. She found herself surprised at how swiftly it had all happened. "Thank you," she blurted as she turned back around to address the keeper. "Thank you, Keeper Orvin."

Keeper Orvin shook his head. "You have your friend Crystara to thank for convincing me," he replied with a smile. "Go on home, young ladies, it's late. The guards will ensure you make it back to your motorcoach unmolested."

As Racquela turned to go, a sense of relief and excitement welled up inside of her.

"Crystara," the keeper said suddenly. Racquela watched as Crystara and the keeper stared at each other in the dark. No words were exchanged, but something unspoken seemed to pass between them.

"I always keep my promises," Crystara said. With a toss of her hair she turned and left for the waiting motorcoach at a brisk pace.

Racquela hustled to catch up. "What promise did he mean, Crys?"

Crystara stopped and looked over the wall at the Old Temple. "I agreed to let him teach me crystal speaking, in addition to my normal studies at the school."

"The keeper, teaching somebody outside of the church? Is that legal?"

Crystara looked into Racquela's eyes. "What we just did wasn't legal. I did this for you, originally, but the keeper is the most powerful speaker in the whole world. This is my chance to make something of myself. I wasn't born rich. Crystal speaking is my best shot."

Racquela detected a note of resentment in Crystara's voice at the mention of wealth, but she let it drop.

"You did all this just for me?" Racquela could think of no other friend who would have risked so much.

"I did it for both of us," Crystara replied.

***

As far as schools went, Central was structured more like an academy than an ordinary finishing school. By the end of their first year, students were expected to declare a major, which was supposed to help on their path toward an intended career.

By the winter of 1894, Racquela was still undecided. There was too much going on at Central School for her to worry about declaring a major until she absolutely had to. Racquela's social life was busier than it had ever been. There were many nobles from other cities whom Racquela was getting to know, and she spent a great deal of time with Crystara outside of classes.

Classes weren't difficult for Racquela. She had the ease of knowing she wouldn't have to worry about emotionally draining classes such as empathy. Crystara often related horror stories of the exercises, especially when paired with somebody who projected their emotions very strongly. Being the only harpist in music class was always enjoyable but it wasn't as fulfilling as it used to be.

Crystara told her that it was because of all the boys. Racquela supposed that the assumption was correct. Crystara cut through to the truth of any matter as though it were clear as crystal. Boys were plentiful at Central School, and they were the best Novem had to offer: the smartest, the richest, the most attractive and the most athletic. A good half of Captus Nove's elite nobles sent their children to Central, and many wealthy merchants, too. Several boys of various social standing had already declared their intentions toward Racquela, and she accepted their gifts and notes or poems graciously but remained strategically undecided. The crystal betrothals were never far from her mind.

Timori was particularly persistent as far as Racquela's admirers went. She would often receive chocolates or poetry from

121

the young man, and she found the poetry quite flattering and well-written. As a candidate, however, Racquela knew that his station was a serious barrier, and although he was very athletic, he wasn't as handsome as his friend Jacoby. Jacoby always seemed aloof around Racquela, however, despite flirting with other girls, including Crystara. Surprisingly, Crystara was tight-lipped on the subject of Jacoby, despite claiming that there was nothing between them. Racquela decided that she hoped neither of the boys would be selected by the Great Crystal. Jacoby seemed to have eyes for half the girls in the school and Timori was far too low-class for her parents ever to be happy with such an arrangement.

Before Central School, class differences had never been so obvious to Racquela. She had attended a prestigious primary school that taught only the most affluent children, but Central was a mixed pot. It had taken all of Racquela's social graces to convince her old friends to accept Crystara.

"She's not even very nice," Bella noted. Her eyebrows, which used to grow thick when she was younger, were always plucked slightly crooked and it drove Racquela insane. Bella, Racquela and Phebe were sharing a picnic lunch in the outer courtyard of Central, under the shelter of a darkoak tree. All three girls wore heavy shawls on top of their school uniforms. It was not a particularly cold winter that year, but it was very damp.

"She is nice," Racquela said. She took a dainty bite of her cheese and tried not to stare at Bella's eyebrows. "We're just not always accustomed to ... her type of honesty."

"It sounds like an excuse," was Bella's rebuttal. "She's never been nice to me, at any rate. She just glares at everybody and doesn't say anything. Or she's reading a book when we try to talk to her."

"Besides which," Phebe added, "she's a miner's daughter. You shouldn't be hanging around her anyway. She doesn't even try to make herself presentable most days. Her clothing is always dirty."

Racquela looked away and said nothing. She wanted to defend Crystara, but it was hard to make other people understand what made her a good friend. Crystara was a good listener and understood Racquela in a way nobody else did. Racquela couldn't afford to lose her more influential friends, however, and so she put up with their criticisms.

"Well, we'll leave your charity case alone for now," Bella said as though she were supremely benevolent.

Racquela found Bella more and more annoying every day. She wondered if life at Central, intermingling with students of all classes, was beginning to change her. Lower and middle-class students were beginning to seem more interesting. They had a lot more to talk about.

"Have you found a new dress for the winter formal yet, Racquela?" Bella asked.

Racquela nodded and sipped her hot cocoa. Nothing excited her more than a formal dance, especially her first one at Central School. The possibilities of it made her feel dizzy if she thought about them too much. She had gone dress shopping with her mother and Crystara as soon as she had found out about the dance. Her gown was blue satin, in the latest form-hugging, low-backed style.

When she caught Crystara examining a similar dress in red and holding it up in front of the boutique mirror, Racquela had secretly returned to the dress store a day later and purchased it for her friend. Crystara, always proud when it came to money, had told Racquela that she couldn't accept the gift, but after ten minutes of arguing Racquela had talked her down to paying her back for the dress someday. Racquela hoped it didn't come to that. Her parents' money had paid for it, anyway.

"Have you found a date yet, Bella?" Racquela asked. She wondered if the spite was noticeable in her voice. Bella was always jealous of Racquela because 'she stole all the boys'.

Bella scowled. "Not yet."

Her response made Racquela feel somewhat better. Phebe, luckily, didn't compete with the other two for male attention. She had been courting the same boy, Alonzo, since late primary school. He went to another finishing school, but he would accompany Phebe to the dance.

Racquela began thinking about the crystal betrothals again and wondered which girls would be chosen other than herself. It wasn't long, however, before she was thinking about the winter formal again.

* * *

The old courtyard served a perfect dual function as a ballroom. Decked out in blue and silver streamers that hung from the ceiling, the bright colours warmed the sombre bricks, and the students and chaperones quickly forgot that they were dancing in a former prison. The band's lively music offered a little bit of something for everybody. There were waltzes for the couples, traditional Noven songs for the teachers and chaperones, and fast-paced 'contemporary orchestra' or *tempo* for the vast majority of students.

As Racquela entered the courtyard with Crystara, she scanned the room for people that she knew. Phebe and Alonzo were dancing alongside Belle, who was doing her best not to seem like a third wheel. Jacoby and Timori were near the band.

Jacoby didn't appear to know much about dancing, but he never lacked girls to dance with. Racquela wondered how many hearts he would break before the end of the school year. Timori was never far from his best friend, but Racquela caught him looking over at her several times. He didn't show much interest in the girls he was dancing with, but, though he looked distracted, he did know how to move his feet.

Racquela spent the early part of the evening with Bella, Phebe and Crystara, socializing more than dancing. Sweaty *tempo* dancing was for the lower-class kids. She hoped that either Jacoby or Timori would invite her to dance at some point during the evening. The inseparable boys were far better conversationalists than most of their peers. Racquela was occupied enough by other young men dancing with her, however, that she soon got caught up in the music and was less concerned with casual conversation.

The band began to play a waltz and Racquela watched Timori in his rumpled, poorly fitting brown suit stride purposefully over to her. His serious expression made Racquela want to giggle. It was just a dance, after all.

"May I have this dance?" he asked. He offered his hand in a graceful masculine gesture.

"Of course," Racquela replied.

Timori held her back firmly and led her around the dance floor. For all his awkwardness in other regards, Timori was an excellent dancer. Racquela found herself getting swept away by the music. Briefly, she looked into Timori's green eyes to find him intensely returning her gaze. Crystara had definitely been correct: Timori was in love with her. Racquela became excited and uncomfortable all at once. Timori drew her in closer and she rested her head lightly on his shoulder. It was a nice feeling. Racquela realized that she was having difficulty deciding exactly what it was that she felt for Timori. Was it attraction, or was she merely flattered by all of the affection he showed to her?

"Racquela," Timori whispered, "I need to tell you something." He was almost panting and his palms were sweaty. Racquela's heart sped up. She pulled away slightly and caught Timori's gaze.

"Not yet."

"I ... what?"

"Please, not yet, Tim. Whatever you have to say, wait until after New Year. At least until after the crystal betrothals. You never know ..."

Timori nodded slowly as his lip trembled. He pulled away from Racquela completely even though the song had not yet ended. "The crystal betrothals ... a simple 'no' would have sufficed."

"Tim, it's not a 'no', it's just that right now isn't the best time. Please understand. Don't you want to finish the dance?"

Timori shook his head and looked away. Racquela was surprised by his reaction. She had always thought that girls were supposed to be the dramatic ones.

125

"No, it's fine, Racquela. I need to get going anyway. My mother is working late and I have to make sure my sisters get to bed. Have a wonderful evening. I'm sorry if I ruined it for you at all."

"Tim ..." But by the time she uttered his name, he had already fled the dance floor.

Racquela tried to enjoy the rest of the evening, but Timori was constantly on her mind, even though she tried to convince herself that she had nothing to feel guilty about. Her friends chatted and danced as she stared at the streamers and the band, holding the same stuffed olive for an hour without taking a bite.

As the dance wound down to an end, Racquela noticed Jacoby approaching her. He looked handsome in a grey pinstripe suit and his hair was neatly combed, for once. Jacoby's eyes always seemed to have a sparkle in them, as though he was thinking about some secret joke. He smiled warmly and touched Racquela on the arm.

"Are you all right?" he asked, loudly. He had to shout to be heard over the band. "You seem upset."

Racquela returned Jacoby's smile. "I'm fine, thank you Jacoby."

"Come with me for a walk. I need to talk to you."

He offered his arm. Racquela's heart raced. Jacoby was usually so aloof, but suddenly he was acting very forward. Containing her excitement, she took Jacoby's arm and they left the dance floor for the relative solitude of the outer courtyard. It wasn't empty. Many young couples strolled through the courtyard, but it offered a decent amount of privacy compared to the dance area. Racquela was surprised that the chaperones weren't patrolling the area.

"Nice night out, warm for the time of year," Jacoby observed as he led Racquela to a quiet spot. They leaned against the cool stone wall. "Listen, I just wanted to talk about Tim for a moment ..."

Racquela sighed. Jacoby wasn't interested in her at all. He was merely looking out for his best friend. Racquela's disappointment surprised her. She didn't realize until he was right in

126

front of her how attractive he was, and he was of a higher class than Timori, besides.

"I didn't mean to upset him."

"I know you didn't. Don't worry about it too much. He'll be fine if you give him a bit of time. He's ... just a lot more sensitive than he appears to be, and he's really smitten with you."

Racquela found that she was having trouble focusing on the conversation. Jacoby's eyes were dark and inviting. "Ah, well, I think it would be unwise for anybody to commit to anything until after we know who is chosen. For the crystal betrothals."

Jacoby nodded. "I understand completely. Timori should, given time as well. All I want to know is ... if neither of you is selected, are you interested in him at all?"

Racquela had to choose her words very carefully. Whatever she told Jacoby would be relayed directly to Timori. She had no wish to hurt the young man's feelings, but at the same time, she already knew that she was going to be selected for betrothal and there was no sense in leading Timori on.

"Honestly, Jake, Tim is shiny, but ..." She searched for the right words, but there was no easy way to put it. He wasn't handsome enough. He wasn't rich enough. He wasn't confident enough. For a moment, Racquela thought that it would be simpler to tell Jacoby about the bribe she had made, but that was a secret she couldn't reveal. Racquela wished that she was an empath so that she could read Jacoby's intentions. Was he just looking out for Timori? He was leaning in awfully close.

"But you're not interested," Jacoby said, finishing the sentence for her. She couldn't stop looking at his lips as he spoke. "It's all right, I understand completely. You can't fault yourself for who you like. After all ..."

Racquela pushed herself forward on the tips of her toes and kissed Jacoby. Her boldness surprised her, but Jaocby's eyes had been beckoning her to do it from the start of their conversation. He must have known, as an empath, just how attractive she found him at that moment or he wouldn't have been looking at her that way.

Jacoby didn't pull away, but his eyes widened in surprise. Racquela's lips left his and she looked up at him.

"I'm sorry. Is this ... is this all right?" she asked.

"I ..." Jacoby paused. He looked into Racquela's eyes and it felt as though he was delving right into her soul. "Yes, it's all right."

They kissed in the courtyard until the faraway din of music ended for the evening.

Chapter 9

The Noven tradition of the crystal betrothals stretched back to the early days of the First Empire, and a history of the betrothals was out of necessity a history of the Great Crystal.

The Great Crystal's origins had always been shrouded in mystery, and the most disputed part of crystal theory concerned the actual history of the Great Crystal's creation. For a millennia and a half, the accepted story was that the crystal had been a gift from the gods so that humans could communicate with their masters who dwelt in the sky and follow their bidding.

During the age of enlightenment, some scholars began to challenge the church's theory, despite persecution. These challenges, along with the Noven church's diminishing power led to a series of altercations between the church and many of Novem's more influential guilds. During the conflict several temples were looted or destroyed, and many church documents were uncovered that suggested the Great Crystal's origins were much older than the accepted crystal calendar year of 0. Many church astronomers tried to defend the Old Temple's position by pointing to astral phenomena, including a large meteorite crash that occurred in Novem in the year 0, but the church was already losing the battle. A loss of faith in the institution of the gods was subsequently a loss of faith in the crystal.

Despite the rise of republican science, the Great Crystal was still under church control and the keepers would not allow it to be studied by outsiders. Any study of the crystal outside of the church was done by hunting down documents of ancient Novem. From those studies, three further theories about the origin of the Great Crystal emerged, although none of them led to a clear understanding of what exactly its function was, if indeed its function was more than as a decorative church figurehead. Only the Noven Church knew the answer to that secret.

The first and most widely accepted theory among anti-theologian scholars was that the Great Crystal was created by the engineers of the Noven Imperium as a sort of oracle. Evidence to back up the theory was found in the fact that the engineers of ancient Novem knew many secrets about crystal speaking that their modern-day counterparts still could not duplicate, but some argued that many of those speaking abilities may have been more myth than fact. The sack of Captus Nove in 553 A.C. and the burning of the original Avati Library effectively destroyed the best chance scholars may have had at uncovering the truth, as well as many long-lost crystal speaking techniques.

The second theory was that the Great Crystal was acquired from a conquered people known as the Dortians, from whom Novem borrowed many aspects of their own culture. It was theorized that Novem may have learned much about crystal speaking from the Dortians, as well. Any proof of such a claim had yet to be discovered, however, and so it remained another theory.

The advent of archaeology led to the discovery of an underground mine east of Captus Nove where a large excavation had taken place. Whether or not it was the site of the Great Crystal's discovery was a matter of conjecture, but the discovery of the dig site led to a third and more radical theory. It was surmised that the Noven Imperium had mined the Great Crystal from the ground, and that it had already been activated as the source of power that it was supposed to be. As opposed to legend, where the Old Temple had been built around the Great Crystal after it had been given to Novem by Jova the Father of the Universe, the Noven Imperium found a way to move the gargantuan rock all the way up Crystus Hill. Most scholars dismissed the mine theory as merely the same story put forth by the church, except that the crystal had come from the ground instead of from the sky.

Despite continual research, only the church knew for certain whether or not the Great Crystal served any real function. The keepers claimed, as always, that the Great Crystal was a direct link to the gods.

Jacoby had assumed that his aptitude for empathy would make it easy for him. On the very first day of class, the teacher warned the students that most of them would be reduced to tears within the first week. She went on to say that some would choose to drop out of the class altogether. While many carried the capacity for empathy, she explained, not everyone had the fortitude.

Jacoby hadn't cried, but the stress of the class was often intense. After the initial hurdles of reaching out to somebody else and trying to dredge through a melange of emotions that swirled around like a vortex, the interpretation of those emotions followed, which was an even more complex process. Some people in the class had no control over their emotions and would project it all upon the reader, with varying results. Oftentimes it would simply end in tears. One student punched the girl that she was reading. Another boy started screaming and ran from the class in hysterics. He didn't return.

"Empathy isn't simply the act of reading what emotion another person is feeling," Miss Telmari explained. Her pinched face and severe widow's peak gave her a mature, hawkish appearance, although she had told the class that she was in her early twenties.

"Anybody can learn how to do that. Empathy is about understanding that emotion ... indeed, understanding all emotions one can feel from another person, and thus understand that person. It is not mind reading, ladies and gentlemen. We empaths cannot see into somebody else's private thoughts and secrets. But with sufficient training you can understand a person's hidden feelings well enough that you won't have to read their mind."

Jacoby felt like Miss Telmari was talking in circles. She never explained clearly enough *how* empathy worked. She was also very quick to point out just how awful Jacoby was at empathy, despite his high test score. Miss Telmari often scolded Jacoby for not projecting his emotions well enough when somebody else was trying to read him, but then she would *tsk* at him for letting his own

131

emotions get in the way when he read somebody else. Miss Telmari explained that the most important skill for an empath was to mask their own emotions, but at the beginning it was important for all students to learn to project so that others could learn how to read them. According to her, Jacoby projected and masked his emotions at exactly the wrong times.

Jacoby found Crystara to be the most frustrating person to work with, in a class that was already difficult for him. Neither he nor Crystara could read each other very well. Crystara would confuse one thing for another and tell Jacoby that he was feeling something that he wasn't. At the same time, Crystara's emotions were confusing and hard to read, as though Jacoby were seeing them through a shroud. It was as if Crystara had a field of repulsion around her that prevented insight. Jacoby suspected that she did it intentionally. She seemed very uncomfortable with people reading her emotions.

For the first few weeks, most class time was spent discussing a topic with a partner and then trying to assess an emotional reaction. Some topics were tamer, such as general questions of morality, but sometimes Miss Telmari asked the students to get more personal. Most would read Jacoby's nervousness more than anything, which meant that they knew he had something to hide. He was fairly certain that Crystara had already figured out his secret, but she never said anything about it, despite being Racquela's best friend.

Jacoby wondered if Timori would ever find out. Racquela had come to him the day after the dance, saying that she couldn't pursue anything because the betrothals were coming up. She begged him to keep it a secret – it was only a kiss or two after all, she said. Jacoby was relieved beyond belief. He had wanted the kiss, not a courtship that would ruin his friendship with Timori. He had still betrayed his best friend's trust, however, and he tried not to think about it during class. According to Miss Telmari, guilt projected more strongly than almost any other emotion.

On the first day back to classes after the New Year, Jacoby was paired up with Lenara for empathy exercises. He found working

132

with Lenara almost as difficult as it was with Crystara, and for similar reasons. Both girls were attractive, and and neither one projected their emotions very well. Lenara, however, was much friendlier than Crystara, which helped to put Jacoby at ease.

Jacoby often wondered if Lenara could read how interested he was in her. Miss Telmari had warned the class early on that many romantic relationships tended to form in empathy class because of the forced emotional closeness of the students. It wasn't just that Lenara was pretty and petite, or that she had the biggest, most beautiful blue eyes Jacoby had ever seen, or even how well they got along in class, laughing and talking about many things as they tried to read each other.

He liked how she always wore a flower in her hair. She said that it was the only way to look unique when everybody had to wear the same sky-blue uniforms. Jaocby didn't believe in love at first sight, but he was beginning to understand the compulsions that brought about romance.

Lenara and Jacoby were working on an exercise to read beyond the most prominent surface emotion. To begin with, Lenara would think about something that elicited an emotional response in her. Then Jacoby would have to try to feel past that initial emotion to find her deeper emotional state.

"Anger," he guessed.

Lenara smiled and shook her head. "You're not even trying, Jacoby."

"All right, let's try again. Um ... sadness?"

Lenara shook her head again. Jacoby was tired of the exercise and gave up his focus. He knew that it would be a long time before he could read Lenara.

"Jealousy," he mused. "Happiness. Confusion. Fear. Something."

Lenara began to laugh.

"Joy. You were laughing. Joy."

Lenara giggled. "That was the surface thought, silly. All right, let's switch. You're being lazy today."

Before they had a chance to continue, an old man entered the classroom without so much as a knock on the door. He was dressed in the white and blue priests' robes of the Old Temple and flanked on either side by men in republican-grey military uniforms. Although Jacoby knew he had done nothing wrong, he found himself avoiding eye contact with the men in uniform.

The priest unrolled an ornate and ostentatious scroll and read aloud from it. "The following students have been chosen by the Great Crystal and are to follow me immediately: Crystara Mita, Lenara De'Marici, Jacoby Padrona."

Jacoby looked at Crystara, then at Lenara. Neither of the girls seemed very surprised. Jacoby felt light-headed. He knew that being chosen for the crystal betrothals had always been a remote possibility, but he was in no way prepared for it. Lenara and Crystara began to rise, and he did the same. He followed the girls and the priest with his guards out of the classroom as though in a dream.

The priest escorted Jacoby and the girls to the front entrance of Central School. The other chosen students were gathered there: Timori, Racquela, and a lanky curly-haired boy Jacoby had never met named Paulo. The six students were explicitly told by the priest not to speak to each other as they left the school and were escorted in a large motorcoach to the Old Temple. Jacoby stared out the window and pondered his rapidly changing future. He wondered what his parents would say to him. They knew that it might happen. Jacoby tried to read Timori's emotions, but he couldn't tell where his own feelings ended and anyone else's began. A pit of nervousness sank into Jacoby's stomach as the motorcoach arrived at the Old Temple. It was all happening so quickly.

The students were ushered through the great hall and crystal hallway. It was the first time Jacoby had ever set foot inside the Old Temple, but he barely had time to admire the richly-coloured stained glass windows as he passed them by. The priest, who seemed to stand in an eternally stooped position, placed a key into the crystal lock for a hallway door and then ushered everyone inside. As everybody crowded into the small office, the priest turned to stand in

134

front of Jacoby and his fellow students with a guard still on either side of him. Every student in the room was holding their breath, waiting to receive their fate.

"You have all been chosen by the Great Crystal for betrothal," the priest said. He ran a hand through his grey hair, which was thin on top, and cleared his throat. "However, you will be given time to prepare. We will take your measurements and provide you with ceremonial robes for the event, which will be this Joveday here at the Old Temple. Per tradition, a priest from the temple will fetch each of you for the ceremony. Central School will also hold a ceremony in your honour the following week. This may seem very sudden to all of you, but the Great Crystal chooses very carefully. You should all feel honoured that you were chosen. Now, are there any questions from any of you?"

Racquela raised her hand, which seemed shaky from where Jacoby was standing. "Well, who are we each betrothed to?"

The priest seemed surprised by the question. "The Great Crystal will tell each of you during the ceremony. Did nobody teach this to you?"

All of the students shook their heads. Religion was no longer something frequently discussed in school.

"The crystal will tell us?" It was Paulo who asked. He had a deep voice for his age. It rang out throughout the small space.

"Are you saying that the Great Crystal *actually* speaks for the gods? I thought it was just a fancy piece of rock."

Jacoby nearly gasped. Paulo was speaking blasphemy by suggesting that the church was lying about the Great Crystal. Many believed that the Great Crystal was more a matter of ceremony than anything, but to say it inside the Old Temple in the presence of a priest was gutsier than Jacoby cared to be.

The priest frowned, which made his thick tufts of eyebrows connect in the middle. "The Great Crystal is not just a symbol, my son. You will see. Are there any more questions?"

"How ... exactly does it work?" Racquela asked. "Does the Great Crystal simply tell us who our betrothed is?"

The priest seemed thankful to receive a less offensive question. "The Great Crystal speaks for the gods, and thus does not speak in a way that is always easy for us to understand. You will each receive a vision upon touching the crystal. Those who share the exact same visions are meant to be betrothed. After receiving the visions, you will each be taken to a separate room and asked what you saw. That is how we determine your betrothed."

Jacoby stared at the priest's desk and let his eyes go blurry. It seemed an odd system to him and not exactly foolproof, but he wasn't about to question the church the way Paulo had, despite being a very secular youth. He barely ever attended church, and was ambivalent to the existence of the gods. He wondered if touching the Great Crystal would create new faith in him, or make him shed any pretence of belief.

The motorcoach ride back to the school was just as silent as the trip up to the Old Temple, although the priest had not forbidden the students to talk. They were dropped off, almost unceremoniously, at Central School's entrance and the motorcoach drove off.

Jacoby stared up at Central. It seemed much less intimidating than it had a mere day ago. He also noticed that all six of them were milling about. Nobody made a move to return to the school.

"Shatters," Paulo muttered. "I sure wasn't expecting this when I woke up this morning."

"Well, we might as well all start getting along," Crystara pointed out. "We still don't know who we're paired with, after all."

They all looked around nervously. In a few days, they would be paired. Jacoby didn't need to reach out with empathy to feel the judgement and fear circulating. A lot of tension would be relieved when they finally found out.

"No sense in worrying about it now," Timori said as he threw a significant glance at Racquela. He was trying to belie his own nervousness, Jacoby knew. "We won't find out until Joveday, and we have no choice in the matter. I'm going back to class." He trudged off toward the school.

"Wait up," Jacoby called after him. He turned back to the rest of the soon-to-be-betrothed and nodded. "Paulo. Ladies. See you all on Joveday. Try not to worry about it too much. We all seem like a clear bunch."

Jacoby ran off wishing that he felt as confident about the betrothals as he projected.

"I can't believe this is happening," Jacoby exclaimed when he caught up to Timori.

Timori's mouth was set in a grim line. "Joveday could be either the best day of my life, or the worst. I'm in love with her, Jake. There's nothing that I can do about it."

"So what are you gonna do if you get paired with somebody else?"

"I have no idea." Timori paused to think about it for a moment. "I have no idea."

Chapter 10

9 Decembra, 1874
My dearest Julio,
I have to write this quickly, I'm doing a double-shift at the factory. Captus Nove has turned into a city of women. Most of the men have been drafted and the rest have been sent to the mines. According to the papers, crystal yields have to triple for the push into Kilgrun.

How have you been? How are your friends? Are you leaving Nilonne soon? I heard a rumour that Longoro might decide to attack Kilgrun sooner than expected. If that's the case, please be safe, my love.

I have nearly thirty dinari saved for our wedding now. I dream of that day constantly.

I have to go. Please write back soon, it's lonely here in the winter. It's always lonely here without you. You're the only decent conversation to be had, besides all your other amazing qualities, my Julio.

Ramona

30 Decembra, 1874
My one and only Ramona,
We have finished our long march south to defend the northern borders of Novem. I pray that this letter reaches you, for the Alliance has cut off many of our communications and supply lines.

The fighting has been thick here in the southern end of Nilonne, and I have tasted my first combat. We were flanked by a Kilgrish army marching westward, and were pinned down by scattershot in a trench for thirteen days. I went to the top of the trench with my battalion several times to fire at the soldiers manning the massive wands, but I doubt that I hit anything. We were finally rescued by a Mikosian battalion, but not before we lost a good

138

hundred men to the fighting. Kilgrish casualties were heavier, but that makes me feel no better.

It is miserable here, and you are so agonizingly close! The once verdant fields are brown and scarred, and when a man dies outside of the trenches it is often days before he can be recovered. I will speak no more of the things that I have seen. I do not know why I tell you of these things, other than to commit them to what little paper I have so that they no longer burden my heart. Is that selfish of me? If so I am sorry, Ramona, but I know that you are the only one who truly understands the deeper things that I express. It gives me strength to know that you will read this and feel pity for me. I need that pity, gods help me.

We are on a constant state of alert here in the trenches. The scattershot rarely ceases and I have been sleeping very little as of late. I have nightmares of being shot, and I often wake up wondering if I am still alive. Is there respite in the abyss, I wonder, or is it much like a battlefield?

My company and I spend very little time together here, and I am all the more lonely because of it. My thoughts return to you constantly. Roberto mans the scattershot wands for twelve hours and then sleeps. Pietro is constantly fixing our battered equipment and scavenging crystals, and Largo is usually sent to scout. The gods have been with him, thankfully. The worst injury that he has sustained is a cut to his arm from a shrapnel wand.

New Year draws nigh and everyone is praying that the Nilonnese and Kilgrish will observe the proper etiquette and cease firing for the day. I fear that they may continue their push south just to spite us and the gods.

I must go, for it is my turn on the turret wand this evening. I hate the sound it makes and the thought that I might actually hit someone with it, but it is better than being on the receiving end.

My love goes with you, always.
Julio

P.S. I will not receive any letters of pay until I am in a more secure location, but as soon as I get them I will send them home to you, as always. I love you Ramona.

***

The republic of Longoro's youth was in a state of disrepair. Heavy taxation had crippled industries and businesses, leading to a recession. Foreign trade was nowhere near as profitable as it was for other nations in Titania, due to Novem's lack of colonial revenue. The rise in popularity of the socialist movement in Titania, furthered by poor working conditions for the lower classes, was oil on the fire of a nation already experiencing unrest.

Longoro and Posco could not have showed up at a more opportune time to turn that unrest to their complete advantage. Longoro's experiences in cabarets and his connections through Posco's socialist friends espoused him well to the socialists. As always, Longoro seemed to empathize more with the common man than those of his own station.

Posco, likewise, had been disillusioned with both the class system and the floundering economy of the republic ever since his father's business had gone under and the shares divided by the nobles who had a stake in it. Posco's father's suicide had been the final nail in the coffin, changing Posco from a dissident into a full-fledged rebel.

Longoro's and Posco's foray into politics perfectly encapsulates their dynamic and the reasons why neither of them could have succeeded without the other. Posco, far more educated than Longoro despite being of a lower station, was the architect of every manoeuvre made, every back-door deal and bribe, every blackmail that furthered Longoro as the figurehead of the National Socialist Party. Posco was also the face of the common man, and being seen with Longoro let the masses know that Longoro had their best interests at heart, as opposed to the interests of those who lived at the tops of Captus Nove's five hills.

Longoro, on the other hand, was the voice of the pair, the charismatic gentleman who represented positive change for the Noven people. His connections through his family and upper-class friends helped fund the NSP's campaigns, as well as their less-than-legal activities that assisted in bringing Novem's underworld powers under Longoro's command.

The crumbling republic merely set the stage for Longoro's rise to power, and to many contemporary observers, such as journalist Mannio Rosso, 'it seemed as though Novem was simply handed to Longoro on a crystal platter, without so much as a furled brow as resistance to his soon-to-be absolute rule'.

***

6 Aprila, 1875

Ramona, my love,

I am certain that my last letter did not reach you, for I have received no reply. Sadly, it has likely disappeared into obscurity somewhere. I hope that you did not worry about me too much during the last month. I am alive and well, and I pray that you are well also. How is the factory? I hope they are not working you too hard. Is your mother well? I send my love to her also.

We are marching, though I am not permitted to say to where. As I'm sure you have read in the newspaper, we successfully defended our homeland and the northward push is nearly complete. Nilonne will soon be entirely under the control of the Noven Empire.

The march has been long, but relatively safe thus far. Much of the countryside is still very beautiful, untouched by the sullying hands of Arus and the war gods. Although it is still very cold this far north in early spring, the long marches keep us warm. Our only difficulties come from conflicts with the locals, who swear at us even when we barter rather than simply take what the army needs and move on. *I feel like a thief, but I cannot contradict the captain or I would find myself in prison. Sometimes I wonder if it would be preferable to another long and bloody battle like the last one, but then you would be left to fend for yourself, and I could never do that to you, love.*

I feel sorry for the people whom we pass by. One farmer took a shot at the captain and was hit by several of our firewands in response, right in front of his daughters. Another man in a village was taken away for refusing to trade with us, and more than once some of the men in the company, even the married ones, have been getting into trouble with local girls, and I fear that the attention is not always asked for. I swear to you that I, at least, would never do such a thing!

Our destination is a mere few days away and the countryside becomes more pockmarked and trench-scarred as we approach. Many farmhouses have been abandoned or destroyed, and already I have seen a field full of unmarked Nilonnese graves, each with a simple stone as marker. The field was already dotted with indigo duskblossoms, and it was breathtaking in a sad sort of way, even though I shudder to think what it would be like to be put into the ground rather than burned so that my spirit can rejoin the gods.

We have stopped for the evening in a small village. The villagers have already surrendered to Novem, but things remain tense as the soldiers drink the local beer for free and eye the local daughters.

I must go, love. Largo is calling for me to have a beer with him, and he never takes 'no' for an answer.

Love,

Julio

P.S. How is the weather back home? Are the whiteoaks budding? I miss my beautiful city by the sea, and my beauty who resides there. Take care, my love.

***

"Jules, you done writing that letter yet?" Largo nagged.

Julio set down his pen and capped the bottle of ink. He rubbed his eyes, for he had been writing by candlelight again. The night still fell early in Nilonne during the spring.

Julio looked over at Largo, who was leaning in the doorframe of the tavern room with a big smile on his unshaven face. Julio imagined that his own face looked much the same. He hadn't bothered to shave during the march, and the first thing he had done upon his arrival at the village was sit down to write a letter to Ramona.

"When's the last time you wrote a letter to Maria?" Julio asked as he sat up from the desk. Other soldiers were still busy scratching away at letters to their loved ones. Most were on the floor of the tavern room, and four shared the bed as they wrote. Julio blew on the ink and then tucked his letter into a pocket of his trench coat so that he could send it with a courier the following day.

"Mind your own business," Largo snapped. By his tone, Julio gauged that the younger, larger man was already drunk. "You comin' downstairs or what?"

"Yes," Julio replied, "though I really could use a bath."

Largo made a loud guffaw and slapped his hand on the doorframe. He was boisterous when he drank, but Largo was too large a man to be taken lightly, even when he was joking.

"So could we all, Jules. Plenty of time for that tomorrow. The colonel's orders are that we stop here for a day so that we're fresh and ready to face Vadon Hill. Come on, the rest of the company is way ahead of you."

Julio followed Largo down the stairs to find that the low-ceilinged taproom was packed to the doors with Noven soldiers from several different battalions. Julio was surprised that he had managed to shut out the din while he was writing his letter.

Largo pushed his way easily through the crowd with Julio right behind him. Julio found his compatriots seated at a corner table, with two old wooden chairs saved by Pietro's and Roberto's legs.

"Nice of you to finally join us," Pietro said. A small pile of cigarette ash was collecting on the table in front of him. "I know it's hard for you to engage in manly pursuits like the rest of us when you left your dick back in Novem."

"Jealous, Pip?" Largo asked as he sat down beside Julio and Roberto. "You've seen that photo of his Ramona. Bet you've jacked off to it, too."

A round of laughter followed, blending with the rest of the raucous noises of the tavern. Julio would have punched Largo for the comment, but he knew that he would likely lose teeth for it.

"Where's the cap?" Julio asked when the others stopped laughing.

"Captain won't be joining us this evening," Roberto said. "He's watching the place like a hawk to make sure nobody tries anything stupid around the locals. He was especially worried about Pip, which is why we're babysitting him."

Roberto's words were followed by another peal of laughter from the table. Ever since Largo had taken to calling the lieutenant 'Pipsqueak', the name 'Pip' had stuck. Pietro took it all surprisingly well, despite the fact that he was never taken seriously by anybody in the company. Nobody followed his orders, either, but Pietro didn't seem to care so long as he was making people laugh, whether it was at his expense or not.

"Babysitting!" Pietro exclaimed. "You pals are just trying to protect the local girls from my godlike looks. Wouldn't want any of them to faint, after all."

Largo rolled his eyes. "Hey, wench! Drinks!" he boomed as he slammed his fist down upon the table fiercely. One of the tavern owner's daughters began making her way through the crowd to their table.

"See, that's how it's done, Pip," Roberto said as he lit a cigarette of his own with a match. "Girls want a man who will dominate them, which is how an ugly dullard like Largo got such a clear beauty like Maria. And orders were to protect *you* from the local wenches. Small town girls are nuts."

144

The small town girl who served Julio's table was fairly plain, in Julio's opinion, but she must have seemed beautiful to most of the men who hadn't seen the face of a woman in months. Julio felt sorry for her. Drunken soldiers had a tendency to be grabby and aggressive, after all, but he felt better knowing that Captain Di'Zotto would ensure that nothing untoward happened to the girls under his watch.

A round of ale was brought to the table in short order, despite the crowd. Over the following two hours, Julio proceeded to get drunk under the encouragement of his friends. Eventually the conversation turned to politics, as it often did, and the tavern was loud enough that Julio didn't have to worry about being overheard by other commanding officers who were likely to take offense to his anti-imperialist views.

"I've told you before, Jules. It's the strongest who rule," Roberto shouted. They were all well into their cups, discussing Emperor Longoro as loudly as they pleased. "Allow everyone to have a vote and you're just asking for every dullard in Novem to make their voice heard and slow down the whole system so that nothing gets done. That's why everything was so fucked up during the republic. Too many idiots running around in the senate, and too many conflicting ideas. It's inefficient."

Julio swigged the last of his ale and proceeded to light a cigarette. He didn't smoke often, but he and his friends weren't gambling that evening and when Julio drank he sometimes felt like smoking.

"And you trust Longoro implicitly?" he asked the engineer. "I could never trust a man who took away my right to vote."

"I do," Roberto replied with a smirk. He only smiled when he drank, it seemed. "I trust him because he's the only man who's smarter than I am."

Julio laughed in spite of himself.

"Odd how you're stuck here with the rest of us, then," Pietro said in a maudlin tone.

"Fuck off, Pipsqueak," Roberto snapped back. "It takes a lot more brains to be an engineer than it does to be a speaker. Anyway, my point is that one man is way more efficient than a big group of representatives who can't agree on dirt."

"Despite the fact that he lied about abolishing the class system?" Largo countered. "I dunno, Rob, anybody who lies to the people to get into power and then takes away their ability to oust him politically is just grabbing for power. I'm with Jules on this one."

Roberto lit a cigarette of his own and nodded slowly. "Sure he's grabbing power. He knows what's best for Novem and won't let some whiny dullards who don't realize what a sham democracy is get in his way. No offense, Jules."

"Sure," Julio replied. He put his mouth up to his glass and then realized that it was empty. "It doesn't bother you, then, the fact that you lost your freedom?"

Roberto looked at his own empty glass. "Girls around here have a curfew or something? Our glasses have been empty for twenty minutes."

"It hasn't been that long," Julio answered. "Besides, it's busy in here. That can't be easy for her."

Roberto pointed an accusatory finger at Julio. "You know what your problem is, Vellize? You're too damned nice. One of these days someone is gonna take advantage of it, mark my words. But I guess it's only natural for a republican to be a bit naïve. Anyway, I guess I can wait for the beer since we're all being so damned reasonable this evening. Uh, what were we talking about again?"

"Freedom," Largo prompted. "I'm gonna go find that wench." Largo stood up and left the table, muttering under his breath.

"Right," Roberto nodded. "Freedom. It's an illusion. This is all pre-ordained by the gods, so there's no sense griping about the emperor since he was chosen to lead us by the Great Crystal itself."

Julio watched Largo make his way unsteadily through the crowd that stood between their table and the bar. "So you don't believe in free will, then?"

"How can I?" Roberto asked. He banged his empty glass on the table for emphasis. "Everything in my life has been somebody else's choice. I didn't ask to be born. That was my mother's accident. I didn't want to become an engineer. That was my father's decision. I didn't ask to get drafted. That was Longoro's law. It's all a hierarchy, see, handed down from the gods. Nobody has any choice in the matter but them. From the gods to the Great Crystal to the keeper to Longoro to us."

Julio gave a noncommittal shrug to Roberto's idea. "I don't know. I just find it hard to believe that the gods would have a vested interest in every tiny aspect of our lives, you know?"

Roberto smiled as though he had suddenly won the debate. "That's because you want to believe that you have a choice. I trust in Longoro because I trust in the gods."

Julio laughed. "You should read your classics, then. Any student of ancient Novem can tell you that the gods are not to be trusted."

Julio expected his remark to be followed up by a quip from Pietro, but there was only silence. He looked over and noticed for the first time that Pietro's seat was vacant.

"Where did the lieutenant go?"

"I dunno. Probably taking a piss."

"Did Largo leave too? I don't remember him leaving."

"Yeah, you watched him go, remember? The dullard was supposed to be getting us more drinks. Probably off fucking that wench or something."

"No, that doesn't sound like him." Julio stood up abruptly. "We should probably go look for Pietro, though. He's bound to get into trouble in his state. And the captain asked us to look out for him."

Roberto lit up a fresh cigarette and put his arms behind his head. "I'm not going anywhere until that ugly cow comes back with more drinks. You go ahead, Jules. I know your conscience demands it."

Exasperated with Roberto's flippant attitude, Julio left the table to search for his other friends. After walking the length of the tavern three times and searching upstairs twice, Julio grabbed his trench coat from his room and braced himself for the frigid Aprila night.

There were many other soldiers out and about in the village that evening. Some were singing patriotic Noven songs around makeshift campfires and others were making their way among the three drinking establishments in the small town. Julio began wandering through the crowds of soldiers, searching for familiar faces and calling for Pietro and Largo loudly by name.

After what seemed to Julio like an hour of searching, he was about to give up when he heard some muffled voices coming from the stables next to the tavern where he had been drinking. Julio approached the voices cautiously. Even in his semi-inebriated state, Julio knew that he was still in the middle of a war, no matter how safe the village felt at that moment. Julio had left his longwand back at the tavern, and only officers were issued the smaller sidearm-sized wands. Cursing his own foolishness and impatience, Julio continued on toward the stable as stealthily as he could manage, his pulse quickening as he did so. Upon reaching the side wall, Julio realized that the voices sounded very familiar.

"You know better," came a bass tone.

Julio took a few paces toward the stable door. The voice that replied was higher-pitched, almost whiny.

"... just want to talk." There was a muffled part that followed, which Julio didn't catch. "... not gonna do anything, just leave me alone."

Julio peered around the stable door. Directly in front of him, back turned, was a large man in uniform. He was holding a wand in one hand and an oil lamp in the other. In the corner of the stables next to an empty stall was Pietro, who had the serving girl from the tavern cornered.

148

"You're not foolin' me, kid," Largo said.

He seemed perfectly calm and unafraid as he aimed his wand at one of his superior officers. It made Julio wonder what the line was between fearless and crazy.

"I can see it on that girl's face, she knows you're here for more than just talk and you've got her scared to shatters. Let her go, kid."

"Stop calling me kid!" Pietro yelled. "And get the fuck out of here. That's an order, private." He turned his attention back to the girl. Largo, unfazed, took a step toward them.

"Let her be or I'll shoot you," he growled. By the light of the lamp, Julio could see that Largo's finger was hovering over the trigger of his wand. As Pietro swung back around, Julio stepped into the stables and placed his hands up in a pacifying gesture.

"Largo, Pietro, calm down, please."

Largo jumped slightly at the surprise but did not fire. He did not take his eyes off of Pietro, however, who had managed to draw his own wand.

"Get out of here, private," Largo commanded. "This doesn't concern you."

"Abyss it doesn't," Julio spat. "Put the wands down, both of you, and let's be sensible about this. The war is out there, Largo. Pietro, think about what you're doing for a minute. Carefully. Is this what you want your first time to be? An unwilling girl that you force yourself upon at wand-point?"

"Not to mention the court-martial when I tell the captain about this," Largo added.

Pietro's face grew twisted with rage. "Fuck you, you dirty son of a whore miner! You wouldn't dare!" He pointed his wand in Largo's direction, shakily.

"This isn't my first time and I am your superior officer, both of you. I'm also a crystal-speaker, in case you forgot. One shot from this little wand and you'll be blown into nothing more than a splatter across those stalls!"

Julio's heart lurched as Largo took another bold step toward Pietro.

"You think I'm afraid to die? I run to the tops of the trenches every day scouting for the company. I've been shot at more times than you can imagine, speaker. I've been in cave-ins, too, and slum fights where I thought that I was gonna die I was hurt so bad. So pull the trigger, if you think you've got the balls. I say that you don't, Pipsqueak."

Julio found his courage and placed himself between his comrades. Both wands were aimed directly at him.

"Stop it! After all the times we've fought and bled together, this is the way we treat each other? Please, guys. Put the wands down and we can all go back into the tavern for another round of drinks."

He looked at Largo first. "Largo, for the gods' sake, think of Maria." He turned to look at Pietro. "Pietro, please. There'll be another time. Let it go."

The wand was shaking visibly in Pietro's hand, and a bead of sweat trickled down his forehead. The girl looked on, still frozen in horror. Julio could not see Largo's expression. For all he knew, his friend was about to shoot him in the back just to stop Pietro.

Largo grunted. "Fine, Jules, you deal with the fucking Pipsqueak. I've had it with his dirt. If either of you tells anybody that I pointed a wand at a fellow soldier, I'll kill you."

He took another step so that he was right beside Julio and pointed an angry finger at Pietro.

"And if you hurt Jules, you little bastard, I'll make you wish that I'd killed you." Largo stormed out of the stables.

Pietro's hands were shaking, but his wand was still pointed at Julio. "Largo is all talk, I'm not afraid of him. Please leave me alone now, Julio. I just wanna talk to her, that's all. Just leave me alone. That's ... that's an order."

"Pietro," Julio replied. He could see the conviction wavering in his friend's eyes. If he could get the boy to put down the wand, he could talk some sense into him.

"Let the girl go. I know that you're afraid to die. I'm afraid to die too, but I swear to you that if you leave here with me right now, I will protect you with my very life. There will be other women, Pietro."

There was a long pause. A horse's nervous whinny filled the silence. Julio could see the conflict between defiance and defeat raging in the lieutenant's eyes.

"Pietro. There will be other women. Let her go."

Pietro's lip trembled and he fell onto the hay that covered the floor.

"I don't want to die!" he wailed.

Julio watched the serving girl flee out the back door. He walked up to Pietro and knelt down beside him. Lieutenant Pietro Garus put his head on Private Julio Vellize's shoulder and cried. For several minutes the pair exchanged no words. Julio merely patted Pietro's back as the boy sobbed.

Chapter 11

Jacoby's parents didn't like the fact that he would not be able to choose his own wife in his own good time. Though they had accepted the possibility long ago, when he applied to Central School, their congratulations were muted and almost melancholy.

Jacoby shared a bottle of wine with his parents as they talked late into the night. They started a second bottle just as Jacoby's mother turned in for the evening, and Jacoby was left alone with his father.

"You be faithful, Jake," his father said as he poured more of the second bottle into Jacoby's glass. The wine was starting to go to Jacoby's head.

"You mean ... about the Great Crystal?" he asked. "I thought you didn't really believe in it, Dad."

Gilliermo Padrona shook his head. "No, no ... be faithful to whoever is chosen for you. I've seen enough arranged marriages to know that they don't always work out very well, especially when you're young. Legally there's nothing that you can do about it, but so as long as you treat her well you should both grow to love each other in time. There's really nothing else you can do about it, unfortunately."

Jacoby nodded. It was good enough advice, but Jacoby was hoping that the betrothal would somehow be romantic, nevertheless. "I just really wasn't expecting this to happen to me," Jacoby sighed. He took a sip of wine. It was bitter in his mouth.

"Life does unexpected things sometimes, Jacoby. It doesn't always have to be bad, though. I wasn't expecting to be brought up to the Masters class, but ..." he gestured around to the house they were living in, filled with much finer things than their previous abode, "the unexpected turn was for the best, in the long run. If you treat this girl right, whichever one she turns out to be, she'll do the same for you and everything should work out in the end. Just don't get so wrapped up in each other that you forget about your schoolwork, Jake. You still need to have a future, after all."

"Yeah, yeah ..."

***

Jacoby was usually the last to leave his history class. Master Vellize wrote incredibly fast notes on the chalkboard for a man with only one hand, and Jacoby's penmanship was sloppy at best, so he had to write painstakingly slow in order to make sense of his notes when he studied them later on. The class had already emptied for lunch, leaving him alone with his teacher.

"It's nice to know there's at least one young person out there who actually cares about Noven history," Master Vellize mused. "Are you an overachiever, Padrona, or does history genuinely interest you?"

Jacoby looked up from his note-taking. Master Vellize was staring at him discerningly with that one good eye, sporting a smile that would have seemed vicious and threatening were it not for the man's peaceful countenance.

"I do like history," Jacoby replied. "And not to sound like I'm kissing up, but I like the stories you tell in class. It makes me feel like I'm really there, experiencing history for myself."

Master Vellize stood up and limped around to the front of his desk, then leaned against the dark wood and folded his arms. "I was there for much of it, my boy. The Great War years, at least. There are a few stories that I won't tell in class, however."

"Why not?" Jacoby asked, even though he knew how naïve the question was. Jacoby's uncle never spoke of the Great War. Gilliermo often told Jacoby that the things his uncle had seen defied explanation or description, and not in a pleasant way.

Master Vellize laughed. "Think of your most secret memory. Would you share it with strangers?"

Jacoby's stomach growled, but he was too interested in what Master Vellize had to say to worry about lunch right away. "I guess not."

"Still," Vellize continued, "I'm sure you're aware that I didn't always look this way."

Jacoby felt uncomfortable acknowledging his teacher's obvious physical deficiencies and didn't know what to say in response.

"I heard about your selection for betrothal," Master Vellize noted. He pointed his hook at Jacoby. "Not sure whether I should congratulate you or pity you."

"I'm not sure what I should feel either," Jacoby said. He quickly copied the last line of notes and closed his notebook so that he could give Master Vellize his full attention. He hoped belatedly that the ink didn't smudge. "I'm nervous, I guess."

"Nervous. Ha!" Vellize laughed in his saw-like rasp. "You should be scared to shatters. To be paired with somebody you don't even know is a terrible throwback in a society of modern, democratic ideals. Not that falling in love is much better, mind you."

"What do you mean?"

"You're stuck either way. One is legally binding. The other, emotionally binding. Beware the pitfalls of love, my boy. It's not ... well, let me just say good luck to you. A betrothal isn't going to be easy."

Jacoby nodded. "That's what everybody keeps telling me. Any advice?"

"Just a warning. Your heart will always betray you, if you let it."

Jacoby had no idea what Master Vellize meant, but he nodded nevertheless. "Thank you, Master. I should get going to lunch. See you tomorrow."

Master Vellize nodded to him as he left the room, but said nothing more. Jacoby smiled. He reminded himself to stay late in history class more often to see if he could elicit a story or two from his teacher.

Jacoby went to his locker to fetch his crystal-speaking textbook and his lunch. As his nose was buried in the depths of the locker, somebody shoved into him and nearly sent his head into the corner of the open locker frame. He wheeled around, red-faced, to see who it was: Roberto Massini, a goon from the football team. The Massinis were middle-class at best, which made Jacoby wonder who suddenly had it out for him. It was likely an upper-class kid with designs on Racquela, he realized, or at the very least a highborn who was put out that a child of 'Class Action' parents had been chosen for the crystal betrothals.

Roberto was far larger than Jacoby in both height and width, so Jacoby chose his words carefully.

"Sorry, didn't mean to get in your way like that, Roberto." The words were like acid in Jacoby's mouth. He hated how much of a coward he was, but standing up to Roberto Massini in the middle of the hallway wasn't a good idea.

Roberto was nonplussed by the apology. Jacoby figured that the lummox would barrel through and stick to whatever he had originally planned to say, regardless of how politely Jacoby handled the situation. Jacoby had learned the hard way from kids like Grigori Marsa that once somebody got it into their head that they hated you, there was little that could be done to change it.

"You're a lowborn picker and don't deserve to be here," Roberto said as he pointed a meaty, accusatory finger in Jacoby's face. "Don't forget that. You'll get what's coming to you."

"Well, thank you for the advance warning," Jacoby said as Roberto hulked away. Jacoby had tried to sound confident, but his voice had wavered and his legs were shaky. He was glad to have a locker to lean up against.

***

Joveday arrived sooner than Jacoby had hoped. The priest who showed up at the door to Jacoby's house was surprisingly young. He handed Jacoby a heavy black wool robe that he had to change into for the ceremony. With a chuckle, Jacoby wondered if he was supposed to put underwear on underneath the robes. He decided for it. Better safe than sorry.

Jacoby's mother cried and gave him a hug at the door. His father shook his hand. As Jacoby left the house and sat down on the cushioned seat of the motorcoach, he felt as though his whole world had become smaller. In a matter of hours, he would be betrothed. One woman for the rest of his life. The idea frightened him.

It was a cold, grey day. Jacoby stared at the overcast sky and wondered what an empath would find if they were to read his emotions just then. They would likely be just as confused as he felt.

The motorcoach turned onto Corti Street, which led all the way through Avati to Crystus Hill. As he passed by his old house, Jacoby thought about what would happen if Timori were paired up with Crystara. At the very least, he mused, they wouldn't have to go very far to see each other. As amusing as the thought was, Jacoby was worried about what would happen if Timori didn't get paired with Racquela. Timori would just have to deal with it, Jacoby supposed.

The Old Temple was brightly decorated with red and blue banners for the ceremony, which brought some colour to the humdrum feel of the day. As the motorcoach drove up to the front entrance, Jacoby noticed that a crowd had gathered. As a very occasional practitioner of the faith, it was easy for Jacoby to forget how devout many Novens were. He reminded himself that most Novens saw the crystal betrothals as a choice laid down by the gods. As the motorcoach came to a halt, Jacoby wondered if the Great Crystal would actually speak to him.

Jacoby exited the vehicle to the cheering of the crowd, who were bundled warmly against the cold but no less jubilant than they would have been on a warmer day. He was led up to a wooden platform in front of the temple, where the other five students were already waiting. The keeper, who turned out to be the priest that Jacoby had met the other day at the temple, began to deliver a very long and very boring speech about tradition and faith. He wondered whether speeches were simply more interesting to adults, or if perhaps people got more boring as they aged.

Jacoby shivered, wishing that he had worn more than just briefs under his robes.

"My balls are freezing," Timori leaned over and whispered into his ear.

"Nervous?" Jacoby asked through chattering teeth.

"Too cold. Wait until we get inside. Then I'll be nervous. We should have placed bets like the rest of the school, made some money."

Jacoby looked at Timori incredulously. "People have been placing bets?"

"They always do," Paulo piped in with a loud whisper. "Top assumptions are you and Lenara, Tim and Crystara, and Racquela and me."

Timori's face soured.

After what seemed a mercilessly long time, the keeper's speech ended to the cheers and exultation of the gathered faithful. Jacoby and the others were ushered into the temple, grateful more for the warmth than the prospect of what was to follow. Jacoby looked around at his fellow students and noticed the only person who looked happy to be there was Racquela.

"Now then..." The keeper said as he rubbed his hands together. They were standing in the great hall, surrounded by other priests and marble pillars and flanked on either side by the stained glass windows that Jacoby hadn't been able to admire during his first visit to the temple. One window depicted the Great Crystal and its discovery by a prophet of the church – Markus? Julian? Jacoby couldn't remember. The other window was an obvious portrayal of Queen Celesta. Jacoby rather liked the scene, even though he found the idea of abandoning regal responsibility in favour of the church silly.

"You will each have half an hour of private reflection before being summoned to the Crystal Chamber," the keeper said. "Then, after a brief ceremony, you will be asked to touch the Great Crystal. Do not touch it before I say so. It could be very dangerous. Once you touch the Great Crystal it will grant you a vision. Please try to remember what you see down to the exact detail. Some of you may experience euphoria or even pass out after the vision. This is normal. Do not be alarmed. After your visions, say nothing. You will be escorted again to private rooms, where we will ask each of you what you saw. Then you will be brought together and the couples announced. After that, the only other ceremony is a ring exchange performed in front of an assembly at the school. Go now, students, and prepare."

"Good luck, pally," Timori muttered to Jacoby before they were led off in separate directions. Jacoby was taken through a winding hallway to a small room with a single wooden chair and a window that looked out onto a brick wall. Jacoby knew that he was supposed to be contemplating something, but his ordinarily busy mind was blank.

In the silence and calm, he could feel somebody reaching out to him emotionally. It was difficult at first to tell if the projection was deliberate or not, but a wave of emotions rolled over him from somewhere nearby: fear, desire, hope ... There was also a strange sense of determination mingled in. The presence behind the emotions felt lost and afraid, in need of reassurance. Jacoby started to reach out with his own emotions to try and reassure the mystery person that it was going to be all right, but the mystery sender abruptly stopped projecting. Jacoby searched, but could not find them anywhere in the murky void that was the physical space among people's feelings. Whoever had projected so strongly, Jacoby had no doubt the person was looking for him. What had confused Jacoby was the sense of determination. It wasn't as though any of them had a choice in the matter.

Jacoby was left alone in the barren room for what seemed like an eternity, contemplating nothing but his own feelings and those of the mystery sender. He went over different betrothal scenarios in his mind several times with varying degrees of optimism and pessimism. Any of the relationships could have poor results: Racquela could be too high-maintenance and resentful to have to marry down in station, Jacoby knew too little about Lenara and she

158

could have some serious flaws that he didn't like (or vice versa), Crystara could turn out to be cheerless for the rest of her life ...

Jacoby shuddered at the negative possibilities and tried to focus on the positive. As his father had pointed out, he didn't have a choice in the matter itself, but he had a choice in how he acted. He would treat his betrothed with all the respect she deserved. Jacoby wanted nothing if not a happy ending. Wasn't that what everybody wanted, after all?

Jacoby tried to reach out and feel for another person's emotions again, but came up with nothing.

A short, swarthy priest opened the door to the solitary chamber. "It is time," he said. The priest's jowls shook when he spoke, and Jacoby had to stifle a laugh.

He followed the large priest out of the room and down the hallway to a great set of double-doors, where several other priests were waiting with Timori, Paulo and Racquela. Timori was sweating, and Jacoby could see Racquela's hands shaking. He was glad to see that he wasn't alone in his nervousness. Paulo didn't appear to be affected at all, and he glanced casually about the hallway as though he were on a field trip. Before long, Crystara and Lenara rounded the hallway to meet up with the rest of them. The keeper, who stood before the whiteoak doors that led to the Crystal Chamber, made a religious gesture with his hands that Jacoby wasn't familiar with, then turned and opened the doors wide to reveal a room that few Novens had a chance to see in their lifetime.

Jacoby was struck by how much larger the Great Crystal was than he expected. By his estimation, it had to have been at least thirty metres in diameter. It took up the entire room apart from the floor, which was only two people wide, and the raised altar overlooking the crystal at the far end for religious ceremonies. Jacoby had to remind himself that the crystal was also half-buried underground. He marvelled at how such an enormous, perfect sphere of crystal could have formed naturally, and he began to understand why many considered it to be a significant religious symbol. It was awe-inspiring.

From what he had read, Jacoby knew that on a clear day the sun shone through the stained glass dome at the top to refract in the crystal and splash a beautiful array of colours across the room. Jacoby wondered if it was a bad omen that the sun was not shining through the clouds on that day.

With the help of the priests, each student was positioned around the Great Crystal at equidistant intervals. The boys were put on one side of the crystal, the girls on the other. The keeper slowly ascended the tall marble steps and took his place behind the raised altar at the far end of the room, with a priest on either side of him. Upon the pulpit in front of the altar was a large tome, which Jacoby knew to be the 'Book of the Gods', the most sacred religious text of the Noven Church. After a brief moment of silence, the keeper began.

"We are gathered here today, in the sight of Jova, his wife and sons and daughters and their voice the Great Crystal, to honour the traditions of our ancestors. Today six of our children will be joined in the most holy of ceremonies, a joining selected by the gods themselves ..."

The ceremony, agonizingly, was much longer than the high priest's speech outside to the masses. Jacoby was thankful that he was no longer cold, but his legs began to ache after a while. He noted after a time that the heat in the chamber seemed to come from the middle of the room, from the crystal itself. He began to anticipate touching the Great Crystal more than anything else. If something actually did happen, would he be forced to consider the existence of the gods, or was it simply a crystal that had been imbued with a speaking technique no longer known to engineers?

Jacoby looked around at his fellow trapped souls. From where he was positioned, he could only see Timori and Paulo, but reflections of the girls' images could be seen in the facets of the Great Crystal. Timori was staring into the crystal, and Racquela seemed to be doing the same. Lenara was glancing up, through the skylight at the clouds. Paulo was checking his nails. Jacoby couldn't see Crystara's reflection from where he was standing.

160

"... until the end of time," the keeper said in a low monotone. The priests began to chant in a four-part harmony. Their voices created a resonance in the chamber that echoed around the space and sent shivers down Jacoby's spine.

Jacoby was startled when he began to feel an increased amount of heat emanating from the Great Crystal. It pulsed and throbbed with it, although the appearance of the crystal itself did not change. Curious, Jacoby reached out with his empathy to see what everyone else was feeling. As he opened his mind, a wave of emotion hit him, and there was no denying the source: it came from the crystal. There was a great sense of *longing* ...

"Now is the time," said a voice from behind him. It was a priest. He seemed so far away to Jacoby. "Touch the crystal."

Jacoby did as he was told.

***

Jacoby stood in a field of green clover. Gone were the overcast skies of Captus Nove, replaced by brilliant blue dotted with flecks of white cloud, like dove feathers. His robes had turned as white as the clouds, and no longer hung heavily off of him as wool, but caressed his skin like silk. A warm feeling of serenity permeated him to his very bones, and he fell back onto the clover as though he weighed no more than a pillow. Jacoby looked up and all that he could see was sky. The view of that endless dome of blue and white brought him comfort. Jacoby knew that there was something he was supposed to be worried about, but he couldn't remember what it was. He lay back with his arms behind his head and took a deep breath. The world smelled of honey and strawberries. Jacoby closed his eyes and made a contented sigh.

When he opened them again, he wasn't alone.

She was lying beside him, wearing pure white robes that matched his own. Her long chestnut hair was splayed out on the clover underneath her, and she was so close that Jacoby could count the freckles on her nose.

"Lenara," he said. She turned to look at him, and he brought up his hand to move a lock of hair out of her eyes. She looked so beautiful, so serene. All Jacoby wanted to do was kiss her. He leaned forward, but she placed her index finger on his lips.

"I'm so sorry, Jake," she whispered. Her eyes, the same colour as the sky, were glistening. He wanted to ask what she was sorry about, but her finger was still upon his lips. He brushed a tear away from her cheek instead.

As Lenara pulled her finger away from Jacoby's lips, he felt a tremor coming from beneath him. Pressing his hand to the earth beneath the clover, Jacoby could feel the vibration slowly grow more intense. He looked over at Lenara, and her eyes were wide with alarm. They both stood up.

An army was marching toward them. They bore uniforms unlike any that Jacoby was familiar with: red and black, with coats of sleek leather and a symbol worn on the arms and hats that Jacoby couldn't quite make out. Their wands were small and black, but powerful-looking. The crystals embedded in the devices pulsed with an ugly green energy that made Jacoby's skin crawl.

The army continued marching forward. At the head of one column, he could see a short blonde girl setting the marching pace with a big bass drum strapped to her uniform. Jaocby realized with a mixture of shock and horror that the girl with the drum was Crystara. As she approached with the army keeping pace behind her, Jacoby could see looks of malice in the eyes of the men. He spun about and looked for somewhere to run, but they were coming up on all sides. He and Lenara were surrounded and without a weapon. Jacoby grabbed Lenara's arm and pulled her to the ground with him. Lying down flat in the clover, he hoped that the army wouldn't see them.

The army marched until they were about twenty metres from Jacoby and Lenara on every side. Crystara ceased drumming, and the army stopped marching. In a singular motion, they held their wands out to the sky, then slammed them against their chests in an aggressive display of power. The sound it made was deafening.

Jacoby threw himself on top of Lenara in the hopes that it would somehow protect her.

Jacoby winced as he looked back up at the army. He expected them to fire upon him at any second. They were lowering their weapons to shoot. Crystara unstrapped the drum and it fell upon the ground. Her blonde hair flowed wildly in the strong breeze. She looked right at Jacoby, and her eyes were wide and pleading.

"Please help me," Crystara said. The men in uniform took aim, and Jacoby's heart lurched into his throat.

"Don't let it happen this way," Lenara whispered.

The army opened fire, and Crystara was engulfed in green spume that shot forth from the wands. When the army ceased firing, the ground was black and steaming where Crystara had once stood. She was nowhere to be seen.

Jacoby awoke from the vision screaming.

***

He was not in the Crystal Chamber when his eyes opened. Jacoby was back in the small room with the wooden chair, accompanied by the fat priest, who was holding him down. Panicked, Jacoby looked up at the man.

"What happened? How did I get here? Why are you holding me down?"

The priest eased his grip, but still held Jacoby firmly by the shoulders. There was a look of concern in his eyes. "You were thrashing from the vision," the old man explained. "We brought you in here after you lost consciousness. Sometimes people cry things out when they pass out from the visions, and that would have ruined the entire process."

"You could've warned me it was going to be that graphic," Jacoby muttered. "Why do you do this whole vision thing anyway? It seems a counterintuitive way to match people up. What if somebody yelled out their vision at the end because they didn't want to get betrothed?"

"That's the way the Great Crystal wants it, and we don't question its decisions on matters of procedure like that. And we don't like to create expectations in people of what their visions may be like. It's different for everyone, and anything we say to you can affect the outcome."

Jacoby folded his arms. Between watching Crystara die in front of his eyes, the incredibly long periods of waiting and having to stand out in the cold, he was very annoyed with the church. "You say it like the crystal has feelings of its own."

"But it does. Didn't you feel it, before you touched it? You are an empath, aren't you? Did you not feel the crystal calling to you?"

Jacoby scratched his head. He had almost forgotten, since the dream had been so intense. "So, the gods are ...?"

"Real," the priest replied. "There is no denying that the Great Crystal is alive. How could any human being create something so powerful?"

Jacoby nodded and took stock of everything that had happened that day. He started to wonder if anybody else's vision had been as jarring as his, and then he realized that at least one other person's had. It had to have been Lenara. That was how the visions were shared ...

"So, do I just tell you what I saw?"

"Whenever you are ready."

Jacoby told him everything that he had seen and felt during the vision, down to the last detail. The priest wrote down everything Jacoby said in a large notebook. The only time the priest seemed surprised was in the description of the army uniforms, but he made no comment about it. Once Jacoby was finished, the priest closed the notebook and stood up.

"All right, Jacoby. Wait here and I will confer with the other priests, then I will take you to your betrothed." Once again, Jacoby was left alone with his thoughts.

He wondered if the vision had any true significance. Was a war coming? Was Crystara going to die? He had to tell her what he

164

had seen. He would have expected any of the others to do the same for him.

The priest re-entered the room without knocking. "Come with me, Jacoby."

Jacoby followed the priest down the hallway once more, this time to another small room. Waiting inside the room was a younger priest and a girl.

A blonde. Jacoby was very surprised to see her there, and not Lenara. She looked up at Jacoby from where she was sitting patiently.

"Hi, Jacoby," she said calmly.

"Hi, Crystara," Jacoby replied. An image flashed in his mind of Crystara being consumed by volleys of a vile green liquid and he shuddered. He tried to put the thought out of his head.

Jacoby felt paralyzed. He had been expecting Lenara, and he couldn't stop thinking about Crystara's death. As he stood there mutely, Crystara stood up and walked over to him. She put her hands in his. They were cold, which reminded Jacoby of the old adage 'cold hands, warm heart'.

"Let's make this work, Jake," she said. "I know we can."

***

Jacoby spat out a wad of seeds and mush onto the road below the bridge. "What would you have done if you'd gotten someone else?"

Timori shook his head and spat out a single seed. Lately he'd been trying to spit them as far as he could.

"Demanded that we do the whole thing again. I dunno. I knew it was meant to be, Jake. I told ya! Gods, I'm so elated right now!" Timori threw his hands up in the air and shook them vigorously. He grinned like a fool, which made Jacoby laugh.

"We're both lucky. I think Crystara's going to work out really well."

"Work out really well?" Timori mocked. "So much for romanticism. Well, she's pretty clear ... and godsdamned mysterious enough to keep a guy like you interested."

Jacoby punched Timori on the arm. "What's that supposed to mean? That was before, pally. A betrothal must be treated with a lot more respect."

Timori popped a seed into his mouth and carefully opened it with his teeth. "I hope you mean that."

"What did you see?" Jacoby asked.

Timori slowly chewed the edible part of the seed and spat the rest out before answering. "We were in a park, and we had a child together."

"That's it?"

Timori nodded. "That's pretty much it."

Jacoby got the feeling that Timori was hiding something, but he decided not to press it.

"So, that means that you and Racquela are gonna ..."

Timori made a dismissive gesture.

"I'm not gonna lie to you and say that the vision wasn't moving, Jake, because it was, but it was just a vision. It doesn't make me believe in the gods any more than before, and it doesn't mean that what I saw is actually going to come true. There are plenty of secrets the engineers of the old Noven Imperium knew that we're still trying to re-create today. What better way to convince a populace to believe in what the church tells them, than with an imbued crystal that actually *speaks*? Crystal-speakers can make a crystal imitate a human voice and project an image, so is it such a stretch to imagine that the engineers of old had some speaking secrets we still haven't re-discovered? Is it so hard to imagine that a crystal could project a person's own feelings, and make it seem like some kind of euphoric vision? I think that's way more likely than a crystal that has a direct link to mysteriously absent gods from the sky. Why wouldn't they just speak themselves? Why would they need a crystal? But the church needs the crystal, that's the point.

People who touch the crystal believe in something because that's what the crystal's intended purpose is."

Jacoby shrugged and shoved a bunch of seeds into his mouth. "That'sh pretty blashphemoush," he said with his mouth full. He pushed the wad of seeds to one cheek so that he could enunciate clearly. "All I know is that even before I touched it I felt something. Maybe it's spiritual, maybe it's just a really powerful imbued crystal. But if you don't believe in the Great Crystal, why do you support the betrothals?"

"Because it's advantageous to me," Timori admitted. "I love her, Jake. Clear as crystal, I love her."

A brief silence followed, broken only by the occasional sounds of motorcoaches rushing by underneath the Memorial Bridge.

"What did you see?" Timori asked.

"Crystara's death," Jacoby admitted.

Timori nearly choked on a seed until he managed to spit it out. "Relax, Jacoby. It's all in your own head."

"Yeah, probably," Jacoby agreed.

Chapter 12

Before Central School, Crystara had touched crystals very rarely. It always struck her as funny because she was named after them. The talent for crystal-speaking seemed to come naturally to her, however. It was far easier than empathy, which gave her headaches.

Crystara has always been fascinated with the science of crystal-speaking. One of her favourite books was about the old Noven engineers. It was they who had first discovered how to make the points of a glow-crystal resonate in a certain way to increase its brightness. Soon they experimented with other crystals, and discovered that if the shape of the crystal was physically altered, the points would oscillate differently with each other, resulting in a different effect. The secret of crystal resonance was the cornerstone of how the First Empire conquered the known world, and crystal-speakers, those who could alter a crystal's frequency at will, were the mighty heroes of the old Noven armies.

With the proper training, Crystara knew she could make crystals do far more than the simple functions that they were engineered to do. It was also her ticket to a better life. She may have been lowborn, but a talented crystal-speaker could become richer than a noble if they discovered the right resonance. All it took was some entrepreneurial tenacity. Crystara certainly wasn't going to let her new betrothed earn all the money for her. She couldn't think of anything more distasteful than leeching off another person.

Crystara was always ahead of the class. It was all so simple to her. She couldn't understand how the other students floundered with something as simple as a light crystal. It was as easy as saying the words and feeling the shape of the crystal. She couldn't believe that some of the students had even been allowed into the class. Were they the best that Novem had to offer? Even Jacoby embarrassed her sometimes by asking her to help him with his speaking.

He was sweet about it, though, and patient with Crystara in empathy class. Crystara found herself liking Jacoby more and more every day.

"You're distracted," Keeper Orvin said. "You're not paying any attention."

"Sorry," Crystara mumbled. "Go on. I'm paying attention."

She was sitting in Keeper Orvin's office, receiving her extra-curricular crystal-speaking lessons from him. She found Keeper Orvin to be gentle, which was a big difference from the way her father treated her, and the keeper's lessons were a welcome challenge.

"As I was saying, the mystery of why crystals work is one that still hasn't been fully unravelled by scientists and engineers. However, what we do know is that crystals are mined out of the ground already imbued with energy and potential. Depending upon the alignment of the crystal, its shape, colour and how many sides it has, the crystal will vibrate with a certain kind of energy. Some crystals have heat energy, some resonate to alter the properties of matter in their vicinity and some, like electron crystals, have been more recently discovered and have properties that can alter particles at their smallest, most basic level. Engineers have spent centuries cataloguing and studying different crystal alignments."

Keeper Orvin cleared his throat and held up a small crystal from his desk.

"Speakers, however, can re-align a crystal, as you already know. This creates nearly limitless potential for a skilled speaker with a crystal in their hand. However, when re-aligning a crystal, the farther away from its original alignment you take the crystal, the more stress it places upon its structure. The more times you alter a crystal's property, the more likely it becomes that the crystal will fail. If a crystal performs only one function, it should theoretically last for decades. Crystals that get altered have a much shorter lifespan."

Crystara tried to stifle a yawn but it came out anyway. She blushed and flinched away from Keeper Orvin. To her surprise, he chuckled.

"You already know all this, don't you? They cover this in your classes. Why do I bother? We should just do some more speaking exercises, shouldn't we? Unless there's anything about crystal history that they didn't cover in your class."

"Is it true that nobody knows why they really work?" Crystara asked.

Keeper Orvin raised his eyebrows. "There are theories. Some scientists think it has to do with the way the world was formed geologically. The theories behind why a speaker can re-align crystals are a little more complex. There is, however, an old legend about crystals that most people don't know about. It's older than the church, even. Do you want to hear it?"

Crystara grinned broadly. "If it means we get to do more crystal-speaking before I go home."

Keeper Orvin chuckled. "You're cheeky today. All right, we'll get back to speaking after the story. The legend goes that crystals are actually the souls of the dead."

Crystara raised an eyebrow. "Really? Doesn't the church teach that the souls of the dead go to the abyss after they're burned out of the body?"

"Didn't I just say it was a legend? Keep it up and I'm likely to toss a silence crystal at you."

Keeper Orvin smiled. The threat was an empty one. Crystara had been surprised and glad to discover early on that she could joke around with the keeper. A part of her was still waiting for the other shoe to drop ... he couldn't be *that* nice, but her experience with men was admittedly limited.

"Anyway, the legend suggested that speakers were originally called speakers because they communed with the crystals. They *spoke* to the dead, and could re-align a crystal because they could connect to the soul within it. When the Great Crystal became a part of the church, many heathen religions believed that it contained the souls of dead gods, hence its power."

"What is the Great Crystal, truthfully? Does it commune with the gods, or is it just controlled by you?" Crystara half-expected the keeper to be offended by the question, but he merely stroked his beard thoughtfully.

"You know, it's funny. When I was a young priest here at the temple, I asked Keeper Maricchio the very same question. He slapped me and told me if I uttered such blasphemy again that I would be excommunicated."

Crystara's eyes widened.

"Two days later he brought me into his office – this office – and told me to follow him to the Crystal Chamber. He instructed me to touch the Great Crystal and ask for forgiveness. I touched the crystal and it spoke to *me*. It asked me what I believed in."

"What did you say?"

"I told it that I believed in finding absolute truth. The Great Crystal replied, 'Then that is what I am'."

"What did the keeper say?"

"Nothing," Keeper Orvin said with a grin. "I lied and said that the Great Crystal accepted my apology. It was wiser to lie than risk excommunication. The point is that the crystal was more interested in what I thought than whatever the truth happens to be. Whether it's imbued to seem sentient or actually is alive in some way, or is a speaker for the gods, I haven't yet discovered in all my years of research. It's more than just a symbol, but it's almost like it doesn't want anyone to know what its true purpose is. I sacrificed the chance at a family and an engineering scholarship so that I could uncover the true mysteries of crystal lore, but with every mystery I unravel a new one shows up in its place. That crystal has an agenda, Crystara, but in all my years as Keeper I still don't know what it might be. I'm getting old and the damn thing only talks when it wants to. Why do you think I started teaching you?"

"I can't join the church," Crystara said vehemently. "I'm betrothed."

Keeper Orvin nodded. "I know, but you're young. You have years ahead of you to study crystals, and by the time you're my age we'll know ten times what we do about crystals now. Besides, it's ... nice to have somebody intelligent to speak with who isn't a part of the church for once. Anyway, that's enough about that for today. You're probably falling asleep from all these old stories. Let's get back to the task at hand: learning how to master crystals so that you can master the world around you. A powerful speaker is like a god among men."

Crystara's face lit up. She hadn't been falling asleep at all. Keeper Orvin was nothing like her father. She would rather stay with him for as long as possible and avoid going home.

"Okay. What's next?"

Keeper Orvin tossed Crystara a small grey crystal from the basket on his desk and she caught it. "Let's work on silence crystals, since I mentioned them earlier. You're already good at sneaking into places where you're not supposed to be, but let's just keep going with that idea."

He smiled, and Crystara recalled how she had first met Keeper Orvin.

"You're great at getting into trouble, Crystara. Let's teach you how to get out of it."

***

Crystara sat in her room and brushed her hair. She was about to go on her first date with Jacoby and she wanted to look her best. She had picked out a dress that she barely ever wore, a white one that had been her mother's, and even put on makeup for once. The makeup had been a gift from Racquela. Crystara couldn't afford any of her own.

Her father suddenly appeared in the doorway, looming over her. Crystara shivered.

"Your mother's dress," he muttered. "Looks good on you."

"Thanks," she said quietly.

"Aren't you a little young for dating? When I was your age we didn't go out until we were eighteen."

Crystara rolled her eyes. "We're betrothed, Dad. It's different."

"Hmph. Well on the clear side he's rich, at least. I want to meet him when he comes to pick you up. See what kind of little twerp my only daughter is marrying."

"You'll meet him, Dad. He's really nice."

Largo scoffed. "I don't care about nice. I care about whether or not he can look after you properly after I die from the black lung or a cave-in."

Crystara seethed. She had no intention of simply letting Jacoby 'look after her', but her father would never understand that. As she prepared a suitably clever rebuttal, there was a knock on the door. Crystara put down her brush and rushed downstairs so that she could answer the door before her father.

Jacoby stood on the front porch dressed in a pressed grey suit. Crystara suspected that it was new. Jacoby had a fresh haircut and looked sublimely handsome. He was smiling and holding roses, which he handed to Crystara.

"Hi," he said. "You look beautiful."

Crystara blushed. She didn't care much for flowers but she took them anyway. She smelled them and gave Jacoby a coy smile. "Thank you, Jake."

Crystara's father appeared behind her, and she could feel his scowl. "So. You're Jacoby. The boy who's taking my girl away from me."

Jacoby, unhindered by the rude comment, held out his hand to Crystara's father. Crystara watched as Jacoby cringed from the handshake. Largo was likely trying to crush Jacoby's hand.

"Nice to meet you, Mr. Mita," he said through gritted teeth.

Largo's laugh boomed down the street. "You're no bigger than Crystara," he bellowed. "Well, Jacoby, you have her back here by ten, you hear? She might be engaged to you, but she still lives in my house and under my rules. I find out about any funny business and you'll answer to me directly."

Jacoby made a polite smile. If he was afraid of Largo, he didn't show it. "Of course, Mr. Mita. No funny business. Back by ten. I promise."

"Hmm." Largo grunted. He shut the door loudly, leaving Crystara alone with Jacoby on the front step.

Crystara sighed. "Sorry about that."

"He's just being protective, I'm sure," he said. "Come on, I know a great restaurant."

Crystara shook her head. "You don't have to spend any money. We can just go for a walk and talk if you want."

Jacoby took Crystara's hand. His grasp was warm. His smile was inviting and full of possibility. "I insist. I already made reservations by telegram anyway. They're expecting us."

Jacoby and Crystara walked up Corti Street to the top of the hill. Jacoby did most of the talking. Crystara was too nervous to know what to say. He asked her a lot of questions about herself and what she was interested in. She asked him about football and how his classes were going.

"Coach Lagheri is brutal," Jacoby said as they approached the restaurant. Jacoby told her Giovanni's was a family-run place his parents used to take him to once a year on his birthday. Affordable for a poor family who saved money well, he explained. Crystara was relieved to know that Jacoby used to be poor. He used to live in her house before she moved in, after all. He would understand her situation well.

"But he's a damn good coach, I have to admit," Jacoby continued. "He said yesterday that he thinks we might actually have a chance at the national championships this year."

"That would be good," Crystara said. She didn't know much about football, and hoped it wouldn't turn out to be the only thing Jacoby ever talked about. "You're a goaltender, right?"

Jacoby nodded proudly. "Only position I've ever been any good at."

174

They approached the entrance of the restaurant and he held the door open for her. It was a hole-in-the-wall kind of place – a converted house with apartments upstairs, wedged between two other, taller buildings. A small painted sign was mounted beside the door. All it said was 'Giovanni's' in fancy red letters. The interior was surprisingly well-furnished and soothing. Dim lights were hung low over cozy, intimate tables, and a piano player coaxed a romantic melody from the corner of the room.

A tall man dressed in slacks and a white shirt approached Crystara and Jacoby at the door and smiled. "Good evening, sir and madam. Do you have reservations this evening?"

"Two, under 'Padrona'," Jacoby said. The host nodded and led them to a table against the far wall.

He handed them each a menu. "The special tonight is mushroom gnocchi, but our house special is the braised lamb." He poured glasses of water from a pitcher for Crystara and Jacoby. "I would recommend the lamb, and Nilonnese burnt cream for dessert. I'll bring you out some bread while you make your choices." The host left Jacoby and Crystara to study their menus.

"Too bad we can't get served wine," Jacoby said over his menu. There was a mischievous look in his eyes which Crystara found endearing. "My parents used to sneak me some when they took me here as a kid, probably to keep me quiet. You should meet them, Crystara, they're great people."

"Yeah," Crystara said meekly. The idea of meeting Jacoby's parents filled her with an inexplicable dread. "No wine for me, though. I had a bad experience in the summer with Racquela."

Jacoby laughed riotously. "Sounds like there's a story behind that. You have to tell me."

Crystara related the entire story to Jacoby. By the end, he was laughing loudly enough that other patrons were looking over to see what was going on. Crystara couldn't remember the last time a boy had been so interested in what she had to say. She found herself smiling by the end of the story, despite how embarrassing it was.

Their waiter had to come back three times because they had barely even glanced at the menus.

Jacoby ordered the lamb. He told her that he always ordered the lamb when he came to Giovanni's, even though he liked to try new things. Crystara had never tried lamb, but wasn't feeling particularly adventurous since her stomach was in knots. She ordered the gnocchi. She enjoyed bread with garlic butter as Jacoby told her stories about his family and the house that Crystara lived in.

Their meals arrived and Crystara dug in happily. It was nice to have a filling and delicious meal for once, even if she felt guilty that Jacoby was paying for it all. Crystara loved food, but was usually stuck with whatever she could scrounge together. She and Jacoby spoke very little as they ate, but it was a comfortable silence. The knot in Crystara's stomach began to disappear as the evening wore on.

The walk home was chilly, and Crystara surprised herself by accepting Jacoby's coat to keep her warm. They walked hand-in-hand down Corti Street, and Jacoby never seemed to run out of things to say.

Finally they arrived at Crystara's doorstep. It was definitely before ten by Crystara's reckoning, but she wished that the night wouldn't end. Jacoby's easygoing confidence and cheerful nature assured her that things were going to turn out all right with the betrothal.

Jacoby looked into Crystara's eyes as he held her hands outside the door. "So, about the vision we shared ..."

"I don't want to talk about that." The knot in her stomach was returning.

"It's just that ... in the vision you ..."

"I said I don't want to talk about it. It was just a shared vision from a big crystal, not a prophecy. Can we drop it?"

Jacoby was silent for a moment. Crystara wondered if the whole evening had been ruined.

"Hey, can I be honest with you?" Jacoby asked.

"I would prefer that to you being dishonest with me," Crystara said, smirking to try and lighten the mood.

"I know I might not show it, but I was actually really nervous about all of this. You and me, at first. I'm still kind of nervous, but I ..."

He inched closer and leaned in for a kiss. Crystara leaned forward as well and their lips met. Time stood still for Crystara. Jacoby put his arm around her and brought her in closer. She melted into him, and the kiss continued.

Jacoby pulled away and smiled. "I should get going home. Not that I want to." They both laughed. "Goodnight, Crystara." He kissed her once again, quickly, and his hand left hers. "See you tomorrow."

Crystara watched Jacoby walk off into the night. For the first time in her life, she felt safe and wanted. She looked up at the sky and prayed that it would last.

***

Crystara had completely forgotten about the betrothal ceremony at Central until a priest came to pull her out of her mathematics class. She briefly considered faking an illness. Standing up in front of the entire school was not an idea that she relished. Her betrothal to Jacoby was a personal thing, not some silly ritual for the benefit of others.

As Crystara followed the priest down the deepstone hallway, he handed her a white robe. They stopped in front of a washroom door and he gestured for her to go inside. Inside the washroom she found Racquela and Lenara, who were in the middle of changing.

"Hey," Racquela said happily. "Are you excited?"

"Not for this," Crystara said as she removed her old cotton dress. "Standing up in front of the school for an hour? No thank you. How is Timori?"

Racquela blushed. "He's great. I'm a lot less nervous about it than I was at first, and Father and Mother both said that they really like him. Father even said that he would make a great addition to the engineer's guild."

She turned to Lenara. "What's Paulo like, Lenara?"

"Hmm?" Lenara said as she donned her robe. "Oh. He's fine. See you out there." She left.

Racquela frowned. "Not very friendly, is she?"

Crystara shrugged and pulled her own robe on, letting it fall to her ankles. "I'm gonna freeze in this thing. This school was cold even at the end of summer. Why do they use silk and not wool for these robes? I don't know if I can even remember the whole vow."

Racquela put a reassuring hand on Crystara's shoulder. "Don't worry. Timori and I go first. I remember the whole thing. Just listen to mine and you should be fine. What's the worst that can happen anyway? It's not like they're gonna take back the betrothals just because you forget some dull words in a dull ceremony."

"Yeah, I just ... I get nervous in front of people. I'm scared that I'll faint or throw up."

Racquela gave Crystara's hand a friendly squeeze. "You'll be just fine, Crys. Come on, let's go."

Crystara exited the washroom with Racquela to find Lenara and the priest waiting. They were led quietly to the stage of the gymnasium, where the boys were already milling about, accompanied by another priest. Crystara could hear muffled voices and the squeaking of chairs on the gymnasium floor through the stage curtain. Keeper Orvin slid through the part in the curtain to stand beside the other priests, and he gave Crystara a soothing smile as she passed him. She instantly felt better. Crystara went to stand beside Jacoby, who was fidgeting with his robes.

"Nervous?" he whispered. "I am. Don't know why. It's just like accepting an award or something, no big deal."

"I'm an award now?" Crystara asked.

"I ... I was just kidding. I'm sorry." He looked down sullenly.

Crystara nudged him. "I was just kidding too."

Jacoby's shoulders relaxed. "You're pretty clear as far as awards go, though," he said with a grin.

The curtains were suddenly pulled back to reveal the entire school assembled before them. Crystara's legs grew shaky. Jacoby placed a hand on her back to steady her and she breathed a sigh of relief. At the very least he would catch her before her head hit the stage if she fainted. Crystara reminded herself that it would all be over with soon.

The ceremony began with a speech by Keeper Orvin, which was more light-hearted than his speech outside the Old Temple had been. He made a few jokes and talked more about love than about tradition and religion. It put Crystara at ease. After he finished the speech, Timori and Racquela were brought up to the front of the stage to say their rehearsed lines in front of the crystal projectophone. Afterward, two priests handed them each crystal engagement rings, which they exchanged with each other as they both beamed.

Crystara was glad that Racquela was so happy. She had been ambivalent about being betrothed to Timori at first. Her bribe had turned out for the best, after all. Crystara was simply glad that she had been paired with Jacoby rather than Timori. Jacoby had better looks and more confidence.

Timori and Racquela receded to the back of the stage as the crowd applauded, and Crystara nervously stepped forward with Jacoby. The assembled students in their seats swayed before her eyes. She wondered if Jacoby could sense her anxiety, because he looked into her eyes and mouthed 'It's all right'.

"The love of the gods," Jacoby began. His voice rang clear and bold. "For men, their children, is the love we now share. The Great Crystal, their servant to us here on this earth, has bade me become a servant to you, and I obey with an open heart."

Crystara wondered if Jacoby truly meant the word 'love'. It was a part of the vow, but Crystara felt odd about proclaiming such a thing so early. She had never known love. How would she recognize it when it truly happened? Jacoby was rapidly insinuating himself into her heart, but was that love? How would she know? Her head felt light as Jacoby continued the rehearsed speech.

"... and in this, uh, betrothal ..." Jacoby said, faltering.

Crystara clenched her teeth. He had forgotten the words, and everyone was watching. She wished the floor would swallow her up. She was already disliked by so many for her station, what could be worse than giving them another reason to despise poor, grubby Crystara? She didn't care about her own popularity, but she cared even less for public humiliation.

"... I'll always be true," Jacoby finished. It was an ad-lib, but it seemed to fit. Crystara breathed a sigh of relief. Jacoby was supposed to say 'our bond will serve as an example to others and a testament to the gods and their chosen people, until the next generation comes to pass', but she liked what Jacoby had said better.

Jacoby shot Crystara an apologetic look. She smiled and began her own speech. Afterward she couldn't recall a single word of it. It was as though she had put herself into a trance in order to blunder through the godsdamned thing. Relieved that it was over, she exchanged rings with Jacoby. Jacoby's hands were hot, but the ring was cool against her finger as he slid it on. Crystara smiled. A crystal ring was a useful thing to have, apart from the bond it represented between her and Jacoby. After the exchange, she receded into the background with Jacoby and watched as Paulo and Lenara stepped forward.

"Sorry about that," Jacoby mumbled. "I kinda screwed up the speech."

Crystara wanted to kiss Jacoby, but too many people were watching. Her affection was for his eyes alone. "I liked your words better," she said. "Let's skip next class and go for a walk together."

Jacoby's eyebrows pushed together to form a disapproving crease. "I really shouldn't be skipping class, Crystara," he whispered.

"Don't be such a pansy," she teased. "What's more important, your history class or me? I'll make it worth your while." She pursed her lips together suggestively.

Jacoby's face softened and she could tell that he was going to relent.

"All right," he agreed, "but you owe me more than just one kiss."

Crystara looked back at Lenara and Paulo. Paulo was delivering his lines nonchalantly, as though it were all just a game to him. He and Lenara weren't even looking at each other.

"I'll give you all the kisses you could ever want, Jake."

Chapter 13

Before Longoro and Posco took control, the National Socialist Party was 'little more than a band of rabble-rousers and poverty-stricken individuals who were dissatisfied with their lot in life, but lacked the direction and funding to effect a change in government', according to Piatto.

Between Longoro's funding and leadership and Posco's political tenacity, the National Socialist Party soon printed out its manifesto and organized rallies, the first of which was in Septembra 1855. Although Longoro urged non-violent action toward earning a more socialist government, his vehement and spirited first speech whipped his followers into a frenzy, resulting in the market riot known as 'Black Venday'. Posco was jailed during the ensuing chaos, but it wasn't long before Longoro had arranged for his release. There is some debate as to whether or not Longoro bribed the judge of Posco's trial, but Posco was acquitted of all charges nevertheless. Longoro's charm and Posco's haplessness were apparent even then – although Longoro had technically caused the riot, no charges were placed against him, and Posco was jailed for the nebulous charge of 'breach of the peace,' even though several eyewitnesses reported that he had remained behind in the cabaret where Longoro had made his speech.

The following two and a half years were spent preparing for the elections of 1858, during which time Longoro and Posco cemented their popularity with the lower classes by spending a great deal of Longoro's inheritance on his famous 'free lunches', which were essentially rallies in and of themselves. Longoro made speeches at nearly every luncheon, and usually received standing ovations. His speeches, written by a journalist named Gieuseppi Galetti who would later go on to become the propaganda minister for Longoro's cabinet, were so effective that 'many young men personally thanked Longoro', wrote

Rosso, 'and some went so far as to offer their lives to his service so that the socialist party could succeed'. Longoro's power over the poor seemed nothing short of godlike, which is likely the first in a chain of events that led to Longoro's megalomaniacal tendencies later in life.

By the time elections rolled around, Longoro had garnered enough support that he could not be ignored by the major political parties, and most polls of the day placed his rating at an astonishing thirty percent of the popular vote – not enough to win a majority government, but enough to gain the seats necessary to begin his bid for presidency.

Longoro was not satisfied with thirty percent, however. Many of his rivals joined the National Socialist Party in the winter of 1857. Although there are few documents that reveal such back-door dealings, surviving accounts show that at least seventeen members of the active senate were bribed, blackmailed or threatened into joining the NSP, thanks to Longoro's extensive connections through the mob, who had been promised a great deal of power once Longoro succeeded. At least three of Longoro's more influential rivals were assassinated, although two of the murders were ruled as 'accidental deaths' and the other case remained unsolved until certain imperial documents surfaced after Longoro's execution.

In the elections of 1858, Longoro won by a landslide 79 percent, although an infamous court inquiry that had been silenced until after the Great War revealed that the vote had been heavily fixed in Longoro's favour. Even so, conservative estimates put his true tally at forty-eight percent.

Having ousted or assimilated most of his political rivals, Longoro quickly began enacting the laws that he had promised, which furthered his support with the lower classes 'to the point where he was openly worshipped', historian Timatta tells us.

Longoro and Posco's plans to dissolve the senate were nearing fruition, but there was one piece of the puzzle that was missing before Longoro could turn an absolute rule into a legacy.

183

Then, in the summer of 1859, he met Lucrezia Bianca.

***

28 Aprila, 1875

My dearest Julio,

I was so relieved to hear that you're alive and well! Your last letter that you mentioned never reached me, and I feared the worst. Still, your name didn't appear on the lists, and I never gave up hope.

Things remain much the same here, though one of my supervisors has been harassing me of late, which is making my job more difficult and the single women are growing hateful of me. I've told him on several occasions that I am yours only, but he persists! When they send you here on leave, amongst all the other things that we must do together, would you let the man know that it would be unsafe to bother me? I don't mean to make you jealous, love, but I'm at my wit's end!

I don't know what news you receive on the front lines, but earlier this month a man made an attempt on the Emperor's life. He failed, and the execution was made public. I didn't witness it, of course, but it still made me sad. Does a man deserve to die for standing up for what he believes in? Of course, he did try to take a life, but much as I disagree with Longoro's policies sometimes, he doesn't deserve to die either. I think of what it would be like for his wife, left alone with her young children. I wouldn't wish that upon anyone, and I know you feel the same way. I think, also, of the obvious love that the Emperor and his wife have for each other.

The first flowers are in bloom, Julio, and I take walks through Avati Hill Park because it reminds me of you. When are you slated for leave, again? It's been a long winter, and I yearn to be with you again, under the shade of that whiteoak where we shared our first kiss.

How are your friends? I hope they're doing well. Mother is getting worse, to be honest. She was even confused when I mentioned that you wished her well. She's forgetting more and more things every day. I've taken her to the doctor, but he says that if her memory is going there's little that I can do for her other than try to keep her mind occupied. Alfonso is off fighting in the war as well, and Fatima is up in Toscetti, so I have to look after her by myself. I don't mind, but I worry about her. I hope that I'm not burdening you with all this. You must have greater concerns where you are.

You'll let me know once your campaign is over, won't you? Two more nations and this war will be over so that you can come home to me forever. I pray that day comes soon.

Love, Ramona

3 Yuna, 1875

My love,

I have not received a letter from you, but I can go no longer without writing again. It is miserable here in the trenches, and thoughts of you are my only solace.

The battle goes on, with no end in sight. Every day it is the same, a concerted strike toward the next trench with the other battalions, but the enemies on the hill are vigilant and always push us back to the same position. We lose somebody with every push we make. It is folly here, and I question Longoro's wisdom in dividing the armies of Novem between here and Milosa when we are clearly losing this front. Is it the same in the west, do you know?

Sadly, Captain Di'Zotto died yesterday. He was the best commander I could ever have had, and I wept for him. We never even saw the sniper who got him, but thankfully he survived long enough to say some last words for his family, which I wrote down, and the priest-corporal was able to perform his final rites. The medic, unfortunately, could do nothing for him and we had to send the body away to be cremated. Burning bodies near the trenches gives our position away to the scattershot wands, so there was no funeral pyre, just as there never is here. It was an ignoble end to a noble man.

I do not wish to burden you with the horror of this war, love, but I fear that if I do not put these words down I shall go mad. There

185

is very little paper left and so I cannot simply write in my journal or I would not be able to write to you, as well. As it stands I have no idea how long it will take for this letter to reach you, if it will even make it back to the safety of the supply train.

The trenches are a desolate place, devoid of natural life thanks to the scouring of scattershot. Novem feels like another world, and I wonder if this place is the abyss and you a dream from another life. The days bleed together, and I sleep very little. When the scattershot wands boom I do not know sometimes if I am asleep or awake. The sound never ceases.

We are all starving, and many of the men have come down with dysentery because there is no more clean water. Pietro has grown edgy since we ran out of cigarettes, and I am thankful that Di'Zotto did not leave him in charge. Largo has begun catching and cooking the rats, which are plentiful right now, but once we all get used to the taste I fear that they will not last long.

I wax poetic in a morose kind of way as I babble to myself on watch, and only thoughts of you can stop the prattle. My love, you are my grip on sanity in this abyssal place where hope goes to die.

The trenches are riddled with filth and bodies, and the stench of death and decay is often unbearable. Many of our men are still topside where they were shot down, bodies already half-consumed by carrion birds. Nobody has the stomach to try and fetch them, for fear of joining their fallen comrades. The wands on the hill are always watching, and so even the dead here find no respite.

Our card games have become the one bit of relief in this place, but I fear that too will be soured when one of us does not return from a charge. The others take greater risks than I in their tasks, but thankfully the gods have seen fit to protect them thus far.

The horn is blowing, and I must prepare for another assault. Write to me, Ramona, of the serenity of Captus Nove and the sea. Lend me your quiet strength, because mine is failing. Write to me of your beauty, for there is none to be found here.

Julio

***

Scattershot boomed like an unholy thunder, the wrath of the gods. Dust and debris flew down into the trench, pelting Julio's helmet. Julio looked over at Pietro, who was shaking violently back and forth. Scattershot had nearly hit him three days ago, and he hadn't stopped rocking since – he had scattershock.

It was daytime, but the clouds cast a lugubrious grey over the world. Rains had nearly flooded the trench on the previous day, and everyone was coated in caked dirt and the rest of the filth that had risen up. Evacuating the trench would have meant death, however, so the troops had weathered it.

Julio turned to Pietro. "Did you get any word from Lieutenant Caracus about progress in the tunnel?"

Julio couldn't tell if Pietro was nodding or if the boy was still shaking. "The rains fucked it all up, but Rob told me yesterday that it should still hold. Largo hasn't slept in two days, the dullard. He says he wants to be the first one through to surprise those Kilgrish assholes. I told him the reinforcements are only a few days away and then we can make the big push, but he's convinced that the tunnel will be done before then. Gotta hand it to the guy. He's a dirty miner but he's got balls."

"He does," Julio agreed. "He says Maria's gonna marry a war hero."

Pietro was silent for a moment. "You guys are lucky, you know. You and Largo. Having beautiful women back home, someone to fight for. I was stuck in military school until the war started. I ..." he hesitated. "I've never even had a girlfriend."

"The girls will be lining up for you once this war is over, Pietro." Julio took care never to call him 'Pip' after what happened in the stable.

Pietro's eyes were glistening. "Yeah, if I make it home. I thought I'd bought it the other day. You only get so many lucky chances like that. The only clear side is that you never hear the one that gets you."

Julio looked at Pietro and could tell that the boy needed more than just a casual reassurance.

"I swore I'd protect you," he said. He was careful not to mention the incident surrounding that promise. "You're like the little brother I never had."

Julio watched as a tear fell down his young friend's cheek.

"I feel the same way, Jules. Thanks." His shaking seemed to subside somewhat. "I don't know where I would be without you and the other guys. You look out for me, even if you tease me a lot. I may know a lot about speaking, but I'm a dullard when it comes to everything else."

Julio shook his head. A burst of scattershot echoed as it hit the ground somewhere above the trenches, and he waited for the noise to subside.

"You know a lot more than you give yourself credit for."

"Not about love," Pietro countered. "What's it like, Jules? Being in love? I ... want to know. In case I don't make it back."

"Don't talk like that. You'll make it back. But if you want, well ... it's different for everyone, I'm sure, but I can tell you what it's like for me and Ramona."

"I'd like that." Pietro settled into the dirt at the bottom of the trench and took a sip of the water that he'd boiled earlier that day.

"When you love someone, Pietro, the colours of the world become brighter. Food tastes better. Happiness consumes you, like an incurable affliction that settles into your smile, your heart and your bones and won't let go. When I look into Ramona's eyes, all the troubles of the world melt away and I am left feeling like I could conquer any obstacle. Ramona ... Ramona has kept me sane throughout all of this, this war. I shudder every time I pick up my wand, but then I think of her face and I remember that it's her I'm fighting for."

"You're never afraid that something might happen?" Pietro asked. "It sounds wonderful, Jules, but they say that nothing lasts forever."

"I will love Ramona forever. Nothing can change that. I ..."

188

Julio's final thought was interrupted as Roberto came tearing down the trench with an impish grin on his face. "Grab your wands, dullards, we're almost through the tunnel. Vadon is gonna eat wandshot soon!"

Julio stood up straight. "Aren't we waiting for reinforcements?"

"Can't wait that long," Roberto said breathlessly. "The tunnel could collapse before they get here and every hour we run the risk of their scouts finding it. Pip, make yourself useful and round up the rest of the troops, then meet me in the tunnel. I set up those crystals for you. They'll never know what hit 'em. C'mon, Jules!"

Julio glanced at Pietro, and they shared a brief moment of quiet understanding. Then he took out his picture of Ramona and gazed at it wistfully while he followed Roberto to the tunnel. "Gods, see me through this," he prayed.

Chapter 14

The regular football season was going well for Central School in the spring of 1895. Coach Lagheri trained his footballers well, and it showed in their teamwork as well as their abilities on the field. Victories were frequent as they played the other finishing schools of Captus Nove, and Timori was sure that his team could finally earn the nationals trophy that Lagheri so craved.

Timori's performance improved whenever Racquela came to watch him play. He had scored eight goals already that season, which put him second behind Filippo in scoring points for Central.

The game against Southron Heights on the fourteenth of Aprila was a rainy one, and the opposing team was putting up a good fight. Their captain was an impossibly tall fifteen-year-old who always seemed to be one step ahead of Timori, and the slick grass didn't help Timori's game any. Trailing by a point with only a few minutes left in the game, Timori knew that he had to outplay the captain if they were to succeed. Unfortunately, Filippo had been trying to showboat for the entire game and never passed to Timori.

The ball entered play and went to Southron's captain. Timori rushed him as he heard an encouraging yell from Racquela in the stands. Timori was mere metres from his adversary when Filippo came in from beside him and nearly knocked him aside as he brushed past. Timori lost his footing and slipped on the grass, landing flat on his back. The next thing he knew, the ball was flying over his head, followed closely by the Southron captain, who easily outran Filippo.

Timori leapt to his feet. "Defence!" he shouted over the din of the assembled crowd of parents and students. He sprinted after the ball, but it was too late. With a fake and a pass, the ball went to another forward who catapulted it in a shot that nearly took the boy off of his feet. The ball sailed toward the top corner of the net, and Timori knew Jacoby could not reach it when he jumped. Jacoby did his best, but his hands fell short and the ball sank into the back of the net.

Seething, Timori strode up to Filippo as the opposing team and the Southron side of the stands cheered and celebrated.

"What in Jova's name was that?" he demanded. "You cut right in front of me when I had everything under control."

Filippo stuck his nose up into the air. "Maybe you shouldn't get in the way of the best player on the team."

Timori shoved an angry finger in Filippo's face as the other team members gathered around them. "Best player? You just cost us a point, you dully!"

Mariano got in Timori's face. "Don't call my brother a dully, you piss-poor picker!"

Suddenly Jacoby was between Timori and Mariano. He gave Mariano a generous shove. "Who are you calling a picker?"

Filippo threw up his arms. "What, you're taking his side, Jake? You're better than he is. We don't belong with dirty trash like him."

"Fuck you," Jacoby spat. "I'd take Tim over you as a friend any day. Talk about class like that again and I'll be sure to tell Coach exactly what you said."

Mariano shoved Jacoby back. Other members of the team hurled insults at each other as the referee blew the whistle. Central's team was holding up gameplay.

"Can't fight your own battles, coward?" Mariano yelled to Timori.

Coach Lagheri appeared out of nowhere, roughly jerking Jacoby and Mariano away from each other with his meaty palms.

"Get back in play, all of you, before you get us carded! I oughta knock all your heads in! Any more fighting like this and I'll have you all suspended from school, do you hear me? Fucking dullards! Jake, learn how to jump! Tim, fucking watch your feet. And Fil, pull another stunt like that and I'll knock you over myself. Go, get out there!"

Central's players returned to their positions on the field. Many were glaring at each other. Filippo pointed at Timori as he ran to take centre position.

"Watch your back, picker."

"Watch your fucking ... face," Timori shot back.

He shook his head angrily and wished that he had come up with a better insult. Play resumed, but Timori was far too distracted to focus. Although the defence held up enough to keep Southron from scoring another goal, Central's offence couldn't cooperate well enough to keep the ball in Southron's zone. The game ended 4-2.

Coach Lagheri was red-faced as he reamed out the team for a solid half hour after the match. Timori zoned out the coach's flurry of insults and spittle, and glared at Filippo instead. Jacoby was trying to stare down Mariano in the meantime. A punch would have been thrown by somebody if Coach Lagheri hadn't been standing there the whole time berating the team further as they changed out of their football uniforms. Timori and Jacoby left the room quickly to find Racquela and Crystara, who waited by the stands under the shelter of a white parasol.

"He's gonna get a fist to the head next time I catch him alone," Timori groused.

"He's not worth your time," Jacoby said.

"He is if we keep losing games like this."

Racquela rushed up to Timori and gave him a firm hug and a kiss on the cheek. Timori's anger and frustration quickly melted away.

"You looked great out there, Tim," Racquela consoled. "Don't worry about those dull northern boys who don't know how to kick a ball. How about a consolation prize of lunch, somewhere out of the rain?" Racquela took Timori's hand.

"I don't have any money," Timori and Crystara said in unison.

"I can spot you," Jacoby and Racquela said at the same time. The two of them laughed as they walked off the field. Timori didn't find it very funny, and by the look on Crystara's face, neither did she.

The two couples walked down the street to find a suitable café for lunch. With Racquela by his side, Timori's mood changed from sullen to boisterous.

"Did I ever tell you about the time Jake lit his hair on fire?" Timori inquired with an impish grin.

"Please don't tell this story," Jacoby moaned. "It's embarrassing."

"Not for me," Timori said.

Racquela looked over at Jacoby. "Come on, Jake. Where's your sense of humour?"

Jacoby rolled his eyes. "It burned up along with my hair. I'm gonna get you back, Tim, as soon as I can remember an embarrassing story about you."

Timori shrugged. "I don't have any embarrassing stories. So anyway, Jake and I got our hands on some cigarettes one time. We were what, twelve years old? Jova knows why we tried it, cigarettes taste like death. Anyway we couldn't find any matches, but Jake's dad was out of town on some business thing and all we could find to light them with was this old crystal sparker. Jake's dad kept it in a case along with some cigars. So we grab this thing and head out to the alley behind our houses to smoke these cigarettes. Trouble is, the sparker won't make a flame no matter how many times we flick the switch. So Jake, he takes the thing and holds it right up to his eyes and says 'Let me take a look at it, it's dark out'. Suddenly the thing flares up like some kind of fire wand right in Jake's face. His hair goes up in flames, and instead of calmly patting it out with his hands, he starts running around the alley screaming like a wraith out of the abyss for me to put it out. So I tackle him to the ground and throw my jacket over his face. When I take the jacket off, his hair is all right except for some singed ends, but something seems a little off with his face."

Jacoby let out a sigh. "Not only did I get reamed out by my dad and grounded for a month, but I had to go to school that way."

193

"What way?" Racquela asked.

Timori laughed. "Jacoby's infamously expressive eyebrows were no more."

Racquela laughed, and Timori felt a twinge of pride well up in him. It was always rewarding to know that he could make Racquela smile.

"He looked surprised for days afterward, no matter how much he tried to frown! I told everyone that it took him that long to get over being startled by the fire."

"What would I do without a friend like you, Tim?" Jacoby said. He stopped in front of a small café and pointed up at the sign. "La'Monti Street Café. This looks good."

"It looks expensive," Timori and Crystara said.

***

Timori was packing up his notebook to leave engineering class when Doctor Ruveldi cast a shadow over his desk.

"Stravida. Hold up for a moment, I want to speak with you."

Timori waited patiently as the other students left the classroom.

"I noticed you didn't sign up for the junior engineers' conference," Ruveldi noted as he stroked his beard.

Timori shrugged. "I'm not a junior engineer."

Ruveldi barked a laugh. "You obviously weren't listening in class when I talked about it, then. It's an open conference, which means anybody who is interested can attend, not just junior engineers. Have you got your head up in the clouds lately, Stravida, or what? Of all the students in this class, you should be the most interested in attending."

"I have no money," Timori said. It was the part that he didn't want to admit. "I can't afford to attend."

Doctor Ruveldi sat down in a chair beside Timori. "Well, why didn't you say so earlier? You need to go to this conference,

194

Timori. I don't normally stroke egos, but you have the most potential out of anybody in this class. I will pay for you to go."

Timori blushed and looked at his desk. "Oh, no, I couldn't," he insisted. He didn't want to accept any charity, especially not from somebody that he looked up to. "I appreciate the offer, Doctor, but I can't."

Doctor Ruveldi chuckled. "You remind me of my friend Julio. Too nice for your own good. That wasn't an offer, Stravida. I'm taking you to this conference because it's for your own good, and there's nothing you can do or say to change my mind about it."

Timori knew that Doctor Ruveldi wasn't the type of person to take no for an answer. He swallowed his pride. "Thank you, Doctor."

"You can thank me by paying attention in class. You've been distracted lately, Stravida."

"I'm in love."

"So much like Julio," Doctor Ruveldi remarked. "Right, I forgot you were one of the betrothed this year. Well, I suppose it's better than being stuck with a legally binding engagement and *not* being in love. You're too young to listen to or believe anything that I might have to say on the subject of romance, so let me just put it to you like this: you're the best student that I've had in years, Timori Stravida. You worked harder than any of the other students to get here. Just don't lose sight of what an education from Central can do for you in the long run. Don't let your heart overrule your head. And do your homework, for Jova's sake."

***

The rain pattered so hard on the windowpane behind Timori that he couldn't hear his fork scraping on his plate. He looked up and smiled at Racquela across the big banquet table. She was wearing a white dress with a matching bow in her hair, which had been done up in cascading ringlets. Racquela always looked stunning no matter what she wore. Timori pictured her covered in mud and somehow the image was still flattering.

Racquela didn't return Timori's smile. She was staring at her pheasant as she cut it into bite-sized pieces. It had taken Timori three dinners at the De'Trini household to learn how to eat his food as befits an upper-class gentleman, even with coaching from Racquela.

The table looked as though it was set for forty instead of four. The long banquet table was filled with covered trays of cooked game birds, three rice dishes in various rich creamy sauces, gravies, breads, spiced mutton, fowl in an orange reduction, olives stuffed with fish and cheese, and more types of soup and salad than Timori even knew existed.

The strict etiquette was almost more than Timori could stand, but he kept his mouth shut for Racquela's sake. As the guest, he was permitted to choose what to put on his plate first, but Racquela had told him that it was rude to take too much right away. Timori knew that it didn't matter. There were trays and trays of food that didn't get eaten at the end of every meal. It was even more difficult not to try and sneak some food away for his sisters and mother. He would never risk alienating Racquela's parents by taking anything, not even a slice of bread.

"How are your studies going, Timori?" Joven De'Trini asked.

Despite his small stature and whisper-quiet voice, Joven De'Trini still made Timori nervous. He asked the same questions every time Timori had dinner at Racquela's, and Timori struggled to think of something new to say in response.

He looked down thoughtfully and turned the cuff of his shirt sleeve to hide the old gravy stain. It was the same shirt he wore on every date, covered by the same ratty brown blazer. It was only a matter of time before Racquela bought him some new clothes, but he would avoid that for as long as possible. He did not want her charity.

"Good," Timori said. He reminded himself to look his future father-in-law in the eyes when he spoke to him. "Sir." He almost always forgot that part. "My engineering teacher, Doctor Ruveldi, took me to the engineers' conference."

Joven took a sip of wine and nodded. "Mm. Good. I missed out on it this year. How was it? I hope you found it enlightening."

Timori wasn't sure how to reply. Most of his time had been spent with Doctor Ruveldi, who muttered to Timori between swigs from a hidden flask of brandy about how this engineer and that engineer were useless. Timori didn't learn much about engineering, but he learned a lot about engineers.

"Oh, very," Timori said. He stabbed a big piece of quail with his fork and almost shoved it into his mouth when he remembered that he wasn't supposed to talk with his mouth full. "I hope to get my doctorate eventually and show them all a thing or two."

Timori didn't add that he would need a sponsorship from somebody like Joven in order to afford an academy. He downed the steaming slice of meat on his fork before another question was asked.

Racquela beamed at Timori and he blushed, looking back down at his nearly empty plate. He knew that getting into her father's good graces made her happy. At Racquela's family dinners he sat across from her and she said very little. Her parents did most of the talking.

Timori found it even more difficult to talk to Jessica than Joven. She looked like an older version of Racquela. Timori was thrilled to know that Racquela would age gracefully like her mother, but being around two beautiful women only compounded Timori's nervousness.

Timori would have felt a lot less nervous if he could have gone on dates with Racquela alone. All dates with Racquela were chaperoned, either by one of Racquela's parents or their old stewardess. Even in school he never had a moment alone with her. She spent most of her time at Central studying, or talking with Crystara. It wasn't fair. Jacoby's parents didn't follow the noble customs and let Jacoby take Crystara out on dates completely unchaperoned. Timori's neck flushed as he thought about how much more interesting kissing could be when nobody else was watching.

The rest of dinner passed in relative silence. Timori listened to the rain as he tried to fill his stomach enough to last him for two days. He briefly considered stuffing a bread roll or two into the pocket of his blazer, but as he had one in his hand he saw Racquela watching him over her wine glass so he shoved the roll into his mouth instead.

As the chef brought around coffee and bowls of fresh fruit with cream, Joven cleared his throat.

"Well it's raining pretty hard out there, Timori. Maybe I should give you a ride home."

"Oh no, I couldn't impose," Timori said, hoping that was the polite way to decline. He grabbed the cream and poured a meagre amount over the berries and grapes in front of him.

"You're not imposing, young man. I insist. You wouldn't want to ruin that suit, after all." Timori wasn't sure if Joven was being condescending, but when he saw Racquela nodding he knew that it would be impolite to refuse.

"Thank you, sir. Is there room for my bicycle? I might need it tomorrow."

"I am sure we can fit it in the trunk. Are you ready to go, Timori?" Joven took a sip of black coffee and pushed his bowl of fruit away. "I'm full to bursting and I'm sure you have homework to get to. You can tell me more about the engineers' conference on the way."

Timori stared at his bowl of fruit and felt his stomach roil. Joven De'Trini wanted to talk to him *alone*? He wondered what would be more embarrassing – Joven giving him the 'not until you're married' talk, or having the head of the alchemists' guild see the hovel Timori called home.

Jessica wished Timori a good evening, and Racquela followed him down the stairs to the foyer as Joven went to bring the coach around to the front entrance.

"You look nervous," Racquela said as she buttoned his jacket for him. Her face was so close to his, he wanted to put his hands on her cheeks and pull her in for a kiss, but she was very reserved when her parents were around.

"Father likes you, Tim. There's nothing to worry about."

Although Racquela was sometimes physically reticent, he could see the affection in her eyes. As she did up his top button, he took her hands in his.

"It's hard not to be nervous around him. He's your father, and an important man, besides. But it's more that I never know the correct way to behave around you and your family. Sometimes I just want to kiss you, but I can't even express my love that way."

Racquela pulled away from Timori and folded her arms. "That's just not how things are done in noble society, Tim." She dropped her voice to a whisper. "When they're not around, that's different."

Timori bent down to lace up his shoes. "They're always around, or somebody else is. We still haven't had a chance to talk about the vision we shared."

"There's not really much to talk about, Tim."

It was a lie and he knew it. It hadn't been a simple romantic picnic in the vision. The feeling of love between himself and Racquela in the dream still made his head swim if he thought about it. More importantly, there had been a child sitting between him and Racquela on the red-and-white checkered picnic cloth, a little boy playing with a toy soldier. Timori didn't believe that the vision was prophetic, but if both he and Racquela shared it, then deep down they must have both been thinking about children.

It was really the ending of the vision that Timori wanted to talk about, however. There was that brilliant flash that made the whole sky go white, and the earth had trembled so violently that Timori had fallen on his back. 'My baby', he had screamed, but the child was nowhere to be seen by that point, and the last part of the vision had been Racquela fleeing the white flash. She was being beckoned by a dark, smiling stranger.

It was the stranger that Timori really wanted to talk about, but Racquela always played to his sensible side and reminded him that it was just a vision, nothing to be taken literally.

Racquela's father opened the front door. "Well Tim, let's get that bicycle into the back of the coach."

Timori observed the proper custom by kissing Racquela on the cheek. "Goodbye, my love."

"I'll see you tomorrow, Tim."

Timori grumbled under the din of the rain as he and Joven hauled the rusty bike into the trunk of the motorcoach.

Chapter 15

Racquela was in her room practicing the harp when she heard a knock on the door.

"Come in," she called. The knob turned and her father peered in. He gave his only daughter a warm smile.

"Hi, sweetheart. How's the harp?" He came in and gave Racquela a kiss on the forehead, his moustache tickling her. Joven De'Trini sat down on the bed.

She studied the instrument carefully. "Looks the same as it did yesterday."

Joven laughed. "How are classes?"

Racquela shrugged. "They're fine."

"How is Timori?"

Racquela hesitated. It was a complicated question. Timori was ... attentive? He wanted to spend every waking minute with Racquela, but she had other concerns, like her friends and her studies. It was difficult to tell him no sometimes because the novelty of their betrothal hadn't yet worn off, and it was so wonderful to be with somebody who was endlessly caring and made her laugh as much as Timori did.

Still, it was nice to have a break from him once in a while. He had his own concerns that Racquela had to remind him about, such as his schoolwork. Racquela didn't regret her decision to bribe her way into the betrothals, but she wasn't single-minded about her future. There was more to it than just Timori, although she was excited for him to be a part of it all. It was her dream for him to be a Doctor of Engineering and she a famous singer. Racquela was hopeful that Timori's love for her would fuel his ambition, rather than stifle it.

"He's good."

Joven De'Trini nodded. "He's a good boy, I like him. The gods chose well for you, I think, regardless of his station. That kid's got quite a brain on him. Thought you should know, and I'll tell Timori this next time he comes for dinner, but I spoke to Nico at the engineers' guild the other day. He said that he would gladly accept Timori for an apprenticeship once he starts his junior studies at an academy."

Racquela plucked a couple of strings on her harp absentmindedly. Timori spoke frequently about how he didn't think that he would ever be able to afford academy studies.

"He said that he might have to be satisfied with basic engineering. He doesn't think he'll be able to get enough money to go to an academy."

Joven De'Trini shook his head. "Nonsense. No son-in-law of mine is going to be stuck in the pits with the pickers. You tell Tim ... or rather, I'll tell him next time he comes over that Joven De'Trini will sponsor him for his doctorate."

Racquela beamed at her father. "Thanks, Dad. I'm glad you like Tim."

Joven stood up and walked over to the door. "I like whatever makes my daughter happy."

***

Racquela exited the school doors to meet Crystara, Jacoby and Timori for lunch. As she passed by the whiteoaks that flanked the front entrance to Central, she noticed a figure out of the corner of her eye.

Paulo stood casually under a whiteoak, smoking a cigarette. He was always so nonchalant, shirt un-tucked and cigarette in hand as though he didn't care whatsoever if he was caught smoking on school grounds. He gave Racquela a solemn nod.

"Racquela," he said. "Nice day out. Join me for a cigarette?"

Racquela approached Paulo. She knew that Timori wouldn't be pleased to know that she was talking to another boy, but it was just harmless conversation. She had forgotten how tall Paulo was until she was standing right next to him.

"Thank you, but I don't smoke," she replied, "especially not on school grounds. Aren't you afraid of getting caught?"

Paulo shrugged and took a deliberate drag on his cigarette. "Not particularly. Aren't you afraid of never doing anything exciting with your life?"

"What?"

Paulo's tone and sly smile were infuriating.

"Nothing. How's Tim?"

"Good. He's great. How is Lenara?"

Paulo shrugged again. "She's Lenara."

Racquela wondered if Paulo cared about anything at all.

"Well, I won't keep you from your lunch date. Must be hard, though, being betrothed to somebody of a much lower station than yourself."

Racquela scoffed. Paulo's rudeness was no longer charming. "Some of us aren't concerned with class, Paulo. Have a nice day." She started to walk away.

"You should be," he called after her. "Just wait and see."

Racquela turned around. "What is that supposed to mean?"

Paulo took one last pull of his cigarette and then put it out on the trunk of the tree.

"I don't believe in a caste system," he replied. "But until it's abolished, no amount of legality or sanctioning of some stupid crystal can stop the inevitable. Besides, Timori couldn't handle a woman like you if he tried."

"A woman like me?" Racquela was tired of Paulo's vagueness. "You don't know anything about me ... or Tim, for that matter."

Paulo tossed the butt of his cigarette away and walked toward the doors of the school. "Don't have to," he said over his shoulder. "I know that you're an alchemist's daughter and he's a miner's son. Anything else is superfluous."

Paulo opened the school door and disappeared.

"What a jerk," Racquela muttered as she walked off.

Despite her best efforts, she couldn't get Paulo out of her head for the rest of the day.

***

The annual country carnival was Racquela's favourite event of the entire year. It was even more exciting than New Year's celebrations.

Every spring the travelling carnival would convene just outside of Captus Nove before it began its summer circuit through the rest of the Noven countryside. Racquela's parents had taken her to the carnival every year for as long as she could remember. This was the first year that she would be going without her parents. It was a double-date with Timori, Crystara and Jacoby. She still didn't know why her father was allowing her to go unchaperoned, but she wasn't going to question the decision.

The carnival let her experience the other side of Noven life. Racquela came from the city and from money. She was a girl of fancy dresses and five-course dinners, vacations to foreign countries and summer tutelage. The country carnival was a place of puppet plays and centima operas, curio museums in brightly coloured tents and rustic meals from all over Novem and beyond. It was rude humour and music that was never heard on any radio. It was fortune-tellers and untrained crystal-speakers who performed tricks on stage. It was a glimpse into the simple life that Racquela had never known personally.

It was like magic.

Racquela bounced in her seat as she sat in the back of her father's motorcoach with Timori beside her. They had passed innumerable horse-drawn buggies on the country road that led to the annual festival, and Racquela could easily recall a time when she had been a passenger in such a buggy, before her father had purchased a motorcoach.

Crystara was silent on the trip, but Racquela busied herself by telling everyone all of the exciting things that they were likely to see at the carnival. Timori interjected quips once in a while, and he talked with Jacoby quite a bit about the football season, but Racquela didn't mind. Nothing could shatter her good mood on that day.

The peaks of the first tents could be seen as they came up over the crest of a hill on the road, and Racquela felt a thrilling chill run up her spine. In the distance she could see people milling about in the great open space of the carnival, and she longed to be amongst them. Timori could sense her excitement and squeezed her hand affectionately. She smiled back at him.

"You're gonna love it, Tim," she said.

"I'm just excited for the food," he replied. "I can smell it from here. I've never tried cat before."

Racquela slapped Timori playfully on the arm. "Stop it," she said with a laugh. "They don't actually do that."

"Damn," Timori exclaimed. "I was hoping to get rid of all the strays in my neighbourhood."

Joven De'Trini drove up to the edge of the fairgrounds and stopped the motorcoach. Everyone exited the vehicle, except for Racquela's father. He handed Racquela some coins with a smile. "All right, have fun and I'll be here to pick you up at sunset."

"You're not coming with us, just for a little bit?" Racquela asked. Joven's usually reserved exterior melted away every year at the country fair.

Joven shook his head. "No, I've got business back in the city today. Just don't go into any strange tents alone." With a smile and a cheerful wave, he drove off.

Racquela jumped up and down with glee. She felt like she was five years old again. "Well, what does everyone want to do first?"

The carnival was vast. There was no way Racquela and her friends would be able to see it all in just one day. The quartet of betrothed youth went straight for the food vendors. Racqela insisted everyone try fresh lamb loins off the grill, along with rye bread. As they ate, they wandered around looking for a spectacle. Some of the shows were free, and they saw a crystal speaker juggling light crystals, as well as a silly puppet show about the Great War. The puppets representing Emperor Longoro and his infamous counterpart

Posco were portrayed as a married couple, much to the delight of the crowd.

The second show was a little more low-brow, but the toilet humour made most of the children in the audience laugh themselves silly. Jacoby and Timori laughed along with them. Racquela noticed that Crystara wasn't too interested in the puppet shows, but Jacoby cheered her up afterward by winning her a stuffed bear from a stand where he had to shoot apples off of the heads of dummies with a bow and arrow.

"I've gotta find the outhouses," Jacoby exclaimed as he danced around comically. "I drank too much of that berry juice."

Racquela pointed to the east end of the carnival. "They should be over there."

Timori followed Jacoby. "Me too. Except I don't dance like a dully when I have to pee."

Racquela giggled. "All right, we'll wait for you here." She turned to Crystara to find her best friend pointing at a painted sign above a tent entrance.

"Fortune telling."

Racquela clapped her hands. She had never been to a fortune-teller at the carnival before. Her father had always referred to them as 'heathen money thieves'.

"Want to go? I'm sure the boys can find us."

Crystara nodded happily and they entered the tent hand in hand.

The interior was smoky and dimly lit by an old oil lamp that hung low from the ceiling of the tent. Through the sickly-sweet incense smoke, Racquela could make out a wizened old woman in ragged skirts and a shawl sitting behind a wooden table.

"Come in, children, come in," she beckoned.

Racquela and Crystara approached cautiously and sat on the other side of the table in rickety old chairs. The old woman regarded each of them carefully and smiled so deeply that her wrinkles folded like an accordion.

"Well, some pretty young things come to visit. Have you come to hear your fortunes from old Luna? One dinari each."

She held out a leathery palm. Racquela drew two coins out of her purse and handed them to the old woman, who accepted them with a nod and made them disappear with a wave of her hand. She pointed at Racquela.

"You first."

Racquela was uncertain of what to do, so she held out her hand. It turned out to be a proper gesture. The old woman grabbed her wrist with a surprisingly strong grip and studied her hand carefully. Then she looked into Racquela's eyes for quite some time. After she broke eye contact, she brought out a small white crystal, which she waved in front of Racquela's face a few times as she hummed to herself in a tremolo voice. Finally she put the crystal away and nodded sagely.

"Interesting. Your life is filled with love, young one, but also with tragedy."

Racquela didn't fully buy into the old woman's 'fortune-telling', but she was hoping for something a little bit more fun. "Tragedy?"

Luna nodded again. "Tragedy. A woman's heart is a tender thing, young one, and a man's heart is that of a wolf. It hunts and it devours. Beware the hearts of men, for they will lead you into despair unless you, too, act as predator rather than prey."

"I don't understand. Are you saying that I'm going to be betrayed?"

Luna studied Racquela's face carefully. "Not necessarily. The future is not a thing of certainties, child. It is a myriad of paths based upon the choices that we make, but I have seen the future of this world and it is not a place of happiness for many. Many of your choices could lead you to despair, and your heart will always betray you if you do not steel it against the wolves who howl at your door. I see a lot of love in you, child. You have so much love for the world, but it is yourself that you must love first."

Racquela frowned. Her fortune wasn't what she had expected at all. It was vague and filled with negative omens. She had been hoping for a glimpse into her future and that of Timori's.

"What about my betrothed? Can you tell me about that?"

The old woman shook her head. "Betrothed. Silly child. Do you think that a woman with beauty and charms such as yourself will have only one love in her life? Love doesn't always go both ways, take it from old Luna. Some men have the hearts of wolves. Others have hearts of crystal. Their feelings are powerful, but they shatter easily. Remember that."

She laughed. "The rest of your fate you must discover on your own."

Racquela looked away, disappointed. Fortune-telling was a sham, just as her father had warned her. She didn't care so much about the money spent, but the woman could have at least made her fortune more interesting and less vague. A fortune such as the one she had received could have applied to anybody.

"What about me?" Crystara said. It sounded like a challenge.

Again Luna studied her subject's hand and looked into her eyes. She brought out the small white crystal and then suddenly stopped.

"No," she said. "I cannot."

"Can't what?" Crystara asked.

"I cannot read you, child. My visions of you are clouded by darkness. Go. I am finished."

The old woman pushed her chair farther away from Crystara. Her nostrils flared and her eyes went wide.

"What do you mean, finished?" Crystara demanded. "You're not going to read my fortune?"

"Don't worry about it," Racquela said. She tugged at Crystara's sleeve. "Let's just go."

"No," Crystara insisted. "If you won't read my fortune, give us that dinari back."

She glared straight into Luna's eyes. After a moment, Luna waved her palm and a gold dinari coin appeared on the table, which clattered and spun. Crystara picked it up.

"Let's go, Racquela."

They left the tent. Crystara looked at Racquela.

"Don't worry about it, that whole thing was a sham. She wasn't even a real crystal-speaker. I can tell."

Timori and Jacoby came around the corner of the tent and greeted Racquela and Crystara with kisses.

"Did we miss anything?" Jacoby asked.

Racquela shook her head. "No."

The four of them continued on to parts of the carnival that they had not yet visited. Racquela tried to forget about the fortune-teller, but the whole time she wondered if someday Timori would betray her and devour her heart like a wolf.

She was even more frightened of the possibility that his heart was one of crystal.

***

The day after the carnival, Racquela went to visit Timori at home after her band practice. Her father was finally allowing her to visit Timori without being chaperoned, but he still insisted on driving her down to the valley. Racquela was grateful for the lift this time. She had brought a large box with her.

Joven dropped Racquela off just outside of Timori's house. Racquela awkwardly set the box down and knocked on the door. To her surprise, it wasn't Timori who answered, but his sister Nicola.

"Hi, Racquela," Nicola greeted. "Tim's not back from football practice yet."

"Oh, that's all right," Racquela said with a smile. "We can spend time together before he gets here, just us girls. Can I come in?"

"Of course," Nicola said as she held the door open wide. Racquela picked up the box and entered the unkempt home of

Timori's family. She heard her father drive away in his motorcoach and found a clean spot on the couch as Nicola closed the door.

Carlotta looked up at Racquela from her spot on the floor. "What's in the box?"

"I'm glad you asked." Racquela smiled. She opened the lid to reveal a pile of folded-up clothes. Carlotta's eyes brightened as she saw the old dresses that no longer fit Racquela. "They're for you and Nicola. Any of them that don't fit either of you can be sold or given away, if you like, but there should be something in there for each of you."

"Thank you!" Carlotta exclaimed as she threw her arms around Racquela. Nicola, meanwhile, began searching through the pile.

"Want to try some on?" Racquela asked.

"Yes!" Carlotta cried gleefully.

Racquela spent the afternoon in the girls' room trying on different dresses and fixing the girls' hair in braids. Their household was sorely lacking in beauty products, but Racquela had brought a makeup kit with her and spent time showing Nicola and Carlotta how to properly apply it. Carlotta insisted on doing her own and wound up looking like a clown, but she seemed perfectly content that way so Racquela didn't say anything. Instead she spoke with Nicola about how much makeup was too much, and how to do an evening look versus a daytime one, as well as coordinating eye shadow with a wardrobe properly. She knew it was better for Nicola to learn about makeup sooner than she needed to rather than not at all. Racquela was happy to note that there were a few dresses in the collection that fit each of the girls fairly well. It felt like time spent with the sisters that she never had.

Timori showed up just as the sun was setting, and Nicola and Carlotta insisted on showing off their new clothes to him before he could even change out of his football uniform. He gave Racquela a kiss when Carlotta and Nicola weren't looking.

"Thanks," he said. "It's been a while since they got any new clothes."

Carlotta kept her eyes pinned on her older brother as she spun around in a green summer dress that had once been one of Racquela's favourites.

"I'm hungry, Tim. What's for supper?"

Timori's smile faded instantly. "I don't know, Lottie. What's in the icebox?"

"Nothing," she replied casually as she continued to spin. The girl stopped spinning and lost her balance. She fell onto her bed laughing.

"Well, I guess nothing's for supper then," Timori said. "You got new clothes. Eat one of the dresses that you don't like."

Racquela gave Timori a reproachful look. "Tim, we can go pick something up."

"I'm not gonna make you pay for our dinner," he whispered. "That's not your responsibility."

"I don't mind," she replied in the same hushed tone. "I'm hungry too. Come on, let's just go up to Corti and get something."

"All right," Timori relented. "But I need you to know that I don't ever expect you to pay for things for me."

"I know, Tim."

Racquela and Timori left the house, heading for the closest deli on Corti Street. They picked up a variety of sliced meats and bread along with some salad and pasta, and brought the lot of it back to Timori's house. It was fun preparing supper with Timori as he joked and stole kisses, even if clean dishes were hard to come by in the tiny kitchen. Timori insisted that he do most of the work himself, so Racquela busied herself teaching Carlotta and Nicola the words to her favourite songs.

Everyone ate around the kitchen table, and Racquela tried to ignore the fact that Timori's family didn't have proper table manners. After dinner they played guessing games, and then Timori told Carlotta that it was time for bed, much to her protestation. Nicola was sensitive enough to know that Racquela and Timori wanted time alone, so she busied herself with homework. Racquela and Timori went to Timori's room.

They began kissing immediately. Timori's kisses were insistent, and his hands began wandering farther than they usually did. Racquela enjoyed the extra attention, but she grew nervous about things progressing so quickly, so soon. Unbidden, thoughts entered her mind about the vision she had shared with Timori in the presence of the Great Crystal. She could still picture the child sitting between them on the linen. She was nowhere near ready for *that*.

Racquela grabbed Timori's hands and pulled away from a kiss to look Timori in the eyes. "Tim, wait. This is ... moving too fast," she said.

Timori nodded. "Sorry. I just ... I can't help myself. I love you, Racquela."

"I know, but I'm just not ready for ... you know. Not yet. I want it to be special, the first time. Don't you?"

Timori gave Racquela an affectionate kiss just below her ear. His face betrayed nothing, but she could see the disappointment in his eyes.

"Every moment that I spend with you is special, Racquela. I could wait a lifetime."

Racquela nodded, but she secretly wondered if what Timori said was true. She wondered, regretfully, when she would be able to say those three words back to Timori. Did she love him?

She certainly hoped so. They were going to be married in two years.

She and Timori talked until late in the evening, and Racquela knew that it was past her curfew but she also knew that her father tended to be lenient with her when it came to Timori. It wasn't long before Timori's eyelids drooped as they sat on his bed and talked. It had been a long day for both of them.

"I should get going," Racquela said. "You're falling asleep."

"Don't go yet," Timori insisted as he lazily tugged on Racquela's arm. "I never want to spend a minute away from you."

Racquela laughed. "You'll be asleep in minutes, Tim. Tell you what. I'll sing you to sleep, and then I have to go."

Timori made a sleepy smile and lay his head down upon his pillow. "That sounds nice," he mumbled. "Sing me your favourite song."

Racquela sat on the bed and stroked Timori's hair as she quietly sang to him.

Take me away, my love
To my city by the sea
Carry me home, my dear
To where nothing bothers me.
Though the road is long and dreary
My strength is by my side
Though the woods are dark and murky
I have my love, my guide.

Costimara.
Costimara.

Though the road is long and dreary
To my city by the sea
And the woods are dark and murky
No, nothing bothers me,
For soon I shall be home with thee.

Costimara.

Racquela looked down at her betrothed. Timori was fast asleep, sighing softly into his pillow.

Chapter 16

Jacoby never expected crystal-speaking to come easily to him, but it turned out to be even more challenging than empathy. If it weren't for Crystara's careful tutelage during their free time together, Jacoby had no doubt that he would struggle to keep up with the other students.

Jacoby's crystal-speaking instructor often allowed him to work with Crystara for team exercises. It was almost magical to Jacoby the way Crystara could manipulate and realign crystals, as though it were all child's play to her. Oftentimes she would demonstrate a technique before the teacher even finished explaining it.

One of the most challenging techniques was the 'double realignment'. One student would alter a crystal's properties without telling their partner what the alteration was, then the other student would have to return the crystal to its original state.

"Just remember the alignment in your mind," Crystara instructed Jacoby. They were holding hands as the crystal sat between them on the shared desk. "It used to be a light crystal. You know that alignment. It's the first one we learned."

Jacoby picked up the crystal in his hand and studied it. It had gone from a brilliant, incandescent yellow to a murky indigo. The new alignment was completely unfamiliar to him and incredibly complex. He had no idea how to speak to the crystal he was holding.

"I don't even know what kind of crystal this is," he admitted as he broke his focus. "How am I supposed to turn it back?"

Crystara shook her head. "You don't have to know, you just have to change it back to the original alignment. It's easy, watch."

Crystara grabbed the crystal out of his hand and muttered something under her breath. Instantly the crystal shone with its own light once more, and the indigo of the rock was swallowed up by bright yellow.

"See? Try again. Don't think about what it is, think about what it's supposed to be."

She handed Jacoby the crystal again. It had changed back to a deep blue without him even noticing.

"How do you do that?" Jacoby asked.

"Jake," Crystara said. "Focus. You're a good speaker, you just have no focus. Change it back to a light crystal."

"But what in the abyss kind of crystal is this?"

Crystara rolled her eyes and threw up her hands. "You don't listen to me. Just do the exercise. You have to know this for the test next week."

"Jova's sake, I'm just curious, Crys. It's not my fault you're way ahead of me." He folded his arms petulantly.

Crystara sighed. "It's an augmentation crystal. It augments the powers of other crystals in its vicinity. I can teach you how to make one later, Jake, but for now can we please just do the exercise?"

Jacoby looked at Crystara with surprise. "How did you even learn that? It's not in the textbook, is it?"

"I just taught myself," she said. "Focus, Jake."

Jacoby thought that he detected the hint of a lie, but his empathy didn't work very well on Crystara. He supposed it was because they were too close. Using empathy tended to distract him during crystal-speaking, as well, so he tried to tone it down. Still, he wondered if Crystara was doing extra reading at the library. She seemed to stay at the head of the class with minimal effort.

"Okay," Jacoby said. He looked at the crystal and focused on realigning it back to a light crystal. As he muttered the old Noven word for 'light', the crystal shattered in the centre and fell to pieces on his desk. The crystal's colour bled away and the shards that remained were clear.

"Oh, shatters," Jacoby exclaimed. He laughed. 'Shatters' was a common curse-phrase in Novem, but he remembered that the term had come from the very mistake that he had just made.

"You broke it completely apart," Crystara said with a frown.

"I know," Jacoby answered. "I couldn't figure out how to reconfigure that old alignment. Sorry, Crys."

Crystara shook her head. "That's fine. I'm just surprised you managed to shatter it completely is all. Usually the crystal just dies."

"So is that good or bad?" Jacoby asked as he gathered the pieces into a little pile.

"I don't know." Crystara picked up one of the fragments and studied it closely. "I'll have to ... look into it."

***

After the first month, empathy started to come more easily to Jacoby. A semester and a half of classes later, he felt as though an entirely new world had opened up to him. It was like he had been living in darkness for his whole life, and was seeing the sun for the first time. The true feelings that people held from each other were no longer a secret to Jacoby, and he often found himself using his empathy to gauge people's reactions or to ensure that he said exactly the right thing. It wasn't exactly like reading a person's mind, but the motivations of others began to seem obvious, and eventually Jacoby wondered how he ever lived without the skill.

He had used empathy to remain friends with Mariano, and had even convinced him to give Timori another chance. Jacoby often manipulated his parents by figuring out what they wanted to hear.

Empathy was especially useful when it came to Crystara. She often appeared to be upset or disinterested, but Jacoby had come to learn that it was merely his betrothed's countenance. Although initially Crystara had been difficult to read, at some point Jacoby had broken through her exterior and she had ceased masking her emotions around him. Her face remained a façade, as always, but Jacoby could always clearly feel her emotions. If anything, it had made them closer. There was an understanding between them that could not have existed without Jacoby's empathy. Crystara was never forthcoming with her own feelings.

Jacoby was not often paired with Crystara in empathy class because of their closeness. It was no longer a challenge for them to know what the other person was feeling. Instead, Miss Telmari split them up and used them to tutor the other students in the class who were experiencing difficulties. It also meant that Jacoby was rarely paired with Lenara, who was the other talented student in the class. Near the end of the second semester, however, Miss Telmari showed the class some more advanced exercises and wanted to see how far they could get, so she frequently paired Jacoby with Lenara.

Jacoby found it odd sitting across from Lenara. After the betrothals she had shut herself off and shied away from most people. Jacoby couldn't deny his continuing attraction to her, but he would never admit such a thing to anybody except Timori. He had no idea what Paulo would do if he was the jealous type, but conversations with other women turned into arguments with Crystara. She always seemed to know about it when Jacoby talked to a girl, even when he had nothing to feel guilty for.

Talking with Lenara didn't make Jacoby feel guilty, but it did make him sad. There was always a bit of melancholy mixed up in whatever Jacoby read from her emotions. As Jacoby sat across from her and tried to look in her eyes, Lenara sagged in her chair and stared at the floor. She was wearing a white flower in her hair that day, but the petals were drooping just like Lenara's shoulders.

The exercise was not normally challenging as far as Jacoby was concerned. They were supposed to speak about any subject they liked, but the object was to lie to the other person so that they had to use empathy to discern what the subject's true feelings were. Working with Lenara was nothing like it had been before the betrothals. Reading her emotions had become a lot more difficult.

"Um," Lenara said shyly. "You start, Jake."

"All right. How do you feel about school right now?"

"It's fine."

Jacoby closed his eyes to help him sense Lenara's emotions. Lenara was not projecting at all, which made things much more challenging for Jacoby. Whatever emotions she was hiding, however, had nothing to do with school. As far as he could tell, Lenara was ambivalent toward her studies. In other words, she was 'fine'.

He raised an eyebrow. "You're not lying," he accused. "Let's try another one. How do you feel about ... me?"

Lenara's eyes opened wide. Jacoby used the surprise to quickly sort through her emotions, but whatever Lenara was feeling was hidden well.

"I hate you, Jake," she said with a smile.

Jacoby laughed. "Well, I have a hard time believing that, but you're really good at blocking when you want to. I'm gonna have to try a lot harder. Your turn."

"All right. How do you feel about ... Crystara?"

Jacoby swallowed hard and tried to think of a lie. How did he *not* feel about Crystara? Was it love? Not yet. Was it infatuation? Perhaps, but he also had an infatuation for Lenara. Jacoby struggled between feelings of being stuck and being ecstatic as a betrothed. Crystara was very loving but very jealous and required a lot of Jacoby's attention, more than he was willing to give sometimes. As Jacoby sorted through his feelings, it occurred to him that he felt a variety of highs and lows with Crystara.

"I haven't decided," he whispered, too quietly for anybody but Lenara to hear.

Lenara smirked. "Neither of us is doing this exercise properly," she said. "I'm trying to block you. You, on the other hand, never have any idea how you feel about anything, so you have no idea how to make up a lie. How are we ever supposed to discover the truth?"

Jacoby shrugged. "This is a stupid exercise. I'd rather just be honest."

As he put his hands down, his fingers accidentally brushed Lenara's and they both pulled away suddenly. Jacoby quickly used the opportunity to try again to read Lenara before she could put up a barrier. He finally delved beyond the melancholy front of Lenara's emotions to discover a deep sense of guilt, mingled with affection. Lenara's emotions seemed to be murky and complex, but he was certain that Lenara felt guilty about something that she never spoke of. Jacoby was also certain that he hadn't misread the sense of affection she had for him.

Jacoby looked her in the eyes. As Lenara blushed, she dropped her gaze to the floor and ran a hand through her chestnut hair. As she did, the flower fell out and landed between Jacoby and Lenara on the desk.

"We're not very good with honesty," she said. "We're both good at hiding things, in our own way. Maybe we aren't a good pairing for this exercise."

"What makes you think we aren't a good pairing?" Jacoby asked.

"We just don't work well together," Lenara replied. As she said it, Jacoby knew that it was a lie. He wondered if Lenara was pushing him away because they worked *too* well together. Jacoby glanced over at Crystara, a few desks away, to find her glaring at him.

***

Crystara had come over to Jacoby's that evening for supper. Afterward they studied crystal-speaking together in the living room. Spare crystals were incredibly expensive, so they simply went through the textbook together.

Crystara had been almost completely silent for the entire day, ever since empathy class. She didn't want to hold Jacoby's hand and didn't even say thank you to Jacoby's parents during dinner. She barely even ate. Instead she sat at the table in sullen silence and moved a mound of rice around her plate with her fork.

It hadn't taken Jacoby long to figure out what her problem was. A quick read of Crystara's emotions told him that his betrothed was angry because she thought that Jacoby had been flirting with Lenara. When Jacoby thought about it, he supposed that he had been flirting a little bit, but it had been completely harmless. He was betrothed to Crystara, after all, and nothing could change that.

Lenara was just interesting to talk to because she was the only person whose emotions were still mysterious to Jacoby, and they tended to find a lot more to talk about than he and Crystara did. Jacoby tried to avoid thinking about what things would have been like with Lenara instead of Crystara whenever his betrothed was around.

Jacoby avoided the issue for as long as he could, but Crystara's mood was like a dark cloud over Jacoby's entire evening. He tried to cheer her up in other ways by making her laugh or giving her kisses, but Crystara would have none of it. She wouldn't even answer Jacoby's questions about crystal-speaking. Jacoby tried to think of another tactic.

"Hey, Crys, remember today when you said that you would teach me about that augmentation crystal? Why don't we do that?"

Crystara's eyes never left the page of her textbook. "We don't have any crystals," she mumbled. "Later."

"Well, you could just explain it for now," Jacoby suggested.

He inched closer to Crystara and put his arms around her. She didn't budge or respond. "Come on, Crys. Talk to me. What's bothering you?"

"You know damn well what," Crystara said coldly. "Or you could just use your damned empathy and find out."

Jacoby pulled away from the awkward embrace and stared long and hard at Crystara. "It doesn't mean anything, Crys," he said. "I was just trying to be nice to Lenara and get her to open up for the exercise."

Crystara stood abruptly. "So you were flirting with her!" she accused. "You knew all along what I was upset about, Jake, and didn't say a godsdamned thing!"

Jacoby cringed. His parents were upstairs and could probably hear everything. "Please, Crystara, keep your voice down."

"No!" she screamed. "How am I supposed to trust you when you flirt with other girls, Jake? Tell me that!"

Jacoby tried to keep his voice calm, hoping that Crystara would follow suit. He didn't want to think about the conversation he would have to have with his parents later about the argument.

"We're betrothed, Crys. I made a promise to you and I intend to keep it." He pointed to his crystal engagement ring.

"That doesn't mean anything," Crystara countered. "It's your actions that matter, not your words. I'm going home, Jake. I don't want to talk about this right now."

Crystara grabbed her textbook and left Jacoby's house, slamming the door as she went. Jacoby was angry enough with Crystara's unreasonable behaviour to consider just letting her go, but he didn't like to leave things unresolved. He followed after her.

Crystara was halfway down the street by the time Jacoby had his shoes on and was out the door. The early evening stars were hidden by clouds, and Crystara's shadow was long in the crystal lamplight.

"Haven't my actions spoken for me already?" he called after her.

Crystara wheeled around. "Not when you flirt with other girls. Stop talking to Lenara. Promise me you will."

Jacoby ran up to Crystara. "What if I get paired with her again in class? I can't help that, Crys. You can't expect me never to talk to any girls except for you, ever."

Jacoby reached out to Crystara with his empathy to help him figure out how to calm her down. He was surprised by what he found: fear.

"Crys ... I'm sorry if I flirted a little, but I don't understand why you're so upset. I made a promise to you, and I've kept it so far. What are you afraid of?"

Crystara began to cry. She stood there in the street as a light rain began to fall. Jacoby put his arms around her and she didn't pull away. He felt so many more emotions from her then: feelings of guilt at not being more confident about Jacoby, feelings of insecurity, and, underneath it all, a fear that Jacoby finally understood, something that underpinned everything Crystara said or did. With her walls down, it was amazing how much Jacoby was able to feel from her.

"Losing you, Jake. I'm afraid of losing you. There are so many girls out there who are prettier than me, and you smile more when you talk to them. I'm afraid that it's only a matter of time before ..."

"Shh," Jacoby said. He kissed Crystara's forehead and held her tight. "That won't ever happen. I promise."

As Jacoby said the words, he remembered Lenara's accusation earlier that day. She had told him that he wasn't a very honest person. Jacoby had made a promise to Crystara, but he hadn't thought about whether or not he was being honest until after the words had already left his mouth.

Jacoby pondered his promise to Crystara until he went to sleep that evening. He was afraid that he was only telling Crystara what she wanted to hear to make her happy. Was it all right to lie if the truth was something that another person couldn't handle? How could Jacoby promise to Crystara – to anybody – if he didn't know what the future would bring?

Chapter 17

There is no doubt in the minds of anybody who witnessed Maximus Longoro and Lucrezia Bianca together that their love was more than just a public display. Although marrying a commoner was a brilliant political move, every memoir and biography written by family, friends and political allies speaks of the adoration and affection that the couple showered upon each other, and I personally remember how fully with child the young bride was at the public parade that followed their wedding.

The nation seemed to be gripped by a fever of love for the young couple, and everywhere they went, parties were thrown in their honour. The people couldn't get enough of the president and his wife, and the president and his wife couldn't get enough of each other. As Rosso relates, 'They had eyes only for each other, Longoro and his wife. At every public function, they often had to be reminded by others that photographs were being taken, for fear that their constant kissing would be seen as indecent. Longoro declared openly that he did not care, and soon all the young couples of Novem were kissing in public, while the senior citizens shook their heads.'

Posco, meanwhile, was left to his own devices. He was practically ignored by Longoro, whose love for his wife left him disinterested in politics entirely. Like any good puppet master, however, Posco knew how to make the best of a bad situation. Longoro was signing anything that Posco passed through the senate, and Posco 'was perfectly happy to play second fiddle', according to Casto, 'while he laid the true foundations of the empire.' Posco knew, as always, that the beloved figurehead was needed for their plans to be successful. Novens would never give up their freedoms to a pudgy second son like Posco, but most of us gave them up readily to Longoro.

The birth of Anastasia in 1861 furthered the rift between Posco and Longoro and the president spent an increasing amount of time with his family. Public appearances were more frequent after the arrival of the baby. As Casto put it, 'Lucrezia and Anastasia consumed his life, and I had never seen him happier.'

Meanwhile, the economy was crumbling further. The national debt was rising. Lowering taxes made the NSP popular and increased trade, but it also ruined the national budget. Cutbacks to public services angered everyone, commoners and nobles alike, and faith in Novem's favourite son began to fade. Due to Novem's relative poverty and Posco's hatred of capitalism, the vice-president saw only one option for Novem's future: total state control.

All Posco needed was to bring back the spark of ambition in his best friend.

***

34 Yuna, 1875

To my brave hero Julio,

Word reached us today of the victory at Vadon! How brave you must have been. I know now that the gods are indeed with us, and my faith in the empire has been restored. It must have been spectacular to take the enemy by surprise and effect so swift a coup after so long a siege. You must have been so relieved to be able to sleep and have a good meal and a bath again, especially given the tone of your last letter. I'm not as prudish as some women, but still your words shocked me, I'll admit. I understand now how hard this war must be on you. All of my love and comfort are yours if you need them, as always.

The rumour is that every soldier will receive a medal for their part in the battle. I hope that perhaps you'll get a promotion as well, but that might be romantic and wishful thinking on my part.

I'm sure that you'll be given some leave soon, at least that's what they say about the heroes of Vadon, and I can't wait to see you again, love. The summer has been mild and sunny, and my days at the factory seem so much easier knowing that you'll be coming home to me soon.

Congratulations, my darling soldier. I anxiously await your return to my arms.

Ramona

***

It was difficult for Julio to be bitter about the battle of Vadon Hill when he was in the presence of Ramona, despite feeling undervalued compared to his compatriots. Largo was promoted to corporal for his bravery in leading the charge, and Roberto received a promotion to sergeant for masterminding the tunnel project that turned the tide of the siege. Pietro was promoted to captain for his brilliant use of crystals that had crippled enemy defences: scattershot charges detonated remotely using paired crystals operated by Pietro himself. Julio was proud of the boy who had become the leader of B Company in his battalion, but he was worried for him all the same. Pietro was growing up too quickly. As a lad of only seventeen, he was in command of two hundred men.

All Julio had received for his part in the battle was a medal, but still he was not bitter. He was home.

Julio and Ramona walked hand-in-hand under the sunlit canopies of black birch and whiteoak trees in Avati Hill Park. Julio had made love with Ramona that morning, then he had visited the factory to ensure that Ramona's supervisor, a squat man who carried an odd smell, wouldn't bother her anymore. Julio had felt manly watching the supervisor grovel before him, apologizing profusely for any 'misunderstanding' he might have caused, but later he felt guilty for intimidating the small man. Julio was no fearsome soldier, in his own eyes. He had felt better about it after Ramona thanked him with a passionate kiss once they had left the factory.

After meeting Roberto and Pietro at a café on Corti Street for lunch, Julio and Ramona made their way up the hill and basked in the summer sunshine and each other's love. It was a perfect day.

225

"He's a sweet young thing, your friend Pietro," Ramona quipped as they passed by a cluster of men in black imperial uniforms. "So polite."

Julio laughed. "In the company of women he's polite. Pietro's a good friend. He seemed quite taken with you. He told me that your picture did no justice to your beauty."

Ramona blushed. "He's nice to say such things. I think he longs for a girl of his own."

"He does," Julio agreed, "although if he's going out carousing with Roberto tonight, he's apt to find the wrong sort."

Ramona stopped at a wrought-iron bench to rest her feet. Julio sat beside her, never letting go of her hand.

"Roberto is far less polite," Ramona noted. "Maybe we shouldn't have left Pietro in his company."

Julio smiled. "He'll be fine. Rob might be brash, but he looks out for the boy, unlike Largo. Besides, call me selfish, but I want to keep you all to myself while I'm here." He gave her a playful kiss on the cheek.

"Largo. You don't talk about him much in your letters anymore. I wonder if I'll ever even meet the man. Has Pietro replaced him?"

Julio shook his head. "Not exactly, but Largo and I have a ... quieter understanding than Pietro and I do. He, like me, could not be pried away from his lady love during vacation for all the crystal in Novem."

Ramona gave Julio a long kiss on the lips. "Are you sure, love? That's a lot of crystal."

Julio shook his head. "The only crystal that I care about is the one that will be on your finger someday soon."

Ramona touched Julio's cheek tenderly with her hand. "Oh, love, a crystal ring? I don't care about expensive things. I just want you to return safely home from this war to me."

Julio kissed Ramona on the forehead. "I will do everything in my power to ensure that you have both, Ramona. You deserve more than I could ever give you."

Chapter 18

Master Vellize let his cane rap loudly against the side of Jacoby's desk. Jacoby jerked his head up. He was copying the last of the notes for the day before heading out to football practice and hadn't even been aware that his teacher was still in the classroom.

"You've been slacking," Master Vellize said, more as a statement than an accusation. Jacoby had grown accustomed enough to Vellize's gruesome face that it no longer seemed threatening. His teacher appeared more concerned than upset.

Jacoby nodded hurriedly and craned his head around the Master so that he could read the chalkboard. "I've been busy," he said absentmindedly. "School work is piling up, plus football practice is almost every day now."

Out of the corner of his eye, Jacoby saw Master Vellize nodding.

"It's nearing the end of the year. Studies always get intense, especially at a school like Central. However, Jacoby ..." Master Vellize positioned himself right in front of Jacoby and waited until he had Jacoby's attention. " ... you seem to have lost some of your focus. Care to let me in on what's going on? I hate to see bright students struggling."

Jacoby hesitated. He had grown quite fond of his history teacher, but he wasn't certain that he wanted to unburden all of his concerns upon him, most of which revolved around Crystara.

"You did warn me about betrothal, Master, and it's ... it's not that I'm miserable. I guess I'm just having doubts, probably the kind that all people have in relationships. However, you told me once that my heart will betray me, if I let it. I still haven't quite figured out what you meant by that statement, but I think about it often."

Master Vellize nodded. He seemed to understand. Instead of replying, he limped back over to the desk at the front of the class and pulled a large book out of a drawer. Under the crook of his arm, he brought the book back over to Jacoby's desk and let it fall onto the surface with a loud thump that seemed to satisfy him.

The book was thick but designed simply in a black jacket with a silver eagle on the cover that Jacoby recognized as the symbol used by the Second Empire. Jacoby looked at the title: *The Rise and Fall of the Second Empire* by Master Julio Vellize. He gazed up at his history teacher.

"I had no idea you wrote a book, Master."

Master Vellize nodded. "I don't really talk about it much, but my colleagues like to. It's a definitive work about the Second Empire, Jacoby. I know you love history, but I can also tell that you're more concerned with other things in your life right now. This might ... rekindle your interest in this class, since it deals with subject matter that we're currently studying. Plus it might give you an advantage in understanding some of the material we've been looking at concerning the Great War. Just don't tell the other students that I lent this to you."

Jacoby ran his hand over the cover, which was faded and well-worn. Jacoby realized that he was likely holding a first edition, possibly even Master Vellize's first copy. He promised himself not to damage the book.

"I don't understand, though. What does this have to do with hearts and betrayal, or were you just trying to change the subject?"

Master Vellize winked. "You'll understand when you read it, I think. The hearts of men betray them in more than just matters of women, and the Second Empire was quite a romance between its leaders and the people of Novem."

Jacoby opened the front cover to reveal a map of Titania, which was half-obscured by a stack of hand-written letters that had been pressed between the cover and the book's pages. Jacoby examined the top letter, which was dated the 16th of Octobra, 1874. He looked up at his teacher, who was rubbing something out of his eye.

"Oh. I completely forgot that those were in there. Um ... maybe I should take those."

"I'm sorry," Jacoby said as he carefully grabbed the stack of letters and handed them to his teacher. Jacoby felt a sense of sorrow coming from Master Vellize. "I'm sure they're private."

"They are." Master Vellize said with a sad nod. He stared at the letters in Jacoby's hand. "Although ... perhaps you should ... No, no that's probably not a very good idea. Then again ..."

He pushed Jacoby's hand and the stack of paper away with his hook. "Give those a read, too. They are private, but you're not the first person to read them. I think you might learn a lot more from those letters than the book even, Jacoby."

"Are they letters you wrote, Master? During the war?"

Master Vellize nodded and looked out the window. "Give them a read, as well as the book, and then come and talk to me. If you're still having doubts then about love or anything else, I'm sure that we'll have plenty to talk about. You should get going to football practice, Jacoby, shouldn't you? Oh, and I'll gut you with my hook if you lose that book or any of those letters."

He had said it with a smile, but Jacoby could tell the letters and the book were more important to Master Vellize than anything else in the world. Jacoby wondered why somebody would ever lend something so intimate to another person. He had never sensed any *emotion* from Master Vellize before that moment.

Jacoby left the classroom and went to fetch his football uniform from his locker. As he pulled out his gym bag and carefully placed the book Master Vellize had lent him on the top shelf, he heard raised voices coming from around the corner of the hallway. They sounded familiar. Jacoby quietly closed his locker and crept closer, hoping to catch a bit of the conversation.

"... don't see why we can't just *pretend* we're a normal couple." It was a female voice.

"I said no." The male voice was deep and resonant. "I have no interest in spending time with those people, or making more of this farce than I already have, unless you've changed your mind about pretending when nobody else is around, too."

Jacoby heard feet shuffling, and then the sound of a sharp smack and lockers rattling.

"Ow," said the male. "You're lucky I don't hit women or you would regret that."

"I already regret this whole relationship."

Jacoby realized that he was listening to Lenara and Paulo. He closed his eyes and reached out with his empathy to see if he could glean more about the argument. He wanted to peek around the corner, but he didn't want to risk being caught eavesdropping.

"Regret? We didn't have any choice in the matter, Lenara."

Jacoby's hair stood on end when he tried to feel Paulo's emotions. The boy wasn't even angry. He was just ... cold.

"If I could've found a way out of this legally, I already would have."

"If we don't have any choice, can't we just play along?" Lenara pleaded. "What are people going to think if we don't at least pretend?" Emotions were pouring out of her, too quickly for Jacoby to sort through them all. "If I refuse Racquela's invitation again, she's going to start to suspect something, and nobles are notoriously nosy."

Although Jacoby knew he had much more to learn about empathy, he was glad to know that he was skilled enough to sense somebody's emotions from a distance. Jacoby felt a mixture of guilt and satisfaction when he realized that Lenara didn't have much affection for Paulo. It made him feel even sorrier for her. She must have been trying hard to make things work. As Paulo had pointed out, they didn't have a choice in the matter.

"What does it matter what anybody else thinks?"

Jacoby was starting to feel something from Paulo – it was like frustration and determination mixed together.

"None of this dirt is important at all. Finishing school, relationships, betrothals ... You're caught up with society's bullshit. You can go ahead and spend all the time you like with the other dullies who bow to that big fake piece of rock and let a defunct church decide their lives for them. I have more important things to do."

Jacoby heard footsteps. He crept back to his locker and pretended to busy himself with the lock. Paulo came around the corner.

"Shouldn't you be at your pointless male bonding ritual?"

Jacoby held up his gym bag. "On my way. How are you, Paulo?"

"Don't pretend you care, Jacoby."

Paulo produced an apple from his school jacket pocket and took a bite. Jacoby fought back a scowl. As Paulo walked away, Jacoby picked up his bag and walked around the corner of the hallway to see if Lenara was still there.

She was gone, but the scent of flowers lingered in the air. Jacoby breathed it in and wondered how Paulo could possibly be cruel to a girl like Lenara.

Chapter 19

"He's just so ... needy," Racquela complained to Crystara during lunch. The two girls were eating sandwiches in a vacant classroom. Ordinarily they ate outside together, but it had been a wet spring. Crystara liked being outside in the rain, especially on foggy days like this, when it seemed to come from all around like a mist, but she knew she would never hear the end of it if Racquela's clothes got ruined.

Racquela rarely sat with her old highborn friends anymore. The betrothals had set them apart. Everyone looked at them differently, and although Racquela professed to be struggling with her new identity as a 'betrothed', she didn't seem to miss her old friends much. Mostly she and Crystara would spend time together, or with Jacoby and Timori. Apart from Racquela's and Timori's occasional bickering, it was more fun when it was just the four of them. They invited Lenara and Paulo out sometimes, but the couple was reclusive. Paulo rarely even attended classes, and Lenara often claimed to be ill.

Crystara could have cared less about Paulo and Lenara, however. She had her best friend and her betrothed. She had never been happier.

"What do you mean, needy?"

"He just ... well, anytime I so much as talk to another boy, sometimes even Jake, he gets all misaligned and jealous about it. I try to explain that I'm just talking, not doing anything else, but he won't even listen." Racquela took a dainty bite of her sandwich.

Crystara shrugged. A little jealousy was good for a relationship, in her opinion. It let the other person know that they were wanted. "He just wants reassurance that he's the most important person to you," Crystara explained.

"He is," Racquela said. She took a small nibble of her bread. "He has to be."

"Isn't this what you wanted?" Crystara asked. She had never told anybody Racquela's secret and she never would, but she could tell just from watching Racquela and Timori together that sometimes Racquela considered it a mistake. Racquela's relationship with Timori wasn't an easy one, and Racquela always liked things to be simple. As a highborn, everything had always come easily to her. Crystara understood Timori's jealousy perfectly well, from a less romantic viewpoint. Racquela had it all and valued none of it.

"Yes, this is what I wanted." Racquela said. Crystara wasn't convinced.

***

The guards and priests of the Old Temple were familiar enough with Crystara that she could pass them all by without being questioned when she came for her lessons with Keeper Orvin. She even knew some of the guards' names. She knew the layout of the temple, including the gardens, and could find her way to Keeper Orvin's office from the front, back and side entrances. The temple had become a second home to her. The idea of working for the church wasn't repulsive to Crystara anymore, but she would never give up her betrothal to Jacoby.

Nobody responded to Crystara when she knocked on Keeper Orvin's office door, which made the hair on her arms stand up. He was always in his office before she got there. Crystara knocked a second time and then tried the doorknob. It was unlocked. Crystara bit her lip as she cautiously peered inside the office.

It was empty.

"Hello?" she called out to the small space. She wondered if he was hiding under his desk, ready to test her by throwing some kind of unusual crystal at her. He had never done anything like that before, but it wouldn't have surprised Crystara too much.

"Keeper Orvin?"

As she approached the Keeper's desk, she noticed the back door that led to the Crystal Chamber was slightly ajar. Crystara's

233

pulse quickened. She had promised Keeper Orvin that she would not go anywhere near the Great Crystal without his permission, even though he admitted to her that she had the skill to bypass his crystal locks.

Crystara walked up to the door and peered through the crack. She could see a sliver of the Great Crystal through the door and a little piece of sky, but nothing else.

"Hello?" she said into the crack. "Keeper Orvin?"

There was no response. She knew that the prudent thing to do was to ask somebody where Keeper Orvin had gone, but she felt a subtle pull coming from the Crystal Chamber. It was calling to her again. She peered through the slit between the door and its frame. It looked inanimate. It made no sound, and it was as clear as glass, but she could *feel* it pulling her in.

Crystara pushed the door open, just a little bit, enough to poke her head in and look around.

She saw Keeper Orvin lying on the floor of the chamber with his eyes closed. The Great Crystal looming beside her was suddenly forgotten.

"Keeper!" she cried out. She ran up to him, fearing the worst. He was breathing. Crystara shook him until his eyes fluttered open.

"Crystara," he said as he smiled. It seemed to take him a moment to figure out where he was, until he looked behind Crystara at the Great Crystal. "You didn't touch it, did you?"

She shook her head. She was so relieved that she could feel tears forming.

"Good," he replied as he sat up. "You're ... not ready yet."

Crystara helped Keeper Orvin to his feet. "What were you doing in here?"

"The Great Crystal gave me a vision, Crystara." His voice was grave as he led Crystara back to his office.

"What was it about?"

Keeper Orvin slumped into his chair. He looked as though he hadn't slept in days. "It was about you."

Crystara felt her legs turn to jelly. She sat down across from her mentor. "And?"

"And the vision was about you, not *for* you."

"That's not fair." She folded her arms.

Keeper Orvin held his hands against his temples. "I might get you to fetch me some tea in a minute. What a headache. Life isn't fair, Crystara, I'm sure you've figured that out by now. The Great Crystal isn't ready to speak with you yet."

"Then why do you keep warning me never to touch it?"

Keeper Orvin paused. Crystara wondered, not for the first time, what secrets Keeper Orvin kept from her about the Great Crystal.

"Because when you touch that crystal, it will communicate with you, whether you and it are ready or not."

***

Summer was in the air and the weather was warming up, so Crystara and Timori walked up the hill to meet up with Jacoby and Racquela at the park for their double date. Crystara was glad that Racquela's parents were finally allowing her to go out unchaperoned. It opened up new possibilities for places to go in the evenings. Timori had spent the whole walk up the hill talking about Racquela, which Crystara found inane, but she said nothing about it. So long as she didn't have to do much talking, she could tolerate any topic of conversation.

As the sun went down, the quartet made their way to Leo's, a restaurant almost exactly halfway down the hill to Avati Valley. Conversation was lively, and although Crystara didn't say much she loved listening to the other three, except when Jacoby and Timori started talking about football.

They shared big bowls of pastas, bread and salad, and, despite her protests, Crystara was secretly relieved when Jacoby and Timori paid the bill. She knew that Timori had picked up a job as a cook in the evenings, mostly to buy things for Racquela that she didn't really need, and between his work, school and football he was starting to look ragged. Crystara felt sorry for him. She hoped that Racquela realized just how much Timori did for her, even when he no longer had to try to win her affections.

Swing dancing at the cabaret came next, and even though Jacoby was a terrible dancer, he made up for it by being fun company. Timori had his usual small fit of jealousy when other boys showed an interest in Racquela, but other than that, the evening of dancing went well. Crystara only wanted to dance with Jacoby, so she was relieved that not many other boys asked her to dance. It didn't surprise her. There was a stigma attached to blondes, after all.

After dancing, Racquela insisted that she had to go home for curfew, which Crystara knew was a code for 'no longer having fun'. Usually it meant that she and Timori were fighting about something. Timori insisted on walking Racquela home, so Crystara and Jacoby said goodbye to the pair and began to walk back to Crystara's house. She wished that her father wasn't home that evening. It would have been a perfect time to take Jacoby inside.

"What's wrong?" Jacoby asked as they strolled slowly down the glistening lane. It had rained while they were in the cabaret, and Crystara wished it would start up again.

"Nothing's wrong," Crystara insisted.

"Oh. You just ... you look mad, like something's wrong."

"I always look that way."

She didn't know how to explain it to him other than that. People always misinterpreted her, thinking that she was angry or something similar. She was surprised that Jacoby's empathy hadn't seen through her façade as it usually did. Jacoby fell silent after her reply, and they walked together hand-in-hand in silence for a time. Jacoby seemed to be searching for something to say. Crystara was fine just walking quietly with him.

"Boy, Timori sure was getting jealous tonight," Jacoby finally exclaimed.

"That was understandable. Racquela gets too flirty sometimes."

"Do you think so? She's just being nice to people, I think. Timori has nothing to worry about."

"Oh, really?" Crystara folded her arms and stopped walking. "How would you like it if I twirled my hair and batted my eyelashes at every boy I saw? Wouldn't you get jealous?"

Jacoby shrugged. "Well, maybe a little bit, but ..."

"A little bit? Jake, do you even care about me at all? A little bit?"

It occurred to Crystara that she was yelling. A part of her didn't care. How was she supposed to make him understand why she and Timori got jealous? Could she say, as she had already done so many times, that she was afraid of losing him, even though they were betrothed legally?

"Of course I care about you," Jacoby said as he put his arms around her. "I just don't think that Racquela is doing anything wrong, is all."

Crystara snorted. "You wouldn't. You kissed her when you knew that Timori liked her. You and Racquela are just so ..."

Jacoby pulled away. "She told you about that? Does Timori know?"

Crystara gritted her teeth. All Jacoby was concerned about was how good a person he appeared to be, not about Crystara's feelings or even his best friend's.

"How the fuck should I know if Timori knows? Why don't you ask your precious Racquela? You talk to her more than me anyway."

Crystara could feel tears stinging her eyes. She looked away from Jacoby.

"Crystara, don't ... don't say that," he cooed. "Look, it happened before the betrothals. That's all it was, was a kiss. I promise. I'm with you now."

He put his arms around her again. This time she melted into him a little bit. All that she needed was a little reassurance, nothing more. So long as Jacoby understood that, there was no need to argue.

Crystara wiped away her tears with a sleeve and kissed Jacoby on the lips. Nothing reassured her more than physical closeness. It was the one thing that she had always lacked in her life.

"Jake ... I don't want to go home yet," she said softly. "Let's go for a walk in the park, okay?"

Jacoby smiled. "That sounds like a great idea."

They went back up the hill, but to Crystara the climb was worth it. Avati Hill Park was sometimes a dangerous place at night, but danger was a part of the fun to Crystara. She and Jacoby wandered through the trees and across the damp grass, talking of school and crystal-speaking, of their fellow betrothed and of summer plans.

Crystara found a secluded spot with a cluster of trees and shrubs. She stopped walking. She couldn't take Jacoby home, but there were still ways to get more physical. She could tell that Jacoby wanted it, too, even if he hadn't said so out loud. Crystara started kissing Jacoby passionately. He held her fiercely and kissed her back.

After a few minutes of kissing and hands exploring, Crystara summoned her bravery and let her hand dip below his belt. Her heart was beating madly, but she could have sworn she could feel Jacoby's heartbeat through her chest as well. Jacoby hardened in her hand, through his slacks.

Crystara stood up on her tip-toes to whisper in his ear. "Jacoby ... I want you. Let's take this farther. We are betrothed, after all."

Jacoby looked around nervously, but Crystara could see the excitement in his eyes. "What ... here? In the park?"

Crystara wished that Jacoby was more aggressive. "Where else are we gonna get the chance? Nobody can see us. Just lie down in the grass with me, and let's ... see what happens."

Slowly, she led Jacoby down to the ground on top of her, kissing him all the while. The grass was wet and cold, but when Crystara shivered and her skin made goosebumps she just pressed herself closer to Jacoby to stay warm. As Jacoby kissed her neck and fondled her breasts through her light cotton blouse, Crystara struggled to remove Jacoby's pants.

Awkwardly, passionately, hungrily, they made love.

Afterward they put their clothes back on in case anybody came by. They lay in the cool, damp grass, panting. It hadn't lasted long, but Crystara had been expecting that for her first time. Jacoby had spent most of their lovemaking focusing on her breasts. It was just like a teenage boy, she thought, but she hadn't actually minded. It had felt better than she expected it to, and all in all much less painful than she had been led to believe. Crystara knew that it would get better with time, and she was looking forward to many more times with Jacoby. Crystara had never felt so close to anybody in her entire life. She rolled over to look at Jacoby.

"I love you," she said. It was the first time that she had spoken those words since her childhood. She had promised herself a long time ago never to say them again to anybody, but Jacoby had made her believe that perhaps there was love in the world, after all. She waited a few moments for Jacoby's reply. It came later than she would have liked, but it still brought a tear to her eye when he said it.

"I love you too, Crystara."

She wanted to believe it.

***

"Where have you been?" Largo Mita roared. He was at the kitchen table, shirtless as usual. Crystara had hoped to sneak by him, but judging by the bottle of Faxon whiskey in his grubby hand he was waiting to pick a fight with her.

"Out," she said. She knew that no explanation would be good enough for him, so there was little point in elaborating.

"Out where? Out carousing with that no-good sleazy Jacoby kid again? Your clothes are all wet and your hair is a mess. What did he do to my little girl?" He slammed his fist down on the table as though it somehow proved that his opinion of Jacoby was correct.

"None of your godsdamned business, Dad!" she screamed. Instantly she was sorry that she had lost her temper. Crystara knew that Largo wouldn't stand for being yelled at by his own daughter. She wished that Jacoby would somehow hear the argument and come in to rescue her, but she had watched him walk away. He would be long gone up Corti Street. Besides which, he was too much of a coward to face Largo. Crystara flinched and prepared for the worst.

Her father nearly tipped the table over as he stood up. Although he stood on a drunkard's wobbly legs and was larger in the middle than in the shoulders, he still managed to frighten her. The memories of a little girl died hard.

"None of my business?" he shouted as he approached her. "You may be betrothed to that little sonofabitch, but you are still my daughter, living under my roof. Do you understand?"

He struck her hard across the face to make his message clear. Crystara clenched down on her teeth, refusing to give him the satisfaction of hearing her cry out in pain. He hit her again with the back of his hand and sent Crystara flying against the wall. She struck her face against the corner beam of the room and felt a tooth loosen. Crystara reminded herself that she was only stuck for a little while longer, before she and Jacoby were married and she was an adult able to live where she wanted to. She reminded herself over and over, as he hit her over and over.

***

After Largo had passed out from the bottle, Crystara spent some time checking her wounds. Racquela would have to help her with the makeup, especially the black eye. She didn't want Jacoby to know. He would be powerless to stop it, in any case. She was still a minor under her father's care, and as such she had to obey his rules or face the consequences. It had been her own choice to be out so late. Crystara was just glad that her loosened front tooth hadn't actually fallen out. There was no way that her father could afford any kind of dentistry.

240

Crystara could hear Largo snoring from his couch by the radio. Cautiously, she tiptoed across the hall from the bathroom to the master bedroom.

It was comforting, sometimes, to be in the presence of her mother's old things. Neither she nor her father visited the room often. Largo usually slept downstairs on the couch, and Crystara was forbidden from entering the room, so she went in when her father was out of the house or passed out.

There was a stale gloom to the chamber, a musty odour of decay and memories long gone to rot. Crystara remembered nothing at all of her mother. Her childhood memories had been pushed down and away, other than the occasional flashback of a beating from her father ... but those had all been the same, so they didn't make much of a difference. Anything before she was five years old was essentially lost to her. But the room sometimes made her feel as though she almost remembered something. It was the same as when she held her stuffed bunny close. No pictures, no thoughts ... but a smell and a feeling. It was like imagining being back inside of a womb, safe from the world and warm and protected by a maternal force.

For years Crystara refused to enter her mother's room despite her curiosity. Maria Mita had died in her bed, after all. When Crystara and her father had moved to the new house, Largo had painstakingly set up all of Maria's things exactly the way they had been in the old house, even though the woman had been dead for ten years. Crystara was wise enough to never ask Largo anything about her mother's death, but she sometimes wondered if he had been different before her mother had passed away. The more jaded part of her mind told her that he was probably as abusive to his wife as he was to his daughter. Crystara had decided that there were some things better left unknown, and some things better left untouched.

She used to look at the pretty baubles on the vanity and admire the yellowing doilies. Lately all she looked at was the wand.

It would have been so simple for her to whisper a word or two to the dark crystal perched atop the sleek grey piece of wood.

The wand would burn up in Largo's hand, or something similar, and be useless to him. Crystara could rework the crystal in such a way that the wand was only good to her, or another speaker who could undo her resonance. She didn't know if her father even remembered that there was a wand in the room, or if he had left it abandoned in the bedside table as another part of the museum of her mother.

One whisper, one shot ... and a sleeping giant would become nothing more than a sticky mess. Her hand reached out to touch it.

Downstairs, her father stirred. A whiskey sleep was a restless sleep. The sound of her father's movement jarred Crystara, and she exited the chamber as quickly and quietly as she could. She looked back at the wand before closing the door.

For the time being, Jacoby was a much better way out.

Chapter 20

"Last class we talked about the upheaval following the problems of the Fourth Republic," Master Vellize said. Timori sighed and Jacoby chuckled beside him. Jacoby loved history class. Timori didn't mind it as much as he used to, but he still preferred his other classes. He would take science and math over history any day. What practical applications did historical facts have, in comparison with crystal theory and calculus?

"With Emperor Longoro's rise in power, and his coup that effectively ended the Fourth Republic, Novem was once again under despotic law. With much of the continent still controlled by monarchs, this created a tense political situation as Novem was once again viewed as a threat to its fellow kingdoms and nations. Old alliances were torn asunder after the Second Empire was forged, which tipped the scales of balance. The Kingdoms of Nilonne and Milosa were still in the midst of a raging conflict, which made them ripe targets for Novem. A feud that had gone back and forth between Nilonne and Novem for centuries, which we discussed last semester, boiled over. The fresh armies of Novem marched into Nilonne without even bothering to officially declare war."

Timori leaned over to Jacoby. "Hey, can I borrow your notes for this later?" he whispered. "I'm doing a special project for engineering that I want to work on. This dirt is boring."

"Boring?" Jacoby whispered back. "Are you kidding me? This stuff is fascinating. I have an uncle who fought in the Great War ..."

"That's great, Jake," Timori muttered. "Notes? Yeah?"

"Fine, fine, just shut up and let me listen or your notes aren't going to be very good."

Timori nodded half-heartedly and pulled out his notes from engineering class. His project was to design a machine that used imbued crystals as catalysts for separating chemicals for industrial distillation. Doctor Ruveldi had told him that it was far more advanced than the material taught in class, and admittedly more advanced than anything taught to engineering students in finishing school, but he wanted Timori to give it a go and see what he came up with. Timori didn't need the flattery of his teachers to know that he was far more gifted intellectually than almost any student who came through Central School. After all, he was the only Central student who hadn't seemed lost and confused during the lectures at the junior engineers' conference.

Timori quickly grew frustrated with the formula he was working on. Something wasn't going quite right. His numbers weren't adding up and he couldn't get Racquela out of his head. The two problems were likely related. He pulled out a fresh sheet of paper. A poem might clear everything out of his head. Poetry always helped him to sort out his thoughts, especially when things weren't going well with Racquela.

He was worried about losing her, even though they were betrothed legally. A highborn like Racquela could always find a way out of something if she wanted to. The thought scared Timori sometimes. Most days, he felt as though he was fighting a losing battle. Not rich enough, not handsome enough. In the end, he knew, it didn't matter what the courts said. If Racquela wanted to find another lover, she would be married to him in name only. What weighed on Timori the most was whether or not he was pushing her away by trying to love her too much, too soon.

How could he not express his love for her, though? It wasn't a thing to be turned on and off at will, like a crystal light. He couldn't hold the force of his own emotions back from himself, so how could he shield another person from them? Did Racquela even understand the way that he felt about her? Were words, gifts and poetry enough?

"That's not right," a voice said in protest. Curious, Timori looked up from his blank sheet of paper to see what the fuss was about. Somebody had tried to correct the teacher. Timori looked around the room. Everybody was looking at one desk in particular. Within it sat Paulo.

244

"Paulo, I am teaching what I am told to teach. This is not a debate class. If you ..."

Paulo stood up. His face was red. "But you're telling the students lies!" he exclaimed. "Why would the leader of the Second Empire deliberately lead his own country to ruin? It makes no sense. He was trying to lead Novem to glory! He was trying to rebuild what had been lost after the fall of the First Empire."

Since Timori hadn't been paying attention, he had no idea what had been said before Paulo's outburst, but the discourse was intriguing.

"I told you, Paulo, this is what I'm teaching the class," Master Vellize said. His scarred face was turning red as well. "Perhaps you wouldn't feel so strongly about the glory of the Second Empire if you had been in those trenches almost two decades ago. Now you can sit down and listen, or you can leave."

Paulo pointed an accusatory finger at Master Vellize. "You're just creating more puppets for the republic who have no idea how to think for themselves. Fuck this class. I'm done with your lies."

Paulo stormed out of the classroom and slammed the door. The teacher took a long breath before continuing the lesson. He tried to act as though nothing had happened, but the murmurs spreading around the classroom bespoke a tension beneath the surface. Was the school portraying the fall of the Second Empire accurately?

"What on earth was that all about?" Timori whispered to Jacoby. "I sort of missed the start of it."

"Well," Jacoby said, "it seems as though Paulo is an Imperialist. Other than that, I couldn't tell you what his problem is."

***

Timori caught up to Racquela after football practice. He knew that she had been avoiding him lately. Racquela didn't make pretences for the way that she did things. Timori had to know why, and he had to know how to fix it.

"Racquela," he called out after her. She was heading down toward the front entrance of the school, probably to get picked up by her father.

She turned around with an exasperated expression on her face. "What? What is it, Timori?"

He was stunned. She had never been so curt with him before.

"Sweetheart," he said as he touched her arm lightly, "what's wrong?"

She pulled away from him. "What's wrong? You've been following me around like a lost child for the last three days, Tim. You ignore your schoolwork and even your best friend. We need time apart from each other sometimes. You have me, all right? We're betrothed. You don't need to follow me around everywhere. It makes me feel like you don't trust me and that you don't want me to do anything else other than fawn over you, like you do to me. Well, I don't want to be fawned over. I want ..."

"What?" Timori demanded. "What do you want? Just tell me and I'll do it."

"Space."

She held her books in front of her like a shield. "I want some space. This year has been really intense. I need some time to myself once in a while. I want to focus on my studies. I want to work on music, take some time for private lessons instead of going on dates all the time. We have our whole lives to spend together. Let me have some time to myself now."

Her words buzzed around in Timori's head. He was certain that there was something he was missing, something she wasn't saying.

"Why would you want so much space? You told me after the betrothal that it was the best thing that ever happened to you. Did that change?"

Racquela sighed. "Nothing has changed. Love ... isn't the only thing in the world, Tim. You need to see that. You can't just focus on me all the time or you're not going to amount to anything ...

and betrothed or not, I can't be with somebody who isn't going to amount to anything."

She turned to go.

"Where are you going?" he demanded, grabbing her arm more roughly than he intended to. Racquela pulled away indignantly.

"I'm going to my locker. Just leave me alone for a few days, Tim. Please."

Racquela stormed off.

Timori's face darkened. He was fooling himself if he thought that the problems he and Racquela faced would simply disappear after they were married. He was about to chase after her when the din of shouting from the football field drew his attention. Timori turned to see what the commotion was.

Boys in football uniforms were punching each other and some were wrestling on the field. Timori saw Jacoby and Mariano rolling around in the grass. Already itching for violence after his dismal failure with Racquela, Timori rushed to his best friend's aid.

Timori threw himself into the fray without knowing what the fight was about or who he was even supposed to be fighting, but there were about twenty boys from the football team punching each other and shouting things like 'dully' and 'picker'. Timori went for Filippo first, swinging like a boxer in the final round. Eventually he bloodied up the kid's face enough that Filippo shouted for mercy, so Tim got up off him and looked for another target. There were plenty of them to go around.

By the time Coach Lagheri came with enough other teachers to break up the fight, Timori had come out with only a lightly bloody nose. Jacoby had a puffy lip and a bruise on his cheek. The coach spent the next ten minutes berating everybody on the team, telling them how he wished he could suspend them all but he couldn't because then he wouldn't have enough members for the game on the weekend.

Timori tried to stifle a laugh at that part. Somehow half of the team had managed to engage in gratuitous violence without any real consequence, other than the 'threat' of suspension if it happened again. Timori knew that it would happen again, just as he knew that Filippo had likely been the ringleader of it all.

Timori and Jacoby headed toward the washrooms to clean up after they were dismissed from the lecture. He felt somewhat better after the fight, but he knew that he was no closer to a solution with Racquela. Not amounting to anything, indeed! Timori was the smartest kid in his class. She was using it as an excuse to pull away, and he had to figure out why or he was going to lose her.

"What started that one?" Timori asked as they made their way down the hallway to the lavatory.

"Oh, you know. Mariano called Louie a lowborn shoveller or something like that, and then fists started flying."

Timori shot Jacoby a look of surprise. "Over that? Why wasn't it just Louie and Mariano fighting?"

"Do you really have no idea what's been going on lately? The miners' strike?"

It all became clear to him: lowborn miners were striking because they weren't making enough money, which drove up the price of everything related to crystals, metals and coal, which put a further rift between the high-class and low-class at Central, because their parents would be on opposite sides of the issue.

Timori pushed open the door to the washroom. The scent of something burning reached his nostrils. He cautiously peered around the door, but there was no fire. Paulo was leaning against the countertop, smoking a cigarette. He didn't seem the least bit concerned that he had been discovered. Rather, there was a smug grin on his face. He looked like a framed poster-picture Timori had seen on Racquela's wall of the Commonwealth actor Frank Leicester. He, like Paulo, was a poster child for rebellion.

"Gentlemen," he said. He took a slow drag on his cigarette as the boys approached the sinks to wash away the blood and dirt. "Quite the fight out there."

"Yeah, thanks for all your help," Timori said. He turned on the faucet and splashed water on his face.

Paulo sucked on his cigarette languidly. As much as Timori found Paulo to be strange and pretentious, he somehow made smoking look shiny.

"Highborn aren't gonna change their minds just because you beat 'em in a fistfight." He said the words as though they were a part of some deep philosophy.

"You want my help? I need people. I'll pay you three times what you're making at that restaurant to come work for me. With that kind of dinari, maybe your feisty fiancée won't be ignoring you so much, hmm?"

Timori had Paulo up against the bricks in a flash, with Jacoby close behind. He held the taller boy by his school tie and had his fist ready for a punch.

"You don't know a fuckin' thing about her, dully," Timori spat. "Leave me the fuck alone or you'll wish you had."

Paulo calmly brought his cigarette up to his lips so that it was less than an inch from Timori's face, took a pull and blew a perfect smoke ring.

"And you don't know a godsdamned thing about me, either. There is nothing you can do to me that would scare me. Not in the least. Just ease up on my collar, and we can talk about this in a civilized manner. Obviously Racquela is a touchy subject for you. I can understand that. There's nothing easy about it when she's a highborn and you're a miner's son. No point in getting angry over facts. I'm not trying to piss you off. I'm just making you an offer. What do you say? You can work for me too, Jake, unless 'Class Action' has turned you into one of them already."

"He said to leave him alone," Jacoby insisted.

Timori eased up his grip on Paulo, but didn't let him go entirely. "You're a sixteen-year-old kid, and you're gonna pay me to work for you? That doesn't make a shard of sense."

Paulo smiled. "Meet me at midnight on Corti Street, right by your house, and I can explain all of it. You're under no obligation, just think about it. I promise you won't regret it, Tim."

Paulo shrugged off Timori's grip, put out his cigarette on the countertop and exited the washroom. Timori stood there for a moment, fist still raised.

Jacoby folded his arms. "That was weird. How does he know where you live? Are you going to meet him?"

Timori laughed. "Are you kidding? The guy's obviously cracked."

***

It was a new moon midnight on Corti Street. Timori stood under a streetlamp in his leather jacket and felt like a fool. It was only sheer curiosity that had made him show up ... and the possibility of actually making money.

Four shadows approached from the darkness of an alleyway. Timori stiffened. It could be Paulo, or it could be a gang. He was fully prepared to make a break for his house if anybody threatening came his way. As they came into the soft glow of crystal lamplight, Timori could make out Paulo's dark curls that framed his chiselled face. The other three were men, much older than Timori and Paulo, and rough-looking. They had the definite appearance of miners: soiled leather boots, brown overalls, thick beards and calloused hands. Each of them carried a bulky burlap sack over one shoulder.

Paulo smiled and shook Timori's hand. "Glad you could make it," he said in a low voice. Timori imagined that women found it sultry, given its deep rumble and confident timbre.

"This way." Paulo and the miners began walking down the street.

"Where are we going?" Timori asked.

"The river docks."

The Avati River had been an important part of Captus Nove's economy since the city's founding. Large enough to berth trade vessels, many seaworthy merchant ships travelled from other coastal ports up the Noven coast and into the Avati River to load and unload cargo in the heart of Captus Nove, the Avati district.

Although the invention of the motorcoach had lessened the burden on the naval mercantile trade, the river nevertheless remained an important part of Captus Nove's trade network, especially for raw, bulk materials such as iron, lumber and crystals.

Timori couldn't stop staring at the crystals as he and the miners took them out of the sacks, then packed and loaded them carefully into crates of fish. From the short wooden pier, one of the miners brought the crates onto a small fishing boat under the cover of darkness. Timori knew that what he was doing was illegal, but he was likely too far in to say or do anything about it. He could only imagine what kind of threats would be made if he tried to leave after witnessing crystal smuggling. Besides which, he really wanted the money. What he couldn't figure out was how sixteen-year-old Paulo was involved in smuggling, and why he appeared to be the boss of the miners. Timori knew that with patience he could discover the truth.

No stranger to physical labour, he hauled the heavy crates at the same pace as the larger miners. Nobody spoke as they worked.

Once the cargo was loaded onto the boat, Paulo went down to the hold and the miners each lit up a smoke as they sat on the edge of the pier. A man offered one to Timori, but he politely refused. He had read somewhere that some football players didn't smoke because it affected their game. Paulo returned and the boat left the dock in the dark without putting its lights on. Timori felt thrilled and dirty.

The miners bade a silent farewell to Paulo and Timori and disappeared into the night, leaving the boys alone together. Paulo lit up a cigarette of his own and began casually strolling up the docks as though nothing had just happened. He whistled as he walked.

"All right, you owe me an explanation at least, if I'm going to do something illegal without complaint."

"Relax, you'll get paid," Paulo said. "And if you want, there's more work like this coming up. It'll take up a lot less time than your restaurant job, too. I could use your help."

"Quit playing dumb, Paulo. I'm not doing anything else for you until I understand exactly how you know so much about me, and how you're involved in this kind of stuff. Those guys were taking orders from you."

Paulo nodded. "And I could find a lot more of them willing to work for dinari during the strike. I didn't ask you to come here because I actually need you to haul crates. I need an engineer."

"I'm a student."

Paulo kicked a small rock that was in his path into the river. "Right now ... but from what I've heard you're the smartest student that Central has seen in a generation. Someday you'll be the best engineer in the nation. That's why I want to help you now, so that you'll help me later."

"Help you what? Who exactly are you?"

There was either something that Timori was missing, or Paulo was delusional.

Paulo stopped walking. The façade of nonchalance was gone from the boy's face, replaced by something more serious, almost frightening. His eyes were cold and hard, his jaw set.

"I'm telling you all of this because I know that you don't give two shards about politics. You want a blissful future with your betrothed and you don't want to worry about money. I can help you get that, if you help me. Tell anybody, including Jacoby, what I'm about to tell you and ... well, why would you? No point in making threats, here. You need to understand what I'm up to if you're going to agree to help me. And I know that you will, Tim. I know it because I know that you'd do anything to keep Racquela. I can see it in your eyes, what it's like to be more passionate about something than even your own life. I feel the same way."

Paulo took a long drag of his cigarette before continuing.

"I'm working for people who want to see the lower classes given the respect that they are due, in short. You're familiar with socialism, yes? This disparity between the classes, it doesn't work anymore. This miners' strike is just the tip of the crystal. The republic screwed it all up after the Great War, not to mention the fact that Novem got blamed for the whole thing and our economy went to dirt. This class system, it's older than the five hills and people are

252

starting to realize that it doesn't work anymore. It's not fair and everyone knows it, but the people on top don't want to give up their money and power, because who would? Smuggling crystals is just the beginning. The miners are the ones making money, and the rich are suffering even more because they're not getting the goods. Sooner or later this whole thing will blow wide open."

"So you're trying to incite a revolt," Timori said.

He wondered if a revolution would truly change things for the better. There had already been four democratic revolutions in Novem's history, and the class system still remained. It wasn't as simple as changing the government. Timori knew that Noven society would have to be rebuilt from the ground up.

"That still doesn't explain exactly where you fit into all of this."

Paulo opened his mouth to reply, but sucked on the filter of his cigarette instead. He blew out smoke rings into the chilly air.

"I can't tell you. Not yet. Suffice it to say that if you help me, I can make sure that Racquela doesn't get hurt. There's no way a revolution isn't coming. This country is hurt too badly, and a lot of highborn and lowborn both are gonna die before it's all said and done."

Timori wondered what he was getting himself into. Was a revolution really approaching? He had never paid attention to those things, but perhaps it was the right time to start, especially if it meant that Racquela could be in danger. He knew that he couldn't really trust somebody like Paulo, but the offer of three times what he was making at the restaurant was too good to refuse.

"Just leave me out of your revolutionary dirt, and I'll help you do your other dirty work. Socialism is a nice idea, but I have more immediate concerns. I just want to do what's best for Racquela."

"Don't worry," Paulo answered. He flicked his cigarette butt into the river gracefully. "I'll help you do just that."

Chapter 21

The summer was bittersweet for Racquela. She had done well in her classes that year, so her parents took her on a vacation to their summer home in the tiny nearby kingdom of Los Maros. She was allowed to take one person along with her. Since she didn't relish the idea of spending most of the summer exclusively with Timori, she asked Crystara to join her.

The argument she had with Timori about the vacation had lasted for hours. In the end he relented, but Racquela knew he wasn't happy about it. She wasn't happy about it either. What exactly did Timori think that she was up to? It was a vacation with her parents and her best friend, but Timori treated it as though she were going to spend all of the time away with strange foreign boys. Racquela was tempted to do just that, to spite him.

Racquela did miss Timori during the vacation, but the sunny beaches and seaside restaurants made up for her longing. It was a chance to prove to herself that she could be happy without her betrothed, that she wasn't reliant on him. Racquela only wished that the opposite would hold true as well, but Timori always claimed, melodramatically, that he couldn't live without her.

Racquela and Crystara did sneak out at night to go dancing a few times, but they behaved themselves despite obvious interest from many boys, some of them of academy age. On their last night out, Racquela wondered if she always had more fun when Timori wasn't around. Such thoughts made her feel guilty and she put them out of her mind. She tried to think of all the times Timori had made her laugh or feel special.

Racquela's return to Captus Nove in late summer was met with an uncomfortable number of gifts from Timori. Did he still think that he needed to buy her affection? Crystara spent the remainder of the summer with Jacoby, which left Racquela with Timori unless she wanted to try and re-forge her failing friendships with Bella and Phebe. Timori came to visit her every day and often brought gifts, which made Racquela wonder how much time Timori was spending working at the restaurant. He came to see her so often that she had taken to disappearing early in the morning and finding new places to spend time. She re-discovered her love of romantic literature and borrowed many books from the library to read in the park. Racquela still spent time with Timori, but not as stifling an amount as he would have liked.

It was the second to last day of summer before school began again, and Racquela was reading a romance novel in the park under her favourite whiteoak. A shadow loomed above her suddenly, obscuring the words on the page.

"So there you are."

It was Timori. His arms were folded. He looked so tense, it frightened Racquela. "I've been looking all over for you."

"You've been following me?"

"You've been avoiding me," he accused.

Racquela tossed the hair out of her eyes and returned Timori's hard stare. "I'm allowed to have some privacy once in a while, Tim. We don't have to spend every waking moment together. There's plenty enough time for that once we're married."

Timori threw up his hands. "Oh, doesn't that sound just horrible? You had the whole summer having fun without me. I want to spend a bit of time with you now, and this is how you treat me?"

"Why not spend some time with Jacoby?" she asked, desperately trying to appease the situation. She had no idea what Timori was after, other than simply to be angry with her.

The blood rushed to Timori's face. "He's busy spending time with *his* betrothed! What a concept!"

"Tim, please stop yelling. What do you want?"

Timori relaxed his shoulders slightly and knelt down to be level with Racquela. His face had softened, but his eyes were no less intense. She tried not to flinch as he grabbed her shoulders.

"I want to spend time with you, my love. You're the only one who really matters to me. Please. Once school starts again we're all going to be busy with our studies and I'll also have football and

255

work. Can't you just spend some time with me, please? I just ... sometimes it feels like this is one-sided. I'm always chasing after you, trying to get your attention, while you're always pulling away. Prove me wrong. Show me that you care about this betrothal, that you love me. Please, Racquela."

There was a note of desperation in Timori's voice. Racquela could have found almost nothing less attractive, but what choice did she have? He had probably spent the entire morning looking for her. Some women may have found that romantic, but Racquela found it creepy. But her betrothed was right in front of her. There was no easy escape.

"All right, Timori. What would you like to do?"

"Whatever you want, my love."

All Racquela wanted to do was be alone.

***

"I can't fucking believe you!" Timori yelled. There were tears streaming down his face. Racquela had seen him angry before, and she had seen him cry before, but never at the same time. They were standing outside of the gates to Racquela's house where Timori had come to confront her. She could always flee inside if she needed to, and her father would not let Timori in if he yelled at Racquela or grew violent.

"Who told you about this?" she asked.

"That doesn't fucking matter." He practically spat the words. "I know it's true. I can't believe you would do this to me. I can't ..." he started to cry again.

"I didn't do anything to you! It was before we were even together, Tim! How can you accuse me of something that happened before the betrothals? I didn't do anything wrong!"

"Jake knew. He knew and he still did it, that dirty picker. My own best friend ..."

Racquela approached him cautiously.

"Tim, please. It was only a kiss, and it happened a long time ago, before we were together. Jacoby doesn't mean anything to me. You do. I love you, Tim."

She was surprised to hear herself say the words, but they were true. In spite of how much Timori smothered her, she still loved him. It was frustrating to know that love didn't make their relationship any less difficult, but it was something that she was willing to work on. Racquela had created her situation, and she had to live with it.

Timori put his arms around Racquela and sobbed into her shoulder. Racquela was overcome with emotion and started crying, as well. They held each other for a long time.

"Please don't be too mad at Jake," Racquela pleaded.

"We'll see," Timori sniffled. There was still a hint of anger in his voice, but there was nothing that Racquela could do about it since it was out in the open. The rest was between Timori and Jacoby. Racquela hoped that she hadn't ruined their friendship.

"Do you ... want to come in and have some tea?" Racquela offered.

Timori shook his head. "No, thank you. I have to get ready for work."

"This late at night? Is the restaurant even open?"

Timori smiled in a way that made Racquela suspect that he was lying.

"No, I've been helping out with cleaning at night, just to make extra money. I have to go, love." He kissed her on the lips. "We'll talk tomorrow. I'm sorry for getting so upset. It was just very shocking is all. But I understand. You're right, it happened before we were together and I have no reason to be angry about it. It's just jealousy. Anyway, I have to get going."

Timori started to walk briskly down the lane. Racquela raised an eyebrow as she watched him leave. Perhaps he'd lost his job and didn't want to admit it to her, but that didn't account for all the money he was still spending on her. Racquela turned and was about to go back inside when she noticed motorcoach lights shining at her.

The machine had the crystal engine running, and a lazy drift of smoke curled out of the rolled-down window. Racquela hurried up the steps to the gatehouse, but looked back at the motorcoach once she reached the door. Somebody had exited the vehicle and was walking toward her. She nearly screamed, but as the lean figure walked into the lamplight she realized that it was Paulo. He was wearing an expensive-looking brown suit and a fedora and was smoking a cigarette. Racquela found the whole look incredibly attractive on him. She had to remind herself how rude he usually was.

"What are you doing here?" she asked.

Paulo shrugged. "Just out for a drive. Do you have a moment?"

She knew in her gut that he was up to something, but Racquela was too intrigued to simply say no. "I have a few. What is it?"

Paulo gestured toward the motorcoach. "Let's go for a drive, actually. It's not too late for you, is it?"

Racquela looked back toward her house. She knew that her parents would say nothing to Timori if they saw her leaving at night in a motorcoach with another boy, but she would be disciplined heavily if she got caught sneaking around. It was just a simple chat, though, and a drive, she told herself. If she loved Timori and wouldn't do anything to hurt him, what could possibly happen?

"I have to be back in an hour, no later," she said.

Paulo nodded and led her over to the motorcoach. He opened the passenger door for her then got into the driver's seat.

"Cigarette?" he offered. Last year, Racquela had thought that smoking was disgusting, but in the summer at Los Maros *everybody* smoked, especially academy students. After a moment's hesitation, she accepted and let Paulo light her cigarette. He even made flicking a match look sexy. They drove.

Paulo chose the winding back roads of Avati Hill, those that coiled their way like serpents across the landscape of estates and old chateaus. Racquela wondered how Paulo could afford a motorcoach, and decided that it had to be his parents'. It occurred to her that she knew very little about the boy. She hadn't even known what social class he was until the suit and motorcoach made it obvious.

Five minutes of driving later, Paulo still hadn't said a single word to Racquela. She looked over at him nervously. "You ... wanted to talk?"

He pulled over to the curb and stopped the engine. "This is a good spot, nice and quiet. Yes, I did want to talk, Racquela. We haven't really talked much, have we?"

She shook her head, still wondering what Paulo was on about. For some reason, she kept staring at his lips. He was so much more handsome than Timori, and it was difficult to ignore that fact.

"It's a shame, really. Out of all of us, the betrothed, I feel like I know you the least ... although I do know a lot about you from talking to others, but who knows how well you can trust that kind of information, right? Anyway, I know about your situation from Timori especially, and I think I know a way that I can help you."

"You ... talk to Tim a lot?"

Paulo nodded. He lit up another cigarette and gave one to Racquela.

"All the time. He's a troubled boy, Racquela, like you wouldn't believe. I'm sure you see enough of it yourself, being betrothed to him and all, but it doesn't really end there. Did you know he's been thinking about dropping out, to make more money? For you?"

Racquela nearly dropped her cigarette. "What? He's never said anything of the kind to me. Are you sure about this?"

Paulo nodded with severity. "I am certain. He confided in me just the other night about it. He says that he's thinking about working the mines, because of the strike. It's good dinari."

Racquela fumed. "The dully. He's so smart. Doesn't he realize his best bet is to stay in school? He doesn't need to buy me

259

gifts, we're betrothed! And besides which, he'd be throwing away
..."

"A lot," Paulo interrupted. "But it's hard to explain that to
him. You have to remember, my dear, that he's seeing things from an
entirely different perspective. He's grown up dirt poor. Money
means everything to him right now, money and you. You have the
perspective to see what's best for him, but he's a lowborn going to a
highborn school and betrothed to a highborn girl. How is he
supposed to compete? Money is the great equalizing factor, but as
ambitious as Timori is, he's incredibly short-sighted."

"So ..."

Racquela took a drag on her cigarette to try and stay calm.
She was glad Paulo had told her all of the things he had. What would
she have done if Timori suddenly left school without her even
knowing?

"... What am I supposed to do? Convince him to stay in
school? He dotes on me, but he's stubborn as granite and won't
listen."

Paulo shook his head. He took a pull of his cigarette and
breathed the smoke out slowly through his nostrils. "The real
problem here is class difference. I've done a lot of research into past
cross-class betrothals, and let me tell you, Racquela, they usually
don't end very well."

"But they're chosen by the Great Crystal. How could they
not end well?"

Paulo shook his head. "Racquela, please. You're too smart to
act so naïve all the time. The betrothals are a machination of the
church, nothing more. An old tradition used as an excuse to mingle
the bloodlines of crystal-speakers and the brilliant of the lower
classes with the nobility. They don't end well because you can't
arrange passion. You'd be doing Timori a favour by fixing things
now rather than later."

"Wait ... what are you saying? That I should ... break up with
Timori? I can't, we're betrothed! And besides, I wouldn't want to. I
love him."

Racquela thought about storming out of the motorcoach, but something held her back. Was she considering what Paulo was saying?

"Racquela." Paulo put his hand on hers. It was electric. Racquela knew that the only decent thing to do was to pull her hand away, but she couldn't bring herself to.

"I know you're not content. I can tell. I see this all the time. People continue on in these unhappy relationships because they're afraid of being alone, afraid of hurting the other person by leaving. Timori claims that you're all he needs, but does he seem fulfilled to you? Really?"

Racquela thought about it for a moment. Timori was usually upset about one thing or another, whether it was about their relationship or something else. Yet he claimed that nothing else made him happier than being with her.

"He is happy! With me, at least."

"What about the argument you had the other day, about Jacoby?"

Racquela rolled her eyes. "Gods, does he tell you everything?"

"Think about it. You kissed Jacoby before the betrothal ceremony, not Timori. I don't think Tim was ever really the one you wanted to be with, but now you feel stuck because of the betrothal. However, you're a very independent woman when it comes down to it. You always know how to get what you want."

"What I want ..." Racquela echoed. "What would you know about that?"

"Plenty." He was still holding her hand, and her palm was growing sweaty.

"You have ambition to do more than just be a wealthy socialite. I can see it in your eyes, and the way you're driven to succeed at school. You don't care all that much about class because you're friends with Crystara, but things are different with Timori because you're betrothed to him. All of these problems you have with him now, you think they'll magically go away someday? His

261

jealousy won't recede. It'll only get worse. His desire to protect and control you will magnify, and I can tell you don't like being controlled. If you don't get out now, it'll be too late. You're set to be married at graduation, remember, and that's less than two years away. Think about it long and hard. Is marriage to Timori really what you want?"

Racquela felt light-headed. Paulo was forcing her to confront so many issues that she had pushed to the back of her mind because they were too challenging to deal with, and they all came down to whether or not she wanted to be with Timori.

"Wait, wait. Why are you saying all of this? Are you really looking out for what's best for Tim? This would devastate him. Not that I can ..."

Paulo took a finger and put it to Racquela's lips. He was pushing his boundaries again, but Racquela didn't stop him. Paulo's dark eyes seemed to look right into her soul. It was exciting and dangerous, and so much more interesting than the way she interacted with Timori.

"You can, my dear. You can appeal to the Great Crystal. The Great Crystal can sanction betrothals and it can also annul them, all perfectly legitimate as far as the gods are concerned. It would be especially easy for you since you bribed your way into this whole mess in the first place ..."

He removed his finger from her lips so that she could speak.

"How ... how do you know about that? Does anybody else know?"

Paulo shrugged. "Not many people, I would guess. I found out from a priest. You'd be surprised at what money can do. Well, maybe you wouldn't. The point is that you can appeal directly to the Great Crystal if you want, and get an annulment for all of this. If that's what you want. You'd be doing yourself and Timori a favour, even if he doesn't realize it. Don't you see that you're not right for each other?"

Racquela sighed. She had considered it, several times, but hadn't thought there was any way out. She didn't think annulments

262

were still allowed, but if they were, she would have to admit that she'd bribed the church.

"What do you get out of all this?" she demanded. "Why are you doing this?"

Paulo leaned in so that he was just a few inches away. He was so close that Racquela could smell mint on his breath and smoke in his hair.

"Because I think that we would make a much better couple, my dear."

The words hit Racquela like a sack of bricks. He was just after her. Her heart pounded fiercely in her chest, and she was torn between her guilt and duty to Timori, and her attraction to Paulo.

"What about Lenara? Your betrothed?"

"What about her? I can't leave her without an annulment. You know, it's funny. I was considering messing with the betrothal when we were in the crystal chamber because I didn't really want to get betrothed in the first place. I can't tell you how disappointed I was when I found out that I was with Lenara and not you."

It was all the affirmation Racquela needed. She leaned in and kissed Paulo.

In the heat of the moment, they were suddenly pulling off each other's clothes, hands exploring. Romance with Timori had never been so passionate. Racquela couldn't help herself. She wanted Paulo.

They made love in the backseat of the motorcoach. Paulo did exciting things that Timori never attempted. He pulled her hair and whispered dirty things in her ear as their passion fogged the windows of the vehicle.

Afterward, clothing rumpled, they smoked cigarettes in the backseat together and mopped up their sweat with handkerchiefs. Racquela knew that she was late for her curfew, but she didn't care. Guilt about that and other things could come later.

"I've been waiting a long time to do that," Paulo admitted. He lazily sucked on his cigarette.

"You've been planning this for a while, then?" Racquela giggled. It was so soon, but she felt something with Paulo that she had never felt with Timori. Was she falling in love? Already? She wondered if she had ever really loved Timori, or just cared about him deeply enough to believe that it was love. She wondered what the difference was. Was it passion or guilt?

"I'm nothing if not strategic," Paulo admitted.

"So you waited for the perfect moment to strike? That's evil."

Paulo shrugged. "What's wrong with going after what you want in life? I'm not going to be unhappy out of guilt for somebody else. Nobody should."

"Unhappy ..." Racquela mused. "You really think this annulment is what's best for Timori?"

"Don't worry about him. Worry about what's best for you. Whichever way you look at it, that annulment is the only way that we can be together. Isn't that what you want?"

Racquela wasn't surprised to discover the truth.

"Yes."

Chapter 22

In all of Posco's machinations to return Novem from its structure as a cluster of re-unified city-states to its former glory as a revered empire, one crucial piece of Noven tradition was missing that had been a cornerstone of the First Empire.

The anti-crystal rebellion of 1691 had left the Church of the Great Crystal a mere shadow of its former grandeur and wealth, and its involvement in politics had lessened considerably. Its keeper in 1862 was Iago De'Locci, a man who was 'obsessed with crystal lore', according to church historian Bellino, '(who) left administration of the Church of Novem entirely up to his high priests'. Bellino's book *De'Locci: Keeper, Engineer* details Keeper De'Locci's contributions to the advancements of crystal technology before and during the Great War.

What passed between Posco and Keeper De'Locci is still a matter of much debate, but some facts are known. In Quinta 1862, Keeper De'Locci declared that the Great Crystal had made a prophecy proclaiming that Longoro would become the first emperor of Novem to rule since the Sundering. This declaration pushed a further rift between Longoro's supporters and those who wanted to see him ousted, as crystal prophecies were controversial at best. Surviving correspondence between Keeper De'Locci and Posco does not directly imply a false prophecy, but it certainly outlines Posco's plans to make the church a central figure of authority for the Second Empire. By 1862, records show that there was undoubtedly a conspiracy brewing among Posco, De'Locci and Galetti, as well as many other members of the presidential cabinet. Whether or not the Great Crystal actually made a prophecy is a matter of religious speculation.

The prophecy became self-fulfilling, regardless. Longoro began writing his book *Dreams of Novem* the following month, which detailed his plans not only to bring Novem back to glory with himself as emperor, but to bring all former Noven-occupied territories back under Novem's banner once again. The book was not published until after Longoro's death in 1879, however, when the Great War was already over.

'The splendour of the First Empire can still be seen in my nation,' Longoro wrote. 'Our ancient architecture, well-maintained, beautiful and awe-inspiring, reminds me of the histories of the emperors of old, philosopher-kings who raised whole cities out of the dirt of this land. Our proud borders once touched the four seas of Titania, bringing enlightenment and the protection of the gods to the four corners of our continent. I can feel in my very bones that it is my destiny to return Novem to that former glory.' Longoro's obsession with the idea of himself as emperor was palpable.

Prominent psychologist Armani Buccari, one of the founding fathers of modern psychology along with Wilhelm Krantz, performed a famous psychoanalysis of Longoro in his book *The Imperial Mind* – although he was never privy to the inner workings of Longoro's thoughts since the two had never met.

'Behind Maximus Longoro's bold exterior lies an urgent longing for the approval of others', Buccari wrote. 'The attention-seeking behaviour of his childhood evolved into a pattern from which he could not escape, and the more the people of Novem loved him, the more of that love he craved. In catering to Posco's dreams of power, the attentions of his family and the adoration of a poor who idolized him, Longoro spent almost no time loving himself. His need for adoration would prove to be his undoing, as his mind slipped farther from reality as time went on. His overfed ego turned a people-pleasing attention-seeker into a megalomaniac.'

By the summer of 1862, Posco had nearly all of the necessary elements in place to effect a coup that would obliterate the vestigial elements of democracy in Novem and allow Longoro to exert complete control over the nation. Longoro and Posco dominated the senate, and they possessed the backing of the church and a prophecy which fed Longoro's need to be loved. The final step was to create a crisis.

***

10 Sexta, 1875
My love,
Alas, our time together seemed all too brief, though it was a wonderful month we spent together, wasn't it? My return to this abyssal war is worth it for the moments that we can share together.

The good news is that we are relatively safe right now. Our battalion has been charged with the defence of a city that is fairly far from the fighting but still a strategic area. The colonel does not expect the empire's advance into Milosa to let up anytime soon, so most of the danger here lies in the possibility of rebellion from the locals. They have no weapons, so the likelihood is remote.

Roberto is convinced that the war will be over by next year. Usually I am not so optimistic, but the last pockets of resistance are falling in Nilonne and our advances into Milosa and Kilgrun seem to continue unchecked. Wouldn't it be wonderful for this all to end? I think about our wedding day constantly, my love.

Pietro also seems to have had a good vacation. He cannot stop talking about the girls back home that he met. He asked me if I would ask you if you had any young, single friends who like a man in uniform. I think he was too shy to ask you himself when you met him, but women seem to be the only subject on my young captain's mind now. Sometimes I feel as though he is a younger brother to me, as I have told him several times. I want to help him find somebody to love. Shouldn't everyone have what we have?

There are many local girls here, but luckily there has been little trouble other than the occasional relationship that seems to occur now and again between a Nilonnese girl and a soldier. I suppose it is not much of an issue since Nilonne will soon be entirely a part of the empire, but it does create some resentment from the local men, few though they are.

Surprisingly, Pietro has shown no interest in the women here. He is convinced that only a Noven girl is good enough, which I can understand. Largo, as well, had eyes only for his Maria back home. Roberto doesn't even look at the girls here, and I am convinced that he should have gone into the priesthood! As for me, well, the girls here might as well be old men as far as I'm concerned. No woman could ever compare to you.

I fear sometimes that the respite here will not last, that we will be attacked or our battalion summoned to the front, but for now things are as peaceful as they could be during a time of war. I am hopeful for Novem's future, and ours.

I love you, Ramona. Write back soon.

Julio

27 Sexta, 1875

My darling Julio,

I'm sure that you got the news before I did, but I have to tell you anyway. Nilonne surrendered! People are cheering in the streets as I write this. Once Milosa and Kilgrun are under Noven control, this war will finally be over and you can return to me.

Pietro is such a sweet boy. A handsome young captain like him will have no trouble finding a girl here, but if he likes I can certainly think of a few friends who would love to meet him the next time your battalion comes back to Novem. Aliza springs to mind as somebody Pietro might fancy. You remember Aliza, don't you? She's a bit on the shy side, but she is very pretty and an excellent cook. Ask Pietro what he thinks.

I hope they don't move you from your current post. I worry for you constantly, even though you say that you're out of harm's way, for the moment.

Are the fall colours nice where you are? Avati Hill is beautiful right now. I go for long walks after my shifts at the factory and pretend that you're walking beside me.

I hate to sour this letter with bad news, but Mother's health is getting worse. She leaves the stove burning all the time and forgets that she's cooking, and I'm scared that she'll burn the house down. On top of it, she asked me the other day what I was doing in her house. She's forgetting who I am and where she is a lot of the time, and it scares me. Doctor Di'Matti says that she might not have much longer. I know that you have your own troubles, ones that I wouldn't ever want to face, but I wish that I didn't have to do this alone. I wish that Father was still alive and that Mother wasn't ill. Most of all, I wish that you were here.

Look after yourself, my love.
Ramona

***

The Elta crisis was a masterpiece of political deception.

It had long been the case in the northernmost region of Novem that there was a large contingent of separatists. Much of the population was, and still remains, Nilonnese, and many times throughout Novem's history, the Duchy of Elta was under the dominion of the Nilonnese Empire. Manufacturing a crisis in the region was simply a matter of convincing the populace that the provincial government was planning to defect to Nilonne, Novem's oldest rival.

False documents were created, implicating Elta's governor, and many members of the senate were bribed into giving false accounts that thoroughly blackmailed Governor Betrozzi and several of his political allies. So thorough was Posco's deception that King Louis the 10th of Nilonne began massing an emergency army to protect the possible interests of their Eltan allies, which was exactly what Posco and Longoro were banking on. A state of military emergency was declared, which froze the powers of the senate and put Longoro in a position of absolute control over the nation and its army. Betrozzi and his allies were denounced, and although some of them managed to flee with their families to the safety of Nilonne, most, including Betrozzi, were captured and hanged for their 'crimes'. The true nature of this event was not revealed until King Louis' death at the end of the Great War.

With Elta 'secured', Longoro swiftly negotiated with King Louis for peace. War with Nilonne was in the works, but Novem was nowhere near ready. The economy was still struggling, and the military was underequipped. Luckily for Posco and Longoro, Nilonne quickly agreed not to go to war, as they were tied up in the Milosan-Nilonnese war that would flare up three more times before the Great War began.

The trick to maintaining absolute power over Novem lay in convincing the populace that they were still in a state of crisis while simultaneously pacifying the fears of other Titanian powers that the nation posed them no threat.

Longoro's famous address in the winter of 1862 achieved that end perfectly. His famous opening line, 'My dream for Novem is a dream we all share', was filled with sentiments from his book. He revealed his idea for a self-sufficient economy, the heart of his socialist doctrine, and outlined plans for a shift toward Noven cultural identity and unity. An uninhibited effort was required, Longoro claimed. Re-opening the senate would stifle any attempt at progress.

The Noven cultural pride and mistrust in foreigners that Longoro and Posco manufactured with the Elta Crisis had the desired effect. Any sentiments of dissidence were quelled either by the hope that Longoro truly would bring prosperity back to Novem, or through the fear of his secret police, who by that time had begun heavy operations to stop any possible attempts at counteracting Longoro's young empire.

For a time, prosperity did return to Novem. Longoro seemed as good as his word.

***

19 Novembra, 1875

Dearest Ramona,

Alas, they have moved us from our safe city. The advance into Milosa is not going so well and our battalion has been called back to the front. Currently we are on the march with three other battalions. The cavalry scouts say that we should be safe until we reach our destination, but it does not make me feel any less nervous.

I am sorry to hear of your mother's health. I know this must be hard for you, and I wish that I could send you more than just my love and meagre pay to help with the doctor's bill. Your mother has been in my prayers every night.

On a happier note, Pietro is growing more and more confident and used to his command with every passing day. Largo remains belligerent around him, but Pietro deals with it as he always has. The rest of the company are respectful of him, and his military training is beginning to show in his ability to lead. He wins at cards a lot more, too.

I told him of your friend, and he says that he would love to meet her. I doubt that we will be on leave again until at least springtime, but Pietro said that he can wait. He models his patience after my own, he says, though I think he underestimates how much I pine for you while I am here.

My next letter might not come for a while. It depends upon how thick the fighting is. I can only pray that the Milosans surrender before the end of winter.

Love, Julio

22 Decembra, 1875

Ramona, my love,

One of our letters must have been intercepted or lost, for I have not heard back from you yet. Our rear guard is being harried by the enemy right now, so I hope that this one reaches you.

Milosa is a mess. We have been pinned down in the ruins of an old town whose name nobody knows, and the Milosans fight like mad heathens with no regard to their own safety. They charge our turret lines daily and we have almost been overrun twice. Their casualties are greater than ours, we figure, but we have lost nearly a full battalion in a month. Our crystal supplies for the wands are dwindling, and Pietro says that relief will not come for at least another week. Luckily we still have lots of food and fresh water.

How is your mother? I hope that she is doing better, and that the factory is treating you well. I try to hold on to hope during this misery. A letter from you would bring some light back to this dark and miserable winter of cold and mud and blood.

Write back soon, love. I must make these letters short until we get more paper supplies.

Julio

***

With his absolute power secured over Novem, Longoro began rebuilding his nation from a stagnant republic into the empire of his forefathers.

His answer to a crippled economy was to fulfill his early promises and follow socialist ideals by turning the industrial focus of Novem inward, toward infrastructure and self-sufficiency. In doing so he managed to satisfy the desires of the lower classes, despite going back on his promise to abolish the class structure entirely. To have done so would have resulted in a swift coup against him from the nobles, who were already upset at Longoro's anti-capitalist policies. Keeping his wealthy contemporaries in check was a juggling act that Longoro managed with the deftness that only a man of his ambition could manage.

As the army of Novem quietly grew, the other wars of Titania during the 1860s kept other nations from taking pre-emptive measures against a suddenly nationalistic country that no longer wished to engage in much trade or diplomacy.

Over the following decade, Novem swung back from a state of poverty. Although its currency had become relatively worthless outside its own borders, the rich of Novem lived like kings in their own land, and the poor no longer lived in complete squalor. Noven crystals were no longer exported to supplement the national budget, and instead were put to every conceivable use. With the help of the church, Novem was once again the world leader in crystal technology.

Longoro's behaviour during this time was non-aggressive. He sired four more children with Lucrezia: Titus, Estefen, Emelia and Cassio. He took a hands-on approach with his empire. Public appearances were frequent. He attended many inaugurations, gave speeches at schools and even continued his tradition of free lunches. He and Posco had manufactured the first successful socialist nation in the world. As weak as their economy was internationally, the people were happy and the nation prospered internally. Many who lived through this time still speak of what Novem might have been, had it not gone to war.

The prosperity was not to last. While Longoro basked in the love of the public, he was privately preparing to invade Nilonne. Posco, as usual, handled the details.

***

3 Maya, 1876

My beloved Ramona,

I was so relieved to get your last letter. The winter was awful and it is heart-warming to hear that you are doing well.

The news you received was a little bit presumptive, but we defeated Milosa nevertheless. I find it humorous that Longoro declared Milosa defeated on the first of Martia, when truly the fighting did not cease until mid-Aprila. Still, we were there in Modira when the king surrendered, though I did not find it as glorious as Roberto and Largo seemed to.

273

On the clear side, we have only to defeat Kilgrun and the war will be over. I cannot wait for us to be wed!

I was hoping to get leave time after Milosa, but they called us to bolster troops in Kilgrun, two days after our victory. Luckily we got to take horses instead of having to trek through the spring rain and mud all the way across three territories of the empire.

Right now we are at Dunsel, a staging ground for the Kilgrun campaign. There are at least three whole brigades here! Soon we will depart for the front, though I wish we weren't leaving without Pietro. Our temporary replacement captain looks upon all of our company with utter disdain, and I have no idea why.

Perhaps I should explain why Pietro is not with us, though if he has gone to visit you already then you will know the reason. Apparently, some groundbreaking new speaking techniques have been discovered by the keeper, and many military speakers have been sent back to Novem for special training. Why they are doing this now, when the war is almost over, is beyond me.

Pietro has told me that he will visit you when he is in Captus Nove, and that he is excited to meet your friend Aliza. I am glad that he is getting a break from the war, but I do miss him. He is a good leader and a good friend. Give him my best when you see him.

I must go now, love. Largo and Roberto are nagging me to play cards against some men from another battalion. Please write back soon.

Julio
17 Maya, 1876
My love,
I have terrible news. Mother passed away last week.

It wasn't unexpected, of course. Her health has worsened over the past month. The funeral was lovely, but I felt so alone without you here. I don't know what I would have done if Pietro hadn't been here to comfort me. He is a dear friend and hopes that you're doing well. He says that he'll be returning soon, and he has many stories to tell you.

He and Aliza didn't exactly hit it off, possibly because I was distraught. I feel selfish for taking up his time while he was here, but he said that he didn't mind. I promised to find him a nice girl when I'm feeling better.

The house feels so empty now, with Mother gone and you away. How goes the war? Surely Kilgrun is almost defeated and you can come home soon.

I have to go. Pietro is taking me out for lunch to cheer me up. Stay safe, my love.

Ramona

***

Ramona felt guilty for not telling Julio more of what had happened in her most recent letter to him, but she had no desire to overwhelm her lover when he had so many things to deal with during the war. On top of her mother's death, she had found her brother Emilio's name in the lists of men killed in action during the war. It was a devastating blow, and she cried and prayed for him as well as her mother at the funeral.

The house had been so lonely with her mother gone, and if it wasn't for Pietro coming to visit, Ramona believed that she would have gone mad. She had poured herself into her work that week, and Pietro's friendship was a bright spot during an otherwise dark time.

He had offered to take her out to lunch that afternoon after she wrote her letter to Julio and she agreed, more for the companionship to stave off loneliness than the fact that she could barely afford to eat after the funeral expenses had been covered. She and Pietro sat out on the patio of a restaurant of Pietro's choosing. Ramona would have picked some place less expensive, but Pietro insisted that Ramona needed cheering up with a fine meal, and she was gorgeous enough to be worth it, besides. She appreciated his compliments. He reminded her of a younger Julio.

"They're sending me back soon," Pietro said as he filled his mouth with bread. He was dipping it vigorously in balsamic vinegar

275

and olive oil. "I wish I didn't have to leave you here all alone, after all that's happened."

"I'll survive," Ramona said quietly. "I always have."

"Part of what Julio sees in you, I suspect," Pietro said. "Apart from your beauty. You're a very strong woman. I respect that."

"Thank you, Pietro," Ramona said as she stared at her mostly full plate. She felt guilty for not eating more when Pietro was the one paying, but her appetite had been reduced to almost nothing since her mother's death.

"You know," he continued, mouth still full, "I'm sorry about Aliza. I know you tried really hard, but I guess it just didn't feel right. She's pretty, but ... well, my heart isn't in the right place."

"What do you mean?"

Pietro stared off at a bird that was picking bread crumbs from underneath a vacant table nearby. "Nothing. Just not the right time, I guess. You can't control your heart, after all."

"That's true."

"He's lucky to have you."

"I'm lucky to have him."

Pietro nodded. "Yes, also true. He's been such a good friend to me. I don't know how I would have made it through this war without him."

Ramona put her napkin on top of her food and pushed her chair back slightly. "I'm sorry, Pietro, this is really a wonderful meal but I'm not hungry in the slightest. Besides which, I should be going to work soon."

Pietro wiped off his mouth with his own napkin. "Think nothing of it. I'm gladder for the company than anything, Ramona. It was probably good for you to get even a little bit of food in your stomach. If you don't mind, I'll walk you to the factory. It's a nice day out."

Ramona nodded and stood up as Pietro went to pay for the meal. He returned and they walked down the hill to the factory by the river. Ramona was mostly silent on the way there, lost in murky

276

thoughts of death. She was sorrowful for those who had just passed away and fearful for those who might die before the war was through. Fears of Julio's death kept her awake many nights and she was beginning to fear for Pietro as well. He was so bright-eyed and eager. It saddened her to think that such a promising youth could be culled from life during his prime.

Pietro talked away as they walked, mostly to fill the silence. He told Ramona stories about Julio to try and cheer her up, and it did, somewhat. As she approached the factory, a pang of anxiety chilled her heart. She was so tired of working, so tired of everything, but there was nothing she could do or she would quickly lose the house. Mostly she was tired of her supervisor, who had not relented in any way even after Julio had personally spoken to him. Ramona set her jaw grimly. There was no option but to continue as she always had. War and rent would wait for no one, she knew. Her task was to carry on until the war was over and things could finally get better for her.

Pietro insisted on following her all the way to the workers' entrance, and gave her a hug that lasted a moment longer than it should have.

"You're late," a snide voice said from the door. Ramona looked over Pietro's shoulder. It was Ralfi Andari.

"I'm not late," Ramona protested. She broke her embrace with Pietro. "My shift starts at three."

Her supervisor shook his head and brought out his pocket watch. "It got changed to two. Weren't you at the meeting?"

"No," Ramona said. She had missed the meeting because of her mother's funeral, but she doubted that Mister Andari would understand that.

"This is the last straw, Ramona," Andari warned. "The owners told me that I only had one option if you showed up late to work after missing that meeting. Consider yourself fired ... unless you'd like to reconsider my offer, that is."

Pietro rushed toward Ralfi like wandshot and grabbed the smaller man by the collar. Ramona wanted to shout out and protest, but by the time she summoned the courage to speak, it was too late.

"How dare you threaten her?" Pietro said, red-faced. "Her mother and brother both just died, you insensitive piece of dirt."

Ralfi Andari looked down at the rank on Pietro's uniform. "My quarrel isn't with you, my good captain. My apologies if I made it seem so. Ramona is late to work, and I have quotas to fill for the Imperial military, your employers. She's been falling behind in her job for a while now, and I'm afraid that it's not my decision to let her go. My hands are tied."

Ramona felt ill. "Please, Mister Andari," she begged. "Isn't there something that I can do? Extra shifts? I really need this job."

Ralfi Andari shook his head. "I'm sorry, Ramona. You know that I hate to see you suffer. And really, I am sorry. I had no idea about your mother and brother."

Pietro eased up on his grip, and Mister Andari straightened his tie and jacket.

"However, I really would hate to see something bad happen to you. There is a way out of this, you know. I could take care of you. Marry me instead of Julio and you'll never have to worry about money again."

Ramona's heart sank. Marrying Ralfi Andari was not an option. She had no interest in him. She told herself that she would have to find another way, have to survive somehow off of the meagre pay she received from her intended.

"She doesn't want anything from you," Pietro spat. "You wormy little dullard, you fire her and then ask for her hand in marriage? Get out of here before I clean your clock."

Ralfi Andari opened his mouth, but he took another look at Pietro and then shut the door.

Ramona shook with anger and confusion. "Pietro," she said weakly. "Walk me home, please."

Ramona made it until she was almost out of sight of the factory before she began to cry. She allowed Pietro to put his arms around her as they walked home in the afternoon sun.

"I'm so sorry, Ramona," Pietro said. "I shouldn't have threatened him like that. This is all my fault."

"No, it's not," Ramona said. "He's had it out for me for a long time, ever since I refused him the first time. Oh, Pietro, what am I going to do now? I can't afford to live on what Julio sends me. I need to find another job."

"I suppose that's true. I could send you some of my pay as well, though. Just until you get a new job, that is."

Ramona stared at the dusty road. She was tired of men bending over backwards for her. "No, Pietro, I could never accept that, but thank you anyway. I can make it on my own."

Pietro lit up a cigarette. "Are you certain? They pay me well as a captain, and there aren't exactly a lot of things to buy in the trenches. You can even pay me back, if you like, once you're back on your feet. I'm just trying to help you out. You're in a really rough spot."

"I know, Pietro."

They walked the rest of the way to Ramona's house in silence. Ramona wanted to say goodbye to Pietro at the door, but she could tell that he wanted to be invited in to talk. He was leaving for the front the next day, after all. Ramona let him inside. She was feeling lonely, anyway, and Pietro was a good listener.

Ramona made tea for the two of them and they sat on the couch together. The house felt so empty without her mother there. She missed Julio so dearly, and she had never needed him home more than she did just then. She tried not to unload too much upon Pietro, but once they began speaking it all came out like an opened floodgate. She talked of having to deal with the deaths of her three closest family members in a matter of less than three years, of having to be alone so much during the war, of how much she missed Julio and how she was afraid of what would happen if he died on the front.

Most of all she spoke of how hard it was to be strong on her own in a man's world.

"I'm afraid to go back," Pietro said after a few moments of silence. He was staring at the fire in the hearth. He continually tried to inch his way toward Ramona. She longed for comfort so badly and Pietro was the only person nearby who could provide it. Eventually she stopped finding excuses to get up and adjust her position on the couch.

"Julio will protect you," Ramona said. "He told me so himself. He promised to."

Pietro gazed into the flames as though he were looking into the abyss.

"He did, but what kind of promise is that to make during a war? Anything could happen, and I'm just as worried about him. He's not a fighter, Ramona. He's a smarter man than I will ever be, and he belongs here doing the things that a smart man should be doing, not out fighting in the dirt with the rest of us."

"He belongs here with me," Ramona sighed. "I miss him so much, Pietro."

Pietro seemed to snap back to reality for a moment. "You're right, Ramona. I'm sorry. I know you're going through a lot more than I am. I just ..."

He looked into Ramona's eyes. He seemed innocent then, not predatory or lecherous.

"I'm afraid. I'm afraid to die, I always have been. Call me a coward, call me what you will, but just because I'm a leader doesn't mean that I'm fearless or anything. I'm afraid that I'll go back to the front and you will be the last woman that I will ever see. I'm afraid that ...".

His face inched closer to Ramona's. Ramona was feeling so alone that she could not bring herself to ask Pietro to watch his distance. She was afraid that he would simply get up and leave. She tried to move her head back but she was almost falling over the arm of the couch.

"... Well, I don't like to admit this to anyone, but I'm afraid that I'll die not ever knowing love." Pietro's lips were suddenly upon Ramona's.

She stood up immediately and kept him at an arm's distance.

"Pietro, please. I can't do this." She stood up. "I'm with Julio. My intended. Your friend. Think about what you're doing. I know you're going through a lot right now, and so am I, but this is the one thing that cannot happen."

Pietro stood up and edged closer. Ramona's back was to the fire. She realized how foolish she had been to let him inside, alone with her.

"I know, Ramona. You're right, I'm being selfish. It's just that ... I think I'm falling in love with you. I tried so hard not to, and I promised myself I would never do anything like that to Julio, but I can't help it. You're everything I've ever wanted in a woman."

Ramona watched Pietro's stance. It was no longer aggressive. She allowed herself to relax slightly.

"Pietro, don't say that. We still barely know each other and ..."

Pietro began to cry. In spite of his chin stubble and his captain's uniform, all Ramona could see was a boy in a man's world, playing at manly things. Ramona knew that she was a complete fool for doing so, but she approached Pietro and held him as he cried. She felt motherly, and it was so nice to have somebody close. It made her forget her own problems, being able to shoulder somebody else's instead. She began to feel strong again.

She had promised herself not to allow anything to happen, but it was already too late. Once his arms were close around her, she knew that he needed her. She promised herself that it was just one time, and then Pietro would be off to war again, possibly never to return. She led him to her tiny bedroom and tried not to think of all the times Julio had slept there beside her.

After they made love, Pietro fell asleep almost instantly. Ramona smiled despite her guilt. Even in sleep Pietro seemed innocent. Ramona stayed up for the rest of the night, pacing back and forth in the kitchen as she tried to figure out how to survive, how to find a new job, and how to tell Julio the truth.

She had to tell him the truth. She loved him too much not to, even though she knew that it would break both of their hearts.

Chapter 23

"Why do you have to go?" Crystara demanded. She stood on the porch outside her house and ran after Jacoby, who was headed to his bicycle.

"Can't you spend some time with me instead?"

Jacoby rolled his eyes. It was the same argument every time he went out anywhere with his football friends. He turned around.

"Because I can't spend all of my time exclusively with you, Crystara. I have friends outside of this relationship, you know. We can do something together tomorrow."

"You always say that. Tomorrow, we'll do something tomorrow. You're always brushing me off. Please, Jake, just this once, stay here with me instead." She tugged at his arm in a childish gesture.

"And what? Sit around and try to think of things to talk about, like we always do? Try to cheer you up because you're always upset? Because that's all we ever wind up doing."

Jacoby was tired of her melancholy façade. Reading Crystara using empathy only revealed further insecurities and jealousy. She was never satisfied with Jacoby's reassurances and was never truly happy no matter how much positive emotion Jacoby tried to pour into the relationship. Sometimes Jacoby likened her to a vortex of negative emotion, but he would never say that to his betrothed's face.

"Why don't you understand how much this means to me?"

Jacoby was fed up. As much as she claimed he didn't listen, she was guilty of the same.

"Why don't you understand how much it means to me to have some time outside of this, as well? Gods, you stifle me sometimes."

"Then why don't you just fucking leave me? It seems to be what you want!" Crystara screamed.

Jacoby held his hands out in an attempt to pacify her. Crystara never cared who could hear an argument when she was upset. He walked up to her and embraced her before she could protest further. He was so tired of fighting with her all the time. It was easier to just give in sometimes than it was to fight against it.

"Shh, Crystara, sweetheart. I don't want to leave you. I don't want to be fighting all the time. I just ... I invite you to come along, but you never seem to have any fun. I'm not trying to exclude you."

"Can't you just stay here with me for once? Please? I feel really depressed today and all you care about is your football friends. I just need some reassurance from you. Your friends will understand. You can see them tomorrow at school."

Jacoby sighed. He wasn't going to win without more fighting. It seemed as though no matter how much he reassured Crystara, no matter how much time he spent with her, she always wanted more.

"All right, Crystara. I'll stay."

Jacoby cursed himself for a dully and went back inside the house with Crystara. He truly was a coward. He couldn't even tell her that he wasn't happy with the way things were going. He would just let them continue on as they always had.

***

It was the first day back to school after the summer break, and Jacoby was more excited to see Timori than anyone else. His best friend had been busy working for most of the summer, as well as spending time with Racquela after she had returned from vacation, so Jacoby had spent most of his time with Crystara. He was also spending a lot of his time with the football boys, especially Mariano and Filippo, who were no longer treating Jacoby like a lowborn. Jacoby wanted to play football alongside Timori, however. He wanted to go back to the bridge and spit seeds and to go on double-dates again.

He spotted Timori approaching him at his locker from across the hallway and gave him a friendly wave. Timori didn't wave back.

Jacoby assumed that his friend hadn't spotted him. Timori continued to approach and stood in front of Jacoby with his arms folded.

"So?" Timori said, curtly. "What do you have to say for yourself?"

"About what, pally?" Jacoby asked.

"You know damned well what," Timori said, his voice seething with hate. Jacoby's heart leapt into his throat. He could think of only one thing that would have Timori so furious with him.

"Well, I'm not sure. Maybe if you tell me, then I can ..."

Jacoby was slammed up against the locker faster than he could blink. Timori's face was a rictus of rage.

"You asshole. You can't even be honest with me. I told you I liked her and you just went behind my back anyway. You didn't even have the balls to tell me."

"Tim ..." Sweat broke out on Jacoby's forehead. He was less concerned with physical violence and more about losing his best friend. It seemed likely that both would happen.

"I didn't want to ruin anything between you and her by telling you. I'm sorry. It was just a kiss, one time."

"How am I supposed to trust you now, after this? You knew I liked her, Jake. You knew!"

"Tim, I ..." Jacoby searched for words, something to say to convince Timori that it was water under the bridge, but nothing came to mind.

"Just don't talk to me anymore," Timori said as he roughly let Jacoby go. "Don't talk to me, and stay away from Racquela if you know what's good for you. Goodbye, Jake."

Jacoby sensed Timori's inner feelings, and he knew that no amount of training with empathy would save their friendship just then. Timori stormed off, leaving Jacoby with his guilt.

***

Jacoby came home that evening to his father waiting up at the kitchen table.

285

"Jake, I want to talk to you about your grades for a second. You slacked off last year, and I really think that ..."

Jacoby had been mulling over what had happened between himself and Timori for hours. He was in no mood to talk about school with his father.

"Not now, Dad. Please."

His father stood up. "No, Jake, you sit here and listen. I told you last year that this school was really important and really expensive and you just goofed off and spent all your time with Crystara when I told you that ..."

"Dad, I said fuck off!" Jacoby yelled.

Gilliermo's face turned more severe. Jacoby ran up the stairs to his room before his father could strike him for saying such words. He slammed the door shut and pressed himself against it so that his father wouldn't be able to get in. He could hear Gilliermo stomping up the stairs. The doorknob rattled.

"Jacoby! You let me in right now!" he shouted. "What in the abyss has gotten into you?"

"I had a bad day, Dad! Can we talk about this tomorrow?"

"No, dammit! We talk about it now. How dare you speak to your own father that way? Haven't I taught you any respect?"

Jacoby sighed. "I'm sorry. I had a fight with Tim, Dad. He said that we weren't friends anymore. I'm sorry for yelling at you."

"If you ever swear at me like that again, Jake, you'll get a lot more than just an earful. Now come downstairs so we can talk about your grades. And Tim."

Jacoby agreed and went back to the kitchen with his father. To Jacoby's surprise, Gilliermo went into the pantry and pulled a bottle from the top shelf. It was whiskey, some kind of commonwealth make.

Jacoby raised an eyebrow. "Whiskey, Dad?"

His father shook his head and took two small glasses out of the cupboard.

"I had my first whiskey when I was your age. Besides, I'm sure you've been drinking once in a while when you're out with your football pallies."

Jacoby's cheeks reddened. His father knew him better than he wanted to admit. Gilliermo poured a meagre amount of caramel-brown liquid into each glass and clinked his against Jacoby's.

"So tell me what happened."

Jacoby related the entire story to his father, starting with the dance the previous winter where he and Racquela kissed and ending with Timori's threats that morning. In the process, he wound up telling his father quite a bit about his troubles with Crystara.

"Timori will get over it," Gilliermo Padrona decided. "He's mad at you right now, which he has a right to be, but you've been friends since before you could talk, Jake. He'll get over it once he stops seeing Racquela through a crystal lens, which might take a little while because he's young, but it will happen."

"I hope you're right about that, Dad. I feel awful."

Gilliermo nodded and sipped his whiskey. Jacoby had barely touched his. It tasted awful and had gone to his head after only a couple of sips.

"You should. I've always taught you to think with your head and not with ... other things. But I think you might have learned your lesson in that your best friend is more important to you than a kiss from a girl. Now, as for Crystara ... Son, you need to be firm with this girl. You can't let her walk all over you, especially since you're getting married to her."

"Well ... how? I've tried, but she always turns it into this huge fight."

"Son, let me explain how it's worked so well for me and your mother all these years. A successful marriage isn't about love. Well, it is, but love isn't the only part of the equation. If it's just about love, then there's passion, but no substance. Part of the thing is to remember that you are both separate people, with separate likes and dislikes. You have to have something that is only yours, a refuge from the other person. Your mother has her garden. I read books.

Without those things you just get wrapped up in each other and it's self-destructive. You lose perspective on the outside world, the real world. You have those outside things, like football, but Crystara doesn't, so she clings to you because right now you're the only thing that matters to her. Jake, you have to help that girl find other things in her life. I can tell that she's troubled, probably isn't very happy with her home life, but you can't be her rescuer. She has to rescue herself from that, find something of her own to live for."

Jacoby let a pause settle in and thought about what his father had said. He took another sip of the terrible whiskey "So ... how do I help her do that?"

"You can't, Jake. She has to find it on her own. All you can do is set boundaries and let her know that your life can't revolve around her. Right now it should revolve around school."

Jacoby let out a laugh. "I knew you would get back to that eventually. I'm sorry, Dad. I'll pick it up this year. I know how much Central costs, and I want to do better this year, besides."

"Don't do it for me, Jake. Do it for yourself. This is your future we're talking about."

Jacoby thought about his future all the time. Guiltily, he wondered what it would be like without Crystara. Sometimes it felt as though all the possibilities that life had in store were stripped away from him, and he was stuck with one. He wondered if any of the other betrothed felt the same way.

As Jacoby stumbled up to his room late that evening, he tripped over something heavy at the foot of his bed. As he cursed and steadied himself on his mattress, he turned around to take a look at the item that had taken advantage of his clumsiness. It was Master Vellize's book. Jacoby's foot had accidentally kicked it open, and the letters within were now scattered across the floor of Jacoby's room. Focusing against his intoxication, Jacoby carefully scooped up the letters and the book and brought them over to his bed.

He thought about everything that his father and Master Vellize had told him about love, and he wondered what further insight the book and letters would give him that he could apply to his

288

relationship with Crystara. He had to find some kind of solution. There was no way that he could let things go on the way that they were going or he would be miserable for the rest of his life.

Jacoby decided to set aside the letters for last. He opened *The Rise and Fall of the Second Empire* to the first page. It read: 'This book is dedicated to my best friend, brother-in-arms and patron of a broken man's dreams, Doctor Roberto Ruveldi, the Second Empire's greatest advocate and its harshest critic.'

The name 'Ruveldi' sounded incredibly familiar, but he couldn't quite remember from where. The dedication gave him hope, however, that perhaps once things settled down he and Timori would be friends again, and remain so into their old age.

Jacoby turned the page.

***

They were waiting for him on the field outside the locker room, five members of the football team. Jacoby knew from the look in their eyes that they meant business. He turned to run, but there was already one behind him. It was Roberto Massi. Jacoby was roughly shoved in the direction of the other five bullies. He looked up with horror to discover that he was being handled roughly by Mariano.

"Sorry, Jake," Mariano whispered. "It's either you or me."

Jacoby tried to read Mariano's emotions to glean some indication as to why he was siding with Roberto Massi, but Jacoby's own inner feelings were coming out too strongly and he could not focus. Jacoby wondered if he was being picked on because of 'Class Action', or because he was simply the smallest on the team.

None of Jacoby's attackers bothered with an explanation. Punches and kicks started flying at Jacoby, and he tried desperately to defend himself and fight back. They called him every name in the book and shoved him back and forth, taking turns pummelling Jacoby in the face and stomach until he couldn't stand anymore and fell to the ground. The beating didn't stop there. He buried his face in his arms and tensed himself to receive their kicks, which hurt all the more from the cleats they wore. Jacoby called out weakly for help, but none came. Timori wouldn't be there to rescue him.

A sudden sharp pain struck Jacoby in the back of his head, and his vision spotted. He saw some blood on the grass beneath him and couldn't tell if it was from his nose, or if he had coughed it up. It was a mistake to take his arms away from his face. A shoe came up to strike him in the temple and he blacked out.

Jacoby wasn't entirely certain how long he was unconscious. He had a vague notion of somebody asking him questions, but he couldn't remember what they asked, or what he said in return. He remembered being dragged, and worrying about getting blood on somebody's clothes. He might have vomited in a motorcoach, or was that a dream?

Jacoby awoke. His head, ribs and crotch throbbed with pain. A wet cloth covered his face. He couldn't see a thing. He tried to speak, but his lips were caked together from blood and something else. Mucus? Vomit? All that escaped his lips was a weak moan.

"Oh my gosh, you're awake," a female voice said.

"Crystara?" Jacoby managed to croak. The cloth towel was removed from his face. Jacoby's right eye opened, but the left was too bruised. With his good eye he could see a blurry figure with dark hair wringing out the cloth in a small basin. He was lying on a bed.

"Racquela? Who ...?"

The figure leaned closer to dab at his facial wounds with the cloth. Jacoby thought he smelled flowers. His eye stung terribly. Once the girl drew close enough, the blurriness subsided. Her blue eyes gazed into his with concern. Jacoby could feel her reaching out with empathy. Relieved that he didn't have to use words, he projected his confusion and fear. Reassurance wafted back to him, along with many other emotions that Jacoby would have to take some time to sort out. She was worried about him, nervous about something she needed to tell him, and sorry about something obscure.

"How did you find me there?" Jacoby rasped.

Lenara touched his cheek lightly. Somehow it didn't hurt.

"I had a vision."

Jacoby tried to sit up, but it was too painful. He grunted and lay back down.

"Unhh ... what do you mean, vision?"

He could sense Lenara's hesitation to answer the question. As usual, it was much easier to read Lenara's emotions than Crystara's.

"Jake, there's so much I need to tell you, but you need to rest. You're so badly hurt I almost took you to the hospital."

"Why didn't you?" Jacoby asked. A hospital seemed the logical place to take somebody in his condition. He felt something from Lenara, hesitation and an anticipation of revealing something to him. She was holding back a very strong emotion from him, but Jacoby was too weak to search for it.

"Please, Jake, sleep for a bit. I'll tell you everything when you wake up."

Jacoby slept.

***

It was fully night-time when Jacoby awoke. He was much more alert than he had been earlier. His discussion with Lenara seemed almost like a dream. As he shook off sleep, Jacoby was startled to find that he was wearing nothing more than his undershorts, but he was too weak to truly protest.

Lenara was suddenly in front of him, and put a cup of tea to his lips. Startled, he drank, spilling much of the warm liquid down his chest. Lenara gently dabbed off the spilled tea with a cloth, which made Jacoby all the more aware of his near-nakedness. He was even more aware of Lenara, who was dressed in only a white nightgown. Her brown locks spilled out over her shoulders and chest sensuously, and Jacoby tried very hard not to stare.

"Does anybody know I'm here?" he asked. Even in admiring Lenara's beauty, he felt guilty that somebody else would find out about it.

Lenara shook her head and sat down beside him on the bed. The sheets were purple and the bed's canopy was done up in mauve lace. Jacoby saw some antique porcelain dolls out of the corner of his eye, staring at him from a shelf.

"My parents are away on business. I haven't told anybody that you're here. Would you like me to send a telegram to Crystara?"

His empathy told him that Lenara was nervous about mentioning Crystara. Lenara probably felt the same from him. They hadn't done anything wrong, but he knew that Crystara would never forgive him if she knew that he was at Lenara's house.

"Not yet, no. I still feel pretty banged up."

Lenara sighed. A waft of strong emotion poured out of her. There was something that she wanted to get off of her chest more than anything else, but Jacoby caught fear emanating from her as well. Whatever she wanted to talk about, it was obviously very important and she was worried about Jacoby's reaction.

"Jake ... I've evaded you for so long, but I can't do it any longer." She toyed with the teacup in her hands. "You have to know something. This vision I had today ... it made me realize that I've been avoiding you, and I can't do that anymore."

"You really have visions?" Jacoby asked. "Is that even possible?"

Lenara shrugged. "I don't know if it's supposed to be, but I do. Only my parents and a couple of other people know. I'm afraid of what the church or the government would do if they found out. But I know that they're real. I think it's sort of like empathy, only different. I knew that you were going to be there, that those boys were going to beat you up. I didn't get there in time to warn you, but I borrowed my dad's motorcoach and brought you here."

"Thank you," Jacoby said. He took Lenara's hand in his without even thinking about it. It felt natural to do so. She smiled at him. "I could have been in serious trouble. Thank you, Lenara."

292

Lenara stared at the teacup in her other hand. "You shouldn't be thanking me," she muttered.

"Why not? You saved me. Who knows how long I would have lain there if you hadn't known to come and get me?"

Lenara shook her head. "Not that," she said.

A wave of unbound sadness rolled off of Lenara. Jacoby watched as a tear fell down her cheek. He could feel her reaching out to him for comfort, for support. Not knowing what else to do, Jacoby put his arms around her. Lenara began to sob softly and leaned into Jacoby. Guilt and shame soaked into him as the warm tears trickled down his shoulder and back.

"What is it, Lenara?" he asked as he stroked her hair.

It was an incredibly forbidden thing for him to do, but in the moment, pressed against her, he couldn't stop himself. She was so close and so vulnerable. There was no flower in her hair, but as he breathed in he could still pick up the scent of lilacs. It stirred him.

Lenara brushed away her tears on the sleeve of her nightgown. Her eyes were red and puffy, but Jacoby still thought she looked beautiful. He imagined that he probably looked a lot worse, anyway.

"I have lots of visions, Jake. Not just about things that are about to happen really soon. I knew about the betrothals and about Paulo ..." Guilt projected from her again.

"What about Paulo?" he asked.

He knew little about Paulo, or his relationship with Lenara. Nobody ever talked about it other than to say it was mysterious, and the two were never seen together. Lenara looked at Jacoby. Although the tears had abated, her lip was still trembling slightly. Jacoby was tempted to kiss that trembling lip, but he remained stalwart. It was bad enough what he had done to Timori, which hadn't even been cheating.

"I tried to make him a good person, really I did, but it's too late now anyway. He doesn't care about me. He doesn't care about anything except for his empire he wants to build. Everybody will think he's crazy but it's really going to happen, Jake, I've seen it. I

293

had a chance to stop it, to stop him but I didn't try hard enough because my heart wasn't in it and ..."

She stopped mid-sentence and began crying again. Jacoby held her close again and tried to sort through her emotions as she babbled. She was making almost no sense to him, and her feelings were coming out just as jumbled. Jacoby felt as though he were missing an important piece of information.

"So wait, Paulo ... wants to build an empire? What exactly are you saying, Lenara?"

Lenara sent Jacoby a grave expression. The talk of sixteen-year-old boys building empires sounded silly to Jacoby, but Lenara didn't seem to think it was.

"Jake. You need to understand who Paulo is. He's Emperor Longoro's son."

Jacoby thought for a moment. It didn't make any sense for Paulo to be Longoro's son. Master Vellize had just told him the other day in class that the entire extended family had been put to death after the fall of the Second Empire. The story would make a good case for why Paulo believed that he could rebuild a new one, but it was too far-fetched for Jacoby to believe.

"That's impossible," he told Lenara. "And even if it were true, how would a teenager expect to topple the republic?"

"I didn't want to believe it myself, but Paulo's always talking to strange people and he has a mysterious benefactor who gives him money ... I think somebody's trying to use him for political gain, but Paulo knows this, and he'll get the upper hand in the end. He's smart, Jake, and ruthless. I've seen what will happen, and I'm telling you that Paulo is going to take over Novem. Not right away. He's still too young, but it's going to happen, and short of somebody killing him nothing will stop it now. The republic is failing, anybody can see that. All it takes is somebody who seems to have all the answers to step in and ..."

"... take control, just like Longoro," Jacoby said, finishing the sentence for her. "It makes sense, Lenara. It's just that ... well, it's a big pill to swallow. Why are you telling me all of this, anyway?"

"Because I can't do this anymore, I can't be with Paulo. He doesn't care about me at all, and if I remain with him things don't end well for me. They don't end well for any of us, Jake. The betrothals were screwed up from the beginning, and now things are getting worse."

"What do you mean, screwed up from the beginning? Do you mean you think the crystal is a lie?"

Lenara shook her head vigorously. "No, Jake, the Great Crystal is real. What I mean is that the process was tampered with. The visions. We didn't all get betrothed to the right people."

Jacoby's eyes widened. "But how?" he demanded. "We each had visions and were interviewed separately. How could anything have been tampered with?"

Jacoby could feel the guilt once again, and watched as Lenara fought back more tears.

"I knew. I knew what was going to happen, and I thought that my visions were telling me something. That if I sacrificed myself, I could change him and stop the war."

"So there is a war coming? My vision was right?"

"Worse than just a war, Jake."

Jacoby scratched his chin, which felt soft and bruised. "Okay, so you knew about this war that's supposedly coming, and about Paulo. But who did you switch with?"

As Lenara burst into tears once again, Jacoby realized that he already knew the answer. She had shared the vision with him, been right there beside him as the army marched up the hill. Lenara tried to continue speaking through her sobs.

"I ... I'm so sorry, Jake. It was you. I was supposed to be with you. We could have been happy all this time ... I ... I ..."

Lenara could no longer speak, but sobbed into Jacoby's chest with abandon. He stared at the blank white walls as everything he had believed since the betrothal came crashing down around him.

Lenara had switched with Crystara. As he thought about it, something was still missing from the equation.

"Lenara, Lenara," he said.

Lenara sniffled and tried to control her tears. She looked up at him, lip trembling once again.

"How did Crystara know?"

"I had a vision about it the night before, and talked to her. She agreed to it. She said she wanted to be with you more, anyway. She chose you. She's a reader, Jacoby. I pretended that I passed out and had no vision, but Crystara read my thoughts and told the priests about the vision that I'd had after touching the crystal, which was the same as yours. Since I'd lied and said I didn't receive a vision, by default I was put with Paulo."

Jacoby was hit by another unlikely revelation. "A reader? Aren't those myth? This is a lot to believe in, all in one day."

"They're incredibly rare, but it's true, Jake. Supposedly Queen Celesta was a reader, too. Haven't you ever noticed how Crystara always seems to know things?"

"Like what?" Jacoby asked, but as he thought about it he realized that Lenara was right. It was likely that Racquela hadn't even told her about the kiss at the winter dance. She had known all along. If it were true, then she knew everything about Jacoby, and everything about what he thought in terms of their relationship. She wasn't an empath at all, which was why she couldn't read Jacoby's emotions. She looked so much deeper than that, into his very thoughts. It was why she was always so worried about their relationship. She must have known every step of the way when Jacoby felt insecure about something, which made her insecure in turn.

She would even know about his conversation with Lenara, as soon as he saw her next. It sent a chill up Jacoby's spine. Nothing he could do would stop what was going to happen. He understood why Lenara had been so hesitant. It was all going to fall apart.

"You'll see as soon as you talk to her next," Lenara said, echoing Jacoby's own thoughts. "She'll know about all of this, what we just talked about. There's no going back now."

"So what do we do?" Jacoby asked. "If Crystara has been keeping this a secret, it means ... she really wants to be with me, despite the fact that she's supposed to be with Paulo."

"We, Jake? What do you want to do?"

"I ..." Jacoby had no idea what to do next. He knew that a choice lay before him, but he was afraid of the consequences either way. He could remain with Crystara and convince her that he didn't care what the Great Crystal's choice was, or he could confront her about it and get an annulment from the church. He knew that such things had happened in the past, if it was revealed that the ritual had been disturbed in some way.

Jacoby knew, though, that he did care what the crystal's choice was. He felt robbed, cheated out of it.

"I have to get an annulment from the church," he told Lenara. "It's the only way to settle this, make it right."

"I'm sorry it came to this, Jake. I thought that you and Crystara were really going to be happy. You seemed so at first."

Jacoby nodded. "We were. But I don't ..."

Jacoby found himself inching closer and closer to Lenara, as though he were drawn in by some unseen magnetism. The thrill, the prospect of Lenara being his chosen wouldn't leave his thoughts. He wanted to know, wanted to feel who she was.

"I don't ... know if I ..."

Their lips touched. Lenara melted into him as though she had always belonged there.

Guilt intermingled with a deep sense of longing and forbidden passion. Slowly and gently they intertwined. Lenara was careful not to disturb too many of Jacoby's many bruises. Their lovemaking was slow and gentle, filled with tender caresses and deep looks into each other's eyes. It was a different experience entirely, knowing what the other person was feeling at every moment. Jacoby could feel Lenara's need to be caressed, her desire to be shown that

297

she wasn't alone and that somebody in the world cared about her. All those times in class, those emotions that Lenara had tried to hold back, were out in the open.

Jacoby and Lenara freed each other from the burdens of restraint and doubt. Without saying a word, they knew that they wanted to be together.

Chapter 24

In the month of Quinta, 1874, Longoro announced the campaign to reclaim all former Noven territories that had once been under the dominion of the First Empire. Although many disagreed with the decision, Longoro's power over Novem was absolute. Nobody dared oppose him lest they risk persecution from his secret police.

A month later, Noven armies were marching across Novem's northern border. Half of Nilonne had fallen by Novembra of the same year. With Novem's allies Mikos, which had declared itself a vassal state of Novem in Aprila of 1874, and Denlund, which had received a guarantee that it would remain a sovereign entity, Nilonne was forced to fight a war on three fronts.

Under the sudden threat from Novem, Milosa and Kilgrun knew that they would be next. Milosa and Nilonne quickly signed a peace accord and the three nations formed an alliance, but it had come too late. By the winter of 1876, Novem's borders were once again what they had been before The Sundering.

Longoro did not seem satisfied with his conquests, however. The military was still active and mobilized, and Novem's supremacy over Titania was unquestioned, but the victory and prosperity of Novem – along with the adoration of his citizens – had gone to Longoro's head. He had become increasingly paranoid and megalomaniacal ever since the attempt on his life in 1875, making fewer public appearances while at the same time commissioning statues of himself to be built all over the empire. In 1877 he declared himself a demi-god and had the church trace his lineage back to Jova himself.

The war could have ended with the fall of Kilgrun, but the great eastern kingdom of Parsu loomed just over the Rhun River from Novem's latest conquest and proved too tempting a target for the emperor, despite its fiercely defended western front. Unconquered since the days of the Hans of the Orient, it was a land rich in resources, culture and crystal. King Pyotyr waited for Longoro's deceit and his armies were more than ready.

Posco begged Longoro to reconsider such a foolish military decision, at least until the Noven military had a chance to replenish its numbers and supplies, but Longoro no longer listened to his second-in-command. As Casto overheard Longoro say to Posco, 'I answer only to the gods now'.

The push into Parsu proved to be Longoro's undoing. King Pyotyr's military front was unyielding, and Parsu had allies that Longoro did not expect: the island nation of Faxon, along with its entire Commonwealth around the world. Troops were landing on Imperial shores along five different fronts, all of which were undermanned by Novem's divided armies, while Noven soldiers were at a standstill along the border with Parsu.

The tide of the war very quickly turned.

***

"Fuck Longoro," Roberto spat.

Julio was playing cards in the trench with Pietro, Roberto and Largo. It was the first day of spring. A standstill had been called for the day out of respect to the gods. Julio was thankful to the Parsish for their generosity. It was nice to have a breather from the war, especially on such a frigid day. The snow wasn't expected to melt until Maya, and it had been a bitterly long winter. Julio found himself missing the rainy winters of Novem, something that he never in a million years thought that he would miss.

Many of Julio's battalion had died that winter of the cold rather than in battle, until the day when Pietro had managed to rig up a system of heat crystals in the trenches with Roberto's help. Largo had already lost the tips of his ears to the cold by that time, and Roberto's right pinkie finger no longer worked well from having to

300

hold his longwand on watch without gloves for so many nights. Roberto never complained about it, however.

"Finally come to your senses, Rob?" Largo asked as he lay his cards down on the snow. The group of them no longer played for cigarettes. There hadn't been any supplies for over a month. Starvation had killed almost as many as the cold and the remaining troops were emaciated and weak. Julio could count all of his ribs and had eaten only shoe leather soup for the past three days.

Roberto threw his own cards down in exasperation. "Threes and nines for twenty-four. Tough luck, Largo. Well, I may have won this round of cards, but you win the debate. This is abyssal misery here, and it's all thanks to Longoro's greed. We were fine when we took Kilgrun, and now this dirt. If we don't all die here, I'll be mighty surprised."

"Well, that's a cheerful thought," Pietro added.

"Nothing cheepful about this situation, Pip," Largo rumbled as he gathered the cards. "You can always go back to the warmth and safety of the command tent back behind the trenches if you don't like it. Here in this hole, we're all griping socialists. It just took Rob a little longer, is all. Must be his pride."

Julio gathered some snow in his helmet and held it over the heat crystal to get water.

"Be nice, Largo," he scolded. "Our captain is here for morale's sake, and he saved us all with these crystals, besides."

Largo stared at Julio but did not reply. For some reason, Julio thought back to the night Largo had almost shot Pietro. He shivered.

"Jules is right," Roberto added. "We've all gotta look out for each other now, 'cause the empire isn't gonna anymore. Deal out those cards, Largo, and I'll explain my thought process behind this change of heart."

Largo began dealing out cards as Roberto continued.

"Longoro made a promise to each and every one of us. Prosperity for Novens, and the reclaiming of our former empire. We had it. We had it with the fall of Kilgrun. We were all supposed to go

301

home and enjoy the fruits of our labours in this war, and enjoy our lives as imperial citizens, the chosen of the gods. Then Longoro got greedy. He set his sights too high, and we're all paying for it. The gods are abandoning us for that greed. That is why I'm officially declaring myself a socialist. This greed we have to fight for and this place of death we have to live in over a piece of dirt land that doesn't belong to us is showing me what it must have been like to grow up poor. Right, Largo? Fighting for your life because somebody else wants more than what they deserve."

Largo scoffed. "Jules is the only other one here who knows what it's like to grow up poor. Welcome to squalor, Rob."

Julio examined his cards and immediately folded. "Do you take back your ideas about the rest of the places we conquered, Rob?"

Roberto shook his head vehemently as he studied his own cards. "No. We won those battles because the gods had granted those lands to us centuries ago. I accepted my draft, and I accepted Longoro's promise, so I have nobody to blame but myself. However ..."

"What if there are no gods?" Julio interrupted. There was a silence.

"That's a pretty heretical thing to say," Pietro answered. "I raise an imaginary cigarette."

Julio looked up at the sky. "I dunno about you guys, but for me it's hard to believe in a lot of things after all that I've seen in this war. Maybe I'm just more sensitive to violence, but eventually it makes you wonder what the point of all the killing is, and why the gods would condone it. Sometimes I just think ... well, I've never seen them, so what proof is there? Some big crystal that nobody's ever seen?"

"I've seen it," Pietro replied. "It's pretty damn big."

"But is that proof?" Julio continued.

"Fuck your existential crisis, Jules, we're talking about mine here," Roberto said. "And I see your imaginary cigarette and raise you another, Pip. My point was that when we set foot on Parsish soil

302

we lost the favour of the gods. Just my opinion here, oh Jules-the-sudden-atheist. Longoro broke his promise, and thus my faith in the empire. He broke my heart."

Largo laughed uproariously. "I hope you don't mean that literally, Rob! You sound like a faggot!"

Roberto reddened and looked away. "It's not that kind of love, you dullard. Longoro represents the kind of man I always wanted to be. He did, anyway, until he betrayed me. Never trust your heart, gentlemen. I learned that when I fell in love for the first, only and last time."

"Was it with a man?" Largo chuckled. Pietro laughed along with him. Julio took a sip of water from his helmet and watched as Roberto glared daggers at his companions.

"I guess socialists can still be assholes," he muttered as he threw his cards down upon the snow. "What I'm saying is that my loss of faith is a lot like Jules'. Get fucked around enough and you stop believing in something."

Roberto stood up. "Anyway, I'm gonna try and get some sleep since the scattershot isn't booming today." He trudged off down the trench without another word.

Largo shrugged. "You still in, Pip? Jules?"

Pietro shook his head. "Nah, I have to write a letter before the fighting starts again. Sorry." He got up and turned to leave.

Julio looked up anxiously at his captain. "You're writing to Aliza again? Could you ask her how Ramona is doing? I haven't received a letter in a long time."

"I will, Jules. I'm sure there's no reason to worry, though. Communication lines are probably being disrupted by the Commonwealth all across Titania. My letter might not even make it back to Novem."

Julio frowned. "You know, it's funny. Ramona said that you and Aliza didn't hit it off that well. I guess she was mistaken."

"We didn't at first," Pietro said quickly. "But we started writing to each other after I got back to the front."

Julio smiled. "Think you've found the one?"

303

Pietro looked away. "We'll see. I've gotta go, Jules." He left at a brisk pace.

Julio looked over at Largo, whose eyes were narrowed. "What is it, Largo?"

"Never liked that kid, and now I know why. Don't you find it strange that Ramona's letters stopped right when Pietro started writing to Aliza?"

Julio's face darkened. "What are you saying?"

Largo shook his head. "Nothing. Yet."

Julio took another sip of frigid water. "I trust Pietro, no matter what you might think. He would never do that to me. Ramona will write back soon, you'll see."

Largo shrugged again. "Whatever you say, Jules. I still think I shoulda killed him that night in the stables."

Julio shivered again, not just from the cold.

***

2 Martia, 1877
Ramona my love,

It has been almost a year since your last letter and I worry. I know that the Commonwealth is making it difficult for correspondences all across the empire, but if you get this letter, then please try to write back to me. I just want to know that you're alive and well.

Pietro says that he has heard no word of you from Aliza, which worries me further. My heart aches, and all the horrors of this war pale in comparison to the pain I feel when I think of what might have happened to you. Is Novem still even safe?

We are under orders to remain here in this dismal place, somewhere in Parsu, but we are losing ground and men weekly. Pietro says there has been talk of breaking orders amongst the commanders. We are losing the war thanks to this Parsu blunder and their alliance with the Faxon Commonwealth. The only clear side is that the war may end, even if it is not in our favour.

This is my last sheet of paper, love. Please write back soon.
Please. I need to know that you are safe and well.
With all of my love,
Julio

Chapter 25

Timori and Paulo sat on the dock, legs dangling out over the murky river water below. Paulo enjoyed one of his usual cigarettes. Timori merely enjoyed the feeling of the warm, late summer breeze across his face. It was nice after a long night of work.

They didn't always smuggle crystals. Sometimes Timori followed Paulo to his meetings with miners and other ragtag socialists in a dimly lighted warehouse. The meetings mostly revolved around the gathering of what was dubbed 'intelligence' and arguments over the optimum time to perform a coup against the republic. Timori also helped Paulo move a great deal of weaponry from one place to another, as well as other goods useful to an army.

He tried once to feel guilty about what he was doing, but he found that he was starting to believe in the ideals of socialism. Why shouldn't he have the same rights and monetary compensation as everybody else? The class ladder was a societal construction, wholly unnecessary. It was exploitative. The more Timori spent time with Paulo, the more he believed in a revolution. They even agreed on matters of religion.

"So I'm not the only one who thinks that the Great Crystal is just a figurehead?" Timori said. "That's a relief."

"Figurehead? Pfft. I didn't even have a vision. I think some people make them up because they want to believe in something."

Timori wondered what it was he wanted to believe in. Was it his love for Racquela? She professed to have seen the same vision, but Timori wondered if it was all an elaborate setup by the church. Nothing was stopping the priests from imbuing a crystal in very specific ways to incite certain illusory sights in people. He wouldn't want it any differently if it meant keeping her, but Timori simply couldn't fathom a crystal being the voice of absent gods. It was a sham, but an advantageous one.

Timori stiffened as Paulo drew a small wand out of his coat. He placed it on Timori's lap.

"Things are going to get more dangerous from here on," Paulo said calmly. He twirled his cigarette between his fingers and looked out at the river. "The operation's getting bigger, which means that the republic is getting wind of it. I know you can handle yourself, but you should keep this on you, just in case."

Timori stared at the wand, cold and grey in his hand. With a simple pull of the trigger he could kill somebody. He slid the wand into his jacket pocket.

"Just in case," he echoed.

Paulo laughed to himself. Sometimes Timori wondered about the man's sanity, but he respected him nevertheless. Paulo was one of the only people that Timori considered to be his intellectual equal.

"Remember when you threatened me in the washroom that one time?" Paulo mused.

Timori remembered it well. Paulo's confidence and fearlessness were the only reasons that Timori hadn't punched him for his comment about Racquela.

"I had a wand in my pocket, then. I wouldn't have used it. I just thought it was funny."

Timori stared at Paulo. There were few people he knew whom he truly considered to be dangerous, but he counted Paulo among them.

"Paulo ... Who are you, really? I know you're not just some kid with ideas of grandeur. Everybody takes orders from you, even though you're just a student from Central."

Paulo was silent for a while, enough time to take several drags of his cigarette. Timori watched the dark water of the river rush by on its way to the sea. He could see it snake like a black ribbon through the slums of Avati. Paulo had told him a story a few nights ago about a killer who had once roamed the streets of Captus Nove and dumped his victims in the river. Timori shuddered to think that he used to go swimming in the Avati River with Jacoby when they were younger. Thoughts of Jacoby filled Timori's mind and he tried to push them away.

Paulo spoke just as Timori was about to let the subject drop.

"My uncle's not my real uncle, but he was a supporter of the Second Empire. I was too young to remember this, but I guess I was under the firing squad along with everybody else in my family."

"So how did you ...?"

"Let me finish," Paulo said abruptly. "Could you shoot an infant, even if you were ordered to? Even if you knew that some day that kid could grow up to try and take over his family's legacy? An innocent child? Well, I guess those soldiers couldn't. There are probably ten or twelve guys out there who know the secret. They must've hoped that I would just wind up some unlucky orphan somewhere to ease their consciences, but Uncle Gordo was a close friend of my family's. He was tenacious enough to avoid being blamed after the Great War, and he found me and took me in. To him I'm just a symbol, a figurehead as empty as the Great Crystal, to be used for his lofty goals. But I'm not just some puppet."

Timori splashed at the water with his boot. "That doesn't tell me who you are."

He wished that he had paid more attention to his history lessons, like Jacoby. Timori reminded himself again to stop thinking about his former best friend.

"It tells you what you need to know."

"So why tell me?" Timori asked. "What if I went to Parliament tomorrow and told them all about you?"

"I don't think you will, Tim. You believe in what I'm doing too much. You believe in equality, and you know what it's like not to have enough to eat some days. I wouldn't have brought you into all this if I weren't certain what kind of person you are. You and I, we're the same in many ways, Timori. We believe in something, not like people like Jacoby who just drift through life without forming a real opinion about anything."

Timori nearly leapt to Jacoby's defence. Jacoby's lie was just one thing in a long list of problems Timori had with his life. Revolution offered an answer.

***

Timori strode onto the path that led from Corti Street to Avati Hill Park. Under the crook of his arm was a box of chocolates. The sun was out, but it was nowhere near as hot as it had been the previous summer. As Timori reminisced about the past year, he thought about his handshake with Jacoby on Memorial Bridge. He thought about the first time he had seen Racquela's face.

She was waiting on a wrought-iron park bench underneath a whiteoak tree with her hands folded in her lap. She looked radiant with her hair done up in curls, and she was wearing a white cotton dress with a red floral print that Timori hadn't seen before. As he approached her, he noted that something about her seemed apprehensive. Not for the first time, Timori wished that he was an empath.

Timori handed Racquela the chocolates and sat down beside her on the bench, then planted a kiss on her cheek.

"Hi, sweetheart," he said. "I'm glad you wanted to spend time together today. I've missed you. You must be feeling better about things. About you and me."

Racquela looked at Timori but didn't meet his gaze.

"Timori ..."

Timori took Racquela's hands in his own. Hers were damp. He wondered what Racquela could possibly be nervous about, but realized that she was probably scared to apologize to him for the way that she had been acting. No harm was done, in Timori's opinion. He was anxious for things to go back to the way they had once been.

"Yes, love?"

"I'm ..." Racquela stopped in the middle of her sentence and her lip began to tremble. Timori felt his guts clench as Racquela simply stared at him speechlessly.

"What is it? Is everyone all right? Are you pregnant?"

"I'm appealing for an annulment of the betrothals," Racquela said. Timori reeled backward as though he had been physically struck.

"What? Why? You can't do that. We're legally betrothed, you can't just leave me."

Racquela swallowed hard and finally looked Timori in the eyes.

"I can, Tim, and I am. I'm sorry, but this isn't working out, and I have to be honest with you about something. I bribed my way into the betrothals. I paid a priest to make sure that I was chosen. Whoever was supposed to be there was replaced by me. I'm sorry, but I'm coming clean about it. All of the betrothals are getting annulled."

Timori tried to hold himself together. He wasn't sure whether he would explode with rage or break down and cry. His world was flying apart in front of him and he was powerless to stop it.

"So? So what if you bribed him? So what about the betrothals? Don't we work well together? I love you, godsdamnit. Doesn't that fucking mean anything to you?"

"Timori, I love you too, but ..."

"But what?" Timori stood up and waved his arms around angrily. A group of young women passing through the park nearby quickly fled the scene. "You just said it yourself, you love me! What else matters?"

Racquela didn't move. "The rest of it, Tim. I'm not happy. We fight all the time, you smother me, and you have no real ambition. Love isn't everything."

"No ambition? I'll be whatever you want me to be! I swear!"

"That's just the problem, Tim. You don't want to be anything for yourself. There's nothing that you can say to change my mind. I just wanted to tell you in person. I'm sorry, Tim, but I have to fix this mistake. Goodbye."

She stood up. Timori grabbed her by the shoulders and spun her around to face him.

"What about Jake and Crystara? You're just going to ruin their relationship too?"

Racquela shook her head. "You know they're not happy either, Tim. If you look at their relationship, you'll see our own. Now let me go, please."

Racquela left the shelter of the whiteoak and began to walk away.

Timori chased after her. "You can't just walk away from me like that! Can't we talk about this?" He grabbed her by the wrist and wrenched her back to him.

"Let me go, Tim, or I'll scream."

Timori did not let go. "Why are you doing this to me?" he demanded.

"I made a mistake, Tim. I have to fix it."

"So that's all I am, then? A mistake? The betrothal means nothing? Our love means nothing?"

Timori's grip tightened. Racquela's eyes narrowed as she struggled against him.

"You never believed in the Great Crystal, Tim. And I do love you, but I don't want to be with you. I think we would be better off as friends." She said the last part through gritted teeth.

"Friends," Timori echoed. He had no idea how Racquela could claim to love him and not want to be with him at the same time. She wanted to be friends. Timori felt worthless. He wasn't even good enough for the girl he was promised to, the girl who claimed to love him. He was a mistake that Racquela had made. He was nothing.

"Tim? You're hurting my arm."

Timori was shaking with rage. "You're destroying my life, Racquela."

"Let me go, Tim. Please."

"I can't. I don't want to."

Racquela twisted her arm and broke out of Timori's grip. For a moment they stared at each other from across the short space between them. As Timori opened his mouth to speak, Racquela turned and ran. Timori wanted to chase after her and convince her somehow not to leave him, but his legs buckled from underneath him.

He wept openly as the first whiteoak blossom of the season began to fall.

***

Timori returned home that evening with dark thoughts on his mind. He had shouted at Racquela from the street in front of the De'Trini estate for an hour until Joven De'Trini threatened to telegram the police if he didn't leave. It was his last shot at convincing her not to appeal for an annulment, and she hadn't even had the decency to talk to him about it. He had never felt so alone. He no longer had a best friend and was soon to lose his betrothed. He had lost her despite his best efforts.

As he walked into the kitchen, he was surprised to find Nicola fixing dinner. Timori examined the fresh pasta in the pot of water on the stove and walked over to the icebox without a word. As he opened the lid, he was amazed to find it full.

"How did Mom afford all these groceries?" he asked.

Nicola looked over at him as she stirred a pot of pasta sauce with the only wooden spoon in the house.

"Racquela brought them over while you were gone. She kept saying 'I'm sorry', but she wouldn't say what for. What's going on, Tim? Is something wrong with you two?"

Timori sat down at the table and buried his head in his arms. "Yes. Something is very wrong. She's leaving me, Nicola."

Nicola stopped stirring. "Why?"

"I don't know, Nicky."

"Well, why did she bring us all this food, then?"

"Because she's a good person, Nicky. Whether we're together or not. It's why I love her."

Nicola frowned. "But she doesn't love you?"

"I'm going to bed," Timori said. "Try and make that food in the icebox last for a while, will you?"

Timori stomped up to his room and sat down on his bed to cry. Without thinking, he pulled the wand out of his pocket. He stared at the cold piece of metal with its bright red crystal for over an hour.

Chapter 26

Originally, Ramona had every intention of telling Julio what had happened with Pietro. She owed that much to him and more. Even though she felt that she didn't deserve him, she secretly hoped that somehow he would bring himself to forgive her.

Then she started to get sick in the morning.

She denied what was happening for as long as she knew was possible before she finally went to see Doctor Di'Matti. After a few simple tests, he congratulated her on her pregnancy. Ramona cried even as she thanked her doctor.

The timing was undeniable. It was Pietro's. Ramona did the only thing that she could think of. She started writing to Pietro. It was his child, after all, and he had a right to know.

Pietro promised in his very first reply to tell Julio everything that had happened, to take the burden off of Ramona's shoulders. She had betrayed Julio so deeply that she couldn't imagine how hurt he would feel, but Ramona saw no other option. Moments after she discovered she was pregnant, she knew that she could never abandon her child. She hadn't been raised that way. Her fate was inextricably tied to the baby inside her, and to Pietro. She didn't know if she could ever love Pietro, but she knew that he loved her, and by her actions she would have to marry him as soon as he returned from the war.

Pietro told her how excited he was, both to marry Ramona and raise their child together, in every letter he sent. He said that Julio had dealt with it well, and was upset but willing to forgive both Ramona and Pietro, for he loved them both. He was too hurt to keep writing to Ramona, though, which brought tears to Ramona's eyes – but she knew it was her own fault, just as she knew that she would never be able to completely forgive herself for what she had done.

Ramona could not find another job. Nobody was willing to hire a pregnant woman. She considered lying about it, but by the time the thought crossed her mind she was already beginning to show too much. Ramona guiltily accepted the pay that both Pietro and Julio sent her and promised herself to pay Julio back once he returned from the war.

She gave birth without complications, assisted by Doctor Di'Matti and a nurse. Aliza was there as well, and held her hand. Her baby boy was born on New Year's Day, the first of Martia, 1877. She named him Drago.

Ramona wrote one last letter to Julio, but she couldn't bring herself to send it.

***

Longoro was convinced that the gods were still with him, even when Milosa was freed by the Faxon Commonwealth in Yuna 1877. General Thessau argued that 'had Longoro pulled his troops from Parsu before the winter of 1876, the Noven military's superior tactics, training and equipment might have saved his empire'. Longoro sacrificed the lives of over 100,000 Noven men to the Parsu front before finally calling the order to pull back in Quinta 1877. With Milosa freed, the Noven Empire was fighting a war on five fronts: the Milosa-Nilonne border, northern Nilonne, southern Kilgrun, eastern Kilgrun (as Parsu advanced westward in assistance to the Commonwealth) and the pitched naval and marine battles that took place near Southern Novem.

The following year and a half were the bloodiest of the war. The Second Empire slowly lost territory and men to the Commonwealth and Parsu, as well as to the fresh volunteers of the three kingdoms that were being freed. The Noven Empire contracted in a similar fashion to how it had expanded, and everybody but Longoro seemed to see it coming.

Back in his palace at Captus Nove, Longoro had grown increasingly paranoid and delusional. An attempt on his life was made in Septembra 1877 by Fiscus De'Lorre, a trusted high-ranking member of Longoro's secret police, and again in Martia

1878 by an unknown sniper who was never caught. Longoro was eating breakfast on a palace balcony with his wife and children. Sadly, Longoro's firstborn son, Titus, was hit by the longwand and he died before he could be rushed to the palace doctor. He was fourteen years old.

There is some conjecture among historians that Titus had been the sniper's target all along. As Emperor Longoro's firstborn son, he was being groomed to become the next emperor and had been trained in politics, the arts and military strategy. While Longoro always claimed not to play favourites with his children, all accounts concur that he spent the most time with Titus.

The 'Titus theory' states that the intent in shooting Longoro's firstborn son was to further unhinge Longoro's sanity and drive him to make grievous errors in the war, thus ending it sooner. Though the sniper's identity, and thus intent, were never verified, Imperial detectives deduced the shot came from the Old Temple's bell tower, which had a clear view of the western palace balcony. The prevailing speculation, then, is that the sniper was likely a member of the Church of the Great Crystal.

After Titus's untimely death, Lucrezia Longoro 'begged (Maximus Longoro) to allow her to escape with the children, for their safety', Casto tells us. The Emperor remained convinced that the palace was the safest place in the world for his family, so long as nobody ever went outside. In fact, it was from that point that Longoro no longer made any public appearances at all. Casto left clues in his memoir, however, that the Empress's desire to escape may have been motivated by fear of Longoro himself as well. Casto spoke of 'a love that has gone sour, like milk left out of the icebox too long. Lucrezia cringes at Max's footsteps. He looks at her like he still loves her, but his eyes are wild and his temper unpredictable. The losses to the Empire's territories are unhinging him, bit by bit.'

Abroad, decisive Alliance victories in Nilonne and Kilgrun spelled defeat for the armies of the empire, and many brigades were wiped out entirely. By Novembra 1878, Novem had been pushed back entirely to its pre-war borders and all efforts were put into homeland defence. The war was expected to end before 1879, but Longoro and his proud supporters held out on Noven soil to the very last.

The militia of Novem held Parsu and the Commonwealth at bay until Martia 1879. It is argued that they might have held out much longer had a large contingent of the militia not surrendered. Some called it cowardly. Others said that it was wise to recognize that the war had already been lost. By the time the Commonwealth invaded Captus Nove, support for Longoro had dwindled down to a few. Everywhere defamatory statements about Longoro were scrawled in graffiti, and in many places the Commonwealth were welcomed with open arms as liberators of an oppressed people.

On the fifteenth of Martia 1879, Commonwealth troops from the United Territories swarmed the Imperial Palace with orders to find the emperor and his entire family, dead or alive. It was Maximus Longoro's forty-seventh birthday.

***

Pietro craned his head over the ruined section of wall, then quickly ducked back behind cover. Julio could hear wandshot ricocheting off of the other side of the bricks and cringed. The remainder of their battalion was nearly surrounded. Julio knew that things were nearing the end, unless they could all find a way to flee. It didn't seem likely. Pinned down in the ruins of a small Nilonnese town, their last turret wand had failed that morning. Pietro had altered the crystal too many times, Roberto said. Pietro carried the company's few remaining replacement crystals, but it was open space between their wall and the turret.

"About thirty metres," Pietro said to his company. There were seven of them remaining: Captain Pietro Garus, who was in command of the entire battalion after the colonel had died, Private

Julio Vellize, Sergeant Roberto Ruveldi, Corporal Largo Mita, Corporal Alfredo Bocco, and two privates whose names Julio couldn't remember. The rest of the other two companies were at the western edge of the town, attempting to cripple the scattershot wands as a part of the retreat operation.

"That's too far to go out in the open," Roberto said as scratched the wandshot scar on his leg, "even with covering fire."

The captain nodded. "I know. No choice, though. I'm the only speaker left, Rob, and if I don't get that turret up again then nobody's getting out of here alive. A and C companies should be taking out those scattershot wands, so all we have to contend with are those godsdamned Faxons over by the sandbags. If I get the turret going, they'll be cut to pieces and it'll buy us enough time to escape. No arguments on this one. This is our last chance to get out of here so I expect my orders to be followed."

He pointed at the two privates leaning against the wall next to Julio.

"Tosci, Pellero, you're with me on this one, providing covering fire. Bocco, as soon as we leave the wall and draw their fire, you need to get over to A Company and let them know what we're doing, and that it's now or never to start the retreat. The rest of you ..."

His face softened as he looked at his closest comrades. "... I expect some damn good covering fire from behind this wall. The whole plan is dirt without the turret anyway. Sergeant Ruveldi is in charge if I don't make it back. Got it?"

"Yes, sir," Roberto agreed. "Just be careful out there, Pip."

Pietro's eyes met with Julio's, and it felt as though the weight of the entire world was in something unspoken between the two of them. Pietro opened his mouth to speak, but for a drawn-out moment, no sound came forth.

"Julio ... Jules, I want you to know that ..."

Julio leaned forward to hear what his captain had to say, knowing that it could well be important. It was likely to be the last time that any of them would speak to each other, unless by some miracle they all escaped unscathed.

As he waited for Pietro to finish his sentence, Julio found himself thinking about Ramona. He had never trusted in Largo's suspicions about Pietro and Ramona. It had all seemed too convenient, and fit in perfectly with Largo's disdain for his captain. Julio had long ago assumed that some terrible fate had befallen his lover, but in the crux of that moment where all of their lives hung in the balance, Julio knew that the first thing he would do if he ever made it back to Captus Nove was to find Ramona, if she still lived.

"Yes, Pietro?" Julio found himself saying. He thought his friend was stalling, searching for words. Brief moments seemed to stretch out when Julio was in a dangerous situation, so he understood Pietro's difficulty. The plan to fix the turret was incredibly dangerous, and Pietro was only slightly braver than Julio, despite all they had been through.

"Captain?" Julio whispered.

Pietro looked down and shook his head with a laugh.

"Nothing. It's not important right now. I'll tell you when we all make it out of here to safety."

Julio nodded. "Right," he said with a smile. "Now's hardly the time for small talk. Good luck, captain. We'll cover you."

Pietro made a brave salute and left the cover of the wall with Tosci and Pellero. Julio brought his longwand to bear along with Roberto and Largo and laid down suppressing fire on the Faxon soldiers across the rubble-littered plaza. Julio breathed a sigh of relief when the Faxon troops sought cover of their own behind the sandbags, which gave Pietro a chance to replace the crystal in the turret.

Julio kept his longwand trained on the sandbags. His finger was a shaky millimetre from the trigger as he watched for the slightest sign of movement from across the open space. He could hear Pietro toiling away as he pried the old, broken crystal out of its socket and began to fetch the fresh one out of his pack. A bead of sweat rolled onto Julio's eyebrow and he wiped it away with his sleeve. He never took his eyes off of the sandbags, but he began muttering for the gods to assist Pietro in his endeavour.

Behind the sandbags and the cover of a broken-down brick building came the deafening, disheartening boom of a scattershot wand. Julio cringed. The other companies had failed in their mission. Faxon soldiers had managed to repair their long-range weapons. The only remaining choice was for Pietro to take out the close-by soldiers with the turret wand and then effect a swift retreat from the area before they were all blown to pieces.

The first round of scattershot landed in the centre of the plaza, scattering dust and debris all over the place. Julio's eyes widened.

"Pietro, get out of there!" he shouted. "Scattershot!"

"One sec!" came the reply. "I'm almost ..."

A second boom echoed throughout the broken city, followed by the tell-tale whistle as the scattershot round sailed through the air toward its destination. Julio's eyes were locked on Pietro as his friend manically shoved the fresh crystal into its compartment on the turret wand.

A fraction of a second later, the scattershot found its target. Pietro never even saw it coming. The turret wand was reduced to debris, and the image of the privates' bodies being torn apart and sent through the air would haunt Julio for the rest of his life.

"Pietro!" Julio screamed in vain. Clouds of dust had been kicked up by the scattershot. He didn't know where his friend had landed, or if he was still alive. The rational part of his mind told him that nobody could have survived a direct hit like that, but another part of him was not prepared to give up on Pietro.

"Oh, gods," Ruveldi muttered. He was shaking.

Julio scarcely noticed as wandshot began to crack and ricochet around him. The enemy had begun to fire upon their position again. A pair of strong hands grabbed the front of his trench coat and hauled him back to the safety of cover. Largo's bearded face was centimetres from his own.

"You heard the captain's orders," he said. "We're getting the fuck out of here. Now."

Julio shook his head slowly. The shock was still settling in.

"Not without Pietro. He still has a girl back home. We have to get him."

Largo shook Julio violently. "Didn't you just see what happened? Pip is dead, and we'll be dead too if we don't get out of here now.

Julio shook his head again, dumbly. "I'm not leaving without him."

Largo gave Julio a wild-eyed glare. "I didn't want to have to do this ..."

Julio expected the corporal to knock him into submission and carry him out of there, but instead Largo began rummaging in his pack.

"Gods, Largo, not now," Roberto pleaded. "We don't have time for this!"

"It's now or never," Largo replied as he produced a few crumpled sheets of paper from the folds of his canvas pack.

"Julio needs to understand why his captain isn't worth saving. This letter was in Pietro's gear. I stole it two days ago."

Largo handed the sheets to Julio, who accepted them as he gave Largo a questioning look. The scattershot wand boomed in the distance.

30 Maya 1878

Pietro,

I fear for you and Julio more and more each day. Despite what the newspapers say, I know that we're losing the war. If only Longoro would surrender, then this could all be over and you could return home to us.

Julio curled up into a ball, choking back sobs. The letter was in Ramona's handwriting, unmistakeably. He couldn't believe it.

Ramona had been alive the whole time. She was alive and writing to Pietro. As he cried, Julio continued to read.

Thank you for telling Julio the truth. He's such a kind person, the best man I know, and didn't deserve any of this. Hopefully in time we can all be friends after the two of you return home.

Drago gets bigger every day. He is so healthy and beautiful, Pietro. He took his first steps last week. You would've been so proud to see him! He looks just like you. I can't wait for you to meet your son. Thankfully he's not old enough yet to start talking and asking about his father. I want you to be home for that.

You boys will look after each other, won't you? Please come home safely.

Ramona

"She's alive," Julio sobbed. "Gods, she's alive."

"Great plan, Largo," Roberto said. The scattershot wand fired again and he waited for the din to subside. "Now we've got a grown man reduced to a blubbering child on top of our dead captain."

Julio looked up at Roberto and wiped the tears from his eyes. "He's not dead. He can't be dead. He has a son."

Julio didn't see Largo's hand coming as it struck him across the face.

"Pull yourself together, Julio! Don't you get it? He betrayed you. He stole your woman, and then lied to you about it. You owe him nothing, and he's dead. We have to get out of here, now."

"I ..." Julio choked back more tears. Could he bring himself to leave Pietro on the battlefield, even after all that he had done? Pietro had a baby back home. The pain of betrayal made Julio's chest hurt, but not quite so much as the thought of leaving somebody to die.

In the silence, a weak voice floated up over the din of the battlefield.

"Help." It sounded like Pietro. "Julio ... Rob ... help me."

Roberto's eyes widened. "Gods, did you hear that? He's still alive."

Julio peered cautiously over the broken wall. As the dust settled, he could see Pietro lying against another wall, several metres from the smashed turret. He was bleeding from several wounds, but he didn't appear to be missing any limbs, although his leg was bent at an odd angle. Julio marvelled at the captain's luck. The two privates had been scattered into pieces across the plaza. Sadly, it was a sight that Julio was used to by then.

"We have to get him," Julio decided. "We'll cross the plaza to him, take cover behind that wall, patch up those holes he's got and flee."

Roberto nodded. "I agree. We can't just leave him here, despite all that he's done to Jules."

Largo threw up his hands. "Have you both gone insane? We are under orders to get out of here, and that piece of dirt completely betrayed you, Jules. He even lied to you to cover up what he did, probably hoping that you would die out here somewhere so that he would never have to own up to his ..."

"Shut up!" Julio shouted. Another tear rolled down his cheek. He didn't bother to wipe it away. Instead he clutched his wand close and prepared to stand.

"Either help us rescue the captain or stay here, like a coward. Pietro has a son, and I could never abandon him, regardless of the circumstances. Call me a dullard, but I still love Ramona. I swore that I would do anything for her, and I still will. Ready, Roberto?"

Roberto nodded. Julio looked over at Largo. The large man was reluctantly getting his longwand ready.

"I'm no coward," he muttered to Julio. "Let's go."

The trio stood up and made a dash across the open street. Julio stopped to lay down suppressing fire upon the Faxon soldiers at the other end of the open area. Roberto was the only one who knew anything about medicine. Julio wanted to make sure that the sergeant made it to Pietro first.

There was a sudden blast of heat, and pain ripped through the entire right side of Julio's body. He found that he was suddenly flying through the air. He hadn't even heard the blast. He hadn't heard anything at all.

The last thing that he saw before he blacked out was Largo approaching Pietro, wand still raised.

***

Emperor Longoro was executed by a wand squad on Crystus Hill Plaza, along with most of the remaining members of his cabinet and family. Notably absent were Lucrezia Longoro and her youngest son, Paulo, as well as Leonardo Posco. Lucrezia was discovered a week later by a Faxon platoon. She was travelling with a small retinue along Novem's Eastern coast, presumably heading for Los Maros. Having identified Lucrezia as the Empress, the platoon executed her and her entire entourage, including her newborn son.

Leonardo Posco was never found. Many theories have surfaced regarding the infamous man's disappearance, but the man himself has not. To this day the fate of Posco remains the 'great mystery of the Great War'.

Longoro's final words before his execution were "The gods will never forgive you for this." His name, glorified and vilified by those of us who remember him, went down in history as one of the greatest and most terrible emperors ever to rule Novem.

This old republican also hopes that he is the last emperor that Novem will ever see. The damage done to Novem has not yet been repaired in the fifteen years since the end of the war. The economy of the 1890s is worse than it was during the Third Republic, thanks to trade embargoes and sanctions that served as Novem's punishment for the war crimes of 1874-1879, combined with the global depression. The poor, just as dissatisfied with the Fifth Republic as they were with the

declining Second Empire, still clamour for a truly socialist government.

Nothing about the Great War taught the common person to have any faith in humanity, or politicians especially. Longoro's punishment may have been swift, but the rest of Novem, culpable by association, is still paying the price.

What drives a man to do the things Longoro did? What made him betray our trust? Is it man's constant yearning for something just out of reach? Was he simply the victim of corrupt power? Did he take the adoration of Novem for granted and use it for his own ends? He crippled his nation, but in the end, it is the nation that has endured.

The story of Emperor Longoro is one of love and betrayal. It is a story of Novem's love for him and his betrayal of that love.

Chapter 27

Crystara knew it was coming from the moment Jacoby approached her in the outer courtyard during lunch. She knew it even before she read his mind. It was in the look on his face and the determined way that he was walking. Jacoby Padrona was going to try to leave her.

She supposed it was only a matter of time. Everybody left her in the end, after all. She leaned against the marble statue of Jova that stood in the middle of the yard and braced herself for the worst.

"Listen, Crystara ... we need to talk."

She noted that his face was unusually passive as he folded his arms.

Crystara wanted to save herself the trouble and sift through his thoughts to find out what the excuse was, but she also wanted to hear what Jacoby had to say first. She bit her lip and waited for whatever he could throw at her. Whatever it was, Crystara knew that they could work past it as long as she could convince him. They loved each other, after all. Anything else just took a little hard work and they could make it through together, she knew.

"What about?" she said finally, playing dumb.

"You ... oh, I thought you would know already," Jacoby said.

"Know what?"

Jacoby shook his head. There was a defiant gleam in his eyes. "Cut it. I know that you're a reader, Crys."

"You ... how did you?"

As she phrased the question, she already knew the answer. Lenara. The bitch had finally betrayed her, just as Crystara thought she might. The worst part about being back-stabbed by Lenara was that it had all been Lenara's idea. Crystara had gone along with it because Jacoby reminded her less of her father than somebody arrogant like Paulo. What a great idea that had turned out to be. She was about to lose Jacoby, regardless.

326

"Aren't you just going to read my thoughts like you always do?"

Crystara fumed. "I don't always do that, Jake. Besides, it's no different from intruding on somebody else's feelings like empathy does. Why don't you just fucking tell me why you're breaking up with me, instead?"

Jacoby let out air through his nose and frowned.

"I'm not happy. I thought that I was stuck with it, not being happy and being with you, but now that I know the truth about the betrothals it doesn't have to be that way. You and I have little in common and we fight all the time. What kind of relationship is that? I wasn't ready for these betrothals, anyway. I'm sixteen years old. I want to live a little, be young. Not be stuck somewhere that only goes one possible direction."

Crystara took Jacoby's hands in hers. She knew that she could change his mind, if she tried. He just wasn't seeing things straight.

"Jake, listen. We can make this work, I know we can. I know what it's like not to be happy, I live with it every day. I can make you happy, we can be happy if you just give me the chance. Tell me what's wrong and I'll fix it, I swear. We can go back to the way things were in the beginning. We were happy then, remember? There's nothing we can't fix if we try. You want me to come out with you more, be more fun? I will. I'll do whatever you want, just please don't leave me. Don't leave me."

Jacoby stood, silent, for an agonizingly long time. Crystara refrained from reading his mind again. She didn't want to if she didn't have to, not this time.

"This isn't something we can fix, Crystara. We're not compatible. No."

Crystara couldn't believe that the boy who said he loved her could be so callous, so devoid of any emotion as he spoke to her. Was he always like that and any compassion he showed was just a façade? It hurt more deeply than any hit she had ever taken from her father.

327

"Jacoby, please! If you love me ... then we can work this out, I know we can. Please, for the love of the gods, please!"

A crowd was starting to gather around the statue to watch the argument, but Crystara didn't care. They could gawk all they liked.

"I ..." Jacoby stared up at the sky and shut his mouth. He was hiding something.

"What aren't you telling me?" she demanded.

"I don't love you." His forest green eyes looked right into hers as he said it, coldly boring into her soul with their gaze. "I don't know if I ever did."

Crystara fell to her knees. Everything sounded far away as she sobbed on the grass. Jacoby continued to speak, saying something about trying to love her and wanting to believe it was true. She wanted to tear out her hair and scream until she lost her voice. Her worst nightmare had become reality. Crystara had given her heart, her body and her soul to the boy standing over her and he was crushing it all under his bootheel. Why would he be so cruel? She wanted to curl up into a ball and die.

Jacoby was still talking, but at a distance, not reassuring her. He was afraid of getting close. He was afraid of actually feeling something, the cold bastard. He was afraid of his emotions being read. Jacoby probably hadn't realized that Crystara couldn't actually read emotions at all, just thoughts.

By Jacoby's continuing string of excuses, Crystara knew that he was still hiding something. She read his mind. Then she screamed.

"Crystara, please. This is a public ..."

Her slap came so quickly, she didn't even realize she had hit him until a collective gasp arose from the gathered crowd. Jacoby stared at her with a shocked expression. Her hand was stinging.

"You cheating sack of dirt!" she screamed. She wanted the whole world to know what he had done. "Get the fuck out of here and go back to your whore."

"Crys, wait, let me ..."

"No," she interrupted. She grabbed him by the shirt. "I never want to see you again. Ever. If you ever come near me, I swear to the gods I will kill you. You know what? I'm glad, now that I know what a cheater and a liar you are. Get out of my sight."

Jacoby left without another word, tail between his legs as she expected. Crystara fled the school, and made it to the safety of solitude before bursting into tears again.

The tears lasted until she fell asleep that evening.

***

Crystara was surprised by a knock at the door the following day. She hadn't gone to school, but she hardly cared about that after what had happened with Jacoby.

Thankfully, her father was away picketing with the other miners for once so she wouldn't be bothered. As she tromped down the stairs in yesterday's clothes and makeup, which had smeared all the way down her face, she found herself hoping that it was Jacoby, come to tell her that he had changed his mind.

Instead it was Racquela.

"Hey," Racquela said. Her concern for Crystara hadn't stopped her from doing her makeup and picking out an expensive-looking silk dress before coming over. "I heard about what happened. How are you doing?"

"Terrible," she admitted. She didn't want Racquela to see her in that condition but it was already too late. Besides, Racquela was the one person left in the world that she could trust.

"Dad's not around. Do you want to come in?"

"Okay," Racquela said as she crossed the threshold. Racquela fidgeted with her purse, but Crystara refrained from reading her best friend's mind to find out what she was nervous about. It was probably something to do with Timori, anyway. Crystara knew that her reading had caused enough trouble already. She led Racquela up to her room.

"Did you hear from everybody at school that Jacoby is a cheating bastard?" Crystara asked. She promised herself that she wouldn't cry anymore, but even as she said the words, she could feel the tears begin to fall. Racquela put her arms around Crystara and let her cry until she was ready to continue.

"Maybe it's for the best," Racquela suggested. "You two didn't seem to be very happy."

"I was happy," Crystara said. "Happier with Jake than I was at any other point in my life. He said that he wasn't, but I know that's not entirely true. He just couldn't deal with any kind of difficulty because he likes things to be easy all the time. The fucking coward."

"Well, if he cheated on you," Racquela began, "maybe this is the way it should be. You can always appeal for an annulment of the betrothals."

Crystara had already thought about appealing for an annulment. She was certain that Keeper Orvin would easily grant one to her. The last thing she wanted, though, was for Jacoby and Lenara to be able to run off and be happy together. She hadn't decided yet if she still loved Jacoby despite what he had done, but if Crystara couldn't be content then she wasn't prepared to allow anybody else to be, either. It wasn't fair otherwise. Crystara didn't know if she could ever forgive Jacoby for his betrayal, but she knew that she could keep him, legally, if she wanted to. He and Lenara could do absolutely nothing about it. As a reader, Crystara could watch Jacoby's every move, and it was her intention to do just that. She would make him love her by giving him no other choice.

"I don't want an annulment," Crystara said. "I want to fix this."

"You want to fix this? After he cheated on you? Don't you want to be with somebody who will treat you the way you deserve, Crystara?"

Crystara looked at Racquela with disdain. A highborn like her would never understand.

"I don't believe that anybody ever will, Racquela. I'll make Jacoby sorry that he ever cheated on me, though, and ensure that he can never do so again."

Racquela looked horrified, but Crystara didn't care. She knew that Racquela had always taken Timori for granted, and although Crystara had never found Timori attractive, she was resentful of how much Timori gave his love to Racquela and how she didn't seem to appreciate it.

"What if ..." Racquela hesitated. "What if somebody else appeals for an annulment? What will you do then?"

"You mean somebody like Lenara? I have other ways of stopping her, if necessary." She thought of Keeper Orvin again.

"What do you mean?" Racquela fidgeted with her crystal ring. Crystara grew suspicious. Racquela could never sit still when she was hiding something. She forced herself, not for the first time that day, to refrain from reading her friend's mind.

"Wait, are you appealing for an annulment?" Crystara said. "Racquela, don't. Please don't. I'm asking you as your friend. I need to keep Jacoby. I might be miserable, but at least I won't be alone. And you can't do this to Timori. I don't know if you have any idea how much he loves you. He would do anything for you. He would die for you, Racquela, and you're just going to throw that away?"

Racquela looked at Crystara pleadingly. "I'm miserable with him, Crystara."

"I'm miserable all the time, and I somehow find a way to carry on. You just take everything for granted, including Timori."

Racquela stood up. "But what you're talking about sounds crazy. Staying with Jacoby just so that he can't be happy? Let him go! It obviously isn't working between you two, and he cheated on you besides. Let me get an annulment and we can all go on with our lives."

"You were the one who wanted this!" Crystara shouted. "You got me to help you get into this betrothal, and now you want out? You're so fucking privileged, Racquela, can't you see how selfish this is? You decide that something is too much effort so you quit?"

"I'm being selfish? You want to stay with Jaocby just to make him miserable! That's selfish!"

Crystara knocked all of the items off of her dresser with a swing of an arm. All of the makeup and jewellery that Racquela had bought her clattered to the floor.

"He cheated on me! And you want to call me selfish? You bitch! Maybe Timori deserves to be free of you. Go on, try and get your annulment then. We'll just see if Keeper Orvin will let you. He'll probably deny any connection to a bribery attempt and you'll be stuck."

Racquela began to cry. "Crystara, please. I don't want to lose you, too."

Crystara glowered. "You should have thought about that before you took Jacoby's side in this. Get out of here. I do not want to be friends anymore."

"Fine, Crystara," Racquela said as she fought back more tears. "If that's the way you want it, then fine." Racquela fled.

Crystara raged about her room for a few minutes, throwing things about and shattering her dresser mirror with a fist before she began to calm down. Certain that Racquela had left for good, Crystara angrily threw on her coat and left the house with a satisfying slam of the door. She had to visit Keeper Orvin before Racquela did.

***

"My hands are tied," Keeper Orvin said as he picked another shard of glass out of Crystara's bloodied knuckles. "There's nothing I can do, Crystara. I'm sorry."

Crystara shifted uneasily in her chair. Even Keeper Orvin was turning against her, it seemed, and he was her last resort, the only person left that she thought she could trust.

"But the Great Crystal sanctioned it!" she argued. "And you were the one who made me join the betrothals as part of the deal! Now you want to take it all back? How can you just allow an annulment? Wouldn't an admission of culpability undermine the church, if Racquela tells everyone that you allowed yourself to be bribed by her?"

Keeper Orvin began to wind gauze around Crystara's injured hand. He looked apologetic, but, as usual, Crystara could glean nothing from his mind.

"Nobody is going to find out about that," Orvin said. "However, you haven't been entirely honest with me, either. Crys, I'm not upset with you, but I know what you and Lenara did."

Crystara bit her lip. "Who did you read? Me? I thought that you couldn't."

Keeper Orvin shook his head sadly. "I can read you sometimes because you're still unpracticed, but in this case I didn't read anybody. The Great Crystal told me, Crys. It's been waiting for this annulment."

Crystara slammed her uninjured hand upon the desk. "The Great Crystal isn't a person! Its opinion isn't worth a shard!"

Keeper Orvin took a tissue out of the first aid kit and began wiping away Crystara's smeared makeup.

"That crystal has more sway over the church than I do, Crystara, regardless of how you feel about it. Gods or no, it has power and influence and a mind of its own. If it wants an annulment of these betrothals, I have no choice but to comply or I would be immediately excommunicated and replaced by another high priest. I'm sorry about this, really I am, but I'm afraid you're just going to have to let Jacoby go. You can do better than him anyway. You're young and beautiful and have your whole life ahead of you. Do you really want to stay with somebody who treats you the way he does?"

Crystara stared at the floor. "No. But I don't want him to just be able to get away with everything he did. He does not deserve to be happy."

Keeper Orvin stood up and walked over to Crystara to give her a hug. "Perhaps not, but you do. You won't be able to focus on your own happiness if you're always so concerned with your own misery. Trust me on this. These feelings will pass, I promise."

"I have never felt so alone," Crystara admitted as she shed a tear.

Keeper Orvin wiped the trickling bead away from Crystara's face and smiled. "You still have me, and I will never leave you. Until I die, at least." He chuckled.

"That's not funny," Crystara said as she flexed her bandaged fingers. "If you won't help me, does that mean the Great Crystal won't, either?"

"You're not allowed to speak to it."

"I know."

"But you're telling me right now that you might try to, anyway?" Keeper Orvin grabbed a small white crystal from his desk and began twirling it through his fingers.

Crystara stared at the door behind Keeper Orvin. "I might." She hoped that such a threat might change his mind about the annulment.

"Then we will both do what we must when the time comes."

***

Crystara cried for days straight. She barely ate. She barely slept. Everything reminded her of Jacoby. Every book she read, there was a character like him. Every time she went outside, she remembered a time that she and Jacoby had shared in that exact same spot. The school was filled with memories of him. No matter where she went, she couldn't escape Jacoby. When she saw him in the hallways or in class, she would pretend that he wasn't there. To do otherwise was to invite fantasies of gory violence.

She dreaded the annulment. It was a waiting finality that she couldn't face. Jacoby could talk all he wanted, he could mess around with Lenara all he wanted, but he was still legally betrothed to

Crystara. She would hold off on the annulment until they came to drag her out of her house, kicking and screaming.

Crystara thought about the betrothals and about the Great Crystal's involvement. She had never received a vision at all, and had instead read Lenara's mind for hers, as had been the plan. Before the betrothal, Crystara had believed the Great Crystal to be false. But if a giant piece of rock could be petitioned for an annulment and dole out marriages, then it could do more than just give out visions and play matchmaker.

Crystara knew exactly how to fix things. More petitions could be made to the Great Crystal than simple betrothals and annulments. For a crystal-speaker, the path was a simple one. If she wasn't going to be happy, neither was anybody else.

Crystara passed her mother's room on the way out of the house and stopped. She cocked an ear to listen for her father. Soft snoring was coming from the couch. She was relatively safe. She crept in and opened the bedside table drawer to reveal her father's wand. She took it in her hand and slid it down the front of her dress.

The only other thing that she needed was a crystal. Crystara slid her ring off of her finger, the one that Jacoby had given to her at the ceremony over a year ago. It would suffice.

Chapter 28

Julio awoke to unfamiliar surroundings. His left eye opened just fine, but his right one was covered by something. The ceiling above him was concrete and bare pipes. He tried to sit up but found that he was too weak. His entire face felt as though it was on fire. He made an attempt to call out for help, but his voice would not come to him. Confused and exasperated, Julio let his head fall to the side. Across from him was a hospital bed, occupied by a man with a cast on his arm and bandages around his waist. It was Roberto Ruveldi. He was sleeping.

"Rob," Julio muttered weakly. His voice sounded like a hacksaw trying to cut through a sheet of metal. Julio tried to reach out to his friend, then gasped in horror at what he saw. Where his hand should have been there was only a lump of bandages. Without thinking, he tried to bring the missing hand to his face to inspect the damage there. What should have been fingers stroking his face was instead an odd sensation, as though his hand was still attached but would not respond. The stump that was his wrist clumsily hit his chin and he sucked in air to fight off the sudden pain. The bandages began to turn red.

Somebody rushed to his side. The young woman was dressed like a nurse, but her uniform was an unfamiliar brown and white. Her hair, done up in curls, was the colour of burnished copper. As Julio fought off the pain and nausea, he realized that he was in a Faxon war hospital. The nurse began to unwind the gauze around Julio's wrist.

"How do you feel?" she asked in Noven. She seemed quite surprised that Julio was awake. Julio found that the woman's thick accent made her difficult to understand, so he switched to Faxish.

"Where am I?" he asked in what he hoped was the nurse's native tongue. It hurt terribly to speak, and he found himself gritting his teeth after each word.

"You are in Alloise," she replied, slowly and in the same language that Julio was using. "Please try not to speak too much. Your face is badly injured and it will interrupt the healing process if you move your jaw."

"Alloise," Julio repeated. The nurse's advice proved to be correct. The whole right side of his face stung with intense pain when he tried to speak. He needed more information from the nurse, though, before he could be satisfied.

"So I'm a prisoner of war, then. How bad are my injuries?"

The nurse gave Julio a pitying look. "You received no life-threatening injuries to your vitals, and you should still be able to walk once you are feeling well enough."

Julio stared, mouth open, as the bandages around his wrist fell away to reveal a throbbing red lump. He was dizzy and thought that he might have blacked out for a moment. When he looked back at the wrist, it was all done up in fresh white bandages.

"You are lucky, sir, that none of your wounds were infected."

Julio laughed at the word 'lucky', despite how much it hurt to do so. He brought his left hand up to his face to inspect the rest of the damage properly. His entire face was covered in bandages, save for one eye, his nostrils and his mouth.

"So I'm missing my right hand, my writing hand. Be honest, my good lady. Does this other eye still work?"

The nurse looked away, toward the white noise of the large hospital room. "I ... we don't know yet," she said.

It sounded to Julio like a lie, but he let it slide. The woman had been kind enough to him, considering he was the enemy.

"One more question, if I could," Julio said. The nurse looked back to him. "Were there any other Noven soldiers brought here at the same time as me and the man in the bed beside me?"

The nurse shook her head, then left to tend to another patient somewhere else in the hospital. Julio could only hope that Pietro and Largo had managed to escape somehow, or had surrendered. Knowing Largo, the surrender possibility didn't seem likely.

Julio had no idea how long he had been unconscious, but he still felt incredibly tired. He drifted off to sleep, even though the pain on the right side of his body was excruciating. He thought about asking a nurse for some duskblossom extract to dull the pain, but by the time the thought appeared in his mind he was already half-asleep.

When he awoke it was dark and silent, apart from a few moans coming from other hospital beds. Julio turned his head to the side to find that Roberto was staring at him from the adjacent bed.

"The nurse told me you woke up today," Roberto whispered. "How do you feel?"

"Like I want to die," Julio said, and he meant it. He tried to speak through his teeth so that his jaw didn't have to move too much. "Wait, what do you mean 'today'? How long was I out for?"

Roberto sat up in bed. Compared to Julio, the engineer's injuries seemed insignificant.

"It's Septembra, Jules. I know that might come as something of a shock to you. I've spoken to the doctor a few times, even though hearing him speak Noven is like listening to a sow in heat. He didn't expect you to wake up at all."

Julio nodded sadly. "Septembra. I've been comatose for two months, then."

He thought about Ramona and Pietro and fought back tears. "What about Pietro and Largo? Did they make it?"

A pained look of regret crossed Roberto's face. "Pip ... didn't make it," he said.

By the look on Roberto's face, Julio could tell that his friend knew the details of Pietro's death. Julio didn't want to know.

"Largo I'm not sure about. He ran off after he ..." Roberto seemed to be searching for the right words to use, "... after Pip died. I went back to get you and then I couldn't find him. I got shot dragging you out of there, which turned out to be a blessing, because they let me surrender. I'm sorry, Jules. It was all for nothing, trying to save him."

Julio wept, shedding tears from the undamaged side of his face. Roberto got out of his bed and took Julio's hand in his own, comforting him as he cried. Julio didn't even feel any pain from the burns or the shrapnel. It was only his chest that hurt. As he cried, Julio thought that he heard weeping coming from other beds, as well. Whatever he was going through, loss of love and limb, he knew that he wasn't alone. He wept for several long minutes. Roberto was silent and grave beside him.

Finally the tears subsided, and Julio mopped his face with the sleeve of his hospital gown.

"Ramona," he said. "I must tell Ramona."

"With all due respect, Jules, you don't owe that bitch anything."

"She's all I have left, Rob."

Roberto squeezed his hand. "You have me," he said. "I won't abandon or betray you like they did. You're so godsdamned naive and kind, Jules ... you just let people walk all over you. Please, Julio. You've already had your heart and your body ripped apart trying to save these people who betrayed you. Don't go back to her. I'm begging you. Her child isn't yours, and she made a choice to be with somebody other than you. She doesn't deserve you."

Julio sighed deeply. He gritted his teeth and fought off the throbbing pain across his body so that he could continue speaking.

"Rob, I know we'll always be friends. You're the only person left that I trust. I just ... I have to see her again. I still love her, Rob. Maybe that's crazy. Maybe it's stupid, but I picture her stuck raising that child all alone and I ..."

Roberto stood up. His face was an emotionless as a mask.

"You're such a dullard. If you haven't learned by now, I don't think you ever will. Go ahead then, go back to the woman who cheated on you. This, Julio ... this is why I don't believe in love." Roberto started to walk away.

"Where on earth are you going?" Julio asked.

Roberto didn't turn around. "To beg the Faxon soldiers for a smoke."

As Julio watched his friend leave, the throbbing across his body became a burning sensation. He could feel the heat from the scattershot blast all over again. It was like his skin had been shorn off on one side by hot knives. Curling up into a ball, he cringed and could not help himself from crying out. It felt to Julio like a dreadfully long time before the nurse arrived.

"What?" she said, not unkindly. Julio's vision was blurry from the pain, but he could tell it was not the same nurse as before. She likely didn't speak much Noven at all.

"Duskblossom," he hissed through his teeth. He repeated the word in Faxish and Nilonnese.

The nurse said nothing, but left Julio's side and returned a moment later with a syringe and injected his good arm with a liquid that Julio hoped was an anaesthetic rather than a sedative. Seconds later, the nurse was gone and the pain was receding. He lay back in bed and tried to collect his thoughts, which were quickly becoming fuzzy.

Roberto returned a few minutes later and sat down on his bed. "Gods, these holes in me hurt," he muttered. "I can only imagine what you're going through."

Julio gave Roberto a dopey smile. "I feel just fine right now. It's easy to see why people get addicted to this stuff."

Roberto nodded and lay back on his bed. "Well, at least they're giving it to you. We're being treated pretty well considering we're prisoners."

Julio laughed. "They let you go outside to smoke, don't they? I'd say this is a pretty fair treatment for military aggressors."

Roberto Ruveldi snorted. "Well, what am I gonna do? Run off into the chilly autumn night in nothing but a backless gown?"

Julio laughed at the mental image. He was surprised to be feeling so well, but he knew that it was probably just the duskblossom extract that made him feel so euphoric. It would subside in time, he knew, and his thoughts would return to his dismal situation.

"Think they'd let me send a letter, Rob?"

"Pff. They gave you a strong dose of that stuff, didn't they? You're gonna have to wait until the war's over, pally. Don't worry. I'm sure it won't be long now."

"The war ... almost over," Julio mused. "I never thought I would feel worse at the end than I did while I was in the middle of it all. Gods, Rob, what am I gonna do with myself now? I won't be able to work. Novem probably won't pay for me to go back and get my master's ..."

Roberto grinned. "Well, seeing as how I'm a socialist now, I might as well share some of that dirty inherited money waiting for me back home. I was looking to go back to school anyway ... show all of those idiots what a real engineer looks like. You might as well come with me, get that history degree. You've got a comprehensive account of the war to write anyway, don't you?"

Julio raised an eyebrow. "What do you mean?"

Roberto leapt up excitedly, then winced and gasped for breath as he clutched his side. After a moment of pacing back and forth cursing, he poked his head under Julio's bed, muttered something about the chamber pot, and produced a familiar-looking leather notebook which he held up for Julio to see.

"They let you keep your war journal, Jules."

***

24 Martia, 1879

Ramona,

There is no easy way for me to write this letter, so I will put everything plainly. Please forgive the messiness of the writing, as well. I am using my left hand.

I am certain that by now, news has reached you of Pietro's death. I am deeply sorry for your loss, as well as my own. Despite the fact that you both lied to me, I have never wished death upon anyone, especially not a friend who had a child back home. I know this must be very hard for you. The war was hard on all of us.

They are sending me home this week. Marching me home, to be exact, along with all of the other prisoners of war in Nilonne. For the past seven months I have been in a military hospital in the Nilonnese city of Alloise. Those who were healthy enough were moved to the prison, such as Roberto, but I still have not fully recovered. I was hit by scattershot and lost my right hand and eye. I almost lost a leg as well, but it still works with some difficulty.

The reason I am telling you this is because I want to prepare you for when I come to see you. I do not look as I once did, and my appearance might seem frightening.

I need you to know that I am not mad at you. I understand what happened, and why you did the things you did. Pietro happened to be there when you were in a very emotional state over the death of your mother. He was there for you when I could not be. Things might have been different if there weren't a child involved, but I understand why you stopped speaking to me. I won't pretend that I wasn't hurt or angry or confused, but that was then. The war is over now and we all have scars, both physical and emotional. All I want is to go home and have things return to the way they were.

So I am coming home to you, if you will still have me. I forgive you, Ramona. I tried to hate you for what happened, but I understand your choice and Pietro's. I still love you. I always will, and nothing will ever change that. Drago shouldn't have to grow up without a father and I cannot be without you.

I should be back in Captus Nove in about two weeks. Please, Ramona, let's work this out. I want to be with you. I love you.

Julio

Chapter 29

Jacoby sat on his bed and read Julio's final letter over again. He couldn't comprehend his teacher's decision to go back to Ramona. Similar to Ramona's situation, Jacoby had cheated on Crystara willingly. He had chosen to be with somebody other than his intended. Ramona's motivations were murky, and something seemed to be missing from the equation. Jacoby sat up, wondering what Master Vellize had to say about the whole thing.

Jacoby carefully placed the letters back into Master Vellize's book and closed the cover, then slid it into his book bag. It occurred to him that he didn't even know if his history teacher was married. Nobody had ever dared to ask him, and Jacoby had never thought to look for a ring on the man's finger. What had happened between him and Ramona, in the end? Jacoby had to know, just like he had to know what Julio Vellize had meant when he said that the heart would always betray. Was it Julio's heart, or Ramona's? Had Jacoby's heart betrayed him, and in turn betrayed Crystara?

Jacoby had no idea if his teacher would be at the school on a weekend, but it was worthwhile to have a look and see. He left his house and got on his bike, pedaling in the rain as fast as he could for Central School.

***

Master Julio Vellize sat in his cramped, bookshelf-filled office, legs up on his desk. Sitting beside him was a man that Jacoby recognized as Timori's engineering teacher. The two of them were smoking pipes and appeared to be in the middle of a conversation when Jacoby entered.

Master Vellize seemed surprised to see Jacoby. "Ah, Jacoby. What brings you here on a weekend? You didn't lose that book I lent you over the summer, did you? Come in and dry off some."

Jacoby shook his hair out and approached his teacher's desk.

343

"Actually, it's the book I wanted to talk to you about ... or the letters, rather." He sat down in the chair that faced the desk.

The engineering teacher glanced over at Master Vellize. "You showed him your letters? Gods, Jules, what for? It's been years."

Master Vellize made a dismissive gesture to the other teacher. "He needed advice, Rob. Kids in love, you know how it is."

"I do," the engineering teacher said.

"Doctor Ruveldi," Jacoby said. "I get it now. You two are still friends after all these years. Maybe there's hope for me and Timori yet."

Doctor Ruveldi nodded and clapped Master Vellize on the back. Julio nearly lost his pipe.

"We've been through a lot together, Jules and I. What's your question, son? We were in the middle of a riveting conversation about republican policy."

Jacoby brought the book out of his bag and laid it upon the desk.

"When you said that my heart will betray me if I let it, you were talking about Ramona, weren't you? Because her heart betrayed her to Pietro. See, things have fallen apart between me and Crystara. My whole relationship with her just left me confused, and I feel like I know less about love now than I did when I started. I don't know if I ever really loved her, or if I even believe in love. I want to believe that I could fall in love with ... with somebody else, but it's the nature of love that eludes me, Master. Is it supposed to be euphoric and perfect, or is it a thing that makes you miserable?"

Doctor Ruveldi burst into laughter. "That's a lot of questions, kid."

Master Vellize nodded. "The letters don't exactly explain what happened in the end, do they? Love is different for everyone, Jacoby. Some people obsess over it. Some are pragmatic about it. Some don't even believe in it."

"What about you?" Jacoby asked. "What do you believe?"

Master Vellize sighed. "I believe in love. However ... well, maybe I should tell you the rest of the story."

"With you and Ramona, you mean?"

"Yes. Ramona. Maybe this will give you further insight into the nature of the human heart, Jacoby ..."

* * *

Julio stood in front of the door, cane poised to knock. He stared at the peeling red paint, same as it had been since his last visit to the house nearly four years earlier. A lark's song filled the silence, cheery despite the chill of dawn. The wind picked up. Something darted past Julio's peripheral vision and he turned to look at it with his one good eye. It was a hummingbird, sucking nectar from a yellow flower under Ramona's windowsill.

It had always been beautiful around Ramona's house, even though it was in the slums. Julio looked back at the door. It had been several minutes, and he had not been able to bring himself to knock. He lifted the cane and let it hover in front of the door again. He sighed.

The march home from Alloise had been arduous, even though Julio had been allowed to ride on horseback most of the way. Every bump made his body ache, and the Nilonnese army medics who accompanied the freed prisoners back to the border refused to give Julio any more duskblossom extract. The withdrawal was the worst on the first week back. He screamed in pain for hours on end until other prisoners threatened to physically silence him. He threw up nearly everything that he ate, which was precious little in the first place.

He was lucky that Roberto had been there to look after him. Julio sometimes suspected that the Nilonnese army would just as soon have left him on the side of the road to fend for himself. Julio felt helpless and useless, and it was only thoughts of returning to Ramona and washing away the past that kept him going.

The Novem that he returned to was not the one that he remembered. Signs of foreign occupation were constant, and a group of Faxish soldiers had spat on the prisoners as they walked by. The northern fort city of Saliara was almost completely demolished. Its castle, which had stood for nearly a thousand years, lay in ruins. Julio reminded himself that it was all a part of history, but reading about the toll that a war took on a nation was different from witnessing it in person.

Captus Nove was in better shape, but not by much. Parts of the city were still filled with rubble, and some of the buildings that Julio had known since childhood had been destroyed, especially ones that had borne a strong link to the empire. Graffiti littered the walls and few people walked the streets. The ones who happened to look at Julio quickly looked away. Julio felt as broken as his city.

He and the rest of the prisoners of war were taken to Crystus Hill, where they were released into the custody of the republican militia. Names were taken down, and any soldiers who had been drafted were immediately released, many to the waiting arms of family and loved ones.

Roberto and Julio had temporarily parted ways there. Roberto went to his mother's house and asked Julio to come by sometime within the next few days. Julio had meant to go straight to Ramona's, but his walk had taken him to Avati Hill and then to the cliffs by the ocean. He had sat there staring at the rolling waves until long after the sun had set. Without a centima to his name and lacking the strength to walk to Roberto's mother's house up in Cateli Hill, Julio slept in the cool grass by the ocean, waking up from nightmares and fits of pain every hour or so.

Julio was jolted awake by a crow before dawn as the dew began to dampen his ragged shirt and pants. He rubbed the sleep out of his eyes with his only hand and began to wander through the barren, broken streets of Captus Nove, heading to Ramona's house. He knew the way by heart.

The sun was rising behind Julio, casting his shadow across the faded red door. He let out a long sigh, summoned his courage and knocked with his cane.

Several moments later, he heard movement behind the door and the sound of a deadbolt sliding. The door swung open and a woman appeared, holding a child in her arms. She was far larger and uglier than Julio remembered Ramona being.

The woman stared at him, mouth agape. So did the child.

"Mama, what's wrong with his face?" the boy asked.

"Hush, child." Her voice didn't sound quite right either. Julio was both relieved and confused. He had the right house, didn't he? The heavyset young woman set the boy down and folded her arms.

"I'm sorry, soldier, but I've got no food, no money and no work for you. We're all on hard times right now. I hear they're looking for dockhands, but that might be difficult for a man in your condition. Sorry I can't help you more."

Julio scratched his scalp where hair used to be. "I'm sorry to bother you, my good lady. I'm looking for Ramona Scaletti. Does she still live here?"

Forgetting his manners, Julio tried to peer inside the house. The woman easily blocked his view and frowned at him.

"Do you rent from her?"

A look of recognition crossed the lady's face. "Wait a minute. Are you Pietro? Ramona mentioned you before she moved."

Julio felt as though he had been slapped. "Pietro is dead," he said. "I'm Julio Vellize. Her first love. Where did she leave to? Please, you must tell me."

The woman's hard, snub-nosed face finally showed some pity. "I can give you the address where I send her letters when they come here. Can't help you any more than that, soldier. Far as I know, she lives at 134 Romadi Street, up on Southron Hill."

Julio's mind reeled with the possible implications of Ramona's departure from her father's old house. He tried to put them from his mind and focus only on his own determination. Julio looked at the woman and nodded grimly.

347

"Thank you, you've been more than kind. Gods be with you in these hard times." The words were bitter in his mouth.

The walk was long and Julio was sore and wheezing by the time he made it up the hill, but he would not allow himself to be defeated. He arrived at 134 Romadi Street, exhausted and anxious. The house was the largest on the street, built of bright red brick. Without hesitating, Julio crossed the small front lawn and rapped on the front door with his cane before he could lose his nerve. His heart pounded in his chest.

The door opened.

She looked a little older and bigger than Julio remembered, but she was Ramona all the same. There were deep bags under her eyes and her hair was dishevelled, but it was nothing compared to how Julio's looks had changed.

Julio's chest clenched. He had been worried about how he would react to seeing Ramona again, whether it would be anger or sorrow or joy, but she was still the same woman that he remembered, and he knew in his heart that he could forgive her and have things return to the way they were supposed to be. He was more worried about how Ramona was going to react to him.

Ramona's jaw dropped as soon as she looked upon him, and she quickly covered her mouth with her hand.

"Ramona," he rasped. His voice had changed, as well, from the piece of shrapnel that had nearly torn open his jugular vein.

Ramona took a step backward. Julio wanted to approach her, to hold her and tell her everything would be all right, that he forgave her for all that she had done. He wanted to do something other than stand awkwardly in her doorway looking like a thing from the abyss, but he needed to know how she'd respond. He needed to know what she felt. Julio would have given anything, even his other hand, to be an empath just then.

"Gods," Ramona gasped. Julio could see fear in her eyes, as though she wanted to scream or slam the door in his face. "Julio, is that you?"

Julio tried his best to smile, even though he was painfully aware of how awful his smile looked. "It's me, Ramona. Did you get my letter?" He took a timid step forward.

Ramona wrapped her arms around Julio, nearly knocking him over. She began to weep.

"They told me you were dead," she sobbed. "They told me you were dead. Oh, Julio, I'm so sorry. I'm so sorry for everything."

They clung together and cried in the doorway. For just a moment, Julio thought everything would be all right again. Julio drank in Ramona's smell and it summoned to his mind all of his fondest memories of her. The heartache of the war and all of the deception that he had suffered seemed to fade away.

"Mama?" said a small voice.

Julio looked down. Clinging to Ramona's skirt was a boy of about two with bright blue eyes and a thumb in his mouth. Julio felt a pang in his heart. The boy looked just like Pietro. Although it pained him to do so, physically and emotionally, Julio knelt down to look at the child who had torn his life asunder.

"Hello, Drago," Julio said. The child screamed and fled in terror.

Ramona looked into the house, then back to Julio. "Don't take it personally, Julio. He has no idea who you are. You just startled him, is all. Come in while I settle him down."

Ramona ushered Julio inside and shut the door. She left Julio standing in the foyer of the house and exited the room to find Drago.

The entryway was roomy and tidy, but there were no decorations to be seen. Julio could tell right away that the owner of the house was wealthy, but thrifty. He checked his face in the foyer mirror and frowned as he tried to push his hair over the scarred side of his face.

"It's not the fact that I'm a stranger that frightened him," Julio called out.

Ramona didn't answer. Julio could hear her in a room down the hall, cooing and hushing her son. She returned a moment later with Drago in her arms.

"See, Drago, there's nothing to be afraid of. This is your father's friend, Julio. Say hello."

The child simply stared at Julio, who tried his best not to feel resentful. He knew that the child was innocent, but to be referred to by Ramona as the boy's father's friend was almost more than he could bear. Julio stood awkwardly in the clean, unwelcoming foyer and wondered what to say next.

"Would you like some tea?" Ramona asked.

Julio smiled. "Tea ... would be great," he said. "We have a lot to talk about."

Julio wanted more than anything to take Ramona into his arms and kiss her, not talk over tea, but it didn't take an empath to feel her hesitance. Julio hoped against the odds that it was merely Ramona's guilt that made her so reserved. The more rational part of Julio told him that it was his face.

Julio sat in a parlour and waited for Ramona to settle Drago down for a nap and bring tea. As he looked at the furnishings and portrait of an unrecognizable moustached man above the mantle, he started to wonder if perhaps Ramona had come to work for a wealthy merchant as a live-in maid. The idea was comforting.

Ramona came in with tea and crackers on a silver tray. Julio was ravenous but too nervous to eat. Ramona set down the tray and poured tea for the two of them, then sat down on the couch opposite Julio. She held her teacup and stared at Julio for a long time before saying anything. She sighed several times and opened her mouth as if to speak, but closed it again and looked away as though she were pondering what to say first. She took a long sip of her tea and sighed again.

"Julio, I'm sorry. Sorry for everything. I completely ruined your life and it's all my fault. Everything ... everything with Pietro happened so quickly, and it's my fault for that too. It was a moment of weakness. Mother had just passed, and I got a letter the same week telling me that Alfonso had died up in Kilgrun, and I was let go from the factory. Pietro just ... happened to be there, you know? And, and I told myself that it was just one time. I promised myself that I

350

would tell you, when you got back from the war so that you didn't have to worry about it when you were away fighting and so that you and Pietro wouldn't hurt each other. And then ..."

She began to cry. "And then I realized I was pregnant. And I couldn't tell you. I'm so sorry, Julio, but I couldn't bring myself to tell you. Pietro offered to do it, and I let him, even though that was selfish of me. And I ... I still loved you, but I tried to convince myself that I loved Pietro instead, so that it would be easier for everyone, so that you could go on and find somebody new, someone who would treat you the way you deserve to be treated because you're such a wonderful, caring person."

Ramona choked back sobs as she struggled to continue. Julio was fighting back his own tears.

"And then ... and then I found out about the battle near Alloise, and the papers said that every soldier in the battalion had been killed and I ... Oh, Julio, I'm just so sorry for everything ..."

Julio limped over to Ramona and held her in his arms. They both cried for several minutes.

"It's all right," Julio whispered as he held his one and only love in his arms. "It's all right, I forgive you. I forgive you for everything, Ramona. Everything's gonna be all right now. I'm back, and the war is over, and we can be together again."

Ramona pulled away from the embrace. "Julio ... we can't. I ..."

Julio cringed. "Is it my face? You told me that nothing would change our love."

"Nothing has," Ramona said. She looked down at her left hand. "I'm married, Julio."

Julio jerked backward. He couldn't believe he hadn't noticed it before. There on her left hand was a crystal ring. He should have known all along from the nice house to Ramona's reticence, but he was just as naïve as he had always been, even after all that he had been through. Roberto had been right all along. Julio was a dullard for thinking that things could ever go back to the way that they were.

"You're married? To whom?"

Ramona stared into her tea. "Ralfi Andari."

"Your supervisor from the factory? The man you rebuked and asked me to tell off for you? The one who must have fired you from that very same factory?"

Ramona couldn't meet Julio's good eye. "Julio, please, you must understand. I had no money. I had to sell my house, and I was living with Drago in ..."

"And so you married him?"

"What was I supposed to do? Pietro was dead, and I thought that you were too. The money that you sent me only lasted so long. I couldn't afford to eat. I had to do something for Drago, Julio. Ralfi took me in, offered to take care of me. Please understand. He's really good to Drago. He's been really good to me as well. I'm sorry, Julio, I know this must be awful for you to hear, but ..."

Julio had fallen prostrate at Ramona's feet. "Please, Ramona, please. You said that you still love me. I know you do. Come away with me. I'll take care of you and Drago, I promise. We can be together again. I know you don't love him, you were just looking after Drago and yourself, but now you don't have to. I'm back. Please, don't do this to me."

He wept, looking up at his love pleadingly. Julio grasped Ramona's hand in his own. "Please, Ramona. Don't cast me out. Don't do this to me. You're the only reason I have left to live in this world."

Ramona bit her lip and looked away. "We've all had to find new reasons to keep on going, Julio. I'm sorry, but I can't be yours anymore. I can't, for Drago's sake. He has a home here now, and so do I. I'm sorry for everything that I've done to you. You didn't deserve any of this, but there's no changing what's already happened. If you want, I can see if Ralfi will lend you some money and ..."

Julio stood abruptly in spite of his injuries. "I don't want anything from him."

He tried to compose himself, push all of his hurt aside. Ramona had made her choice, and no amount of pleading would change it. If it weren't for his face, he knew that Ramona would have chosen differently, even if she could never admit it.

"I should leave, then, before this broken shell of a man embarrasses himself any further. Just tell me one thing, Ramona, and please be honest this once. Did you ever really love me?"

Ramona stood and stared at Julio for a moment, then kissed him fully on what was left of his lips.

"I will always love you, Julio."

Julio gave Ramona a sad smile. "I wish you hadn't said that."

He picked up his cane and limped slowly to the front door.

Ramona followed him. "Julio ... please don't give up on life. There are ... there are things more important than love, sometimes. I'm the last person who should be worthy of your love, anyway. You should hate me for what I've done to you."

Julio turned around to look at the love of his life. "That's not for you to decide, Ramona."

***

Julio Vellize stared out the window at the rain as he finished his story. "You can't help who you love, Jacoby. You can't help it if you don't love your betrothed, and she can't help it if she loves you. It's not something easily controlled. I still love Ramona, after all these years ... not that it changes the way things are. She's still married, and I'm still alone."

Jacoby thought about Master Vellize's story. "So she gave you all of the letters back? You still speak to her?"

Doctor Ruveldi smirked. "They're still friends, the dullards. Old Andari wanted those letters out of his house, so Ramona gave them to Jules."

"And Largo," Jacoby said, "that's Crystara's father, isn't it?"

Julio Vellize scowled at the mention of Largo's name.

"I pity her, you know, having him as a father. A part of me still suspects that he killed Pietro after I got hit with scattershot, but he denies it."

Jacoby was aghast. "Why are you still on speaking terms with him?"

Master Vellize lit up another cigarette with help from Doctor Ruveldi. "I'm not a man who holds a grudge, Jacoby. I never was, and we all went through a lot together in that war. Anyway, Largo's not the point."

Jacoby frowned. "What is the point, then? All I've learned was that the Great War was really horrible and ruined people's lives."

Master Vellize nodded slowly as he puffed on his pipe.

"It was horrible. I pray that something like it never happens again. But I didn't give you the letters so you could learn about war, or history. Those letters are about love. Love is an inevitable part of the human condition. It can make you happy or miserable or both, and it will force you to make some terrible mistakes in your life, but we all make mistakes, Jacoby. The point is not to hold those against people. Life is too short to despise others for the choices that they make."

"I don't hate Crystara," Jacoby admitted. "I just ... want to be free of her. I just want to live my own life without having anything decided by someone else, or some damn crystal."

Master Vellize smiled. "I told you that you would learn something from those letters. Go on, I'm sure you have better things to do than sit around talking to a couple of old soldiers on a weekend."

Jacoby left Master Vellize's office in better spirits. As he walked to the front entrance of the school, he was surprised to see Racquela and Paulo moving at a brisk pace down the hallway.

"I don't think he's here," Paulo said as he checked his fingernails.

Racquela was in tears. "But we've looked practically *everywhere!*" She didn't see Jacoby until she ran right into him. "Jake! What are you doing here?"

"I could ask you the same thing."

He glanced at Paulo, who acknowledged Jacoby with a short nod. Jacoby quickly reached out with his empathy to try and understand why on earth Racquela was spending time with Paulo. He was glad that Paulo wasn't an empath. Jacoby had slept with Paulo's betrothed.

Any other emotions were overwhelmed by the anxiety pouring forth from Racquela. Jacoby didn't have the skill to look any deeper.

"We're looking for Tim," Racquela said as she accepted a handkerchief from Paulo. "He just sent me a telegram. I ... I think he's going to do something terrible." She wiped away tears and smeared makeup.

Jacoby tried not to panic. "Like what? What did he send you?"

Paulo produced a small piece of paper for Jacoby to read. Printed on it were the words 'you'll be sorry'.

"Um ... did anything prompt this, other than the breakup?"

He looked at both Racquela and Paulo. He thought he detected a note of guilt from Racquela, but nothing from Paulo, as usual. Jacoby wondered sometimes if the boy even *had* emotions.

"Do you have any idea where he might be?"

"He's not at home, or at any of the other places he would usually be," Racquela said. "Do you have any ideas? Please, I'm so worried about him. If he's not with Paulo or you then something terrible might have happened."

"Why would you know where he is?" Jacoby asked Paulo.

"We work together," Paulo said.

Jacoby didn't have time to ask more about that. "Racquela, you have to tell me everything that happened if you want me to help find him," he insisted. "It could be important. Why would he send you that telegram?"

"All right, I told Tim, I don't see why I can't tell you. I bribed my way into the betrothals, and I'm using that fact to try and get an annulment. Tim knows. It's definitely what set this off."

Jacoby's eyes widened. It made him feel a lot better about his indiscretion with Lenara. He looked at Paulo cautiously.

"You're all right with this?"

Paulo shrugged. "This annulment benefits everybody. Even Tim, though he doesn't know it yet."

Jacoby was surprised by Paulo's response, until he carefully reached out to sense Racquela's emotions again. He looked at her tear-filled dark eyes, then back to Paulo's deep icy-blue ones. He couldn't believe that he hadn't realized it right away.

"Doesn't know it yet," Jacoby breathed. Some things could wait until he at least knew that Timori was safe and sound.

"I can't believe you're trying to get an annulment. I was about to do the same thing in a couple of days. What fucked up lives we live."

A thought struck him. "All right, I think I know where to look. You go see if you can get your dad's motorcoach and drive around a bit. I'll meet you at Avati Hill Park at sunset if I can't find him. Paulo ... I guess you should go with Racquela."

Paulo snorted. "I have my own motorcoach, thank you."

"Oh," Jacoby said. "Well, why don't you just go with Racquela, then?"

"I'm not going to look for him at all." He was playing with something in the pocket of his coat. "Somebody has to get this annulment before things get any crazier."

Jacoby nodded and turned around. He sprinted down the hallway toward the school entrance.

"Jake!" Racquela shouted. "Where are you going?"

"Lenara's."

***

She was waiting outside her house for Jacoby as though she already knew that he was coming. Her chocolate locks of hair were damp and looked almost black. The whiteoak blossom in her hair was drooping from the rain. Jacoby slammed on the brakes of his bicycle and skidded to a halt in front of her, then gave her a quick kiss.

"I saw a bridge, Timori was there," she said. "How did you know I would be here?"

"Racquela told me about Tim. I was hoping you'd have the answers I needed. I have to go help him." Jacoby got ready to pedal off toward the Memorial Bridge.

"Jake, wait," Lenara said. "This might be really soon, but ... I love you. I just wanted you to know." She gave him another kiss, much more passionate than the first. "I have a bad feeling about tonight."

Jacoby took his feet off of the pedals and grasped her hand firmly in his. "Are you in danger?"

"I don't know. Somebody is, one of the betrothed, I think. It's vague, damned visions aren't always what they're cracked up to be," she laughed darkly. "It could be Timori if you don't hurry, though. Just go!"

Jacoby kissed her one last time. "Be safe."

***

Jacoby couldn't count on his fingers and toes the number of hours he had spent with Timori at Memorial Bridge. Admittedly, most of them involved sunflower seeds, but it was that very special place the two of them had always shared, a haven of sorts that nobody else had ever been a part of.

Timori was standing on the precipice of the bridge, holding a wand to his own head. A crowd had gathered and the police were there trying to negotiate with Timori. He was shouting at them to get back or he would shoot.

357

Jacoby ditched his bike on the side of the road and pressed his way through the crowd to the police officer who was talking to Timori.

"Let me talk to him," Jacoby said. Tension was written all over the officer's face. Jacoby gave the officer a pleading look.

"Please, he's my best friend. He'll listen to me. Let me go up and talk to him."

"He's got a wand, kid," the officer said. "I can't. He points it at anybody other than himself and we have to shoot him."

"What are you doing here?" a desperate voice called out. "I told you to stay away from me."

Gasps and murmurs circulated in the crowd. The officer looked at Jacoby, who had no choice but to respond since he had been spoken to.

"Tim," he said. He struggled with what to say next. "Please, don't do this."

"Why not?" Timori demanded. "My betrothed is leaving me. My supposed best friend betrayed me. My mom would be better off without another mouth to feed, and I'm a lowborn picker who can't handle his own fucking life. Why shouldn't I just do the world a favour, Jake?"

"Because ..."

Jacoby thought of so many things that he could say. He could argue with Timori all afternoon about his friend's good qualities, but Timori would likely refute every single one. Bringing up Racquela was a bad idea, as well. Timori couldn't easily be reasoned with, and the jumbled emotions coming from him did little to give Jacoby an idea of what to say.

"Tell him you love him," a girl said from behind Jacoby. Jacoby craned his head. It was Crystara standing behind him.

"Crystara," he whispered. "What are you doing here?"

"Helping you save his life," she said. "I can read his thoughts. I know exactly what to say to him. Tell him you love him. Hurry, Jake, there isn't much time."

Jacoby took a step forward. "I love you, Tim."

358

Timori seemed to hear the words, but the wand didn't move from its place beside his head. Jacoby looked back to Crystara pleadingly.

"Remind him of all of the good times you've had together. All of the reasons why he matters to you. All of the reasons why he's your best friend and why you love him. Why he has a reason to live."

Jacoby swallowed his panic and turned back to Timori.

"You're my best friend, and you have been ever since I can remember. We used to spit seeds off of this bridge for hours, remember? We would spit them and die laughing when we hit somebody on a bicycle. I can't think about doing that with anybody else. I want to do that with you when we're old men and have nothing else to do with our lives."

He thought of Master Vellize and Doctor Ruveldi. He wanted to have that, too.

"I know I made a mistake, and I'm sorry. I know you're hurting right now, and it hurts me too."

Jacoby began sobbing, but he tried to keep talking, anything to keep the conversation going and stop his best friend from making a mistake he wouldn't have the chance to regret.

Timori sniffled. "Godsdamnit, Jake, why did you do it? Just tell me that."

"Why did you, Jake?" Crystara inquired.

"I ... I don't know," Jacoby admitted. "I just know that I'm sorry. Please, don't do this. I love you too much to see you do this. You're more important to me than any girl. You're my best friend, and you always will be. I know that I made a mistake. Gods know we've both made a lot of them this last year, but I'm just asking you to forgive me. Please, Tim, forgive me and forgive yourself ... You're not a fuck-up, you're just going through a rough time. There are a lot of great things about you that you've forgotten. Just put the wand down and we can fix all of this. Please."

Timori's hand wavered, but he did not let the wand drop.

"I lost her, Jake. She's going to annul the betrothals. What do I do without her? She was my everything."

"The betrothals don't have to be cancelled," Crystara muttered behind Jacoby.

Jacoby couldn't tell that to Timori. He wanted the betrothals annulled as well. He decided to try a different approach, something that he learned from Master Vellize.

"Love ... Timori ... isn't all there is to this life," Jacoby said.

He didn't know if Timori would believe him, but he had no idea what else to say. He had nothing reassuring to tell Timori about Racquela.

"You just have to find something else to live for."

Jacoby saw Timori swallow hard. He stared at Jacoby across the space between them, and it was like they were looking at each other for the first time.

"If you can make me a promise, I will put the wand down," Timori said. Jacoby heard a collective breath of relief from the crowd.

"Anything," Jacoby agreed. He wondered if he meant it. What was a life worth?

"Promise me," Timori insisted.

"Promise him," Crystara echoed.

"What is it?" Jacoby asked, both to Crystara and Timori.

Timori hesitated. "I can't tell you here, in front of these people. Promise me and I'll put the wand down."

Jacoby's gut clenched. Whatever the promise was, it was worth his friend's life.

"I promise you, Timori," he said, before Crystara had the chance to whisper it to him.

The wand clattered to the concrete. Timori's firm composure crumpled and he lay on the ground, weeping. Jacoby tried to rush over to him, but the policemen were there first. Timori would have to be processed. Jacoby wondered where Timori had found the wand.

Broken and defeated, Timori was led to the police motorcoach to be taken in for disturbing the peace, and possibly possession of a weapon in public. The crowd dispersed just as the rain was letting up. Jacoby turned to Crystara.

"Thank you, Crys. I couldn't have done that without you. We saved his life."

Crystara stared at Jacoby and grasped his hands in hers.

"Jake ... I forgive you. I'm willing to give you another chance. We can be together again. Please, I need you. I can't live without you. I love you."

Jacoby had no idea what to do. After everything that had happened with Timori, his nerves were on edge. He thought about what it would mean to go back to Crystara. She had done so much for him, and he knew that she cared for him possibly more than anybody else in the world, but would things simply return to the way they were?

He thought of Julio Vellize. Jacoby wondered if he could sacrifice his happiness for another person. He discovered that he already knew the answer.

"I'm sorry, Crystara. My mind is already made up. Thank you for this ... I hope we can still be friends, but ..."

Crystara dropped Jacoby's hands and turned away. "Forget it. I should have known. Nothing is ever good enough for you, Jake. Goodbye."

Crystara left.

Jacoby felt a pang of guilt, but he reminded himself that he had done the right thing. Timori was safe, and all that was left to do was to get an annulment from the church. He left on his bicycle to find Racquela.

Chapter 30

"You ..."

Crystara stared across the room to the entrance of the Crystal Chamber. There Lenara stood, dressed in a simple black gown.

Crystara briefly considered ignoring her and touching the crystal, but speaking to the Great Crystal could be a lengthy process, and she had no idea what Lenara was up to, other than to probably try and stop her. Why else would a girl with visions follow her to the Crystal Chamber? Crystara couldn't take any chances. She scanned the girl's mind to discover what she was up to.

Lenara did not plan to stop Crystara physically. She merely wanted to reason with her. Crystara snorted. She was not in any mood to be reasoned with, especially not by a boyfriend-stealing slut. Not by the girl who had orchestrated something that had worked out so well for Crystara, only to snatch it away like the selfish bitch she was.

"I know why you're here," Crystara called across the room. Her voice echoed deeply against the walls. "And you can fuck right off. I'm not interested in talking. Go away. I'm not afraid to hurt you if you don't."

As if to prove the point to herself, she fingered the wand in the hidden pocket of her cloak. She kept her hand there, just in case.

Lenara didn't move. "Crystara, please don't do this," she begged. "I have a bad feeling about it."

Crystara glared at Lenara. "Oh, you have a bad feeling about it? Like you had a bad feeling about Paulo and the betrothals, so you switched with me? At what point are you going to change your mind about your bad feeling and fuck me over again, you heartless bitch?" Crystara was shaking with fury.

"Please, you have to understand. That was all a mistake. The annulment will fix it."

Crystara took a step toward Lenara. "I don't want the fucking annulment!" she screamed.

She was probably waking up the entire temple with her yelling, but she couldn't control her rage anymore.

"I wanted Jacoby, but you took him away from me. I wanted to be happy, but it was dangled in front of my face just to get snatched away, as always. You don't give a shit what I want, though, do you, Lenara? You just care about your cheating new boyfriend and your precious Great Crystal and your stupid visions that cause nothing but problems. And before you say anything about it, I know exactly what you're thinking so don't even bother."

She inched closer to Lenara with every word she spoke. She would have to act quickly, or she would lose her only chance with the crystal.

"Nobody has ever cared about what I want ... You only chose to switch because it was advantageous to you, and once it no longer was, you thought you could switch back. Well now you have to deal with the consequences of *my* actions, since I had to deal with the consequences of yours. So you fucking stand still and watch as I fix this godsdamned crystal once and for all."

Crystara reached out to touch the crystal. As her hand inched forward, she felt a presence inside her mind.

"Crystara," it said. It sounded like a million voices calling out as one.

"Crystara, don't," Lenara called out. "Please. We have no idea what will happen."

"Shut up." She reached out with her hand again.

"Free us," said the voices. *"Do it."*

Crystara hesitated. As she pulled her hand away slightly, the multitude of voices no longer seemed to call out as one. Whispers and phrases coursed through her mind, most of them too quiet or jumbled for her to understand clearly.

"Shatter us ..."

"We have foreseen this ..."

"Don't do it ..."

"There will be great sorrow if you follow through with this," a voice warned Crystara. It rang out in her mind clearer than the rest. She tried to ignore it and reached out again.

"Crystara."

"Crystara." A different voice.

"The fate of your future and that of Novem hangs in the balance. Do not do this."

"Do it."

"Blood ..."

"There can be no happiness if you alter this crystal."

"I have never known happiness," Crystara whispered. All of a sudden Crystara could hear footsteps down the hall from the open doorway. She reached for the Great Crystal. Lenara grabbed her arm to stop her.

"Don't!" she screamed. "You'll destroy ..."

"Crystara!" a voice shouted. It was Keeper Orvin, standing right behind Lenara.

Startled, Crystara's finger slid into the crystal trigger of her wand. Shrapnel exploded out of her cloak, tearing it to shreds. Something wet splashed across her face and into her eyes. Blown backward by the force of the modified wand's shot, Crystara was slammed against the wall.

A bright light permeated the chamber, followed by a low thrum. In the piercing flash, bright as day, Crystara could see a dark splotch of something smeared across the face of the Great Crystal. Out of the corner of her eye, she saw two priests enter the chamber with horror written on their faces.

Crystara looked at the priests, then at the Great Crystal. A series of cracks was forming in the centre of the dark smear. On the floor, a black gown and a white robe were tattered and smeared with blood and viscera.

"It is done."

"The sacrifice is made."

"Soon we shall be free."

Crystara's mind was overwhelmed with voices. She screamed out, clutching her temples, as the priests approached.

The cracks continued to spread across the Great Crystal as Crystara's vision spotted, then faded to black.

Epilogue

It was overcast on the day of the funeral, but the sky refused to rain.

Family and friends gathered at Avati Hill Park, all dressed in black. The whiteoak blossoms were falling freely now, sweeping across the chilly grey sky as the six priests in their funeral robes stacked black birch to build the pyre. The Reverie had come and gone. Autumn was in the air. The falling leaves and dying flowers were visual reminders of mortality.

Jacoby met Lenara's parents for the first time at the funeral. They had few words for him. Their faces were as bleak as the autumn weather. They did not blame him, though, even though Paulo told them what happened. Nobody blamed him, they said, but Jacoby still felt that he was at fault. He knew that he should have gone right to the Old Temple after the incident with Timori at the bridge. He should have petitioned for the annulment before Crystara went to the Great Crystal.

Crystara was not at the funeral. She was in a jail cell somewhere. The newspapers said that she was awaiting execution for the grisly murders of Keeper Orvin and Lenara De'Marici. Jacoby did not want her to die. As he watched the priests carry Lenara up to the pyre, inside a black birch box covered in a shroud, he knew that he would not wish death upon anyone.

Jacoby wanted to see her face one last time, but the box had already been sealed. He knew from what the papers had told him that the stolen wand Crystara had used carried a modified crystal. The details were sparse, but the printed story suggested that the remains had been difficult to sort through.

It should have made Jacoby break down and cry. It should have made him angry. Instead he merely felt numb. Timori stood beside Jacoby and put a hand on his shoulder. Jacoby was grateful for his friend's presence, but he knew that Timori was watching Racquela.

Even at a funeral, under a grey sky, Racquela was radiant as she stood slightly away from the crowd. Her dress was simple and respectful, but her ebon hair was done up in flowing curls under a wide-brimmed felt hat. There was a dyed black rose tied to the ribbon of the hat, and when Jacoby saw it he felt his lip tremble. It was the closest he had come to tears since the day Lenara died.

The priests laid the box on the pyre and stepped aside. Before the fire was lit, attendees could choose to place a flower on the pyre, or an item of personal significance. Jacoby watched the line form as the six priests sang their funeral dirge in a tremulous baritone. Students from Central and relatives of Lenara's dabbed their eyes with handkerchiefs as they placed books, jewellery, letters, trinkets and flowers all around the box.

Jacoby watched Paulo approach the pyre. Somehow he managed to appear just as bored at the funeral as he did in a classroom. Jacoby didn't try to reach out with empathy to see if Paulo was even capable of *feeling*. He was afraid of what he might find, and he was afraid that he would completely lose his composure as soon as he opened himself to the torrent of sorrow that was no doubt lingering on the hill that day.

Paulo laid a whiteoak blossom on the pyre. It was a thoughtless gesture. There were hundreds of them scattered across the lawn of the hill, blowing around in the breeze. The lanky youth adjusted his tie and tossed his dark curls out of his eyes. He muttered something to Lenara's parents as he passed them by, but to Jacoby he said nothing.

Jacoby was reminded of Lenara's warning. Paulo was going to take over all of Novem someday. Looking into those cold eyes, Jacoby no longer thought the idea was so far-fetched.

Jacoby reached the front of the line. The box containing Lenara's remains was right in front of him on the stacked wood, surrounded by keepsakes and flowers. There were so many flowers. It smelled like Lenara. Jacoby bit his lip and brought the crystal ring out of his pocket. He had exchanged the vows with Crystara, but it was supposed to be with Lenara. The ring represented a love that was supposed to be, that was never allowed to blossom. The ring represented Lenara's sacrifice. She had chosen Paulo, selflessly, and had paid the price for it.

He stared at the small, clear band and wondered what things would have been like if Lenara and Crystara hadn't switched places. He liked to believe that they would have turned out for the best, but he would never know.

Jacoby leaned forward to place the ring on top of the box. He breathed in the scent of chrysanthemums and memories came rushing back to him. Lenara brushing Jacoby's fingers with hers in empathy class. Lenara lying on a bed of clover, with lilies in her hair. Lenara kissing his bruised and battered body as he stroked the nape of her neck.

Jacoby broke down and wept. A few moments later, Timori came and carried him away from the pyre as he continued to weep into the shoulder of Timori's faded brown blazer. He barely heard the priest begin his speech above the din of his wracking sobs.

"Jova, father of all the gods and creator of man, we commend our daughter Lenara De'Marici to your care. May she find eternal solace in the endless halls of the abyss. We petition also the keeper of the dead, Lutias, to accept her soul and care for it as we release it to the sky and the home of the gods."

The other five priests stepped forward and placed orange crystals around the base of the pyre. Flames began to lick up the sides of the wood. The crackling fire soon became a blaze.

It no longer smelled like flowers. Jacoby ceased weeping and uncurled his fists. The crystal ring was still in his hand.

***

Timori spat out a seed and looked at his best friend. Jacoby's black suit fit him well. The noble image was ruined, however, when Jacoby spat out a giant glob of seed goo off of the bridge. Timori shuddered when he remembered that a few days ago he had almost killed himself at the exact spot where Jacoby was leaning against the railing.

Jacoby didn't laugh when the wad splattered against the road below. He needed to laugh, Timori thought, but then Timori was guilty of the same problem. There was no room for laughter in their world, not for a while, anyway. Timori put a hand on Jacoby's shoulder and watched his friend shed two tears that followed the seeds down to the road below.

"It was a nice funeral," Jacoby said. "No rain is supposed to be a good omen."

Timori didn't know what to say to that. "And it was nice seeing Racquela again, even if she is a bitch."

Timori had hoped that, at least, would make his friend laugh, but no luck.

"She did nothing worse than I did," Jacoby said glumly.

"I know, pally, I just ..." Timori went silent.

"I just keep thinking ..." Jacoby began. He sobbed for a moment, but Timori waited patiently. It was the least he could do for the friend who had saved his life.

"Sorry. Um ... I just keep thinking, what are all the things I'm going to miss out on? I barely got to know her, who she really was. There was this whole life suddenly ahead of us, all fresh and new, and then it was gone in an instant. I should've ..."

"I would trade places, if I could," Timori offered. "You could have stayed with Lenara that night."

"Don't say that," Jacoby scolded. "What's done is done. I can't change it, but I can't change how I feel about it either. I just ... I feel like if I'd stayed with Crystara, none of this would have happened. Or if they'd never switched places, then everybody would still be happy. And alive. Lenara's gone, and soon Crystara will be too."

"Maybe things would have been better," Timori agreed. "Maybe not, though, who's to say? That whole betrothal was fucked up from the get-go." He spat a seed. "And so was Crystara. So am I, for that matter. You can't hold yourself responsible for the actions of others, Jake. Maybe you were a catalyst for all of it, and maybe you weren't. But your intention wasn't to hurt Crystara."

"Well, I did cheat on her, Tim. I am at fault for that. Maybe a lot of this is my fault."

"But Lenara's death isn't," Timori reminded him. "You have to remember that. No more than my death would have been Racquela's. I made my own choice. We all do."

"Let's talk about something else," Jacoby said. He popped a handful of seeds into his mouth and began to chew.

"What was that promise you were talking about?" he said with his mouth full.

Timori looked over at his best friend. "You like history, right Jake? What do you think about being a part of history?"

"Since when are you interested in politics?" Jacoby asked as he pushed his hair out of his eyes.

"Since I started working with Paulo." Timori cracked open a seed with his teeth.

"Oh, right. Racquela told me about that." Jacoby leaned over the railing and gazed at the memorial plaque on the bridge. "Listen, there's something you need to know about Paulo."

Timori raised an eyebrow. "What about him?"

Jacoby pushed back from the railing and shoved his hands into the pockets of his jacket. "Well, the thing is ... it's also about Racquela."

***

Paulo strolled leisurely through Avati Hill Park with Racquela, arm-in-arm. It was a beautiful autumn day, if a little colder than usual for the time of year, and the gold and red leaves trailed by lazily in the breeze. Paulo was dressed in a black-and-white pinstripe suit with a matching trilby, looking deliberately understated compared to Racquela's brightly coloured autumn dress and red parasol.

The annulment had been completed earlier that day. It had been a private affair rather than a big ceremony at the Old Temple. A priest had come over to Racquela's house and signed documents with her and her parents. He hadn't even asked for the crystal ring back, but Racquela would have been more than glad to be rid of it. Bitterly, she wondered if Timori had kept his. There was a heavy feeling in her chest when she thought of him. She would have to break the news to him eventually, and she was afraid of what he would do. Racquela wondered if it would be better to wait until Timori found somebody new before telling him.

After the annulment, Racquela had met Paulo at the park so that they could celebrate their newfound freedom. It was a bittersweet walk, and Racquela couldn't stop thinking of terrible things. Lenara was dead, Timori didn't know the truth about Paulo, and Crystara was awaiting execution.

Racquela often wondered if she had let her friend down, not been there for her enough. Was it madness that had driven Crystara to murder, or had it been an accident? Racquela didn't want to think about it. Her friend was going to die and she couldn't help but feel partially to blame. Racquela entertained wild fantasies of rescuing Crystara and being forgiven, but she knew it was just a silly daydream. Crystara had killed two people and Racquela was no rescuer, besides. She was glad that it wasn't to be a public execution, at least.

"What are you thinking about?" Paulo asked.

"Crystara."

"Hmm." Paulo nodded. "It's really too bad, for both her and Lenara."

"Really too bad?" Tears stung Racquela's eyes and she pulled away from Paulo. "Is that all you have to say about it?"

"What else is there to say about it?" Paulo shrugged. "It is a tragedy, yes, but what's done is done. Dwelling on it won't accomplish anything."

He lit a cigarette and smoked it with enthusiasm. "We should be talking about us instead and focusing on the positive things. I'm happy about the annulment. Aren't you?"

"Of course I am. You know that."

Paulo gestured wildly with his free arm, which made smoke trails in the cold fall air. "We're free to do as we wish, no more forced betrothals."

Racquela gave Paulo a sideways glance. "You could at least pretend to show some sadness about Lenara, Paulo."

Paulo nodded. "I'm sorry, you're right. I'm just too busy thinking about you. About us. About everything that I've been waiting my whole life for, and now that I've found you, you can be a part of it, too."

"A part of what?" Racquela playfully tapped Paulo on the head with the edge of her parasol. He was so energetic that it was hard for her to remain negative.

Paulo suddenly got down on one knee. "A part of my dream come true. Marry me, Racquela."

***

The jail cell was made of cold, rough deepstone. A chamberpot was in one corner, a mouldy mattress in the other. Her surroundings were foul, which matched her mood perfectly. She paced the cell anxiously, wishing that they would just get it over with already. She wanted to die. She had accidentally killed her last friend in the world, as well as Lenara, who should have stayed out of the way. She was a murderer, reviled by society. She had been trying to do them a favour, though. The priests would likely cover it up as best they could, but Crystara knew that their precious Great Crystal was messed up forever.

So was Jacoby, and everybody else. Messed up and miserable. It was the only solace for Crystara in her own misery. Her only real regret was that she hadn't killed her father before she had left for the Old Temple. He was the only one who really deserved it.

When Crystara had first awakened, her thoughts were muddled and confused. She had called out for help, but nobody answered. Her cell must have been very secure, because they hadn't even bothered to post a regular guard. They had left her in her bloodstained clothes and cloak, but all of her possessions had been taken, including her crystal ring. It would have been foolish to leave a speaker with an item like that.

As the memories came rushing back to her, Crystara huddled into a corner and wept. She couldn't banish the image from her mind of Keeper Orvin's face right before he died. He hadn't even seemed surprised. His hand had been outstretched to her, his eyes pleading with her to calm down, but it had been too late. He had startled her and the wand had gone off.

They left her in the cell for what seemed like days before somebody came to give her food and water. The jowly guard refused to speak with her, but she had read his mind to discover that her trial was to be private, conducted by the church. He didn't carry any other useful information.

The trial had been mercifully quick. Evidently they thought she was dangerous because four men had come into her cell to chain her up. They didn't even bother to give her a change of clothes. In a small room without windows, surrounded by priests, covered in dried blood, Crystara had little to say in her defence other than to claim that it was an accident. Evidence was stacked against her on all sides: her wand, blood all over her clothes, fingerprints in the Old Temple.

Her appointed lawyer had done his best, but Crystara had known from a liberal reading of the jury that she was doomed. She didn't care. It was justice. She was being punished for killing Keeper Orvin, who hadn't deserved what she had done to him. Crystara just wanted to greet her fate with open arms. An eternity of nothing was preferable to a life of misery, the life that she had always led. The world wouldn't miss her, and she wouldn't miss anybody in the world. Not anymore.

Footsteps came down the hall. Was it dinnertime already? She didn't think that they were going to execute her yet. There was supposed to be a last supper or something like that, and a priest was supposed to come and do some last rites. She wondered if perhaps they would refuse to send one because she had killed the keeper.

It was a priest. Perhaps she was going to get her last rites, after all. The guards flanking him didn't allow the man into her cell. They left the priest alone in the hall. He looked old, even older than Keeper Orvin. His face was pockmarked, and his fingers were bony and crooked in some places. He stared at Crystara for a long time.

"What?" she asked. She tried to read his thoughts.

There was nothing there to read. He was just like Keeper Orvin.

"You're not bad," he said in a deep, clear voice. "But you're impulsive. You push too hard, and it telegraphs."

"What are you talking about?" Crystara demanded. "Tell me what you're here for or go away. I don't give a shard about last rites."

The wrinkled priest smiled. His face looked like crumpled paper.

"Last rites? Oh, child. You're not going to die. You're far too valuable for that."

"Did you forget that I killed your keeper?" Crystara walked up to the bars. The priest did not flinch or step back. "Maybe I want to die."

"Then it's a just punishment that you have to live instead. You have to help us fix the crystal that you damaged."

Crystara spat at the priest's feet. "Fuck your crystal, and fuck you."

"I'm afraid you have no choice in the matter. You are going to fix the crystal, Speaker, and then you are going to learn how to read properly. We have a revolution to quell."

Author photograph: Tara Juneau

About the Author

Born and raised near Calgary, Alberta, James Funfer is proud to call Vancouver Island his home. He wrote his first novella-length story at age twelve and hasn't stopped writing since. He writes short fiction in many genres and novel-length works in science fiction and fantasy. When he isn't haunting coffee shops, he can often be found trail running.

Like James on Facebook at:
https://www.facebook.com/#!/JamesFunferAuthor
Or visit his webpage: http://jamesfunfer.com/

Today we have the oppurtunity to interview James Funfer, author of Crystal Promise. James, can you tell us a bit about yourself?

It's odd how this was the most difficult question for me to answer. Let's see...I was writing since I was old enough to read, and I knew from a very young age that it was something I always wanted to do. I find that some people express themselves more easily through the written word than they do in conversation, and I'm certainly no exception. I'm also a little bit of a nerd (aren't most writers?) and my main nerdy passion is role-playing games. I do a lot of hiking and barefoot-style running, and I love to cook. I'm a bartender at a local pub, where I make a mean whiskey sour. Ok, I lied before. I'm *very* nerdy.

Where did your inspiration for Crystal Promise come from?

My primary source of inspiration was early 20th-century European history, primarily the rise of socialism and fascism and their influence on the political climate. The Great Depression became a part of my research, too. My biggest source of material was William L. Shirer's *The Rise and Fall of the Third Reich,* but I was also interested in the story of Grand Duchess Anastasia Nikolaevna of Russia (and the later pretenders to her title), as well as the Roman culture (particularly Roman Catholicism). A bit of inspiration came from a video game called *Valkyria Chronicles.* Finally, I wanted to write about passionate, angst-ridden, hormonal adolescent relationships, but I wanted to make the stakes higher and add some class struggle, and, knowing that young adults might eventually read the book, I didn't want to present young love as something 'pure' or 'simple', but frame it in a more realistic fashion.

You chose a small press for your debut--what led to that?

It was certainly a conscious decision for me to start small. Instead of seeking an agent or sending the manuscript to bigger publishers, I wanted to get my feet wet in the industry and get a feel for how my writing would be received. Originally *Crystal Promise* was the winner of a writing contest and was supposed to be published through a group called 'Vicious Writers' (also known as 'Key Publications') but when that on-line community folded I was left with a manuscript I really liked and I didn't want to rest on my laurels. Fortunately I'd made a lot of good contacts through Vicious Writers, and two former members, Genie Rayner and Jim Vires, had started up a small press called Branch Hill Publications. The rest was the usual query process, then editing and so on.

What was your favorite part of Crystal Promise? What scene did you struggle to write?

It's tough for me to choose a favourite part of the story, mainly because I don't really have a favourite character either...I love them all. However, my favourite scene in *Crystal Promise* is probably the 'big reveal', which is also somewhat of a love scene. The best part of almost any novel, to me, is the twist - the crossroads of choice upon which the story rests.

Writing is often a struggle, I think, even for the dedicated and successful among us, but for me the toughest chapters to write were Julio's. The love letters were easy, but writing about a war is challenging when you've lived a life of peace in a first-world country that doesn't involve itself much in foreign conflicts, except in a peacekeeping capacity. Even with help from personal and literary sources, living through a conflict such World War I or II and serving in the military are experiences that change your very outlook on life.

Did publishing with a small press live up to your expectations, why and why not?

Absolutely. It's a compromise between self-publishing, where you do *all* the work, spend all the money and take all the risks, and working with the big publishers, who take a bigger cut and allow you less creative control. My expectation is to get my name out there, and through consignment and internet sales I should be able to do just that. The great part about working with a small press is that the editing process is still very professional, and the relationship with the publishers becomes one of trust. There aren't any hard-line negotiations. One of the best parts about publishing *Crystal Promise* was being able to choose my own cover artist.

Tell us a little bit about your writing process?

Well, I wrote most of *Crystal Promise* in a basement suite in my old brown housecoat. Nowadays I mostly do the stereotypical thing and take my laptop to a café. I like the white noise. Honestly, my writing process is fairly linear. I start at the beginning and work my way to the end. I don't write outlines because I like things to be mutable and have a sense of fluidity. I let my characters take control of the story. They do unexpected things if you let them express themselves as you've imagined them, rather than forcing them to make pre-determined choices. I find that my writing becomes more organic, and I know that if I'm enjoying it because I don't know what's going to happen next, a reader will be even more thrilled.

I try to write two thousand words a day. Usually I work a little bit on something else first just to loosen up, like a blog post, poem or short story.

What's next for you in your career?

Well, the publication of *Crystal Promise* means a lot of pavement-pounding on my part, keeping up with social media and trying to do as many book signings and readings as possible. I'm currently working on the sequel, *Crystal Empire*, and once that manuscript is finished I'm planning on seeking out an agent.

Favorite dessert ever?

You know, I don't often eat dessert. My sweet tooth went away some time ago and left me with a deep-seated hunger for salty foods. Sometimes I enjoy a plate of sweet fruit, without whipped cream. I've never liked cake that much, but ice cream cake doesn't count as real cake, and I could never say 'no' to a piece of that.

Last question (everyone gets this one): One piece of advice you wished you had been given when you started writing?

Network. I always knew that you have to be dedicated to be successful, but nobody ever expressed to me the importance of knowing people in the industry. I'm only just catching up now. Things have changed with the rise of big social media sites like Facebook and Twitter, but there's a value in having industry contacts that you can count on to answer difficult questions or help you with your career. Go to events like conventions and writing festivals, book signings by other authors, or volunteer to be a slush-pile reader for a publishing company. Make contacts and make friends. There is a false perception that, as a writer, you're a glamorous soloist, but in this industry nobody is an island.

Thanks so much, James, for answering our questions.

You can learn more about the Writerly Rejects at: http://www.writerlyrejects.blogspot.com/

Made in the USA
Charleston, SC
13 August 2012